FROM WORD TO STORY

WALLACE GRAVES

San Fernando Valley State College

WILLIAM G. LEARY

California State College, Los Angeles

HARCOURT BRACE JOVANOVICH, INC.

New York / Chicago / San Francisco / Atlanta

FROM WORD TO STORY

COPYRIGHT ACKNOWLEDGMENTS

The authors thank the following publishers and copyright holders for their permission to use the selections reprinted in this book.

J. M. DENT & SONS LTD: PUBLISHERS. For "Amy Foster" from *Typhoon and Other Stories* by Joseph Conrad. Reprinted by permission of J. M. Dent & Sons Ltd: Publishers and by permission of the Trustees of the Joseph Conrad Estate. For "A Story" from *Prospect of the Sea* by Dylan Thomas. Reprinted by permission of J. M. Dent & Sons Ltd: Publishers and by permission of the Trustees for the copyrights of the late Dylan Thomas.

E. P. DUTTON & CO., INC. For "War" from *The Medals and Other Stories* by Luigi Pirandello. Translated by Michael Pettinati. Copyright 1939 by E. P. Dutton & Co., Inc. Renewal © 1967 by E. P. Dutton & Co., Inc. Reprinted with permission of the publishers.

DOUBLEDAY & COMPANY, INC. For "The Valiant Woman." Copyright 1947 by J. F. Powers. From *Prince of Darkness and Other Stories* by J. F. Powers. Reprinted by permission of Doubleday & Company, Inc.

ENCYCLOPAEDIA BRITANNICA. For the selection from "Plague," *Encyclopaedia Britannica,* 1966.

ANGEL FLORES. For "Espuma y nada más" by Hernando Téllez. For "Just Lather, That's All" by Hernando Téllez. Translated by Donald A. Yates. From *Great Spanish Short Stories,* selected and introduced by Angel Flores. Copyright © 1962 Dell Publishing Co., Inc. Reprinted by permission of Angel Flores.

HARCOURT BRACE JOVANOVICH, INC. For *"Magic"* from *Flowering Judas and Other Stories* by Katherine Anne Porter. Copyright 1930, © 1958 by Katherine Anne Porter. Reprinted by permission of Harcourt Brace Jovanovich, Inc.

INTERNATIONAL FAMOUS AGENCY, INC. For "The Portable Phonograph" by Walter Van Tilburg Clark from *The Watchful Gods and Other Stories.* Reprinted by permission of International Famous Agency, Inc. Copyright 1941, © 1969 by Walter Van Tilburg Clark.

ALEXANDER R. JAMES. For "The Tree of Knowledge" by Henry James.

ROBERT LANTZ–CANDIDA DONADIO LITERARY AGENCY, INC. For "Exodus" by James Baldwin. Copyright 1952.

WILLIAM MORRIS AGENCY, INC. For "King of the Bingo Game" by Ralph Ellison. Reprinted by permission of William Morris Agency, Inc. on behalf of the author. Copyright 1944 by Ralph Ellison.

continued on page v

ISBN: 0-15-529225-0

Library of Congress Catalog Card Number: 78-145652

Printed in the United States of America

continued on page vi

PREFACE

As experienced teachers will testify, short stories and short poems are by far the most popular genres for introducing students to literature. They make brevity a virtue, and they provide ideal bases for classroom discussions on literary power and art. It is not surprising, then, that many books seek to introduce students to the pleasures of these two literary forms. But until now, none of the textbooks on short fiction has sought to examine the story fully, using the detailed analysis customarily given the short poem. *From Word to Story* seeks to do this.

Fiction, like poetry, begins with the word. A critical response that first attends to the words of fiction (as it commonly attends to the words of poetry) and then looks to the larger elements will reveal how short-story writers achieve their various effects. Our table of contents discloses the successive stages in this critical process. It may not, however, reveal other distinctive features of this book.

In Part One we have deliberately chosen briefer short stories to illustrate the several elements of fiction. Each chapter introduces a discrete element and is designed for a single class period. The reading assignments are realistically short, and the demands made on the student's insights and memory are kept within suitable limits. Moreover, because these stories are brief, the student may read and study more than one in a single lesson, thus gaining the opportunity to examine each principle in at least two contexts with all the advantages that comparison and contrast can offer. Although each chapter is designed as a separate lesson, cross-references to other chapters help to establish important connections.

The questions that follow each story are integrated with the discussions that introduce each chapter. We have kept these questions specific and focused usually on a single topic, but have, at the same time, sought to ground them in matters of general significance. We have purposely included more questions than any one student may be asked to answer, to give range and flexibility to both instructor and class.

The authors in this collection are major ones: Joyce, Conrad, and Lawrence among others represent England; Tolstoy and Chekhov represent Russia; Maupassant and Camus represent France. Among American authors we include nearly all the best known: Irving, Poe, Hawthorne, Melville, Twain, James, Crane, Hemingway, Faulkner, Anderson, Porter, and such contemporaries as Ellison, Powers, and Baldwin. The book includes one Soviet author and one widely published Spanish American author, whose story also appears in the original Spanish for comparison.

Deliberately, our selections present few surprises. They were chosen not for their novelty but for their literary quality, their teachability, and their brevity. In Part Two, six longer stories appear unaccompanied by any editorial matter. These representative works of acknowledged masters provide a bridge to longer fiction and offer students the chance to apply to several longer masterworks the insights they have acquired through a study of the shorter stories in Part One.

The brief expository essays that introduce each of the chapters in Part One comprise the critical spine of the book. Inevitably they reflect our debt to all who have written about fiction. We are also indebted to Professors Sidney Richman and Wirt Williams of California State College, Los Angeles, Marvin Klotz of San Fernando Valley State College, and Peter Markman of Fullerton Junior College, for their attentive readings of the manuscript in various stages of its development; and to Miss Dorothy Mott and Miss Lynne Lumsden for their judicious editorial help.

October, 1970

W. G.
Northridge, California

W. G. L.
Los Angeles, California

CONTENTS

PART ONE

1
WHAT IS FICTION?

real aspects	artificial aspects

Fiction is the telling of events in such a way that the reader not only understands them, but feels that he was there to experience them as they unfolded. People want to feel, as well as to know, and fiction humanizes facts.

Yet fiction's way of telling is almost always in the past tense, which suggests that the events are over and done with and all the facts in before the story is written. This means that the author has had a chance to organize the facts and therefore to place some pattern of his own invention upon them. Even when the story is told in the present tense so that the facts seem to be coming at the reader in an immediate way, the author has previously planned the order in which these facts are experienced.

Thus we see at the start that fiction has two aspects: a real one, and an artificial one. It not only draws from real life, but it places an artificial order, unity, and compression on those real events.

In this book we will be looking at how writers of fiction create this partly-real, partly-artificial experience for us, in the hope of understanding fiction better, and therefore getting more—and more lasting—pleasure from it. We will treat fiction with the same care one usually bestows on poetry, beginning in the next chapter with *words,* and moving progressively from words to larger patterns.

But before we begin our analysis, let us demonstrate how fiction is real, as well as artificial. We will have to blot out the world around us for a moment and listen to the voice of a professor at the University of California at Berkeley as he tells us about something fantastic that once happened to him:

> The Scarlet Death broke out in San Francisco. The first death came on a Monday morning. By Thursday they were dying like flies in Oakland and San Francisco. They died everywhere—in their beds, at their work, walking along the street. It was on Tuesday that I saw my first death—Miss Collbran, one of my students, sitting right there before my eyes, in my lecture-room. I noticed her face while I was talking. It had suddenly turned scarlet. I ceased speaking and could only look at her, for the first fear of the plague was already on all of us and we knew that it had come. The young women screamed and ran out of the room. So did the young men run out, all but two. Miss Collbran's convulsions were very mild and lasted less than a minute. One of the young men fetched her a glass of water. She drank only a little of it and cried out:
>
> "My feet! All sensation has left them."
>
> After a minute she said, "I have no feet. I am unaware that I have any feet. And my knees are cold. I can scarcely feel that I have knees."
>
> She lay on the floor, a bundle of notebooks under her head. And we could do nothing. The coldness and the numbness crept up past her hips to her heart, and when it reached her heart she was dead. In fifteen minutes, by the clock—I timed it—she was dead, there, in my own classroom, dead. And she was a very beautiful, strong, healthy young woman. And from the first sign of the plague to her death only fifteen minutes elapsed. That will show you how swift was the Scarlet Death.

Notice the *real* aspects of this piece of fiction. It is told by someone identified as "I," and is therefore a personal experience of an individual, just as our own real lives are a succession of personal experiences. Its setting is the San Francisco Bay area, a real place, and the streets, the lecture-room, the glass of water, the notebooks, are all things familiar to us. The sights and the sounds in the story are immediately recognizable—the flushed, scarlet face of fever, the young women's screams, the victim's convulsions, the coldness of her limbs—all these sense impressions are taken from the real world.

But there are also *artificial* aspects. In three short sentences we have leapt from Monday to Thursday, and in two more we are suddenly at Tuesday. This summary treatment of time is absolutely unlike our own second-by-second sense of time. So too with the setting: we hop from San Francisco to Oakland, to beds, to work, to the streets, to the Berkeley lecture-room, all at a mad and unreal pace. Finally, we notice that the reader is shown only a few details of Miss Collbran's death; had we really been in the lecture-room that day, we would have been bombarded with many more impressions than we are shown here. The author has been highly selective and has artificially restricted the experience to suit his purpose. This excerpt is from a short book called *The Scarlet Plague* written by Jack London in 1912, telling about events that are supposed to have happened in the year 2013. Nothing could be more "artificial" than this; yet people continue to read and to enjoy such fiction.

To demonstrate the importance of artificial aspects of fiction, let us turn to another plague—this time a real one—which ravaged London in the years 1664–65. We have an eyewitness report of this plague in the diary of Samuel Pepys. Pepys was not a professional writer, but he had the makings of one, as this entry from his diary for August 3, 1665 suggests:

> 3d. Up, and betimes to Deptford to Sir G. Carteret's, where, not liking the horse which had been hired by Mr. Unthwayt for me, I did desire Sir G. Carteret to let me ride his new £40 horse; and so to the ferry, where I was forced to stay a great while before I could get my horse brought over, and then mounted, and rode very finely to Dagenhams. All the people, citizens, walking to and fro, enquire how the plague is in the City this week by the Bill; which, by chance, at Greenwich, I had heard was 2,020 of the plague, and 3,000 and odd of all diseases; but methought it was a sad question to be so often asked me. Coming to Dagenhams, I there met our company coming out of the house, having stayed as long as they could for me; so I let them go a little before, and went and took leave of my Lady Sandwich, good woman, who seems

very sensible of my service in this late business, and having her directions in some things . . . took leave of her, and down to the buttery, and eat a piece of cold venison pie, and drank, and took some bread and cheese in my hand; and so mounted after them, Mr. Marr very kindly staying to lead me the way. By and by met my Lord Crewe returning; Mr. Marr telling me by the way how a maid-servant of Mr. John Wright's, who lives thereabouts, falling sick of the plague, she was removed to an outhouse, and a nurse appointed to look to her; who, being once absent, the maid got out of the house at the window, and ran away. The nurse coming and knocking, and, having no answer, believed she was dead, and went and told Mr. Wright so; who and his lady were in great strait what to do to get her buried. At last, resolving to go to Brentwood, hard by, being in the parish, and there get people to do it. But they would not: so he went home full of trouble, and in the way met the wench walking over the common, which frightened him worse than before; and was forced to send people to take her, which he did; and they got one of the pest-coaches, and put her into it, to carry her to a pest-house. And, passing in a narrow lane, Sir Anthony Browne, with his brother and some friends in a coach, met this coach with the curtains drawn close. The brother, being a young man, and believing there might be some lady in it that would not be seen, and the way being narrow, he thrust his head out of his own into the coach, and to look, and there saw somebody look very ill, and in a sick dress, and stunk mightily; which the coachman also cried out upon. And presently they come up to some people that stood looking after it, and told our gallants that it was a maid of Mr. Wright's carried away sick of the plague; which put the young gentleman into a fright had almost cost him his life, but is now well again. . . . I, by and by, by boat to Gravesend, where no news of Sir G. Carteret come yet; so back again, and fetched them all over, but the two saddle-horses that were to go with us, which could not be brought over in the horse-boat, the wind and tide being against us, without towing; so we had some difference with some watermen, who would not tow them under 20*s*., whereupon I swore to send one of them to sea, and will do it. Anon some others did it for 10*s*. By and by comes Sir G. Carteret, and so we set out for Chatham;

> in my way overtaking some company, wherein was a lady, very pretty, riding singly, her husband in company with her. We fell into talk, and I read a copy of verses which her husband showed me, and he discommended, but the lady commended: and I read them, so as to make the husband turn and commend them. By and by he and I fell into acquaintance, having known me formerly at the Exchequer. . . . We promised to meet, if ever we come both to London again; and, at parting, I had a fair salute on horseback, in Rochester Street, of the lady, and so parted. Came to Chatham mighty merry and anon to supper.

As we see, Pepys was something of an artist; he captured the experience he lived through and saved it for us. We not only learn the facts, we have a sense of having been there. Pepys has humanized the events for us by the vividness of his writing and by coming alive as a human being himself. He reveals his love of good horseflesh, money, eating, drinking, pretty women, and poetry; and he shows his flair for human drama.

But few people have read the whole 1,500 pages of his diary from start to finish, for despite the good qualities, it is a tedious work. Some of the tedium is revealed in this entry for August 3. Parts of it are more interesting than others, the part about the plague-ridden servant probably being the most interesting of all; but much of the rest seems to lead nowhere. What is apparent from this entry is that Pepys's diary masterfully evokes the *reality* of experience. But it does not compress this reality into the order and unity that we expect from fiction, which explains why excerpts from Pepys's diary, the "good parts," have always been more popular than his full work. Had the diary been more artificial, had Pepys molded reality more thoroughly into an art form, the complete work would have been more appealing.

As a third demonstration of the real and artificial aspects of fiction, let us read what the *Encyclopaedia Britannica* (1966) has to say about "Plague."

> The Great Plague of London in 1664–65 was not an isolated phenomenon. Plague had recurred frequently throughout Europe in the 15th, 16th, and 17th centuries, but London had been unusually free of it in the preceding years. It was not mentioned in the bills of mortality until the autumn of

> 1664 (Nov. 2). A few isolated cases were observed in Westminster, and a few in the following winter, which was severe. About May 1665 the disease again became noticeable and spread, but somewhat slowly. The total number of deaths from the plague in that year, according to the bills of mortality, was 68,596 in a population estimated at 460,000. This number is probably an underestimate, since it is likely that many of the 6,432 deaths attributed to spotted fever were really caused by the plague. In December the mortality fell suddenly and continued down throughout the winter, but in 1666 nearly 2,000 deaths were recorded. From London the disease spread widely over the country, but from 1667 on there was no epidemic of plague in any part of England, though sporadic cases appeared in bills of mortality up to 1679. The disappearance of plague from London has been attributed to the Great Fire, but it also subsided in other cities without such cause. The decline has also been ascribed to quarantine, but effective quarantine was actually not established until 1720. The cessation of plague in England must be regarded as spontaneous.

Notice that this time the events have been arranged artificially to give a summary report of what happened—but despite the careful arrangement, we are given only the facts, without any personal experience or humanizing of these facts. Therefore this account does not work as fiction.

How, then, does fiction differ from biography and encyclopedia entries when these are taken from real life and use many of the techniques of fiction? The answer lies in the writer's implied response to the following question: By what *authority* do you tell your story? When a writer's authority rests solely on his skill of invention, we call it fiction. When his authority depends on exterior events, known or believed by the writer and the reader to exist as facts, we call it biography or history or some other form of nonfiction.

In the next chapter you will find a story about another plague, "The Masque of the Red Death," by Edgar Allan Poe. Like all fiction, Poe's story is drawn partly from reality. But here the reality is artfully transformed by the author into patterns of his own invention, patterns that are not likely to occur in real life. Nonetheless, this story gives the reader a strong sense of being there, which the *Encyclopaedia Britannica* article does not; at the same time, it is highly compressed and tightly unified, unlike the entry from Pepys's diary. It is, in short, an example of the partly-real, partly-artificial pattern of words known as prose fiction.

In a successful short story, those aspects of fiction we have been calling artificial and those aspects we have termed real are fused into an artistic whole. Not only are the best authors able to keep things sounding real, but at the same time they are able to shape a story around a subtly implied attitude toward their subject. This implied attitude—a reflection of the human concerns of a man talking to other men—is what is commonly called a *theme* in a story. A theme is the hub around which the wheel—in this case the story—turns. In the following chapters we will study how the various *techniques* of fiction operate. Like the spokes in a wheel, techniques point to the story's hub, its central theme, and thus reveal the author's attitude. The first of these "spokes" is the indispensable stuff of all writing—the *words*.

2
WORDS

denotation	euphony
ambiguity	cacophony
connotation	repetition

If you read a story in the newspaper with normal attention, you usually absorb all of it the first time. If you reread it, you learn little more. With fiction, you are likely to discover many new and surprising things on the second and third readings. This is because writers of fiction deliberately choose words with fuller meanings and place these words carefully to get the most out of them.

Every word has a *denotation*—that is, a dictionary definition—and in good fiction each word is chosen with careful attention to its denotation, or dictionary meaning. Some words, however, have many denotations, with widely varied meanings. For example, the word "fast" means "speedy"; but it also means "to cease eating," and, for a boat at the dock, it may mean "tied securely." Occasionally authors will use such words to create a deliberate *ambiguity*. That is, they will use a single word to suggest two or more meanings each of which "fits" that situation or makes sense in that context. Notice the use of the word "lie" in the following couplet:

> Here lies my wife: so let her lie!
> Now she's at rest—and so am I.

How many meanings can be read into the word "lie" as it appears in this couplet? Is the poet talking about falsehood? death? sleep?

rest? sex? All are possibilities. Obviously, the greater number of meanings a writer can suggest with a single word, the more he can say in a short space. This is one of the ways he achieves compression in his art.

Another way of achieving compression is to use words that, in addition to their denotations or dictionary meanings, have also highly suggestive associative meanings, or *connotations*. For example, if you wish to flatter a girl who is underweight, you call her "slender"; if you wish to hurt her feelings, you call her "skinny." The two words denote the same thing, but each connotes something quite different.

Note the connotations in this verse:

> There is no frigate like a book
>   To take us lands away,
> Nor any coursers like a page
>   Of prancing poetry.

If we substitute "sailboat" for "frigate," we lose a romantic connotation; and "horses" would not do the connotative job of "coursers," though both denote the same animal. Emily Dickinson, who wrote the lines above, chose words carefully for such associative meanings. Short-story writers often exercise as much care in choosing their words as do poets.

So far we have been talking about the *sense* of words. But the meanings of words may also be conveyed through *sounds*. Hence words can create music. Through patterns of rhythm and repetition their music can add to the meaning. When words and verbal rhythms sound pleasant, smooth, and melodious, they are called *euphonious;* but when they are rough, harsh, and hard to mouth they are called *cacophonous*. Alexander Pope put it this way:

> True ease in writing comes from art, not chance,
> As those move easiest who have learned to dance.
> 'Tis not enough no harshness gives offense,
> The sound must seem an echo to the sense;
> Soft is the strain when Zephyr gently blows,
> And the smooth stream in smoother numbers flows;
> But when loud surges lash the sounding shore,
> The hoarse, rough verse should like the torrent roar:

Each of the last four lines above matches sound with meaning in a different way. This difference is achieved through choosing words with the desired sounds and placing them deliberately for a euphonious or cacophonous effect.

Repetition, as well as placement, contributes to the music of language. We are all familiar with the repeated sounds in poetry called *rhyme,* such as "chance" and "dance" in Pope's excerpt above. This excerpt is also rich in two less obvious patterns of repeated sound: *alliteration* (repeated consonants, usually at the beginning of words) and *assonance* (repeated vowels). Notice the alliterative *s* sounds beginning with line four. Lines four and five also use assonance in the repeated *e* of "echo," "sense," and "Zephyr gently." All the musical devices of rhythm and repetition used in poetry are also available to prose, though the more formal ones, such as rhyme, and the regular rhythm known as "meter," are not often used.

In the second paragraph of the first story, "The Masque of the Red Death," we will discover the musical devices of rhythm and repetition at work. The first sentence of this paragraph, "But the Prince Prospero was happy and dauntless and sagacious," rambles easily off the tongue, with its repeated *and*'s and its alliteration of *P*'s. We can be sure, too, that Poe's musical ear was at work in: "When his *d*ominions were half *d*epopulated," and in "the deep *s*ecLusion of one of hi*s* ca*s*teLLated abbey*s*."

Notice that while these words create their own music through rhythm and repetition, they are also rich in denotative and connotative meanings. "Dominion" comes from the Latin *dominus,* which denotes "the lord," as well as mastery; "minion," from the French *mignon,* means "servile favorite of the prince," and as part of the larger word, echoes an associative meaning relevant to the story's plot. "Castellated" means "built like a castle with turrets and battlements," and therefore accurately denotes what Poe intends; it also sounds like "castle," and when it is followed by the word "abbey," which denotes a "religious cloister," Poe has connoted—and contrasted—worldly and supernatural power in a few words.

Through careful denotation, conscious ambiguity, and connotation, and through euphony, cacophony, and repeated sounds, Poe achieves a remarkable singleness of effect that makes his fantastic tale almost believable. We are persuaded not so much by the reality of the events as by the peculiar power of the words.

Because Poe's story is fantastic, it is not so much true *to* life as it is true *of* life. But that is only one way to write a story. Alter the pattern of words, and you may achieve an effect that is both true *of* life and true *to* life—as Hemingway does in the second story in this chapter. One story is not more artful than the other, but their artistic patterns—and therefore their achieved effects—are strikingly different.

Edgar Allan Poe

THE MASQUE OF THE RED DEATH

The "Red Death" had long devastated the country. No pestilence had ever been so fatal, or so hideous. Blood was its Avator and its seal—the redness and the horror of blood. There were sharp pains, and sudden dizziness, and then profuse bleeding at the pores, with dissolution. The scarlet stains upon the body and especially upon the face of the victim, were the pest ban which shut him out from the aid and from the sympathy of his fellowmen. And the whole seizure, progress and termination of the disease, were the incidents of half an hour.

But the Prince Prospero was happy and dauntless and sagacious. When his dominions were half depopulated, he summoned to his presence a thousand hale and lighthearted friends from among the knights and dames of his court, and with these retired to the deep seclusion of one of his castellated abbeys. This was an extensive and magnificent structure, the creation of the prince's own eccentric yet august taste. A strong and lofty wall girdled it in. This wall had gates of iron. The courtiers, having entered, brought furnaces and massy hammers and welded the bolts. They resolved to leave means neither of ingress or egress to the sudden impulses of despair or of frenzy from within. The abbey was amply provisioned. With such precautions the courtiers might bid defiance to contagion. The external world could take care of itself. In the meantime it was folly to grieve, or to think. The prince had provided all the appliances of pleasure. There were buffoons, there were improvisatori, there were ballet-dancers, there were musicians, there was Beauty, there was wine. All these and security were within. Without was the "Red Death."

It was toward the close of the fifth or sixth month of his seclusion, and while the pestilence raged most furiously abroad, that the Prince Prospero entertained his thousand friends at a masked ball of the most unusual magnificence.

It was a voluptuous scene, that masquerade. But first let me tell of the rooms in which it was held. There were seven—an imperial suite. In many palaces, however, such suites form a long and straight vista, while the folding doors slide back nearly to the walls on either hand, so that the view of the whole extent is scarcely impeded. Here the case was very different; as might have been expected from the duke's love of the *bizarre*. The apartments were so irregularly disposed that the vision embraced but little more then one at a time. There was a sharp turn at every twenty or thirty yards, and at each turn a novel effect. To the right and left, in the middle of each wall, a tall and narrow Gothic window looked out upon a closed corridor which pursued the windings of the suite. These windows were of stained glass whose color varied in accordance with the prevailing hue of the decorations of the chamber into which it opened. That at the eastern extremity was hung, for example, in blue—and vividly blue were its windows. The second chamber was purple in its ornaments and tapestries, and here the panes were purple. The third was green throughout, and so were the casements. The fourth was furnished and lighted with orange—the fifth with white—the sixth with violet. The seventh apartment was closely shrouded in black velvet tapestries that hung all over the ceiling and down the walls, falling in heavy folds upon a carpet of the same material and hue. But in this chamber only, the color of the windows failed to correspond with the decorations. The panes here were scarlet—a deep blood color. Now in no one of the seven apartments was there any lamp or candelabrum, amid the profusion of golden ornaments that lay scattered to and fro or depended from the roof. There was no light of any kind emanating from lamp or candle within the suite of chambers. But in the corridors that followed the suite, there stood, opposite to each window, a heavy tripod, bearing a brazier of fire that projected its rays through the tinted glass and so glaringly illumined the room. And thus were produced a multitude of gaudy and fantastic appearances. But in the western or black chamber the effect of the firelight that streamed upon the dark hangings through the blood-tinted panes, was ghastly in the extreme, and produced so wild a look upon the countenances of those who entered, that there were few of the company bold enough to set foot within its precincts at all.

It was in this apartment, also, that there stood against the western wall, a gigantic clock of ebony. Its pendulum swung to and fro with a dull, heavy, monotonous clang; and when the minute-hand made the circuit of the face, and the hour was to be stricken, there came from the brazen lungs of the clock a sound which was clear and loud and deep and exceedingly musical, but of so peculiar a note and emphasis that, at each lapse of an hour, the musicians of the orchestra were constrained to pause, momentarily, in their performance, to hearken to the sound; and thus the waltzers perforce ceased their evolutions; and there was a brief disconcert of the whole gay company; and, while the chimes of the clock yet rang, it was observed that the giddiest grew pale, and the more aged and sedate passed their hands over their brows as if in confused revery or meditation. But when the echoes had fully ceased, a light laughter at once pervaded the assembly; the musicians looked at each other and smiled as if at their own nervousness and folly, and made whispering vows, each to the other, that the next chiming of the clock should produce in them no similar emotion; and then, after the lapse of sixty minutes (which embrace three thousand and six hundred seconds of the Time that flies), there came yet another chiming of the clock, and then were the same disconcert and tremulousness and meditation as before.

But, in spite of these things, it was a gay and magnificent revel. The tastes of the duke were peculiar. He had a fine eye for colors and effects. He disregarded the *decora* of mere fashion. His plans were bold and fiery, and his conceptions glowed with barbaric lustre. There are some who would have thought him mad. His followers felt that he was not. It was necessary to hear and see and touch him to be *sure* that he was not.

He had directed, in great part, the movable embellishments of the seven chambers, upon occasion of this great *fête;* and it was his own guiding taste which had given character to the masqueraders. Be sure they were grotesque. There were much glare and glitter and piquancy and phantasm—much of what has been since seen in "Hernani." There were arabesque figures with unsuited limbs and appointments. There were delirious fancies such as the madman fashions. There was much of the beautiful, much of the wanton, much of the *bizarre,* something of the terrible, and not a little of that which might have excited disgust. To and fro in the seven chambers there stalked, in fact, a multitude of dreams. And these—the dreams—writhed in and about, taking hue from the rooms, and causing the wild music of the orchestra to seem as the echo of their steps. And, anon, there strikes the ebony clock which stands in the hall of the velvet. And then, for a moment, all is still, and all is silent save the voice of the clock. The dreams are stiff-frozen as they stand. But the echoes of the chime die away—they have endured but an instant—and a light, half-subdued laughter floats after them as they depart. And now again the music swells, and the dreams live, and writhe to and fro more merrily than ever, taking hue from the many tinted windows through which stream the rays from the tripods. But to the chamber which lies most westwardly of the seven, there are now none of the maskers who venture, for the night is waning away; and there flows a ruddier light through the blood-colored panes; and the blackness of the sable drapery appalls; and to him whose foot falls upon the sable carpet, there comes from the near clock of ebony a muffled peal more solemnly emphatic than any which reaches *their* ears who indulge in the more remote gayeties of the other apartments.

But these other apartments were densely crowded, and in them beat feverishly the heart of life. And the revel went whirlingly on, until at length there commenced the sounding of midnight upon the clock. And then the music ceased, as I have told; and the evolutions of the waltzers were quieted; and there was an uneasy cessation of all things as before. But now there were twelve strokes to be sounded by the bell of the clock; and thus it happened, perhaps, that before the last echoes of the last chime had utterly sunk into silence, there were many individuals in the crowd who had found leisure to become aware of the presence of a masked figure which had arrested the attention of no single individual before. And the rumor of this new presence having spread itself whisperingly around, there arose at length from the whole company, a buzz, or murmur, expressive of disapprobation and surprise—then, finally, of terror, of horror, and of disgust.

In an assembly of phantasms such as I have painted, it may well be supposed that no ordinary appearance could have excited such sensation. In truth the masquerade license of the night was nearly unlimited; but the figure in question had out-Heroded Herod, and gone beyond the bounds of even the prince's indefinite decorum. There are chords in the hearts of the most reckless which cannot be touched without emotion. Even with the utterly lost, to whom life and death are equally jests, there are matters of which no jest can be made. The whole company, indeed, seemed now deeply to feel that in the costume and bearing of the stranger neither wit nor propriety existed. The figure was tall and gaunt, and shrouded from head to foot in the habiliments of the grave. The mask which concealed the visage was made so nearly to resemble the countenance of a stiffened corpse that the closest scrutiny must have had difficulty in detecting the cheat. And yet all this might have been endured, if not approved, by the mad revellers around. But the mummer had gone so far as to assume the type of the Red Death. His vesture was dabbled in *blood*—and his broad brow, with all the features of the face, was besprinkled with the scarlet horror.

When the eyes of Prince Prospero fell upon this spectral image (which with a slow and solemn movement, as if more fully to sustain its *rôle,* stalked to and fro among the waltzers) he was seen to be convulsed, in the first moment, with a strong shudder either of terror or distaste; but, in the next, his brow reddened with rage.

"Who dares?" he demanded hoarsely of the courtiers who stood near him—"who dares insult us with this blasphemous mockery? Seize him and unmask him—that we may know whom we have to hang at sunrise, from the battlements!"

It was in the eastern or blue chamber in which stood the Prince Prospero as he uttered these words. They rang throughout the seven rooms loudly and clearly—for the prince was a bold and robust man, and the music had become hushed at the waving of his hand.

It was in the blue room where stood the prince, with a group of pale courtiers by his side. At first, as he spoke, there was a slight rushing movement of this group in the direction of the intruder, who at the moment was also near at hand, and now, with deliberate and stately step, made closer approach to the speaker. But from a certain nameless awe with which the mad assumptions of the mummer had inspired the whole party, there were found none who put forth hand to seize him; so that, unimpeded, he passed within a yard of the prince's person; and, while the vast assembly, as if with one impulse, shrank from the centres of the room to the walls, he made his way uninterruptedly, but with the same solemn and measured step which had distinguished him from the first, through the blue chamber to the purple—through the purple to the green—through the green to the orange—through this again to the white—and even thence to the violet, ere a decided movement had been made to arrest him. It was then, however, that the Prince Prospero, maddening with rage and the shame of his own momentary cowardice, rushed hurriedly through the six chambers, while none followed him on account of a deadly terror that had seized upon all. He bore aloft a drawn dagger, and had approached, in rapid impetuosity, to within three or four feet of the retreating figure, when the latter, having attained the extremity of the velvet apartment, turned suddenly and confronted his pursuer. There was a sharp cry—and the dagger dropped gleaming upon the sable carpet, upon which, instantly afterwards, fell prostrate in death the Prince Prospero. Then, summoning the wild courage of despair, a throng of the revellers at once threw themselves into the black apartment, and, seizing the mummer, whose tall figure stood erect and motionless within the shadow of the ebony clock, gasped in unutterable horror at finding the grave-cerements and corpse-like mask which they handled with so violent a rudeness, untenanted by any tangible form.

And now was acknowledged the presence of the Red Death. He had come like a thief in the night. And one by one dropped the revellers in the blood-bedewed halls of their revel, and died each in the despairing posture of his fall. And the life of the ebony clock went out with that of the last of the gay. And the flames of the tripods expired. And Darkness and Decay and the Red Death held illimitable dominion over all.

QUESTIONS

1 Vocabulary: *Avator:* look up in your dictionary under avatar. *improvisatori:* Italian for entertainers who improvised their words and actions. *decora:* look up in your dictionary under decor. *Hernani:* a spectacular romantic tragedy by Victor Hugo. *out-Heroded Herod:* a phrase used by Hamlet (*Hamlet,* III, ii, 15) to describe a blustering, ranting style of acting and speaking on the stage.

2 Look up the words "masque" and "mask" in your dictionary. What possible deliberate ambiguity does Poe use in his title "The Masque of the Red Death"?

3 Poe's story begins: "The 'Red Death' had long devastated the country." Look up "devastate," "decimate," and "ravage." Considering the denotation, as well as the history and language source, of each word, how do you explain Poe's choice? From what you are told in paragraph 2, why would "decimated" have been the wrong choice?

4 Poe's second sentence reads: "No pestilence had ever been so fatal or so hideous." What are the denotations and connotations of "pestilence" compared with those of possible substitutes like "disease" and "infection"? Why do you think Poe used "pestilence"? Why did he use the word "hideous" instead of "ugly"?

5 In the third sentence what special meaning and effect does Poe achieve by the phrase "its Avator and seal"?

6 Toward the end of paragraph 2, Poe lists what he calls the "appliances of pleasure." What are the customary denotations and connotations of "appliances"? What does Poe's use of this word to describe people as well as ideas and things tell you about Prince Prospero?

7 Paragraph 4 begins: "It was a voluptuous scene, that masquerade." Look up "voluptuous" in your dictionary. Given Poe's characterization of the Prince, why is this word appropriate here?

8 Poe's characteristic diction may be described as baroque: the words are sometimes odd and often showy; their sounds press insistently on the ear; they are always very much in the foreground, and we are always conscious of them. What are some *odd* words in this story? some *showy* words? some words conspicuous for their sound effects?

9 How many repetitions of *p* and *d* sounds do you find in the fourth sentence of the story? Do these form any recognizable patterns? Do these repeated sounds support the sense of the words in which they appear?

10 How does alliteration contribute to the sentence (near the end of the next-to-last paragraph of the story) that describes the Prince's death?

11 What two different forms of repetition establish both the sound and the sense of the story's final sentence?

12 Poe saw ideal Beauty as distinct from beauty revealed through physical things. To achieve ideal Beauty, he believed, physical matter must be discarded. Thus, for Poe, physical death was not a termination but a prologue to an ideal state. How does Poe's disgust with physical matter help to account for the words he chose to describe the symptoms of the "Red Death" in paragraph 1?

13 Time is a finite concept. It applies to the things of this earth. Again, given Poe's curious attitude toward earthly things, how do you account for his choice of cacophonous words to describe the clock in the opening lines of paragraph 5? What words and what sounds does Poe use to produce in the reader the same effects that the striking of the clock produces in the dancers? Why did Poe use "stricken" instead of the more familiar "struck" when he wrote "and the hour was to be stricken"?

14 Retaining the same wording as the original, convert Poe's second paragraph, or another paragraph that you find especially musical, into verse, divided by lines instead of sentences. Read it aloud. How effective is it?

15 Compare the passage in Chapter 1, from Jack London's *The Scarlet Plague,* with any equal number of words in Poe's story. Comment on the two authors' use of words, using the topics discussed in this chapter to measure the variety and complexity of the two styles. How many words, unusual in either sound or sense, does Poe use, compared to London, in the given length Can you successfully convert London's prose into verse?

Ernest Hemingway

A CLEAN, WELL-LIGHTED PLACE

It was late and every one had left the café except an old man who sat in the shadow the leaves of the tree made against the electric light. In the day time the street was dusty, but at night the dew settled the dust and the old man liked to sit late because he was deaf and now at night it was quiet and he felt the difference. The two waiters inside the café knew that the old man was a little drunk, and while he was a good client they knew that if he became too drunk he would leave without paying, so they kept watch on him.

"Last week he tried to commit suicide," one waiter said.

"Why?"

"He was in despair."

"What about?"

"Nothing."

"How do you know it was nothing?"

"He has plenty of money."

They sat together at a table that was close against the wall near the door of the café and looked at the terrace where the tables were all empty except where the old man sat in the shadow of the leaves of the tree that moved slightly in the wind. A girl and a soldier went by in the street. The street light shone on the brass number on his collar. The girl wore no head covering and hurried beside him.

"The guard will pick him up," one waiter said.

"What does it matter if he gets what he's after?"

"He had better get off the street now. The guard will get him. They went by five minutes ago."

The old man sitting in the shadow rapped on his saucer with his glass. The younger waiter went over to him.

"What do you want?"

The old man looked at him. "Another brandy," he said.

"You'll be drunk," the waiter said. The old man looked at him. The waiter went away.

"He'll stay all night," he said to his colleague. "I'm sleepy now. I never get into bed before three o'clock. He should have killed himself last week."

The waiter took the brandy bottle and another saucer from the counter inside the café and marched out to the old man's table. He put down the saucer and poured the glass full of brandy.

"You should have killed yourself last week," he said to the deaf man. The old man motioned with his finger. "A little more," he said. The waiter poured on into the glass so that the brandy slopped over and ran down the stem into the top saucer of the pile. "Thank you," the old man said. The waiter took the bottle back inside the café. He sat down at the table with his colleague again.

"He's drunk now," he said.

"He's drunk every night."

"What did he want to kill himself for?"

"How should I know."

"How did he do it?"

"He hung himself with a rope."

"Who cut him down?"

"His niece."

"Why did they do it?"

"Fear for his soul."

"How much money has he got?"

"He's got plenty."

"He must be eighty years old."

"Anyway I should say he was eighty."

"I wish he would go home. I never get to bed before three o'clock. What kind of hour is that to go to bed?"

"He stays up because he likes it."

"He's lonely. I'm not lonely. I have a wife waiting in bed for me."

"He had a wife once too."

"A wife would be no good to him now."

"You can't tell. He might be better with a wife."

"His niece looks after him."

"I know. You said she cut him down."

"I wouldn't want to be that old. An old man is a nasty thing."

"Not always. This old man is clean. He drinks without spilling. Even now, drunk. Look at him."

"I don't want to look at him. I wish he would go home. He has no regard for those who must work."

The old man looked from his glass across the square, then over at the waiters.

"Another brandy," he said, pointing to his glass. The waiter who was in a hurry came over.

"Finished," he said, speaking with that omission of syntax stupid people employ when talking to drunken people or foreigners. "No more tonight. Close now."

"Another," said the old man.

"No. Finished." The waiter wiped the edge of the table with a towel and shook his head.

The old man stood up, slowly counted the saucers, took a leather coin purse from his pocket and paid for the drinks, leaving half a peseta tip.

The waiter watched him go down the street, a very old man walking unsteadily but with dignity.

"Why didn't you let him stay and drink?" the unhurried waiter asked. They were putting up the shutters. "It is not half-past two."

"I want to go home to bed."

"What is an hour?"

"More to me than to him."

"An hour is the same."

"You talk like an old man yourself. He can buy a bottle and drink at home."

"It's not the same."

"No, it is not," agreed the waiter with a wife. He did not wish to be unjust. He was only in a hurry.

"And you? You have no fear of going home before your usual hour?"

"Are you trying to insult me?"

"No, hombre, only to make a joke."

"No," the waiter who was in a hurry said, rising from pulling down the metal shutters. "I have confidence. I am all confidence."

"You have youth, confidence, and a job," the older waiter said. "You have everything."

"And what do you lack?"

"Everything but work."

"You have everything I have."

"No. I have never had confidence and I am not young."

"Come on. Stop talking nonsense and lock up."

"I am of those who like to stay late at the café," the older waiter said. "With all those who do not want to go to bed. With all those who need a light for the night."

"I want to go home and into bed."

"We are of two different kinds," the older waiter said. He was now dressed to go home. "It is not only a question of youth and confidence although those things are very beautiful. Each night I am reluctant to close up because there may be some one who needs the café."

"Hombre, there are bodegas open all night long."

"You do not understand. This is a clean and pleasant café. It is well lighted. The light is very good and also, now, there are shadows of the leaves."

"Good night," said the younger waiter.

"Good night," the other said. Turning off the electric light he continued the conversation with himself. It is the light of course but it is necessary that the place be clean and pleasant. You do not want music. Certainly you do not want music. Nor can you stand before a bar with dignity although that is all that is provided for these hours. What did he fear? It was not fear or dread. It was a nothing that he knew too well. It was all a nothing and a man was nothing too. It was only that and light was all it needed and a certain cleanness and order. Some lived in it and never felt it but he knew it all was nada y pues nada y nada y pues nada. Our nada who art in nada, nada be thy name thy kingdom nada thy will be nada in nada as it is in nada. Give us this nada our daily nada and nada us our nada as we nada our nadas and nada us not into nada but deliver us from nada; pues nada. Hail nothing full of nothing, nothing is with thee. He smiled and stood before a bar with a shining steam pressure coffee machine.

"What's yours?" asked the barman.

"Nada."

"Otro loco mas," said the barman and turned away.

"A little cup," said the waiter.

The barman poured it for him.

"The light is very bright and pleasant but the bar is unpolished," the waiter said.

The barman looked at him but did not answer. It was too late at night for conversation.

"You want another copita?" the barman asked.

"No, thank you," said the waiter and went out. He disliked bars and bodegas. A clean, well-lighted café was a very different thing. Now, without thinking further, he would go home to his room. He would lie in the bed and finally, with daylight, he would go to sleep. After all, he said to himself, it is probably only insomnia. Many must have it.

QUESTIONS

1 Vocabulary: *peseta:* the most common Spanish silver coin. *hombre:* man. *bodegas:* wine shops. *Nada y pues* may be translated as "nothing and so . . ." *Otro loco mas* may be translated as "another crazy one." *copita:* a small glass of beverage. *bar:* in Spain a stand-up counter where coffee, cognac, and other drinks are served; not the same as an American bar.

2 Select at random ten full lines from this story. Count the number of words in each line, then count the number of one-syllable words in each. What is the proportion of one-syllable words to the total? What effect does this proportion produce?

3 Examine those passages in the story that are used to describe the café, the street, the old man, the bar. Count the number of nouns and then the number of adjectives used. What is the proportion of one to the other? Does this proportion suggest a stark, or a rich, use of words?

4 Find examples of passages where, within just a few lines, some words and phrases are constantly repeated. Is there a connection between the effect achieved by this deliberate repetition and the number of one-syllable words and nouns used? What effect is achieved by means of all three of these verbal devices?

5 The word *clean* runs through this story like a refrain. Examine carefully the passages in which this word occurs. Look up "clean" in your dictionary. How many of its denotations apply to this story?

6 Most of the sentences in this story are short and simple. How does the rhythm of these sentences heighten the effect achieved by the author's choice of words?

7 In what specific ways do the bare words and simple sentences of this story reflect the characters, their situation, and their values?

8 The revelation of this story comes into sharpest focus in the elder waiter's parody of the Lord's Prayer, his vision of a world devoid of any ultimate meaning. How does Hemingway's use of the word "nada" and the effect of its frequent repetition help to illuminate this theme? Compare this parody with the original prayer—Matthew 6:9–13.

9 The Hemingway hero often is faced with the problem of how to preserve dignity in the face of defeat. In what ways does Hemingway's style contribute to the dignity of the drunken old man and the elder waiter?

10 Because this story is presented like a play, there is no obvious narrator. Does Hemingway indirectly supply a comment by the way he makes his characters speak? by the way he describes the world they occupy? How, then, does the style of the story serve as a substitute for the narrator?

11 The contrast between the writing styles of Poe and Hemingway is extreme. Poe's style, as we have seen, is baroque; Hemingway's style is bald. Does this mean that Hemingway draws more sparingly than Poe on the armory of verbal devices available to any writer—denotation, ambiguity, connotation, euphony, cacophony, repetition of sounds? Give specific examples from the story to support your answer.

3
IMAGERY

sight | sound | smell | taste | touch

All of us, at one time or another, have become so engrossed in a story that we forgot where we were and completely missed things that were happening around us. When you think about it, isn't it amazing that a storyteller can so interest you in a pattern of black markings on a piece of paper that your sense of the real world is utterly blotted out? You have become absorbed in another world with its own sights, sounds, smells, tastes, and touch; you have willingly suspended your disbelief in the sensations of a story world, and have allowed them, temporarily, to replace physical reality.

One way an author accomplishes this marvel is to make the sights and sounds, the taste, touch, and feel of the story world, so vivid that the story world becomes more real than your own. The author's eyes see for you things you might have overlooked, or things you never suspected existed; his ears hear sounds that have special meanings; and, at times, he can make your flesh rise with terror or desire, your mouth water, or your nose sniff as if the very smells he writes about were in the room. The things that activate these senses are called images, and often *imagery* is the key to the story's power.

Images are details that play upon the senses. In doing so they often reveal the author's attitude. The simplest way to discover whether imagery is at work in a story is to underline every detail or description that calls attention to one of the five senses: sight, sound, touch, smell, or taste. If you do this, you will soon discover that sight images outnumber all the others combined, since the world of fiction is, like the real world, largely a world of seen things. After all, if a reader cannot *see* what is happening, fiction will falter; even the dream world of closed eyes and the world of revery or reflection are lit by sight.

Therefore, your analysis of imagery in fiction may be sharpened by underlining or noting only those images of sight that pay particular attention to color, or to lightness and darkness, or to size and shape. In so limiting yourself, you will be doing precisely what many writers do when they seek to bring their stories alive through the five senses: they work consciously and hard at weaving these five senses into the story. Since sight images are so dominant, the writer's special attention is often focused on images appealing to the other four senses, and in the case of sight images to particular patterns of color, or lightness or darkness, or shape.

For example, Poe used a sight pattern emphasizing color—reds and blacks—in "The Masque of the Red Death." Note the reds in the first paragraph. You may recall other stories by Poe in which the circular shape of vortexes and whirlpools plays an important part, again with deliberate intent.

Imagery may appear either in the *literal description* of things, or within *figurative language* that describes things not actually present in the setting. Whether literal or figurative, if it is imagery at work, it plays with equal power upon your senses.

Once you have underlined or noted the imagery in a story—the words that appeal to your sense of sound, touch, smell, taste, and sight when particularly directed to color, brightness, or shape—you may then ask: What special effect is the author attempting through these images? Is he trying to convey a sharply drawn experience? Or is he, perhaps, trying to express a particular belief—that veiled attitude, that "hub of the wheel," commonly called a theme? Having noted the images and raised these questions, very often you can see that the images cluster around certain colors, shapes, or sounds, and that these clusters contribute strongly to a significant idea or revealing experience that is central to the story. Images do not really go to work in a story unless they act upon something, or are acted upon. Therefore, you should look for images with an eye to what *relevance* they have to the story's controlling idea or experience.

Ask yourself, too, why the narrator, or a particular character, happens to see or hear only certain details or images from among the thousands that constantly bombard him. We tend to see what we want to see. No eyewitnesses ever describe an event in the same way. Everything a character notices reveals something about his personality. A certain artistic economy operates here; images tell us not only about the person or object seen, but about the person who sees. In short, images contribute strongly to the way we regard the story's people.

Images are sometimes woven in with value judgments, but the difference between images and value judgments should be sharply preserved. Do not confuse a judgment like "She's a real beauty," which says nothing at all about "her," but only about the observer, with images that clearly convey specific information garnered by the senses: "The light from the lamp opposite our door caught the white curve of her neck, lit up her hair that rested there and, falling, lit up the hand upon the railing. It fell over one side of her dress and caught the white border of a petticoat, just visible as she stood at ease." Nor should you confuse images with "feelings," which have to do with a person's reaction to situations. Thus the boy narrator in the next story, "Araby," sees Mangan's sister in the images just quoted. But his feelings when she first speaks to him are expressed without imagery: "I was so confused that I did not know what to answer."

James Joyce

ARABY

North Richmond Street, being blind, was a quiet street except at the hour when the Christian Brothers' School set the boys free. An uninhabited house of two storeys stood at the blind end, detached from its neighbours in a square ground. The other houses of the street, conscious of decent lives within them, gazed at one another with brown imperturbable faces.

The former tenant of our house, a priest, had died in the back drawing-room. Air, musty from having been long enclosed, hung in all the rooms, and the waste room behind the kitchen was littered with old useless papers. Among these I found a few paper-covered books, the pages of which were curled and damp: *The Abbot,* by Walter Scott, *The Devout Communicant* and *The Memoirs of Vidocq.* I liked the last best because its leaves were yellow. The wild garden behind the house contained a central apple tree and a few straggling bushes under one of which I found the late tenant's rusty bicycle-pump. He had been a very charitable priest; in his will he had left all his money to institutions and the furniture of his house to his sister.

When the short days of winter came, dusk fell before we had well eaten our dinners. When we met in the street the houses had grown sombre. The space of sky above us was the colour of ever-changing violet and towards it the lamps of the street lifted their feeble lanterns. The cold air stung us and we played till our bodies glowed. Our shouts echoed in the silent street. The career of our play brought us through the dark muddy lanes behind the houses where we ran the gauntlet of the rough tribes from the cottages, to the back doors of the dark dripping gardens where odours arose from the ashpits, to the dark odorous stables where a coachman smoothed and combed the horse or shook music from the buckled harness. When we returned to the street, light from the kitchen windows had filled the areas. If my uncle was seen turning the corner we hid in the shadow until we had seen him safely housed. Or if Mangan's sister came out on the doorstep to call her brother in to his tea we watched her from our shadow peer up and down the street. We waited to see whether she would remain or go in and, if she remained, we left our shadow and walked up to Mangan's steps resignedly. She was waiting for us, her figure defined by the light from the half-opened door. Her brother always teased her before he obeyed and I stood by the railings looking at her. Her dress swung as she moved her body and the soft rope of her hair tossed from side to side.

Every morning I lay on the floor in the front parlour watching her door. The blind was pulled down to within an inch of the sash so that I could not be seen. When she came out on the doorstep my heart leaped. I ran to the hall, seized my books, and followed her. I kept her brown figure always in my eye and, when we came near the point at which our ways diverged, I quickened my pace and passed her. This happened morning after morning. I had never spoken to her, except for a few casual words, and yet her name was like a summons to all my foolish blood.

Her image accompanied me even in places the most hostile to romance. On Saturday evenings when my aunt went marketing I had to go to carry some of the parcels. We walked through the flaring streets, jostled by drunken men and bargaining women, amid the curses of labourers, the shrill litanies of shop-boys who stood on guard by the barrels of pigs' cheeks, the nasal chanting of street-singers, who sang a *come-all-you* about O'Donovan Rossa, or a ballad about the troubles in our native land. These noises converged in a single sensation of life for me: I imagined that I bore my chalice safely through a throng of foes. Her name sprang to my lips at moments in strange prayers and praises which I myself did not understand. My eyes were often full of tears (I could not tell why) and at times a flood from my heart seemed to pour itself out into my bosom. I thought little of the future. I did not know whether I would ever speak to her or not or, if I spoke to her, how I could tell her of my confused adoration. But my body was like a harp and her words and gestures were like fingers running upon the wires.

One evening I went into the back drawing-room in which the priest had died. It was a dark rainy evening and there was no sound in the house. Through one of the broken panes I heard the rain impinge upon the earth, the fine incessant needles of water playing in the sodden beds. Some distant lamp or lighted window gleamed below me. I was thankful that I could see so little. All my senses seemed to desire to veil themselves and, feeling that I was about to slip from them, I pressed the palms of my hands together until they trembled, murmuring: *"O love! O love!"* many times.

At last she spoke to me. When she addressed the first words to me I was so confused that I did not know what to answer. She asked me was I going to *Araby*. I forgot whether I answered yes or no. It would be a splendid bazaar, she said she would love to go.

"And why can't you?" I asked.

While she spoke she turned a silver bracelet round and round her wrist. She could not go, she said, because there would be a retreat that week in her convent. Her brother and two other boys were fighting for their caps and I was alone at the railings. She held one of the spikes, bowing her head towards me. The light from the lamp opposite our door caught the white curve of her neck, lit up her hair that rested there and, falling, lit up the hand upon the railing. It fell over one side of her dress and caught the white border of a petticoat, just visible as she stood at ease.

"It's well for you," she said.

"If I go," I said, "I will bring you something."

What innumerable follies laid waste my waking and sleeping thoughts after that evening! I wished to annihilate the tedious intervening days. I chafed against the work of school. At night in my bedroom and by day in the classroom her image came between me and the page I strove to read. The syllables of the word *Araby* were called to me through the silence in which my soul luxuriated and cast an Eastern enchantment over me. I asked for leave to go to the bazaar on Saturday night. My aunt was surprised and hoped it was not some Freemason affair. I answered few questions in class. I watched my master's face pass from amiability to sternness; he hoped I was not beginning to idle. I could not call my wandering thoughts together. I had hardly any patience with the serious work of life which, now that it stood between me and my desire, seemed to me child's play, ugly monotonous child's play.

On Saturday morning I reminded my uncle that I wished to go to the bazaar in the evening. He was fussing at the hallstand, looking for the hat-brush, and answered me curtly:

"Yes, boy, I know."

As he was in the hall I could not go into the front parlour and lie at the window. I left the house in bad humour and walked slowly towards the school. The air was pitilessly raw and already my heart misgave me.

When I came home to dinner my uncle had not yet been home. Still it was early. I sat staring at the clock for some time and, when its ticking began to irritate me, I left the room. I mounted the staircase and gained the upper part of the house. The high cold empty gloomy rooms liberated me and I went from room to room singing. From the front window I saw my companions playing below in the street. Their cries reached me weakened and indistinct and, leaning my forehead against the cool glass, I looked over at the dark house where she lived. I may have stood there for an hour, seeing nothing but the brown-clad figure cast by my imagination, touched discreetly by the lamplight at the curved neck, at the hand upon the railings and at the border below the dress.

When I came downstairs again I found Mrs. Mercer sitting at the fire. She was an old garrulous woman, a pawnbroker's widow, who collected used stamps for some pious purpose. I had to endure the gossip of the tea-table. The meal was prolonged beyond an hour and still my uncle did not come. Mrs. Mercer stood up to go: she was sorry she couldn't wait any longer, but it was after eight o'clock and she did not like to be out late, as the night air was bad for her. When she had gone I began to walk up and down the room, clenching my fists. My aunt said:

"I'm afraid you may put off your bazaar for this night of Our Lord."

At nine o'clock I heard my uncle's latchkey in the halldoor. I heard him talking to himself and heard the hallstand rocking when it had received the weight of his overcoat. I could interpret these signs. When he was midway through his dinner I asked him to give me the money to go to the bazaar. He had forgotten.

"The people are in bed and after their first sleep now," he said.

I did not smile. My aunt said to him energetically:

"Can't you give him the money and let him go? You've kept him late enough as it is."

My uncle said he was very sorry he had forgotten. He said he believed in the old saying: "All work and no play makes Jack a dull boy." He asked me where I was going and, when I had told him a second time he asked me did I know *The Arab's Farewell to His Steed*. When I left the kitchen he was about to recite the opening lines of the piece to my aunt.

I held a florin tightly in my hand as I strode down Buckingham Street towards the station. The sight of the streets thronged with buyers and glaring with gas recalled to me the purpose of my journey. I took my seat in a third-class carriage of a deserted train. After an intolerable delay the train moved out of the station slowly. It crept onward among ruinous houses and over the twinkling river. At Westland Row Station a crowd of people pressed to the carriage doors; but the porters moved them back, saying that it was a special train for the bazaar. I remained alone in the bare carriage. In a few minutes the train drew up beside an improvised wooden platform. I passed out on to the road and saw by the lighted dial of a clock that it was ten minutes to ten. In front of me was a large building which displayed the magical name.

I could not find any sixpenny entrance and, fearing that the bazaar would be closed, I passed in quickly through a turnstile, handing a shilling to a weary-looking man: I found myself in a big hall girdled at half its height by a gallery. Nearly all the stalls were closed and the greater part of the hall was in darkness. I recognised a silence like that which pervades a church after a service. I walked into the centre of the bazaar timidly. A few people were gathered about the stalls which were still open. Before a curtain, over which the words *Café Chantant* were written in coloured lamps, two men were counting money on a salver. I listened to the fall of the coins.

Remembering with difficulty why I had come I went over to one of the stalls and examined porcelain vases and flowered tea-sets. At the door of the stall a young lady was talking and laughing with two young gentlemen. I remarked their English accents and listened vaguely to their conversation.

"O, I never said such a thing!"

"O, but you did!"

"O, but I didn't!"

"Didn't she say that?"

"Yes. I heard her."

"O, there's a . . . fib!"

Observing me the young lady came over and asked me did I wish to buy anything. The tone of her voice was not encouraging; she seemed to have spoken to me out of a sense of duty. I looked humbly at the great jars that stood like eastern guards at either side of the dark entrance to the stall and murmured:

"No, thank you."

The young lady changed the position of one of the vases and went back to the two young men. They began to talk of the same subject. Once or twice the young lady glanced at me over her shoulder.

I lingered before her stall, though I knew my stay was useless, to make my interest in her wares seem the more real. Then I turned away slowly and walked down the middle of the bazaar. I allowed the two pennies to fall against the sixpence in my pocket. I heard a voice call from one end of the gallery that the light was out. The upper part of the hall was now completely dark.

Gazing up into the darkness I saw myself as a creature driven and derided by vanity; and my eyes burned with anguish and anger.

QUESTIONS

1 Vocabulary: *The Devout Communicant:* a Roman Catholic manual popular in the nineteenth century. *The Memoirs of Vidocq:* a sensational book of crime written by a reformed criminal, a Frenchman named Vidocq. *Come-all-you:* a narrative ballad form, often beginning with the words "come all you. . . ." *The Arab's Farewell to His Steed:* a poem by Caroline Norton about an Arab who sells his steed for gold. *Café Chantant:* a restaurant where singers perform.

2 Underline all the images of color in the story. These tend to cluster into images of darkness and images of light. Are the darkness images usually descriptive of the area close to or within the boy, or are they usually descriptive of things farther away? Are the light images descriptive of things close to the boy, or of things usually farther away?

3 What does your answer to question 2, above, suggest about the boy's attitude toward his physical world and his mental world? Which one is bright and which one dark?

4 Underline all of the images of (a) smell, (b) taste, (c) touch, and (d) sound in the story. Of these four types, which one predominates? Does it predominate by a little, or by a great deal? What is the significance of this predominant imagery?

5 At one point in the story, the boy reports hearing his uncle's latchkey, hearing him talking to himself, and hearing the hallstand rocking from the weight of his uncle's overcoat. He says, "I could interpret those signs." What do these sound images tell the boy—and you?

6 In paragraph 5, beginning with "Her image accompanied me . . . ," Joyce provides many images and details, some that are literally present in the setting and some that are figurative. Determine which are literal, which figurative. Is the boy's love for Mangan's sister realistic or idealized? How do the details and images in this paragraph prepare us for the intensity of the boy's disillusionment expressed in the final paragraph?

7 Running through the story are many references to religion. Which references help to establish the real world in which the boy lives? Which help to establish the ideal world that he creates for himself?

8 The last paragraph tells directly of the boy's attitude toward himself; the paragraph just before it contains several images. How do these images heighten the attitude expressed in the final paragraph?

9 As you sit in one place, write down all the sensory impressions (except *visual* ones) that you experience during one minute of existence. What does this experiment suggest about your everyday awareness of your world—or lack of it—as compared to the world an author is aware of?

John Updike

A & P

In walks these three girls in nothing but bathing suits. I'm in the third checkout slot, with my back to the door, so I don't see them until they're over by the bread. The one that caught my eye first was the one in the plaid green two-piece. She was a chunky kid, with a good tan and a sweet broad soft-looking can with those two crescents of white just under it, where the sun never seems to hit, at the top of the backs of her legs. I stood there with my hand on a box of HiHo crackers trying to remember if I rang it up or not. I ring it up again and the customer starts giving me hell. She's one of those cash-register-watchers, a witch about fifty with rouge on her cheekbones and no eyebrows, and I know it made her day to trip me up. She'd been watching cash registers for fifty years and probably never seen a mistake before.

By the time I got her feathers smoothed and her goodies into a bag—she gives me a little snort in passing, if she'd been born at the right time they would have burned her over in Salem—by the time I get her on her way the girls had circled around the bread and were coming back, without a pushcart, back my way along the counters, in the aisle between the checkouts and the Special bins. They didn't even have shoes on. There was this chunky one, with the two-piece—it was bright green and the seams on the bra were still sharp and her belly was still pretty pale so I guessed she just got it (the suit)—there was this one, with one of those chubby berry-faces, the lips all bunched together under her nose, this one, and a tall one, with black hair that hadn't quite frizzed right, and one of these sunburns right across under the eyes, and a chin that was too long—you know, the kind of girl other girls think is very "striking" and "attractive" but never quite makes it, as they very well know, which is why they like her so much—and then the third one, that wasn't quite so tall. She was the queen. She kind of led them, the other two peeking around and making their shoulders round. She didn't look around, not this queen, she just walked straight on slowly, on these long white prima-donna legs. She came down a little hard on her heels, as if she didn't walk in her bare feet that much, putting down her heels and then letting the weight move along to her toes as if she was testing the floor with every step, putting a little deliberate extra action into it. You never know for sure how girls' minds work (do you really think it's a mind in there or just a little buzz like a bee in a glass jar?) but you got the idea she had talked the other two into coming in here with her, and now she was showing them how to do it, walk slow and hold yourself straight.

She had on a kind of dirty-pink—beige maybe, I don't know—bathing suit with a little nubble all over it and, what got me, the straps were down. They were off her shoulders looped loose around the cool tops of her arms, and I guess as a result the suit had slipped a little on her, so all around the top of the cloth there was this shining rim. If it hadn't been there you wouldn't have known there could have been anything whiter than those shoulders. With the straps pushed off, there was nothing between the top of the suit and the top of her head except just *her,* this clean bare plane of the top of her chest down from the shoulder bones like a dented sheet of metal tilted in the light. I mean, it was more than pretty.

She had sort of oaky hair that the sun and salt had bleached, done up in a bun that was unravelling, and a kind of prim face. Walking into the A & P with your straps down, I suppose it's the only kind of face you *can* have. She held her head so high her neck, coming up out of those white shoulders, looked kind of stretched, but I didn't mind. The longer her neck was, the more of her there was.

She must have felt in the corner of her eye me and over my shoulder Stokesie in the second slot watching, but she didn't tip. Not this queen. She kept her eyes moving across the racks, and stopped, and turned so slow it made my stomach rub the inside of my apron, and buzzed to the other two, who kind of huddled against her for relief, and then they all three of them went up the cat-and-dog-food-breakfast-cereal-macaroni-rice-raisins-seasonings-spreads-spaghetti-soft-drinks-crackers-and-cookies aisle. From the third slot I look straight up this aisle to the meat counter, and I watched them all the way. The fat one with the tan sort of fumbled with the cookies, but on second thought she put the package back. The sheep pushing their carts down the aisle—the girls were walking against the usual traffic (not that we have one-way signs or anything)—were pretty hilarious. You could see them, when Queenie's white shoulders dawned on them, kind of jerk, or hop, or hiccup, but their eyes snapped back to their own baskets and on they pushed. I bet you could set off dynamite in an A & P and the people would by and large keep reaching and checking oatmeal off their lists and muttering "Let me see, there was a third thing, began with A, asparagus, no, ah, yes, applesauce!" or whatever it is they do mutter. But there was no doubt, this jiggled them. A few houseslaves in pin curlers even looked around after pushing their carts past to make sure what they had seen was correct.

You know, it's one thing to have a girl in a bathing suit down on the beach, where what with the glare nobody can look at each other much anyway, and another thing in the cool of the A & P, under the fluorescent lights, against all those stacked packages, with her feet paddling along naked over our checkerboard green-and-cream rubber-tile floor.

"Oh Daddy," Stokesie said beside me. "I feel so faint."

"Darling," I said. "Hold me tight." Stokesie's married, with two babies chalked up on his fuselage already, but as far as I can tell that's the only difference. He's twenty-two, and I was nineteen this April.

"Is it done?" he asks, the responsible married man finding his voice. I forgot to say he thinks he's going to be manager some sunny day, maybe in 1990 when it's called the Great Alexandrov and Petrooshki Tea Company or something.

What he meant was, our town is five miles from a beach, with a big summer colony out on the Point, but we're right in the middle of town, and the women generally put on a shirt or shoes or something before they get out of the car into the street. And anyway these are usually women with six children and varicose veins mapping their legs and nobody, including them, could care less. As I say, we're right in the middle of town, and if you stand at our front doors you can see two banks and the Congregational church and the newspaper store and three real-estate offices and about twenty-seven old freeloaders tearing up Central Street because the sewer broke again. It's not as if we're on the Cape; we're north of Boston and there's people in this town haven't seen the ocean for twenty years.

The girls had reached the meat counter and were asking McMahon something. He pointed, they pointed, and they shuffled out of sight behind a pyramid of Diet Delight peaches. All that was left for us to see was old McMahon patting his mouth and looking after them sizing up their joints. Poor kids, I began to feel sorry for them, they couldn't help it.

Now here comes the sad part of the story, at least my family says it's sad, but I don't think it's so sad myself. The store's pretty empty, it being Thursday afternoon, so there was nothing much to do except lean on the register and wait for the girls to show up again. The whole store was like a pinball machine and I didn't know which tunnel they'd come out of. After a while they come around out of the far aisle, around the light bulbs, records at discount of the Caribbean Six or Tony Martin Sings or some such gunk you wonder they waste the wax on, sixpacks of candy bars, and plastic toys done up in cellophane that fall apart when a kid looks at them anyway. Around they come, Queenie still leading the way, and holding a little gray jar in her hand. Slots Three through Seven are unmanned and I could see her wondering between Stokes and me, but Stokesie with his usual luck draws an old party in baggy gray pants who stumbles up with four giant cans of pineapple juice (what do these bums *do* with all that pineapple juice? I've often asked myself) so the girls come to me. Queenie puts down the jar and I take it into my fingers icy cold. Kingfish Fancy Herring Snacks in Pure Sour Cream: 49¢. Now her hands are empty, not a ring or a bracelet, bare as God made them, and I wonder where the money's coming from. Still with that prim look she lifts a folded dollar bill out of the hollow at the center of her nubbed pink top. The jar went heavy in my hand. Really, I thought that was so cute.

Then everybody's luck begins to run out. Lengel comes in from haggling with a truck full of cabbages on the lot and is about to scuttle into that door marked MANAGER behind which he hides all day when the girls touch his eye. Lengel's pretty dreary, teaches Sunday school and the rest, but he doesn't miss that much. He comes over and says, "Girls, this isn't the beach."

Queenie blushes, though maybe it's just a brush of sunburn I was noticing for the first time, now that she was so close. "My mother asked me to pick up a jar of herring snacks." Her voice kind of startled me, the way voices do when you see the people first, coming out so flat and dumb yet kind of tony, too, the way it ticked over "pick up" and "snacks." All of a sudden I slid right down her voice into her living room. Her father and the other men were standing around in ice-cream coats and bow ties and the women were in sandals picking up herring snacks on toothpicks off a big glass plate and they were all holding drinks the color of water with olives and sprigs of mint in them. When my parents have somebody over they get lemonade and if it's a real racy affair Schlitz in tall glasses with "They'll Do It Every Time" cartoons stencilled on.

"That's all right," Lengel said. "But this isn't the beach." His repeating this struck me as funny, as if it had just occurred to him, and he had been thinking all these years the A & P was a great big dune and he was the head lifeguard. He didn't like my smiling—as I say he doesn't miss much—but he concentrates on giving the girls that sad Sunday-school-superintendent stare.

Queenie's blush is no sunburn now, and the plump one in plaid, that I liked better from the back—a really sweet can—pipes up, "We weren't doing any shopping. We just came in for the one thing."

"That makes no difference," Lengel tells her, and I could see from the way his eyes went that he hadn't noticed she was wearing a two-piece before. "We want you decently dressed when you come in here."

"We *are* decent," Queenie says suddenly, her lower lip pushing, getting sore now that she remembers her place, a place from which the crowd that runs the A & P must look pretty crummy. Fancy Herring Snacks flashed in her very blue eyes.

"Girls, I don't want to argue with you. After this come in here with your shoulders covered. It's our policy." He turns his back. That's policy for you. Policy is what the kingpins want. What the others want is juvenile delinquency.

All this while, the customers had been showing up with their carts but, you know, sheep, seeing a scene, they had all bunched up on Stokesie, who shook open a paper bag as gently as peeling a peach, not wanting to miss a word. I could feel in the silence everybody getting nervous, most of all Lengel, who asks me, "Sammy, have you rung up their purchase?"

I thought and said "No" but it wasn't about that I was thinking. I go through the punches, 4, 9, GROC, TOT—it's more complicated than you think, and after you do it often enough, it begins to make a little song, that you hear words to, in my case "Hello (*bing*) there, you (*gung*) hap-py *pee*-pul (*splat*)!"—the *splat* being the drawer flying out. I uncrease the bill, tenderly as you may imagine, it just having come from between the two smoothest scoops of vanilla I had ever known were there, and pass a half and a penny into her narrow pink palm, and nestle the herrings in a bag and twist its neck and hand it over, all the time thinking.

The girls, and who'd blame them, are in a hurry to get out, so I say "I quit" to Lengel quick enough for them to hear, hoping they'll stop and watch me, their unsuspected hero. They keep right on going, into the electric eye; the door flies open and they flicker across the lot to their car, Queenie and Plaid and Big Tall Goony-Goony (not that as raw material she was so bad), leaving me with Lengel and a kink in his eyebrow.

"Did you say something, Sammy?"

"I said I quit."

"I thought you did."

"You didn't have to embarrass them."

"It was they who were embarrassing us."

I started to say something that came out "Fiddle-de-doo." It's a saying of my grandmother's, and I know she would have been pleased.

"I don't think you know what you're saying," Lengel said.

"I know you don't," I said. "But I do." I pull the bow at the back of my apron and start shrugging it off my shoulders. A couple customers that had been heading for my slot begin to knock against each other, like scared pigs in a chute.

Lengel sighs and begins to look very patient and old and gray. He's been a friend of my parents for years. "Sammy, you don't want to do this to your Mom and Dad," he tells me. It's true, I don't. But it seems to me that once you begin a gesture it's fatal not to go through with it. I fold the apron, "Sammy" stitched in red on the pocket, and put it on the counter, and drop the bow tie on top of it. The bow tie is theirs, if you've ever wondered. "You'll feel this for the rest of your life," Lengel says, and I know that's true, too, but remembering how he made that pretty girl blush makes me so scrunchy inside I punch the No Sale tab and the machine whirs "pee-pul" and the drawer splats out. One advantage to this scene taking place in summer, I can follow this up with a clean exit, there's no fumbling around getting your coat and galoshes, I just saunter into the electric eye in my white shirt that my mother ironed the night before, and the door heaves itself open, and outside the sunshine is skating around on the asphalt.

I look around for my girls, but they're gone, of course. There wasn't anybody but some young married screaming with her children about some candy they didn't get by the door of a powder-blue Falcon station wagon. Looking back in the big windows, over the bags of peat moss and aluminum lawn furniture stacked on the pavement, I could see Lengel in my place in the slot, checking the sheep through. His face was dark gray and his back stiff, as if he'd just had an injection of iron, and my stomach kind of fell as I felt how hard the world was going to be to me hereafter.

QUESTIONS

1 A swift look reveals the prevalence of sight images in this story. A closer look discloses an important pattern of sight imagery—color images. What, for example, are the colors most closely associated with Queenie? What are the traditional connotations of these colors? Do these connotations correspond with the way Sammy, the young narrator, views her? Why does the author specify the color of Sammy's shirt as he leaves the store in disgust? What color is associated with the manager? How do these sets of opposing colors reflect the principal conflict in the story?

2 Do other details and images support this pattern of color imagery? Consider the description of Queenie's walk and the way she carries herself; the manager's back as seen by the narrator; images of sound, such as the song of the cash register; images conveyed by figurative language, such as those used by Sammy to describe the supermarket customers?

3 An important form of sight imagery in this story has to do with shapes—not only the explicitly described shapes of the girls, but also the shapes in the store: the parallel checkout slots, the grid of aisles, the pyramids of packaged goods. How do these contrasting images of shape—those of the girls, and those of the store—reveal the conflict disclosed by the opposing color images?

4 List some of Sammy's value judgments, that is, his personal opinions. In what specific ways does the imagery he uses support these judgments? Pay particular attention to the images found in his figurative language. What do these images tell us about a narrator who only relates these particular ones from among all those available to him?

5 Sammy uses many slangy, highly connotative words. He begins in paragraph 1 with "can" and "witch" and later in the story refers to the girls as Queenie, Plaid, and Big Tall Goony-Goony. He describes the butcher McMahon as "sizing up their joints" and departs by telling the manager Lengel, "Fiddle-de-doo." Do you consider these expressions mild, or crude? Choose, in each case, a milder expression than Sammy uses. Choose a cruder expression. Comment on how the new choices affect your opinion of Sammy's attitude.

6 In Chapter 5 we will discuss and illustrate irony at some length. For now it is enough to say that irony is often achieved by having a narrator reveal more about himself—by the words he uses, by the ways he sees things, by the opinions he expresses—than he is himself aware of. On the evidence of his language, imagery, and opinions, how would you describe Sammy's view of himself? How does the author view him? How, in turn, do you view him?

7 What is the theme of the story—the author's attitude as expressed through this experience he has created for our entertainment and enlightenment?

4
COMPARISONS

allusion | figurative language | cliché

Imaginative writing depends heavily on *comparisons* to sharpen or enrich its meanings. Comparisons (including the kind we call contrasts) may take different forms. Sometimes this comparison or contrast is made through a reference, or *allusion,* to known persons or events. For example, "She's no Raquel Welch, but what do you expect from somebody who's another Einstein?" means "Not much on looks but plenty of brains." Although an allusion can say a great deal effectively, it runs the danger of falling flat if the reader does not understand the reference. If someone were to say, "She's no Aphrodite, but what do you expect from someone who's another Archimedes?" you might have trouble understanding him, though consulting a dictionary would solve the difficulty. Aphrodite is the Greek name for Venus, and Archimedes was the greatest mathematician of the ancient world.

Allusions are commonly historical, literary, mythological, or Biblical. They may take the form of direct quotations from other works, or they may actually name persons and events from the past, or merely refer to them. "The little Corsican," for example, refers to Napoleon, who was born in Corsica; the phrase also means cocky, authoritarian, perhaps a little mad, to most readers.

You probably did not know what *Hernani* or *Herod* alluded to in "The Masque of the Red Death" when you read it. *Hernani* is a famous play by Victor Hugo, first staged in 1830. More particularly, it has become a synonym for exaggerated romantic drama with excessively spectacular theatrical effects. Herod was a king of Judea who, in 4 B.C., according to the book of Matthew, decreed that all the babies in Bethlehem should be slaughtered. This decree led Joseph and Mary to make the famous flight into Egypt carrying the infant Jesus. But Poe's reference is not to the historical Herod, but rather to the stage figure—a blustering, roaring bully—who came to represent him on the Elizabethan stage. And the expression "out-Heroded Herod" is a direct reference to Hamlet's description of such a ranting actor in his advice to the players (*Hamlet,* III, ii, 15). If his readers know this, Poe's allusions are successful; if they do not, these special effects are lost.

Allusions, in one sense, may be said to flatter the reader: they invite him into a kind of partnership of understanding with the author. But thoughtful writers do not use allusions as mere intellectual adornments. They use them, rather, to enrich and broaden the story's meaning. Sometimes, as in "The Portable Phonograph," which follows, they use allusions as the principle technique for telling their story.

Walter Van Tilburg Clark

THE PORTABLE PHONOGRAPH

The red sunset, with narrow, black cloud strips like threats across it, lay on the curved horizon of the prairie. The air was still and cold, and in it settled the mute darkness and greater cold of night. High in the air there was wind, for through the veil of the dusk the clouds could be seen gliding rapidly south and changing shapes. A queer sensation of torment, of two-sided, unpredictable nature, arose from the stillness of the earth air beneath the violence of the upper air. Out of the sunset, through the dead, matted grass and isolated weed stalks of the prairie, crept the narrow and deeply rutted remains of a road. In the road, in places, there were crusts of shallow, brittle ice. There were little islands of an old oiled pavement in the road too, but most of it was mud, now frozen rigid. The frozen mud still bore the toothed impress of great tanks, and a wanderer on the neighboring undulations might have stumbled, in this light, into large, partially filled-in and weed-grown cavities, their banks channelled and beginning to spread into badlands. These pits were such as might have been made by falling meteors, but they were not. They were the scars of gigantic bombs, their rawness already made a little natural by rain, seed, and time. Along the road, there were rakish remnants of fence. There was also, just visible, one portion of tangled and multiple barbed wire still erect, behind which was a shelving ditch with small caves, now very quiet and empty, at intervals in its back wall. Otherwise there was no structure or remnant of a structure visible over the dome of the darkling earth, but only, in sheltered hollows, the darker shadows of young trees trying again.

Under the wuthering arch of the high wind a V of wild geese fled south. The rush of their pinions sounded briefly, and the faint, plaintive notes of their expeditionary talk. Then they left a still greater vacancy. There was the smell and expectation of snow, as there is likely to be when the wild geese fly south. From the remote distance, towards the red sky, came faintly the protracted howl and quick yap-yap of a prairie wolf.

North of the road, perhaps a hundred yards, lay the parallel and deeply intrenched course of a small creek, lined with leafless alders and willows. The creek was already silent under ice. Into the bank above it was dug a sort of cell, with a single opening, like the mouth of a mine tunnel. Within the cell there was a little red of fire, which showed dully through the opening, like a reflection or a deception of the imagination. The light came from the chary burning of four blocks of poorly aged peat, which gave off a petty warmth and much acrid smoke. But the precious remnants of wood, old fence posts and timbers from the long-deserted dugouts, had to be saved for the real cold, for the time when a man's breath blew white, the moisture in his nostrils stiffened at once when he stepped out, and the expansive blizzards paraded for days over the vast open, swirling and settling and thickening, till the dawn of the cleared day when the sky was thin blue-green and the terrible cold, in which a man could not live for three hours unwarmed, lay over the uniformly drifted swell of the plain.

Around the smoldering peat, four men were seated crosslegged. Behind them, traversed by their shadows, was the earth bench, with two old and dirty army blankets, where the owner of the cell slept. In a niche in the opposite wall were a few tin utensils which caught the glint of the coals. The host was rewrapping in a piece of daubed burlap four fine, leatherbound books. He worked slowly and very carefully, and at last tied the bundle securely with a piece of grass-woven cord. The other three looked intently upon the process, as if a great significance lay in it. As the host tied the cord, he spoke. He was an old man, his long, matted beard and hair gray to nearly white. The shadows made his brows and cheekbones appear gnarled, his eyes and cheeks deeply sunken. His big hands, rough with frost and swollen by rheumatism, were awkward but gentle at their task. He was like a prehistoric priest performing a fateful ceremonial rite. Also his voice had in it a suitable quality of deep, reverent despair, yet perhaps at the moment, a sharpness of selfish satisfaction.

"When I perceived what was happening," he said, "I told myself, 'It is the end. I cannot take much; I will take these.'

"Perhaps I was impractical," he continued. "But for myself, I do not regret, and what do we know of those who will come after us? We are the doddering remnant of a race of mechanical fools. I have saved what I love; the soul of what was good in us is here; perhaps the new ones will make a strong enough beginning not to fall behind when they become clever."

He rose with slow pain and placed the wrapped volumes in the niche with his utensils. The others watched him with the same ritualistic gaze.

"Shakespeare, the Bible, *Moby Dick, The Divine Comedy,*" one of them said softly. "You might have done worse, much worse."

"You will have a little soul left until you die," said another harshly. "That is more than is true of us. My brain becomes thick, like my hands." He held the big, battered hands, with their black nails, in the glow to be seen.

"I want paper to write on," he said. "And there is none."

The fourth man said nothing. He sat in the shadow farthest from the fire, and sometimes his body jerked in its rags from the cold. Although he was still young, he was sick and coughed often. Writing implied a greater future than he now felt able to consider.

The old man seated himself laboriously, and reached out, groaning at the movement, to put another block of peat on the fire. With bowed heads and averted eyes, his three guests acknowledged his magnanimity.

"We thank you, Doctor Jenkins, for the reading," said the man who had named the books.

They seemed then to be waiting for something. Doctor Jenkins understood, but was loath to comply. In an ordinary moment he would have said nothing. But the words of *The Tempest,* which he had been reading, and the religious attention of the three made this an unusual occasion.

"You wish to hear the phonograph," he said grudgingly.

The two middle-aged men stared into the fire, unable to formulate and expose the enormity of their desire.

The young man, however, said anxiously, between suppressed coughs, "Oh, please," like an excited child.

The old man rose again in his difficult way, and went to the back of the cell. He returned and placed tenderly upon the packed floor, where the firelight might fall upon it, an old portable phonograph in a black case. He smoothed the top with his hand, and then opened it. The lovely green-felt-covered disk became visible.

"I have been using thorns as needles," he said. "But tonight, because we have a musician among us"—he bent his head to the young man, almost invisible in the shadow—"I will use a steel needle. There are only three left."

The two middle-aged men stared at him in speechless adoration. The one with the big hands, who wanted to write, moved his lips, but the whisper was not audible.

"Oh, don't!" cried the young man, as if he were hurt. "The thorns will do beautifully."

"No," the old man said. "I have become accustomed to the thorns, but they are not really good. For you, my young friend, we will have good music tonight.

"After all," he added generously, and beginning to wind the phonograph, which creaked, "they can't last forever."

"No, nor we," the man who needed to write said harshly. "The needle, by all means."

"Oh, thanks," said the young man. "Thanks," he said again in a low, excited voice, and then stifled his coughing with a bowed head.

"The records, though," said the old man when he had finished winding, "are a different matter. Already they are very worn. I do not play them more than once a week. One, once a week, that is what I allow myself.

"More than a week I cannot stand it; not to hear them," he apologized.

"No, how could you?" cried the young man. "And with them here like this."

"A man can stand anything," said the man who wanted to write, in his harsh, antagonistic voice.

"Please, the music," said the young man.

"Only the one," said the old man. "In the long run, we will remember more that way."

He had a dozen records with luxuriant gold and red seals. Even in that light the others could see that the threads of the records were becoming worn. Slowly he read out the titles and the tremendous dead names of the composers and the artists and the orchestras. The three worked upon the names in their minds, carefully. It was difficult to select from such a wealth what they would at once most like to remember. Finally, the man who wanted to write named Gershwin's "New York."

"Oh, no," cried the sick young man, and then could say nothing more because he had to cough. The others understood him, and the harsh man withdrew his selection and waited for the musician to choose.

The musician begged Doctor Jenkins to read the titles again, very slowly, so that he could remember the sounds. While they were read, he lay back against the wall, his eyes closed, his thin, horny hand pulling at his light beard, and listened to the voices and the orchestras and the single instruments in his mind.

When the reading was done he spoke despairingly. "I have forgotten," he complained; "I cannot hear them clearly.

"There are things missing," he explained.

"I know," said Doctor Jenkins. "I thought that I knew all of Shelley by heart. I should have brought Shelley."

"That's more soul than we can use," said the harsh man. "*Moby Dick* is better.

"By God, we can understand that," he emphasized.

The Doctor nodded.

"Still," said the man who had admired the books, "we need the absolute if we are to keep a grasp on anything.

"Anything but these sticks and peat clods and rabbit snares," he said bitterly.

"Shelley desired an ultimate absolute," said the harsh man. "It's too much," he said. "It's no good; no earthly good."

The musician selected a Debussy nocturne. The others considered and approved. They rose to their knees to watch the Doctor prepare for the playing, so that they appeared to be actually in an attitude of worship. The peat glow showed the thinness of their bearded faces, and the deep lines in them, and revealed the condition of their garments. The other two continued to kneel as the old man carefully lowered the needle onto the spinning disk, but the musician suddenly drew back against the wall again, with his knees up, and buried his face in his hands.

At the first notes of the piano the listeners were startled. They stared at each other. Even the musician lifted his head in amazement, but then quickly bowed it again, strainingly, as if he were suffering from a pain he might not be able to endure. They were all listening deeply, without movement. The wet, blue-green notes tinkled forth from the old machine, and were individual, delectable presences in the cell. The individual, delectable presences swept into a sudden tide of unbearably beautiful dissonance, and then continued fully the swelling and ebbing of that tide, the dissonant inpourings, and the resolutions, and the diminishments, and the little, quiet wavelets of interlude lapping between. Every sound was piercing and singularly sweet. In all the men except the musician, there occurred rapid sequences of tragically heightened recollection. He heard nothing but what was there. At the final, whispering disappearance, but moving quietly so that the others would not hear him and look at him, he let his head fall back in agony, as if it were drawn there by the hair, and clenched the fingers of one hand over his teeth. He sat that way while the others were silent, and until they began to breathe again normally. His drawn-up legs were trembling violently.

Quickly Doctor Jenkins lifted the needle off, to save it and not to spoil the recollection with scraping. When he had stopped the whirling of the sacred disk, he courteously left the phonograph open and by the fire, in sight.

The others, however, understood. The musician rose last, but then abruptly, and went quickly out at the door without saying anything. The others stopped at the door and gave their thanks in low voices. The Doctor nodded magnificently.

"Come again," he invited, "in a week. We will have the 'New York.' "

When the two had gone together, out towards the rimed road, he stood in the entrance, peering and listening. At first, there was only the resonant boom of the wind overhead, and then far over the dome of the dead, dark plain, the wolf cry lamenting. In the rifts of clouds the Doctor saw four stars flying. It impressed the Doctor that one of them had just been obscured by the beginning of a flying cloud at the very moment he heard what he had been listening for, a sound of suppressed coughing. It was not near-by, however. He believed that down against the pale alders he could see the moving shadow.

With nervous hands he lowered the piece of canvas which served as his door, and pegged it at the bottom. Then quickly and quietly, looking at the piece of canvas frequently, he slipped the records into the case, snapped the lid shut, and carried the phonograph to his couch. There, pausing often to stare at the canvas and listen, he dug earth from the wall and disclosed a piece of board. Behind this there was a deep hole in the wall, into which he put the phonograph. After a moment's consideration, he went over and reached down his bundle of books and inserted it also. Then, guardedly, he once more sealed up the hole with the board and the earth. He also changed his blankets, and the grass-stuffed sack which served as a pillow, so that he could lie facing the entrance. After carefully placing two more blocks of peat upon the fire, he stood for a long time watching the stretched canvas, but it seemed to billow naturally with the first gusts of a lowering wind. At last he prayed, and got in under his blankets, and closed his smoke-smarting eyes. On the inside of the bed, next the wall, he could feel with his hand the comfortable piece of lead pipe.

QUESTIONS

1 Vocabulary: *darkling:* threateningly dark. *wuthering:* blowing with a dull roaring sound. In a story so rich in allusions, it is not surprising to discover allusions behind these strange words. *Darkling* is used with extraordinary effectiveness in Matthew Arnold's poem "Dover Beach." And *wuthering* appears in the title of Emily Brontë's *Wuthering Heights.*

2 In this story allusions are made to all of the following: Shakespeare, the Bible, *Moby Dick, The Divine Comedy, The Tempest,* Gershwin's "New York," Shelley, and a Debussy nocturne. Can you identify all these names and titles? If not, consult a good dictionary or encyclopedia.

3 Why are all of the above, taken collectively, appropriate allusions for this story? What do they suggest or stand for?

4 Some of these allusions have particular as well as general significance. Why, for example, given the situation that confronts these four men, would Gershwin's "New York" be too painful to listen to? Why did the writer say of Shelley, "That's more soul than we can use"? And, speaking again of Shelley, why did he say, "It's no good; it's no earthly good"? And why did he add, "*Moby Dick* is better. By God, we can understand that"?

5 More subtle than these allusions is the reference to the professor's reading aloud from *The Tempest.* This is a very rich allusion that permits those readers who are familiar with Shakespeare's play to discover several possible comparisons. First, in what way is the title alone suggestive? Second, in what respects may the professor be likened to the play's main character, the wise old magician Prospero? Third, in what ways might the conflict between Ariel and Caliban in the play be likened to the situation in which the professor finds himself at the end of the story?

6 Although the Bible is referred to only once, in a general way, this allusion, too, is suggestive. Review the Book of Ecclesiastes, especially Chapter 1. Can you find there passages appropriate to the theme of this story?

7 An author's choice of allusions must be made as carefully as his choice of images and words. Sometimes a word he chooses contains a buried allusion of which even he is unaware at the time. Clark once wrote an explanation of how he came to select the word "comfortable," which appears in the story's final sentence, and which has been much admired. It must have been, he says, an unconscious echo of Juliet's statement to Friar Lawrence when, waking in the tomb and not yet aware that Romeo is dead, she says drowsily, "Oh, comfortable friar." The comparison is instructive: neither Juliet nor the professor in Clark's story will ever experience comfort again, but neither realizes this. Clark ends his account with a statement that reveals a good writer's intention —to raise disturbing questions, not provide pat answers. "And I was sure," he says, "that at least the ghost of that old, warm, trusting 'comfortable' would lurk to trouble the reader as it had troubled me."

FIGURATIVE LANGUAGE

When a thing or an image is substituted for something essentially unlike it, this substitution is called a *metaphor.* "She's a witch."

A *simile,* on the other hand, does not substitute, but names both the literal thing and its figurative counterpart. "My body was like a harp." "As" or "like" is usually the joining word of the simile, though it should be pointed out that just because "as" or "like" appears, a simile is not necessarily present. Language is full of comparisons like this old political saying: "As Maine goes, so goes the nation." But unless a comparison of essentially unlike objects is conjured up, it is not called a simile.

Metaphor and simile, like allusion, are effective because they broaden the world of the story beyond the confines of its setting. "Figurative" language means "not literally present in the setting," and this is how you test for metaphor and simile. In the first sentence of "The Portable Phonograph," the phrase "cloud strips like threats" reveals that cloud strips are literally present; threats are not. Thus, figurative language is at work.

The next story, "An Episode of War," is rich in figurative language, in imagery, and in artfully chosen words. Thus it affords an opportunity to study the interplay in fiction of all the techniques to which you have so far been introduced.

Stephen Crane

AN EPISODE OF WAR

The lieutenant's rubber blanket lay on the ground, and upon it he had poured the company's supply of coffee. Corporals and other representatives of the grimy and hot-throated men who lined the breastwork had come for each squad's portion.

The lieutenant was frowning and serious at this task of division. His lips pursed as he drew with his sword various crevices in the heap, until brown squares of coffee, astoundingly equal in size, appeared on the blanket. He was on the verge of a great triumph in mathematics, and the corporals were thronging forward, each to reap a little square, when suddenly the lieutenant cried out and looked quickly at a man near him as if he suspected it was a case of personal assault. The others cried out also when they saw blood upon the lieutenant's sleeve.

He had winced like a man stung, swayed dangerously, and then straightened. The sound of his hoarse breathing was plainly audible. He looked sadly, mystically, over the breastwork at the green face of a wood, where now were many little puffs of white smoke. During this moment the men about him gazed statuelike and silent, astonished and awed by this catastrophe which happened when catastrophes were not expected—when they had leisure to observe it.

As the lieutenant stared at the wood, they too swung their heads, so that for another instant all hands, still silent, contemplated the distant forest as if their minds were fixed upon the mystery of a bullet's journey.

The officer had, of course, been compelled to take his sword into his left hand. He did not hold it by the hilt. He gripped it at the middle of the blade, awkwardly. Turning his eyes from the hostile wood, he looked at the sword as he held it there, and seemed puzzled as to what to do with it, where to put it. In short, this weapon had of a sudden become a strange thing to him. He looked at it in a kind of stupefaction, as if he had been endowed with a trident, a sceptre, or a spade.

Finally he tried to sheathe it. To sheathe a sword held by the left hand, at the middle of the blade, in a scabbard hung at the left hip, is a feat worthy of a sawdust ring. This wounded officer engaged in a desperate struggle with the sword and the wobbling scabbard, and during the time of it he breathed like a wresler.

But at this instant the men, the spectators, awoke from their stone-like poses and crowded forward sympathetically. The orderly-sergeant took the sword and tenderly placed it in the scabbard. At the time, he leaned nervously backward, and did not allow even his finger to brush the body of the lieutenant. A wound gives strange dignity to him who bears it. Well men shy from this new and terrible majesty. It is as if the wounded man's hand is upon the curtain which hangs before the revelations of all existence—the meaning of ants, potentates, wars, cities, sunshine, snow, a feather dropped from a bird's wing; and the power of it sheds radiance upon a bloody form, and makes the other men understand sometimes that they are little. His comrades look at him with large eyes thoughtfully. Moreover, they fear vaguely that the weight of a finger upon him might send him headlong, precipitate the tragedy, hurl him at once into the dim, grey unknown. And so the orderly-sergeant, while sheathing the sword, leaned nervously backward.

There were others who proffered assistance. One timidly presented his shoulder and asked the lieutenant if he cared to lean upon it, but the latter waved him away mournfully. He wore the look of one who knows he is the victim of a terrible disease and understands his helplessness. He again stared over the breastwork at the forest, and then, turning, went slowly rearward. He held his right wrist tenderly in his left hand as if the wounded arm was made of very brittle glass.

And the men in silence stared at the wood, then at the departing lieutenant; then at the wood, then at the lieutenant.

As the wounded officer passed from the line of battle, he was enabled to see many things which as a participant in the fight were unknown to him. He saw a general on a black horse gazing over the lines of blue infantry at the green woods which veiled his problems. An aide galloped furiously, dragged his horse suddenly to a halt, saluted, and presented a paper. It was, for a wonder, precisely like a historical painting.

To the rear of the general and his staff a group, composed of a bugler, two or three orderlies, and the bearer of the corps standard, all upon maniacal horses, were working like slaves to hold their ground, preserve their respectful interval, while the shells boomed in the air about them, and caused their chargers to make furious quivering leaps.

A battery, a tumultuous and shining mass, was swirling toward the right. The wild thud of hoofs, the cries of the riders shouting blame and praise, menace and encouragement, and, last, the roar of the wheels, the slant of the glistening guns, brought the lieutenant to an intent pause. The battery swept in curves that stirred the heart; it made halts as dramatic as the crash of a wave on the rocks, and when it fled onward this aggregation of wheels, levers, motors had a beautiful unity, as if it were a missile. The sound of it was a war-chorus that reached into the depths of man's emotion.

The lieutenant, still holding his arm as if it were of glass, stood watching this battery until all detail of it was lost, save the figures of the riders, which rose and fell and waved lashes over the black mass.

Later, he turned his eyes toward the battle, where the shooting sometimes crackled like bushfires, sometimes sputtered with exasperating irregularity, and sometimes reverberated like the thunder. He saw the smoke rolling upward and saw crowds of men who ran and cheered, or stood and blazed away at the inscrutable distance.

He came upon some stragglers, and they told him how to find the field hospital. They described its exact location. In fact, these men, no longer having part in the battle, knew more of it than others. They told the performance of every corps, every division, the opinion of every general. The lieutenant, carrying his wounded arm rearward, looked upon them with wonder.

At the roadside a brigade was making coffee and buzzing with talk like a girls' boarding school. Several officers came out to him and inquired concerning things of which he knew nothing. One, seeing his arm, began to scold. "Why, man, that's no way to do. You want to fix that thing." He appropriated the lieutenant and the lieutenant's wound. He cut the sleeve and laid bare the arm, every nerve of which softly fluttered under his touch. He bound his handkerchief over the wound, scolding away in the meantime. His tone allowed one to think that he was in the habit of being wounded every day. The lieutenant hung his head, feeling, in this presence, that he did not know how to be correctly wounded.

The low white tents of the hospital were grouped around an old schoolhouse. There was here a singular commotion. In the foreground two ambulances interlocked wheels in the deep mud. The drivers were tossing the blame of it back and forth, gesticulating and berating, while from the ambulances, both crammed with wounded, there came an occasional groan. An interminable crowd of bandaged men were coming and going. Great numbers sat under the trees nursing heads or arms or legs. There was a dispute of some kind raging on the steps of the schoolhouse. Sitting with his back against a tree a man with a face as grey as a new army blanket was serenely smoking a corncob pipe. The lieutenant wished to rush forward and inform him that he was dying.

A busy surgeon was passing near the lieutenant. "Good morning," he said, with a friendly smile. Then he caught sight of the lieutenant's arm, and his face at once changed. "Well, let's have a look at it." He seemed possessed suddenly of a great contempt for the lieutenant. This wound evidently placed the latter on a very low social plane. The doctor cried out impatiently: "What mutton-head had tied it up that way anyhow?" The lieutenant answered, "Oh, a man."

When the wound was disclosed the doctor fingered it disdainfully. "Humph," he said. "You come along with me and I'll 'tend to you." His voice contained the same scorn as if he were saying: "You will have to go to jail."

The lieutenant had been very meek, but now his face flushed, and he looked into the doctor's eyes. "I guess I won't have it amputated," he said.

"Nonsense, man! Nonsense! Nonsense!" cried the doctor. "Come along, now. I won't amputate it. Come along. Don't be a baby."

"Let go of me," said the lieutenant, holding back wrathfully, his glance fixed upon the door of the old schoolhouse, as sinister to him as the portals of death.

And this is the story of how the lieutenant lost his arm. When he reached home, his sisters, his mother, his wife, sobbed for a long time at the sight of the flat sleeve. "Oh, well," he said, standing shamefaced amid these tears, "I don't suppose it matters so much as all that."

QUESTIONS

1 Underline all the *nouns* in the story that name things or events not actually present in the story's setting, such as "trident" in paragraph 5. Which are metaphors and which are similes?

2 Because a metaphor involves the substitution of one image for another, it seems somehow less artificial than a simile: the comparison is only implied. With a simile the comparison is made explicit: the two images being compared are set forth like the two parts of an equation. You will have discovered in your answer to the preceding question that Crane resorts to the artificial-sounding simile with great frequency. Given the effect his story achieves, why is the very artificiality of the simile an asset to him?

3 A form of figurative language closely related to metaphor is *personification.* Personification may be defined as (1) the representation of an abstract quality or idea by a human figure (such as the abstraction "civilized man" as personified by Dr. Jenkins in "The Portable Phonograph"), or (2) the endowment of an inanimate object with human qualities. Can you find examples of this second sort of personification in Crane's treatment of the wood from which the shot was fired?

4 Some of Crane's similes are commonplace—for example, "statue-like." Can you find others that are commonplace? These come very close to being clichés. On the other hand, some of his similes are startlingly novel—for example, "He looked at it (his sword) . . . as if he had been endowed with a trident, a sceptre, or a spade." Can you find other similes that are novel?

5 Is this pattern of commonplace similes on the one hand, and unusual ones on the other, paralleled by other patterns of the commonplace and the unusual—in the choice of imagery, for instance? in the choice of words? in the different scenes the lieutenant witnesses as he walks to the field hospital? in the treatment he is accorded by the various men he meets on his way? or even in his own different views of himself and his arm? Consider in this connection the different and alternating effects this story has on you as a reader: are you alternately reassured by the commonplace one moment, and jolted by the unusual the next?

6 Remember that in the best stories all the elements of fiction at once reflect and contribute to the story's theme. Do the curious rhythms of the commonplace alternating with the unusual, suggested by all the foregoing patterns, indicate the author's attitude toward the experience of war? What is that attitude? What, then, is the story's theme?

CLICHÉ

Figurative language is used by everyone, not just by writers of fiction or poetry. Everyday slang is full of figures of speech and allusions, but by the time these become slang they are generally so common and so trite that they have lost most of their force. Inexperienced writers often use metaphors, similes, or allusions that they have picked up from others, but because these expressions have been overworked, they make the writer sound thoughtless rather than artful. Because this is so, skilled writers often put trite expressions into the mouths of characters whom they want to undercut, or make to look naive or insensitive. If a trite expression, or cliché, appears in the mouth of a character—if, for example, the checker, Stoksie, in "A & P" says, on seeing the pretty girl: "Oh Daddy, I feel so faint"—we can be sure the author is making some sort of judgment of this character and inviting us to do the same. However, if a trite expression appears from the author himself, he is either being slyly ironic, or else revealing himself as a lazy and thoughtless writer. This, at least, is today's usual judgment: novelty of phrase, including brilliant and apt new figures of speech, is highly regarded; its presence or absence is often used as a measure of modern fiction. Ironically, the best of these new phrases become tomorrow's clichés.

James Thurber

THE SECRET LIFE OF WALTER MITTY

"We're going through!" The Commander's voice was like thin ice breaking. He wore his full-dress uniform, with the heavily braided white cap pulled down rakishly over one cold gray eye. "We can't make it, sir. It's spoiling for a hurricane, if you ask me." "I'm not asking you, Lieutenant Berg," said the Commander. "Throw on the power lights! Rev her up to 8,500! We're going through!" The pounding of the cylinders increased: ta-pocketa-pocketa-

pocketa-*pocketa-pocketa.* The Commander stared at the ice forming on the pilot window. He walked over and twisted a row of complicated dials. "Switch on No. 8 auxiliary!" he shouted. "Switch on No. 8 auxiliary!" repeated Lieutenant Berg. "Full strength in No. 3 turret!" shouted the Commander. "Full strength in No. 3 turret!" The crew, bending to their various tasks in the huge, hurtling eight-engined Navy hydroplane, looked at each other and grinned. "The Old Man'll get us through," they said to one another. "The Old Man ain't afraid of Hell!" . . .

"Not so fast! You're driving too fast!" said Mrs. Mitty. "What are you driving so fast for?"

"Hmm?" said Walter Mitty. He looked at his wife, in the seat beside him, with shocked astonishment. She seemed grossly unfamiliar, like a strange woman who had yelled at him in a crowd. "You were up to fifty-five," she said. "You know I don't like to go more than forty. You were up to fifty-five." Walter Mitty drove on toward Waterbury in silence, the roaring of the SN202 through the worst storm in twenty years of Navy flying fading in the remote, intimate airways of his mind. "You're tensed up again," said Mrs. Mitty. "It's one of your days. I wish you'd let Dr. Renshaw look you over."

Walter Mitty stopped the car in front of the building where his wife went to have her hair done. "Remember to get those overshoes while I'm having my hair done," she said. "I don't need overshoes," said Mitty. She put her mirror back into her bag. "We've been all through that," she said, getting out of the car. "You're not a young man any longer." He raced the engine a little. "Why don't you wear your gloves? Have you lost your gloves?" Walter Mitty reached in a pocket and brought out the gloves. He put them on, but after she had turned and gone into the building and he had driven on to a red light, he took them off again. "Pick it up, brother!" snapped a cop as the light changed, and Mitty hastily pulled on his gloves and lurched ahead. He drove around the streets aimlessly for a time, and then he drove past the hospital on his way to the parking lot.

. . . "It's the millionaire banker, Wellington McMillan," said the pretty nurse. "Yes?" said Walter Mitty, removing his gloves slowly. "Who has the case?" "Dr. Renshaw and Dr. Benbow, but there are two specialists here, Dr. Remington from New York and Mr. Pritchard-Mitford from London. He flew over." A door opened down a long, cool corridor and Dr. Renshaw came out. He looked distraught and haggard. "Hello, Mitty," he said. "We're having the devil's own time with McMillan, the millionaire banker and close personal friend of Roosevelt. Obstreosis of the ductal tract. Tertiary. Wish you'd take a look at him." "Glad to," said Mitty.

In the operating room there were whispered introductions: "Dr. Remington, Dr. Mitty. Mr. Pritchard-Mitford, Dr. Mitty." "I've read your book on streptothricosis," said Pritchard-Mitford, shaking hands. "A brilliant performance, sir." "Thank you," said Walter Mitty. "Didn't know you were in the States, Mitty," grumbled Remington. "Coals to Newcastle, bringing Mitford and me here for a tertiary." "You are very kind," said Mitty. A huge, complicated machine, connected to the operating table, with many tubes and wires, began at this moment to go pocketa-pocketa-pocketa. "The new anesthetizer is giving way!" shouted an interne. "There is no one in the East who knows how to fix it!" "Quiet, man!" said Mitty, in a low, cool voice. He sprang to the machine, which was now going pocketa-pocketa-queep-pocketa-queep. He began fingering delicately a row of glistening dials. "Give me a fountain pen!" he snapped. Someone handed him a fountain pen. He pulled a faulty piston out of the machine and inserted the pen in its place. "That will hold for ten minutes," he said. "Get on with the operation." A nurse hurried over and whispered to Renshaw, and Mitty saw the man turn pale. "Coreopsis has set in," said Renshaw nervously. "If you would take over, Mitty?" Mitty looked at him and at the craven figure of Benbow, who drank, and at the grave, uncertain faces of the two great specialists. "If you wish," he said. They slipped a white gown on him; he adjusted a mask and drew on thin gloves; nurses handed him shining. . . .

"Back it up, Mac! Look out for that Buick!" Walter Mitty jammed on the brakes. "Wrong lane, Mac," said the parking-lot attendant, looking at Mitty closely. "Gee. Yeh," muttered Mitty. He began cautiously to back out of the lane marked "Exit Only." "Leave her sit there," said the attendant. "I'll put her away." Mitty got out of the car. "Hey, better leave the key." "Oh," said Mitty, handing the man the ignition key. The attendant vaulted into the car, backed it up with insolent skill, and put it where it belonged.

They're so damn cocky, thought Walter Mitty, walking along Main Street; they think they know everything. Once he had tried to take his chains off, outside New Milford, and he had got them wound around the axles. A man had had to come out in a wrecking car and unwind them, a young, grinning garageman. Since then Mrs. Mitty always made him drive to a garage to have the chains taken off. The next time, he thought, I'll wear my right arm in a sling; they won't grin at me then. I'll have my right arm in a sling and they'll see I couldn't possibly take the chains off myself. He kicked at the slush on the sidewalk. "Overshoes," he said to himself, and he began looking for a shoe store.

When he came out into the street again, with the overshoes in a box under his arm, Walter Mitty began to wonder what the other thing was his wife had told him to get. She had told him twice, before they set out from their house for Waterbury. In a way he hated these weekly trips to town—he was always getting something wrong. Kleenex, he thought, Squibb's, razor blades? No. Toothpaste, toothbrush, bicarbonate, carborundum, initiative and referendum? He gave it up. But she would remember it. "Where's the what's-its-name?" she would ask. "Don't tell me you forgot the what's-its-name?" A newsboy went by shouting something about the Waterbury trial.

. . ."Perhaps this will refresh your memory." The District Attorney suddenly thrust a heavy automatic at the quiet figure on the witness stand. "Have you ever seen this before?" Walter Mitty took the gun and examined it expertly. "This is my Webley-Vickers 50.80," he said calmly. An excited buzz ran around the courtroom. The judge rapped for order. "You are a crack shot with any sort of firearms, I believe?" said the District Attorney, insinuatingly. "Objection!" shouted Mitty's attorney. "We have shown that the defendant could not have fired the shot. We have shown that he wore his right arm in a sling on the night of the fourteenth of July." Walter Mitty raised his hand briefly and the bickering attorneys were stilled. "With any known make of gun," he said evenly, "I could have killed Gregory Fitzhurst at three hundred feet *with my left hand*." Pandemonium broke loose in the courtroom. A woman's scream rose above the bedlam and suddenly a lovely, dark-haired girl was in Walter Mitty's arms. The District Attorney struck at her savagely. Without rising from his chair, Mitty let the man have it on the point of the chin. "You miserable cur!". . .

"Puppy biscuit," said Walter Mitty. He stopped walking and the buildings of Waterbury rose up out of the misty courtroom and surrounded him again. A woman who was passing laughed. "He said 'Puppy biscuit,' " she said to her companion. "That man said 'Puppy biscuit' to himself." Walter Mitty hurried on. He went into an A & P, not the first one he came to but a smaller one farther up the street. "I want some biscuit for small, young dogs," he said to the clerk. "Any special brand, sir?" The greatest pistol shot in the world thought a moment. "It says 'Puppies Bark for It' on the box," said Walter Mitty.

His wife would be through at the hairdresser's in fifteen minutes, Mitty saw in looking at his watch, unless they had trouble drying it; sometimes they had trouble drying it. She didn't like to get to the hotel first; she would want him to be there waiting for her as usual. He found a big leather chair in the lobby, facing a window, and he put the overshoes and the puppy biscuit on the floor beside it. He picked up an old copy of *Liberty* and sank down into the chair. "Can Germany Conquer the World Through the Air?" Walter Mitty looked at the pictures of bombing planes and of ruined streets.

. . ."The cannonading has got the wind up in young Raleigh, sir," said the sergeant. Captain Mitty looked up at him through tousled hair. "Get him to bed," he said wearily. "With the others. I'll fly alone." "But you can't, sir," said the sergeant anxiously. "It takes two men to handle that bomber and the Archies are pounding hell out of the air. Von Richtman's circus is between here and Saulier." "Somebody's got to get that ammunition dump," said Mitty. "I'm going over. Spot of brandy?" He poured a drink for the sergeant and one for himself. War thundered and whined around the dugout and battered at the door. There was a rending of wood and splinters flew through the room. "A bit of a near thing," said Captain Mitty carelessly. "The box barrage is closing in," said the sergeant. "We only live once, Sergeant," said Mitty, with his faint, fleeting smile. "Or do we?" He poured another brandy and tossed it off. "I never see a man could hold his brandy like you, sir," said the sergeant. "Begging your pardon, sir." Captain Mitty stood up and strapped on his huge Webley-Vickers automatic. "It's forty kilometers through hell, sir," said the sergeant. Mitty finished one last brandy. "After all," he said softly, "what isn't?" The pounding of the cannon increased; there was the rat-tat-tatting of machine guns, and from somewhere came the menacing pocketa-pocketa-pocketa of the new flame-throwers. Walter Mitty walked to the door of the dugout humming "Auprès de Ma Blonde." He turned and waved to the sergeant. "Cheerio!" he said. . . .

Something struck his shoulder. "I've been looking all over this hotel for you," said Mrs. Mitty. "Why do you have to hide in this old chair? How did you expect me to find you?" "Things close in," said Walter Mitty vaguely. "What?" Mrs. Mitty said. "Did you get the what's-its-name? The puppy biscuit? What's in the box?" "Overshoes," said Mitty. "Couldn't you have put them on in the store?" "I was thinking," said Walter Mitty. "Does it ever occur to you that I am sometimes thinking?" She looked at him. "I'm going to take your temperature when I get you home," she said.

They went out through the revolving doors that made a faintly derisive whistling sound when you pushed them. It was two blocks to the parking lot. At the drugstore on the corner she said, "Wait here for me. I forgot something. I won't be a minute." She was more than a minute. Walter Mitty lighted a cigarette. It began to rain, rain with sleet in it. He stood up against the wall of the drugstore, smoking. . . . He put his shoulders back and his heels together. "To hell with the handkerchief," said Walter Mitty scornfully. He took one last drag on his cigarette and snapped it away. Then, with that faint, fleeting smile playing about his lips, he faced the firing squad; erect and motionless, proud and disdainful, Walter Mitty the Undefeated, inscrutable to the last.

QUESTIONS

1 This story presents alternating scenes of fantasy and reality. Much of the humor in the scenes of fantasy stems from Thurber's echoing of the clichés so common once in pulp fiction and now on TV. How many of these clichés can you discover in each of the five scenes of fantasy?

2 The scenes of reality are also full of clichés—this time the clichés of everyday life and talk. How many clichés can you discover in each of the four scenes of reality?

3 Thurber makes good use of other devices besides clichés to hold his scenes of fantasy and reality together. Can you discover, for example, certain phrases and certain images that parallel or echo each other from one scene of fantasy to another?

4 "Gloves" are used to link the scene of reality (paragraph 4) to the scene of fantasy (paragraph 5). Can you find other details Thurber uses to establish links between his scenes of fantasy and reality? What special "sound effect" runs through nearly every fantasy scene like a refrain?

5 If, as we have said, a story's theme reflects the attitude of its author, then we have to know Thurber's attitude toward Walter Mitty in order to understand the story. How would you define his attitude toward his dreamer? Do you find any evidence of deliberate ambiguity in the final sentence of the story?

5
IRONY

irony of situation | irony of style | dramatic irony

People often say, "Isn't that ironic?" meaning, "Isn't it odd that things turned out that way?" When the reverse of what is expected takes place, irony is present. Isn't it ironic, for example, that the industries that supply us with things for the good life also threaten that good life by adding to pollution? People are quick to recognize such ironies of situation, for these ironies act as powerful reminders that nothing in life is thoroughly predictable, and that just when our expectations are about to be fulfilled, they may go down in defeat.

A person who recognizes *irony of situation* sees two things: first, what actually happened, and, second, what one erroneously expected to happen. The tension created in a mind pondering these two ideas simultaneously gives rise to a sense of irony. This awareness of irony requires an intellectual response from the observer, though the person who is the object of irony often reacts emotionally. For example, in "Araby," the boy's experience at the bazaar is very different from what he expected, but while we see the contrast intellectually, he, of course, sees it as tragic and reacts emotionally.

Not all irony is tragic or even somber. Much of it is humorous. In fact, irony lies at the root of all situation comedy. Laughter may appear to be an emotional response, but its origin is intellectual, for we are inclined to laugh when we see a person's expectations jolted. This jolt of the unexpected, and the need to adapt to it, are covered by laughter. In "The Secret Life of Walter Mitty," for example, our humor is stirred when Walter Mitty in his fantasy as a famous surgeon does *not* perform a crucial operation on a millionaire banker, but instead is jolted back into reality by the words of the parking-lot attendant, "Back it up, Mac! Look out for that Buick!"

Irony of situation is only one of several ways authors set up tensions between what we normally expect and what actually happens. Another way is through *irony of style,* wherein a trivial matter is described in a very formal or pompous style, such as the one that characterizes Walter Mitty's cliché-ridden fantasies. Irony of style also exists when a serious subject is presented in a style of naive simplicity, as in "A & P," where Sammy's flippant and slangy style masks the strong idealism that prompts his reckless defense of Queenie.

Irony of style occurs sometimes in real life, quite apart from fiction: something that looms as large as death may be talked about in the simplest of language. We have already encountered "A Clean, Well-Lighted Place," in which the subject of death is treated by Hemingway with studied simplicity. One of Hemingway's great powers as an author was that he wrote so simply of such serious things. The tension created by the contrast between style and subject leads one to sense that Hemingway's narrator feels these events so strongly that if he allowed himself the luxury of talking about them in a more complicated way, he would cheapen the emotion.

Conversely, when someone is embarrassed by the triviality of his thoughts, he often tries to conceal their shallowness from his audience by using big words and complicated sentences to try and fake a dignity that his ideas do not deserve. There is a strong suggestion of this in the remarks of the fat man in Pirandello's "War," which you will read in this chapter.

Besides irony of situation and irony of style, a third form called *dramatic irony* is often at work. You may have noticed that the boy in "Araby" did not know, as we do, that bazaars can be dull and tawdry affairs; his dreams and actions would have been very different if he had known this. When fiction gives us the chance to play God, letting us in on things that the characters themselves are ignorant of, dramatic irony is at work. With dramatic irony, as with irony of situation (where the expected and the unexpected are in tension) and irony of style (where the form is in tension with the content), we receive simultaneously two opposing impressions—the limited appearance (as known by the character) versus the larger reality (as known by us). The tension between these two gives us the same intellectual pleasure we enjoy in irony of situation and irony of style.

In addition to the three kinds of irony that appear in the *structure* of stories, we may encounter *verbal ironies*—statements that are not intended to be taken at face value. These may take the form of *overstatement, understatement,* or *opposite statement.* They are ironic because, as with the other forms of irony, the reader is supposed to know the truth and thus will get intellectual satisfaction in recognizing how the statement differs from the truth.

Examples of verbal ironies are not difficult to find. The young grocery-store checker in "A & P" is fond of using *overstatements* to describe the customers: "I bet you could set off dynamite in an A & P and the people would by and large keep reaching and checking oatmeal off their lists. . . ." By contrast, a poignant example of *understatement* is found in the final words of Crane's young lieutenant, who says of his amputated arm: "Oh, well, I don't suppose it matters as much as all that." And Thurber provides a good example of *opposite statement* when he concludes with: "Walter Mitty, the Undefeated, inscrutable to the last."

These verbal ironies may be distinguished from other forms of irony in two ways: they are expressed very succinctly; and the story's total effect is not dependent on them as it is on irony of situation, dramatic irony, and, often, irony of style. Verbal ironies are small, textural details in a story; the others are large structural elements.

Mikhail Zoshchenko

THE WESTINGHOUSE BRAKE

The main reason, probably, was that Volodka Bokov was a little high. Otherwise, of course, he would never have dared such a crime. He'd had a few.

If you really want to know, Volodka Bokov, just before the train, had downed a double shot of Erivan vodka—plus a little beer. And as far as food was concerned, do you know what he had eaten? One whole wienie. Can you call that food?

Well, the fellow got carried away a bit. Because all that stuff produces a pretty corrosive mixture. And the old noggin swims a bit, and in one's breast all sorts of ideas begin to ripen, such as the desire to make the public sit up and take a bit of notice.

Well, Volodka got into the train and right away began to make himself felt. To the effect that, sure enough, he was the kind of character who could get away with anything. That even the People's Court, should something really develop, would back him up to the end. Because—and let's get this straight—he was of the most absolutely first rate origins. His own grandfather had been a cowherd and his mother the simplest of country women. . . .

And so Volodka beats his gums—it just streamed out—he wanted to show some pride. But here, across from Volodka, some sort of citizen turns up. Cotton stuffing in the ears, cleanly dressed, even stylish. And he says:

"You," he says, "you yak on like that much longer, and they'll haul you in at the next stop."

Volodka says:

"Don't you meddle with my self respect. They can't haul me in—because I'm a member of the proletariat. It doesn't matter beans what I do—I'll get off for anything."

Well, that was the mood he was in. And drunk, too.

But the public began to express its displeasure. And those who were really mean began to egg him on a bit. And one character in a blue peaked cap, a real bastard, says to him:

"And you, pal," he says, "you just try smashing that window, and we," he says, "we'll just look on and see whether they haul you in or whether nothing will happen. Or, better yet, don't bother about the windows, but just stop the train—with that handle there. . . . That's the brake. . . ."

Volodka says:

"With what handle? You, you parasite, just try to make yourself clearer."

Old blue-cap answers:

"That one there. That's a Westinghouse brake. Pull it from the left, this way. . . ."

The public and the citizen with cotton stuffing in his ears began, of course, to try to stop the instigator. Ought to be ashamed of himself, making serious suggestions like that to somebody blind drunk.

But Volodka Bokov jumped up and yanked the handle across from left to right.

At this point everyone suddenly became silent. General speechlessness among the passengers. The only sound was the clicking of the wheels. Nothing else.

The joker in the blue cap, he just gasped.

"Christ Almighty—you stopped it!"

Here a number of passengers began to jump up. The character in the blue cap tried to run out onto the vestibule to get away from the crime. But the passengers wouldn't let him.

And the one with cotton stuffing in his ears, he says:

"This is hooliganism. Right now the train's going to stop. . . . That's how the equipment gets worn out. Time's lost, too."

Even Volodka Bokov got a little scared.

"Grab him," he says, "that guy in the blue cap. Let 'em lock us both up."

But the train, in the meantime, didn't stop all at once.

The public began to talk.

"A train can't stop right away. Even though it's a commuter, it's still allowed 175 feet after first application. More, if the rails are wet."

But the train—it just kept on going.

Over half a mile, and no stopping was noticeable.

And the one with cotton in the ears, he says:

"That brake," he says, "it seems . . . well. . . ."

Volodka says:

"I tell you, nothing can happen to me. Get it?"

Then he sat down. And at the stop he went out onto the vestibule for a little fresh air. And when he came home he was sober. Sober as glass.

QUESTIONS

1 This little story is a tissue of comic reversals. What is the principal one? What form of irony does this comic reversal illustrate?

2 Can you discover other, lesser ironies? What of the story's final sentence, for example? And what about the conduct of the bold joker in the blue cap? Does the drunken Volodka ever reverse his attitude? Finally, what happens, by implication, to our (the reader's) expectations concerning the outcome of drunken behavior?

3 In the remarks of which character does the author reveal irony of style? Is this an instance of a trivial action being talked about in a pompous manner, or the reverse—a serious topic spoken of lightly?

Guy de Maupassant

THE PIECE OF STRING

It was market-day, and over all the roads round Goderville the peasants and their wives were coming towards the town. The men walked easily, lurching the whole body forward at every step. Their long legs were twisted and deformed by the slow, painful labors of the country:—by bending over to plough, which is what also makes their left shoulders too high and their figures crooked; and by reaping corn, which obliges them for steadiness' sake to spread their knees too wide. Their starched blue blouses, shining as though varnished, ornamented at collar and cuffs with little patterns of white stitch-work, and blown up big around their bony bodies, seemed exactly like ballons about to soar, but putting forth a head, two arms, and two feet.

Some of these fellows dragged a cow or a calf at the end of a rope. And just behind the animal, beating it over the back with a leaf-covered branch to hasten its pace, went their wives, carrying large baskets from which came forth the heads of chickens or the heads of ducks. These women walked with steps far shorter and quicker than the men; their figures, withered and upright, were adorned with scanty little shawls pinned over their flat bosoms; and they enveloped their heads each in a white cloth, close fastened round the hair and surmounted by a cap.

Now a char-à-banc passed by, drawn by a jerky-paced nag. It shook up strangely the two men on the seat. And the woman at the bottom of the cart held fast to its sides to lessen the hard joltings.

In the market-place at Goderville was a great crowd, a mingled multitude of men and beasts. The horns of cattle, the high and long-napped hats of wealthy peasants, the head-dresses of the women, came to the surface of that sea. And voices clamorous, sharp, shrill, made a continuous and savage din. Above it a huge burst of laughter from the sturdy lungs of a merry yokel would sometimes sound, and sometimes a long bellow from a cow tied fast to the wall of a house.

It all smelled of the stable, of milk, of hay, and of perspiration, giving off that half-human, half-animal odor which is peculiar to the men of the fields.

Maître Hauchecorne, of Bréauté, had just arrived at Goderville, and was taking his way towards the square, when he perceived on the ground a little piece of string. Maître Hauchecorne, economical, like all true Normans, reflected that everything was worth picking up which could be of any use; and he stooped down—but painfully, because he suffered from rheumatism. He took the bit of thin cord from the ground, and was carefully preparing to roll it up when he saw Maître Malandain, the harness-maker, on his door-step, looking at him. They had once had a quarrel about a halter, and they had remained angry, bearing malice on both sides. Maître Hauchecorne was overcome with a sort of shame at being seen by his enemy looking in the dirt so for a bit of string. He quickly hid his find beneath his blouse; then in the pocket of his breeches; then pretended to be still looking for something on the ground which he did not discover; and at last went off towards the market-place, with his head bent forward, and a body almost doubled in two by rheumatic pains.

He lost himself immediately in the crowd, which was clamorous, slow, and agitated by interminable bargains. The peasants examined the cows, went off, came back, always in great perplexity and fear of being cheated, never quite daring to decide, spying at the eye of the seller, trying ceaselessly to discover the tricks of the man and the defect in the beast.

The women, having placed their great baskets at their feet, had pulled out the poultry, which lay upon the ground, tied by the legs, with eyes scared, with combs scarlet.

They listened to propositions, maintaining the prices, with a dry manner, with an impassible face; or, suddenly, perhaps, deciding to take the lower price which was offered, they cried out to the customer, who was departing slowly:

"All right, I'll let you have them, Mâit' Anthime."

Then, little by little, the square became empty, and when the *Angelus* struck midday those who lived at a distance poured into the inns.

At Jourdain's the great room was filled with eaters, just as the vast court was filled with vehicles of every sort—wagons, gigs, char-à-bancs, tilburys, tilt-carts which have no name, yellow with mud, misshapen, pieced together, raising their shafts to heaven like two arms, or it may be with their nose in the dirt and their rear in the air.

Just opposite to where the diners were at table the huge fireplace, full of clear flame, threw a lively heat on the backs of those who sat along the right. Three spits were turning, loaded with chickens, with pigeons, and with joints of mutton; and a delectable odor of roast meat, and of gravy gushing over crisp brown skin, took wing from the hearth, kindled merriment, caused mouths to water.

All the aristocracy of the plough were eating there, at Maît' Jourdain's, the innkeeper's, a dealer in horses also, and a sharp fellow who had made a pretty penny in his day.

The dishes were passed round, were emptied, with jugs of yellow cider. Every one told of his affairs, of his purchases and his sales. They asked news about the crops. The weather was good for green stuffs, but a little wet for wheat.

All of a sudden the drum rolled in the court before the house. Every one, except some of the most indifferent, was on his feet at once, and ran to the door, to the windows, with his mouth still full and his napkin in his hand.

When the public crier had finished his tattoo he called forth in a jerky voice, making his pauses out of time:

"Be it known to the inhabitants of Goderville, and in general to all—persons present at the market, that there has been lost this morning, on the Beuzeville road between—nine and ten o'clock, a pocket-book of black leather, containing five hundred francs and business papers. You are requested to return it—to the mayor's office, at once, or to Maître Fortuné Houlbrèque, of Manneville. There will be twenty francs reward."

Then the man departed. They heard once more at a distance the dull beatings of the drum and the faint voice of the crier.

Then they began to talk of this event, reckoning up the chances which Maître Houlbrèque had of finding or of not finding his pocket-book again.

And the meal went on.

They were finishing their coffee when the corporal of gendarmes appeared on the threshold.

He asked:

"Is Maître Hauchecorne, of Bréauté, here?"

Maître Hauchecorne, seated at the other end of the table, answered:

"Here I am."

And the corporal resumed:

"Maître Hauchecorne, will you have the kindness to come with me to the mayor's office? M. le Maire would like to speak to you."

The peasant, surprised and uneasy, gulped down his little glass of cognac, got up, and, even worse bent over than in the morning, since the first steps after a rest were always particularly difficult, started off, repeating:

"Here I am, here I am."

And he followed the corporal.

The mayor was waiting for him, seated in an arm-chair. He was the notary of the place, a tall, grave man of pompous speech.

"Maître Hauchecorne," said he, "this morning, on the Beuzeville road, you were seen to pick up the pocket-book lost by Maître Houlbrèque, of Manneville."

The countryman, speechless, regarded the mayor, frightened already by this suspicion which rested on him he knew not why.

"I, I picked up that pocket-book?"

"Yes, you."

"I swear I didn't even know nothing about it at all."

"You were seen."

"They saw me, me? Who is that who saw me?"

"M. Malandain, the harness-maker."

Then the old man remembered, understood, and, reddening with anger:

"Ah, he saw me, did he, the rascal? He saw me picking up this string here, M'sieu' le Maire."

And, fumbling at the bottom of his pocket, he pulled out of it the little end of string.

But the mayor incredulously shook his head:

"You will not make me believe, Maître Hauchecorne, that M. Malandain, who is a man worthy of credit, has mistaken this string for a pocket-book."

The peasant, furious, raised his hand and spit as if to attest his good faith, repeating:

"For all that, it is the truth of the good God, the blessed truth, M'sieu' le Maire. There! on my soul and my salvation I repeat it."

The mayor continued:

"After having picked up the thing in question, you even looked for some time in the mud to see if a piece of money had not dropped out of it."

The good man was suffocated with indignation and with fear:

"If they can say!—if they can say . . . such lies as that to slander an honest man! If they can say!—"

He might protest, he was not believed.

He was confronted with M. Malandain, who repeated and sustained his testimony. They abused one another for an hour. At his own request Maître Hauchecorne was searched. Nothing was found upon him.

At last, the mayor, much perplexed, sent him away, warning him that he would inform the public prosecutor, and ask for orders.

The news had spread. When he left the mayor's office, the old man was surrounded, interrogated with a curiosity which was serious or mocking as the case might be, but into which no indignation entered. And he began to tell the story of the string. They did not believe him. They laughed.

He passed on, button-holed by every one, himself button-holing his acquaintances, beginning over and over again his tale and his protestations, showing his pockets turned inside out to prove that he had nothing.

They said to him:

"You old rogue, *va!*"

And he grew angry, exasperated, feverish, in despair at not being believed, and always telling his story.

The night came. It was time to go home. He set out with three of his neighbors to whom he pointed out the place where he had picked up the end of string; and all the way he talked of his adventure.

That evening he made the round in the village of Bréauté, so as to tell every one. He met only unbelievers.

He was ill of it all night long.

The next day, about one in the afternoon, Marius Paumelle, a farm hand of Maître Breton, the market-gardener at Ymauville, returned the pocket-book and its contents to Maître Houlbrèque, of Manneville.

This man said, indeed, that he had found it on the road; but not knowing how to read, he had carried it home and given it to his master.

The news spread to the environs. Maître Hauchecorne was informed. He put himself at once upon the go, and began to relate his story as completed by the *dénouement*. He triumphed.

"What grieved me," said he, "was not the thing itself, do you understand; but it was the lies. There's nothing does you so much harm as being in disgrace for lying."

All day he talked of his adventure, he told it on the roads to the people who passed; at the cabaret to the people who drank; and the next Sunday, when they came out of church. He even stopped strangers to tell them about it. He was easy, now, and yet something worried him without his knowing exactly what it was. People had a joking manner while they listened. They did not seem convinced. He seemed to feel their tittle-tattle behind his back.

On Tuesday of the next week he went to market at Goderville, prompted entirely by the need of telling his story.

Malandain, standing on his door-step, began to laugh as he saw him pass. Why?

He accosted a farmer of Criquetot, who did not let him finish, and, giving him a punch in the pit of his stomach, cried in his face: "Oh you great rogue, *va!*" Then turned his heel upon him.

Maître Hauchecorne remained speechless, and grew more and more uneasy. Why had they called him "great rogue?"

When seated at table in Jourdain's tavern he began again to explain the whole affair.

A horse-dealer of Montivilliers shouted at him:

"Get out, get out you old scamp; I know all about your string!"

Hauchecorne stammered:

"But since they found it again, the pocket-book!"

But the other continued:

"Hold your tongue, daddy; there's one who finds it and there's another who returns it. And no one the wiser."

The peasant was choked. He understood at last. They accused him of having had the pocket-book brought back by an accomplice, by a confederate.

He tried to protest. The whole table began to laugh.

He could not finish his dinner, and went away amid a chorus of jeers.

He went home, ashamed and indignant, choked with rage, with confusion, the more cast-down since from his Norman cunning, he was, perhaps, capable of having done what they accused him of, and even of boasting of it as a good trick. His innocence dimly seemed to him impossible to prove, his craftiness being so well known. And he felt himself struck to the heart by the injustice of the suspicion.

Then he began anew to tell of his adventure, lengthening his recital every day, each time adding new proofs, more energetic protestations, and more solemn oaths which he thought of, which he prepared in his hours of solitude, his mind being entirely occupied by the story of the string. The more complicated his defence, the more artful his arguments, the less he was believed.

"Those are liars' proofs," they said behind his back.

He felt this; it preyed upon his heart. He exhausted himself in useless efforts.

He was visibly wasting away.

The jokers now made him tell the story of "The Piece of String" to amuse them, just as you make a soldier who has been on a campaign tell his story of the battle. His mind, struck at the root, grew weak.

About the end of December he took to his bed.

He died early in January, and, in the delirium of the death-agony, he protested his innocence, repeating:

"A little bit of string—a little bit of string—see, here it is, M'sieu' le Maire."

QUESTIONS

1 Vocabulary: *va!*: go on! or oh, go on, now.

2 There is dramatic irony in this story. Name the characters who are ignorant of something the reader knows all about. What, in each case, does the reader know?

3 What is the central irony of situation in this story? How does the author develop this initial irony into a series of revelations that converts a potentially comic story into a painfully grim one?

4 Consider the images that Maupassant has so carefully detailed in the first five paragraphs. How do they help to explain why Maître Hauchecorne became the victim of the central ironic situation?

5 How do the remarks of the mayor illustrate one form of irony of style?

6 What is Maupassant's attitude toward the experience he narrates here? The answer to this question should lead you to the story's theme. To measure your understanding of the theme, test your conclusion against the evidence afforded by all of the elements of fiction we have so far discussed—words, imagery, comparisons, and irony. The best statement of theme will be the one most strongly supported by evidence from all of the story's techniques.

Luigi Pirandello

WAR

The passengers who had left Rome by the night express had had to stop until dawn at the small station of Fabriano in order to continue their journey by the small old-fashioned local joining the main line with Sulmona.

At dawn, in a stuffy and smoky second-class carriage in which five people had already spent the night, a bulky woman in deep mourning was hoisted in—almost like a shapeless bundle. Behind her, puffing and moaning, followed her husband—a tiny man, thin and weakly, his face death-white, his eyes small and bright and looking shy and uneasy.

Having at last taken a seat he politely thanked the passengers who had helped his wife and who had made room for her; then he turned round to the woman trying to pull down the collar of her coat, and politely inquired:

"Are you all right, dear?"

The wife, instead of answering, pulled up her collar again to her eyes, so as to hide her face.

"Nasty world," muttered the husband with a sad smile.

And he felt it his duty to explain to his traveling companions that the poor woman was to be pitied, for the war was taking away from her her only son, a boy of twenty to whom both had devoted their entire life, even breaking up their home at Sulmona to follow him to Rome, where he had to go as a student, then allowing him to volunteer for war with an assurance, however, that at least for six months he would not be sent to the front and now, all of a sudden, receiving a wire saying that he was due to leave in three days' time and asking them to go and see him off.

The woman under the big coat was twisting and wriggling, at times growling like a wild animal, feeling certain that all those explanations would not have aroused even a shadow of sympathy from those people who—most likely—were in the same plight as herself. One of them, who had been listening with particular attention, said:

"You should thank God that your son is only leaving now for the front. Mine has been sent there the first day of the war. He has already come back twice wounded and been back again to the front."

"What about me? I have two sons and three nephews at the front," said another passenger.

"Maybe, but in our case it is our *only* son," ventured the husband.

"What difference can it make? You may spoil your only son with excessive attentions, but you cannot love him more than you would all your other children if you had any. Paternal love is not like bread that can be broken into pieces and split amongst the children in equal shares. A father gives *all* his love to each one of his children without discrimination, whether it be one or ten, and if I am suffering now for my two sons, I am not suffering half for each of them but double. . . ."

"True . . . true . . ." sighed the embarrassed husband, "but suppose (of course we all hope it will never be your case) a father has two sons at the front and he loses one of them, there is still one left to console him . . . while . . ."

"Yes," answered the other, getting cross, "a son left to console him but also a son left for whom he must survive, while in the case of the father of an only son if the son dies the father can die too and put an end to his distress. Which of the two positions is the worse? Don't you see how my case would be worse than yours?"

"Nonsense," interrupted another traveler, a fat, red-faced man with bloodshot eyes of the palest gray.

He was panting. From his bulging eyes seemed to spurt inner violence of an uncontrolled vitality which his weakened body could hardly contain.

"Nonsense," he repeated, trying to cover his mouth with his hand so as to hide the two missing front teeth. "Nonsense. Do we give life to our children for our own benefit?"

The other travelers stared at him in distress. The one who had had his son at the front since the first day of the war sighed: "You are right. Our children do not belong to us, they belong to the Country. . . ."

"Bosh," retorted the fat traveler. "Do we think of the Country when we give life to our children? Our sons are born because . . . well, because they must be born and when they come to life they take our own life with them. This is the truth. We belong to them but they never belong to us. And when they reach twenty they are exactly what we were at their age. We too had a father and mother, but there were so many other things as well . . . girls, cigarettes, illusions, new ties . . . and the Country, of course, whose call we would have answered—when we were twenty—even if father and mother had said no. Now at our age, the love of our Country is still great, of course, but stronger than it is the love for our children. Is there any one of us here who wouldn't gladly take his son's place at the front if he could?"

There was a silence all round, everybody nodding as to approve.

"Why then," continued the fat man, "shouldn't we consider the feelings of our children when they are twenty? Isn't it natural that at their age they should consider the love for their Country (I am speaking of decent boys, of course) even greater than the love for us? Isn't it natural that it should be so, as after all they must look upon us as upon old boys who cannot move any more and must stay at home? If Country exists, if Country is a natural necessity, like bread, of which each of us must eat in order not to die of hunger, somebody must go to defend it. And our sons go, when they are twenty, and they don't want tears, because if they die, they die inflamed and happy (I am speaking, of course, of decent boys). Now, if one dies young and happy, without having the ugly sides of life, the boredom of it, the pettiness, the bitterness of disillusion . . . what more can we ask for him? Everyone should stop crying; everyone should laugh, as I do . . . or at least thank God—as I do—because my son, before dying, sent me a message saying that he was dying satisfied at having ended his life in the best way he could have wished. That is why, as you see, I do not even wear mourning. . . ."

He shook his light fawn coat as to show it; his livid lip over his missing teeth was trembling, his eyes were watery and motionless, and soon after he ended with a shrill laugh which might well have been a sob.

"Quite so . . . quite so. . . ." agreed the others.

The woman who, bundled in a corner under her coat, had been sitting and listening had—for the last three months—tried to find in the words of her husband and her friends something to console her in her deep sorrow, something that might show her how a mother should resign herself to send her son not even to death but to a probably dangerous life. Yet not a word had she found amongst the many which had been said . . . and her grief had been greater in seeing that nobody—as she thought—could share her feelings.

But now the words of the traveler amazed and almost stunned her. She suddenly realized that it wasn't the others who were wrong and could not understand her but herself who could not rise up to the same height of those fathers and mothers willing to resign themselves, without crying, not only to the departure of their sons but even to their death.

She lifted her head, she bent over from her corner trying to listen with great attention to the details which the fat man was giving to his companions about the way his son had fallen as a hero, for his King and his Country, happy and without regrets. It seemed to her that she had stumbled into a world she had never dreamt of, a world so far unknown to her and she was so pleased to hear everyone joining in congratulating that brave father who could so stoically speak of his child's death.

Then suddenly, just as if she had heard nothing of what had been said and almost as if waking up from a dream, she turned to the old man, asking him:

"Then . . . is your son really dead?"

Everybody stared at her. The old man, too, turned to look at her, fixing his great, bulging, horribly watery light gray eyes, deep in her face. For some little time he tried to answer, but words failed him. He looked and looked at her, almost as if only then—at that silly, incongruous question—he had suddenly realized at last that his son was really dead—gone for ever—for ever. His face contracted, became horribly distorted, then he snatched in haste a handkerchief from his pocket and, to the amazement of everyone, broke into harrowing, heart-rending, uncontrollable sobs.

QUESTIONS

1 Irony of situation usually involves a single reversal: we expect something to happen, and something else happens instead. In this story there is a double reversal, a shift in attitudes of both the fat man and the grief-stricken woman. Can you chart precisely the change in attitude of each? What precipitated the change in the woman's attitude? In the fat man's attitude? How does this compound the irony?

2 The author introduces irony of style into the speech of one of the characters. Which one? Is this an example of a pompous style masking a shallow sentiment, or of a simple style used to handle a big subject?

3 Because the fat man is articulate and gives such full expression to his original attitude, the author must be careful to make his subsequent shift in attitude convincing. What images does Pirandello use in his descriptions of the fat man that prepare us to accept his seemingly sudden change? By what very different means does he explain the shift in the woman's attitude? Why are these different means well suited to the different characters?

4 Once again we return to theme—the hub of the author's attitude. If the old woman's original stance represents unreasoning emotion, and the fat man's original stance represents a code of reasoned behavior, what are we to say of the author's attitude? How does this story's principal technique—the use of a double reversal of situation—assist us to find the answer? How do irony of situation and irony of style operate as two "spokes" in the wheel to lead us toward the hub, or theme?

6
SYMBOL

literary symbolism | allegory | personification

Some people are so literal-minded they find it difficult to believe that two stories can be told simultaneously by the same words, or that a character in a story can represent not only himself, but something else at the same time. Yet, this is so. When the surface action of a story does not seem to add up to a satisfying conclusion, very often the most important pattern is not the obvious action, but what this action symbolizes.

Stories containing *literary symbolism* have four noteworthy characteristics. First, certain objects or actions with a concrete meaning carry an additional abstract meaning. For example, in "A & P" the neatly pyramided packaged goods are not only foodstuffs; they also symbolize the dehumanized aspect of a society that values a sterile order in things at the expense of a healthy disorder in people.

Second, this combined concrete-abstract meaning in one object or action is repeated with others to set up a *pattern* of symbolic meaning. Thus a pyramid of foodstuffs, which symbolizes a sterile emphasis on orderly things, is later coupled with shoddy, plastic toys neatly wrapped in cellophane, which symbolize the mindless quality of human behavior when it is more concerned with the container than with its contents.

Third, the pattern of these symbolic objects or actions must remain logically consistent throughout the story. If the neatly lined-up foodstuffs and deceptively-packaged plastic toys symbolize sterility and mindlessness at one point in the story, they cannot, later on, symbolize something contrary.

Fourth, this symbolic pattern may have more than one possible interpretation. You may argue with equal validity, for example, that the contrast between human qualities and dehumanized order serves to symbolize the generation gap, or the struggle for individualism in a mass society, or the dangers of automation, or the results of a profit-oriented system. These various interpretations will supplement and support, rather than undercut or contradict each other.

Symbolism might be said to be a prolonged metaphor, except that symbolic meaning does not substitute for surface meaning, but simply adds another dimension to it. It might be considered a prolonged simile, except that a comparison is not plainly stated. Symbolism is also like a prolonged allusion, except the thing alluded to is usually never named. Thus symbolism differs from figurative language: instead of having a cross-reference between two things, it has only a single reference with added levels of meaning. It is most nearly a prolonged connotation.

Allegory is a simpler and less subtle form of symbolism. If we think of symbolism as a prolonged connotation, we might think of allegory as a prolonged double denotation, in which the most important things and events in a story consistently denote at least two things instead of one. *Personification* (see the definition of personification on page 59) can illustrate such a double denotation. In "The Portable Phonograph" the name Dr. Jenkins denotes the professor himself, but it also denotes the abstraction "civilized man." There is little doubt that this double denotation was intentional. When such personifications become part of a prolonged action, we call it allegory. "The Lightning-Rod Man," which is the next story, and "Young Goodman Brown," in Chapter 13, illustrate patterns of allegory. In each, the abstraction of human behavior known as "evil" has been made a concrete character and this character has engaged in the action.

Symbols and symbolic action are usually subtle companions to the story's characters and what they do. If, as was pointed out before, the surface action is difficult to understand, or if the reader at the conclusion cannot easily understand the story's total significance, there could well be a symbolic pattern contained in this action that can illuminate this significance.

Life itself is full of symbols and symbolic action—full of additional meanings and prolonged connotations (such as the flag one salutes or the way one wears his hair). This fact throws light on an important question: How intently should the reader search for symbols in explaining or analyzing literature? If prose fiction is about life, and if life itself is full of oft-repeated symbolic patterns, then naturally such symbolic patterns will appear in literature. We may find symbolic relationships in almost any story. The reader, however, must learn to distinguish between natural symbols and the deliberate literary symbols that call attention to themselves through repetition or through an internally consistent pattern.

Some readers can sense these underlying symbols almost immediately, as if symbolic writing were a natural way of talking about things. Other readers find it difficult to look beyond the literal statements in the story to achieve the free associations necessary to respond to symbolic writing. Failure to notice the important symbols in a story can be crippling to the literal-minded reader's understanding. But finding symbolic significance where it is not intended may seriously distort a story's meaning and confuse the reader's understanding. The overingenious reader should learn to exercise more tact, more prudence, more modesty. He must let the story instruct him, instead of trying to instruct the story. The literal-minded reader by reminding himself of the presence of symbols and symbolic action in his everyday life can alert himself to the presence of this symbolic process operating in literature as well. To both kinds of readers we offer the same advice: do not be too easily convinced that something "stands for" something else, and therefore, that symbolism is at work; insist on consistency and continuity of the symbolic pattern. If the story makes sense on the literal level, without a symbolic interpretation, appreciate it literally, without unnecessary hunting for something beneath the surface—even though symbol-hunters often find what they look for.

The most useful approach to symbolism takes account of (1) the presence in almost all stories of natural symbols that are easy to understand and to recognize (for example, the conventional use of the chill autumn scene in "The Portable Phonograph" to suggest not only the approaching death of the year but also the impending death of civilization); (2) the presence in some stories of a deliberate pattern of literary symbolism that deserves analysis (such as the implied multiple meanings of the packaged goods in "A & P," mentioned earlier in this chapter); and (3) the presence in a very few stories of a private symbolism that only special study can clarify (such as the elaborate private symbols Edgar Allan Poe used to bring out his central idea, that the achievement of true Beauty depends on the dissolution of the material into the ethereal).

Sometimes writers become so intrigued with a symbolic pattern that the symbolism becomes more important to them than the literal story. This seems to be true in the next story, "The Lightning-Rod Man," which is implausible and not very interesting on the literal level but both plausible and interesting when read as a carefully constructed pattern of literary symbolism.

Herman Melville

THE LIGHTNING-ROD MAN

What grand irregular thunder, thought I, standing on my hearthstone among the Acroceraunian hills, as the scattered bolts boomed overhead, and crashed down among the valleys, every bolt followed by zigzag irradiations, and swift slants of sharp rain, which audibly rang, like a charge of spear-points, on my low shingled roof. I suppose, though, that the mountains hereabouts break and churn up the thunder, so that it is far more glorious here than on the plain. Hark!—some one at the door. Who is this that chooses a time of thunder for making calls? And why don't he, man-fashion, use the knocker, instead of making that doleful undertaker's clatter with his fist against the hollow panel? But let him in. Ah, here he comes. "Good day, sir:" an entire stranger. "Pray be seated." What is that strange-looking walking-stick he carries: "A fine thunderstorm, sir."

"Fine?—Awful!"

"You are wet. Stand here on the hearth before the fire."

"Not for worlds!"

The stranger still stood in the exact middle of the cottage, where he had first planted himself. His singularity impelled a closer scrutiny. A lean, gloomy figure. Hair dark and lank, mattedly streaked over his brow. His sunken pitfalls of eyes were ringed by indigo halos, and played with an innocuous sort of lightning: the gleam without the bolt. The whole man was dripping. He stood in a puddle on the bare oak floor: his strange walking-stick vertically resting at his side.

It was a polished copper rod, four feet long, lengthwise attached to a neat wooden staff, by insertion into two balls of greenish glass, ringed with copper bands. The metal rod terminated at the top tripodwise, in three keen tines, brightly gilt. He held the thing by the wooden part alone.

"Sir," said I, bowing politely, "have I the honor of a visit from that illustrious god, Jupiter Tonans? So stood he in the Greek statue of old, grasping the lightning-bolt. If you be he, or his viceroy, I have to thank you for this noble storm you have brewed among our mountains. Listen: That was a glorious peal. Ah, to a lover of the majestic, it is a good thing to have the Thunderer himself in one's cottage. The thunder grows finer for that. But pray be seated. This old rush-bottomed arm-chair, I grant, is a poor substitute for your evergreen throne on Olympus; but, condescend to be seated."

While I thus pleasantly spoke, the stranger eyed me, half in wonder, and half in a strange sort of horror; but did not move a foot.

"Do, sir, be seated; you need to be dried ere going forth again."

I planted the chair invitingly on the broad hearth, where a little fire had been kindled that afternoon to dissipate the dampness, not the cold; for it was early in the month of September.

But without heeding my solicitation, and still standing in the middle of the floor, the stranger gazed at me portentously and spoke.

"Sir," said he, "excuse me; but instead of my accepting your invitation to be seated on the hearth there, I solemnly warn *you,* that you had best accept *mine,* and stand with me in the middle of the room. Good heavens!" he cried, starting—"there is another of those awful crashes. I warn you, sir, quit the hearth."

"Mr. Jupiter Tonans," said I, quietly rolling my body on the stone, "I stand very well here."

"Are you so horridly ignorant, then," he cried, "as not to know, that by far the most dangerous part of a house, during such a terrific tempest as this, is the fire-place?"

"Nay, I did not know that," involuntarily stepping upon the first board next to the stone.

The stranger now assumed such an unpleasant air of successful admonition, that—quite involuntarily again—I stepped back upon the hearth, and threw myself into the erectest, proudest posture I could command. But I said nothing.

"For Heaven's sake," he cried, with a strange mixture of alarm and intimidation—"for Heaven's sake, get off the hearth! Know you not, that the heated air and soot are conductors;—to say nothing of those immense iron fire-dogs? Quit the spot—I conjure—I command you."

"Mr. Jupiter Tonans, I am not accustomed to be commanded in my own house."

"Call me not by that pagan name. You are profane in this time of terror."

"Sir, will you be so good as to tell me your business? If you seek shelter from the storm, you are welcome, so long as you be civil; but if you come on business, open it forthwith. Who are you?"

"I am a dealer in lightning-rods," said the stranger, softening his tone; "my special business is—— Merciful heaven! what a crash!—Have you ever been struck—your premises, I mean? No? It's best to be provided;"—significantly rattling his metallic staff on the floor;—"by nature, there are no castles in thunder-storms; yet, say but the word, and of this cottage I can make a Gibraltar by a few waves of this wand. Hark, what Himalayas of concussions!"

"You interrupted yourself; your special business you were about to speak of."

"My special business is to travel the country for orders for lightning-rods. This is my specimen-rod;" tapping his staff; "I have the best of references"—fumbling in his pockets. "In Criggan last month, I put up three-and-twenty rods on only five buildings."

"Let me see. Was it not at Criggan last week, about midnight on Saturday, that the steeple, the big elm, and the assemblyroom cupola were struck? Any of your rods there?"

"Not on the tree and cupola, but the steeple."

"Of what use is your rod, then?"

"Of life-and-death use. But my workman was heedless. In fitting the rod at top to the steeple, he allowed a part of the metal to graze the tin sheeting. Hence the accident. Not my fault, but his. Hark!"

"Never mind. That clap burst quite loud enough to be heard without finger-pointing. Did you hear of the event at Montreal last year? A servant girl struck at her bed-side with a rosary in her hand; the beads being metal. Does your beat extend into the Canadas?"

"No. And I hear that there, iron rods only are in use. They should have *mine,* which are copper. Iron is easily fused. Then they draw out the rod so slender, that it has not body enough to conduct the full electric current. The metal melts; the building is destroyed. My copper rods never act so. Those Canadians are fools. Some of them knob the rod at the top, which risks a deadly explosion, instead of imperceptibly carrying down the current into the earth, as this sort of rod does. *Mine* is the only true rod. Look at it. Only one dollar a foot."

"This abuse of your own calling in another might make one distrustful with respect to yourself."

"Hark! The thunder becomes less muttering. It is nearing us, and nearing the earth, too. Hark! One crammed crash! All the vibrations made one by nearness. Another flash. Hold!"

"What do you?" I said, seeing him now, instantaneously relinquishing his staff, lean intently forward towards the window, with his right fore and middle fingers on his left wrist.

But ere the words had well escaped me, another exclamation escaped him.

"Crash! only three pulses—less than a third of a mile off—yonder, somewhere in that wood. I passed three stricken oaks there, ripped out new and glittering. The oak draws lightning more than other timber, having iron in solution in its sap. Your floor here seems oak."

"Heart-of-oak. From the peculiar time of your call upon me, I suppose you purposely select stormy weather for your journeys. When the thunder is roaring, you deem it an hour peculiarly favorable for producing impressions favorable to your trade."

"Hark!—Awful!"

"For one who would arm others with fearlessness, you seem

unbeseemingly timorous yourself. Common men choose fair weather for their travels: you choose thunder-storms; and yet——"

"That I travel in thunder-storms, I grant; but not without particular precautions, such as only a lightning-rod man may know. Hark! Quick—look at my specimen rod. Only one dollar a foot."

"A very fine rod, I dare say. But what are these particular precautions of yours? Yet first let me close yonder shutters; the slanting rain is beating through the sash. I will bar up."

"Are you mad? Know you not that yon iron bar is a swift conductor? Desist."

"I will simply close the shutters, then, and call my boy to bring me a wooden bar. Pray, touch the bell-pull there."

"Are you frantic? That bell-wire might blast you. Never touch bell-wire in a thunder-storm, nor ring a bell of any sort."

"Nor those in belfries? Pray, will you tell me where and how one may be safe in a time like this? Is there any part of my house I may touch with hopes of my life?"

"There is; but not where you now stand. Come away from the wall. The current will sometimes run down a wall, and—a man being a better conductor than a wall—it would leave the wall and run into him. Swoop! *That* must have fallen very nigh. That must have been globular lightning."

"Very probably. Tell me at once, which is, in your opinion, the safest part of this house?"

"This room, and this one spot in it where I stand. Come hither."

"The reasons first."

"Hark!—after the flash the gust—the sashes shiver—the house, the house!—Come hither to me!"

"The reasons, if you please."

"Come hither to me!"

"Thank you again, I think I will try my old stand—the hearth. And now, Mr. Lightning-rod man, in the pauses of the thunder, be so good as to tell me your reasons for esteeming this one room of the house the safest, and your own one standpoint there the safest spot in it."

There was now a little cessation of the storm for a while. The Lightning-rod man seemed relieved, and replied:—

"Your house is a one-storied house, with an attic and a cellar; this room is between. Hence its comparative safety. Because lightning sometimes passes from the clouds to the earth, and sometimes from the earth to the clouds. Do you comprehend?—and I choose the middle of the room, because, if the lightning should strike the house at all, it would come down the chimney or walls; so, obviously, the further you are from them, the better. Come hither to me, now."

"Presently. Something you just said, instead of alarming me, has strangely inspired confidence."

"What have I said?"

"You said that sometimes lightning flashes from the earth to the clouds."

"Aye, the returning-stroke, as it is called; when the earth, being overcharged with the fluid, flashes its surplus upward."

"The returning-stroke; that is, from earth to sky. Better and better. But come here on the hearth and dry yourself."

"I am better here, and better wet."

"How?"

"It is the safest thing you can do—Hark, again!—to get yourself thoroughly drenched in a thunder-storm. Wet clothes are better conductors than the body; and so, if the lightning strike, it might pass down the wet clothes without touching the body. The storm deepens again. Have you a rug in the house? Rugs are non-conductors. Get one, that I may stand on it here, and you, too. The skies blacken—it is dusk at noon. Hark!—the rug, the rug!"

I gave him one; while the hooded mountains seemed closing and tumbling into the cottage.

"And now, since our being dumb will not help us," said I, resuming my place, "let me hear your precautions in traveling during thunderstorms."

"Wait till this one is passed."

"Nay, proceed with the precautions. You stand in the safest possible place according to your own account. Go on."

"Briefly, then. I avoid pine-trees, high houses, lonely barns, upland pastures, running water, flocks of cattle and sheep, a crowd of men. If I travel on foot—as to-day—I do not walk fast; if in my buggy, I touch not its back or sides; if on horseback, I dismount and lead the horse. But of all things, I avoid tall men."

"Do I dream? Man avoid man? and in danger-time, too."

"Tall men in a thunder-storm I avoid. Are you so grossly ignorant as not to know, that the height of a six-footer is sufficient to discharge an electric cloud upon him? Are not lonely Kentuckians, ploughing, smit in the unfinished furrow? Nay, if the six-footer stand by running water, the cloud will sometimes *select* him as its conductor to that running water. Hark! Sure, yon black pinnacle is split. Yes, a man is a good conductor. The lightning goes through and through a man, but only peels a tree. But sir, you have kept me so long answering your questions, that I have not yet come to business. Will you order one of my rods? Look at this specimen one? See: it is of the best of copper. Copper's the best conductor. Your house is low; but being upon the mountains, that lowness does not one whit depress it. You mountaineers are most exposed. In mountainous countries the lightning-rod man should have most business. Look at the specimen, sir. One rod will answer for a house so small as this. Look over these recommendations. Only one rod, sir; cost, only twenty dollars. Hark! There go all the granite Taconics and Hoosics dashed together like pebbles. By the sound, that must have struck something. An elevation of five feet above the house will protect twenty feet radius all about the rod. Only twenty dollars, sir—a dollar a foot. Hark!—Dreadful!—Will you order? Will you buy? Shall I put down your name? Think of being a heap of charred offal, like a haltered horse burnt in his stall, and all in one flash!"

"You pretended envoy extraordinary and minister plenipotentiary to and from Jupiter Tonans," laughed I; "you mere man who came here to put you and your pipestem between clay and sky, do you think that because you can strike a bit of green light from the Leyden jar, that you can thoroughly evert the supernal bolt? Your rod rusts, or breaks, and where are you? Who has empowered you, you Tetzel, to peddle round your indulgences from divine ordinations? The hairs of our heads are numbered, and the days of our lives. In thunder as in sunshine, I stand at ease in the hands of my God. False negotiator, away! See, the scroll of the storm is rolled back; the house is unharmed; and in the blue heavens I read in the rainbow, that the Deity will not, of purpose, make war on man's earth."

"Impious wretch!" foamed the stranger, blackening in the face as the rainbow beamed, "I will publish your infidel notions."

The scowl grew blacker on his face; the indigo-circles enlarged round his eyes as the storm-rings round the midnight moon. He sprang upon me; his tri-forked thing at my heart.

I seized it; I snapped it; I dashed it; I trod it; and dragging the dark lightning-king out of my door, flung his elbowed, copper sceptre after him.

But spite of my treatment, and spite of my dissuasive talk of him to my neighbors, the Lightning-rod man still dwells in the land; still travels in storm-time, and drives a brave trade with the fears of man.

QUESTIONS

1 Vocabulary: *Acroceraunian:* acro means "on top" and ceraunian comes from the Greek word for thunder and lightning. *Jupiter Tonans:* Latin epithet meaning "Jupiter the Thunderer."

2 "The Lightning-Rod Man" is not only a literal story—in this instance about a peddler during a thunderstorm—but also a story of abstract forces. Melville presents both the literal and the symbolic simultaneously. Hints of this dual meaning appear in the proper names, the imagery, and the situation. List all the capitalized names throughout the story. Some, like Montreal, are real; others are not. Does Melville take us from, or toward, the real?

3 In symbolic stories, certain concrete objects or actions also have symbolic meaning, but this meaning is often not clear until you have read the whole story. At the end of this story, who does the narrator "stand at ease in the hands of"? By contrast, who might the Lightning-rod man symbolize? List the imagery that describes him. Does this imagery support his symbolic identity?

4 In symbolic stories, there has to be a consistent pattern of action on the symbolic as well as on the literal level. Taken literally, the lightning-rod peddler's attack on the narrator does not make sense. But on the symbolic level, it makes perfect sense. Explain the story's symbolic meaning, based on the last few paragraphs.

5 In symbolic stories, the pattern of symbolism must remain constant: A single character cannot symbolize two opposing abstractions in the same story. Comment on the consistency (or lack of it) of the imagery, actions, and epithets by which Melville presents the Lightning-rod man.

6 Symbolic stories are often open to several interpretations that tend to support one another. (a) In this story Melville refers to a part of Canada that is predominantly French Catholic. Does the Lightning-rod man sell his wares in Canada? What metal is used there? Is the Canadian metal as effective against lightning? What happened to the servant girl? What metal was her rosary made of? Does a rod with a "knob at the top" conjure up any religious personage? Based on this image, what does Melville think about the effectiveness of Catholicism to fend off lightning? What does "lightning" symbolize in this story? (b) The narrator says that in Criggan last week three things were hit by lightning. What was damaged? The Lightning-rod man claims to have had a rod on top of the steeple, but lightning struck it; on whom does he blame the event? Explain the symbolic, as well as the literal meaning of this. (c) Explain, symbolically, the statements "But of all things, I avoid tall men," and "Man avoid man? and in danger-time, too?"

7 The last paragraph is obviously about much more than lightning-rod peddlers. Explain Melville's theme, as symbolically presented in this last paragraph.

Langston Hughes

ON THE ROAD

He was not interested in the snow. When he got off the freight, one early evening during the depression, Sargeant never even noticed the snow. But he must have felt it seeping down his neck, cold, wet, sopping in his shoes. But if you had asked him, he wouldn't have known it was snowing. Sargeant didn't see the snow, not even under the bright lights of the main street, falling white and flaky against the night. He was too hungry, too sleepy, too tired.

The Reverend Mr. Dorset, however, saw the snow when he switched on his porch light, opened the front door of his parsonage, and found standing there before him a big black man with snow on his face, a human piece of night with snow on his face—obviously unemployed.

Said the Reverend Mr. Dorset before Sargeant even realized he'd opened his mouth: "I'm sorry. No! Go right on down this street four blocks and turn to your left, walk up seven and you'll see the Relief Shelter. I'm sorry. No!" He shut the door.

Sargeant wanted to tell the holy man that he had already been to the Relief Shelter, been to hundreds of relief shelters during the depression years, the beds were always gone and supper was over, the place was full, and they drew the color line anyhow. But the minister said, "No," and shut the door. Evidently he didn't want to hear about it. And he *had* a door to shut.

The big black man turned away. And even yet he didn't see the snow, walking right into it. Maybe he sensed it, cold, wet, sticking to his jaws, wet on his black hands, sopping in his shoes. He stopped and stood on the sidewalk hunched over—hungry, sleepy, cold—looking up and down. Then he looked right where he was—in front of a church. Of course! A church! Sure, right next to a parsonage, certainly a church.

It had *two* doors.

Broad white steps in the night all snowy white. Two high arched doors with slender stone pillars on either side. And way up, a round lacy window with a stone crucifix in the middle and Christ on the crucifix in stone. All this was pale in the street lights, solid and stony pale in the snow.

Sargeant blinked. When he looked up, the snow fell into his eyes. For the first time that night he *saw* the snow. He shook his head. He shook the snow from his coat sleeves, felt hungry, felt lost, felt not lost, felt cold. He walked up the steps of the church. He knocked at the door. No answer. He tried the handle. Locked. He put his shoulder against the door and his long black body slanted like a ramrod. He pushed. With loud rhythmic grunts, like the grunts in a chain-gang song, he pushed against the door.

"I'm tired . . . Huh! . . . Hongry . . . Uh! . . . I'm sleepy . . . Huh! I'm cold . . . I got to sleep somewheres," Sargeant said. "This here is a church, ain't it? Well, uh!"

He pushed against the door.

Suddenly, with an undue cracking and screaking the door began to give way to the tall black Negro who pushed ferociously against it.

By now two or three white people had stopped in the street, and Sargeant was vaguely aware of some of them yelling at him concerning the door. Three or four more came running, yelling at him.

"Hey!" they said. "Hey!"

"Uh-huh," answered the big tall Negro, "I know it's a white folks' church, but I got to sleep somewhere." He gave another lunge at the door. "Huh!"

And the door broke open.

But just when the door gave way, two white cops arrived in a car, ran up the steps with their clubs, and grabbed Sargeant. But Sargeant for once had no intention of being pulled or pushed away from the door.

Sargeant grabbed, but not for anything so weak as a broken door. He grabbed for one of the tall stone pillars beside the door, grabbed at it and caught it. And held it. The cops pulled and Sargeant pulled. Most of the people in the street got behind the cops and helped them pull.

"A big black unemployed Negro holding onto our church!" thought the people. "The idea!"

The cops began to beat Sargeant over the head, and nobody protested. But he held on.

And then the church fell down.

Gradually, the big stone front of the church fell down, the walls and the rafters, the crucifix and the Christ. Then the whole thing fell down, covering the cops and the people with bricks and stones and debris. The whole church fell down in the snow.

Sargeant got out from under the church and went walking on up the street with the stone pillar on his shoulder. He was under the impression that he had buried the parsonage and the Reverend Mr. Dorset who said, "No!" So he laughed, and threw the pillar six blocks up the street and went on.

Sargeant thought he was alone, but listening to the *crunch, crunch, crunch* on the snow of his own footsteps, he heard other footsteps, too, doubling his own. He looked around, and there was Christ walking along beside him, the same Christ that had been on the cross on the church—still stone with a rough stone surface, walking along beside him just like he was broken off the cross when the church fell down.

"Well, I'll be dogged," said Sargeant. "This here's the first time I ever seed you off the cross."

"Yes," said Christ, crunching his feet in the snow. "You had to pull the church down to get me off the cross."

"You glad?" said Sargeant.

"I sure am," said Christ.

They both laughed.

"I'm a hell of a fellow, ain't I?" said Sargeant. "Done pulled the church down!"

"You did a good job," said Christ. "They have kept me nailed on a cross for nearly two thousand years."

"Whee-ee-e!" said Sargeant. "I know you are glad to get off."

"I sure am," said Christ.

They walked on in the snow. Sargeant looked at the man of stone.

"And you have been up there two thousand years?"

"I sure have," Christ said.

"Well, if I had a little cash," said Sargeant, "I'd show you around a bit."

"I been around," said Christ.

"Yeah, but that was a long time ago."

"All the same," said Christ, "I've been around."

They walked on in the snow until they came to the railroad yards. Sargeant was tired, sweating and tired.

"Where you goin'?" Sargeant said, stopping by the tracks. He looked at Christ. Sargeant said, "I'm just a bum on the road. How about you? Where you goin'?"

"God knows," Christ said, "but I'm leavin' here."

They saw the red and green lights of the railroad yard half veiled by the snow that fell out of the night. Away down the track they saw a fire in a hobo jungle.

"I can go there and sleep," Sargeant said.

"You can?"

"Sure," said Sargeant. "That place ain't got no doors."

Outside the town, along the tracks, there were barren trees and bushes below the embankment, snow-gray in the dark. And down among the trees and bushes there were makeshift houses made out of boxes and tin and old pieces of wood and canvas. You couldn't see them in the dark, but you knew they were there if you'd ever been on the road, if you had ever lived with the homeless and hungry in a depression.

"I'm side-tracking," Sargeant said. "I'm tired."

"I'm gonna make it on to Kansas City," said Christ.

"O.K.," Sargeant said. "So long!"

He went down into the hobo jungle and found himself a place to sleep. He never did see Christ no more. About 6:00 A.M. a freight came by. Sargeant scrambled out of the jungle with a dozen or so more hobos and ran along the track, grabbing at the freight. It was dawn, early dawn, cold and gray.

"Wonder where Christ is by now?" Sargeant thought. "He musta gone on way on down the road. He didn't sleep in this jungle."

Sargeant grabbed the train and started to pull himself up into a moving coal car, over the edge of a wheeling coal car. But strangely enough, the car was full of cops. The nearest cop rapped Sargeant soundly across the knuckles with his night stick. Wham!

Rapped his big black hands for clinging to the top of the car. Wham! But Sargeant did not turn loose. He clung on and tried to pull himself into the car. He hollered at the top of his voice, "Damn it, lemme in this car!"

"Shut up," barked the cop. "You crazy coon!" He rapped Sargeant across the knuckles and punched him in the stomach. "You ain't out in no jungle now. This ain't no train. You in jail."

Wham! across his bare black fingers clinging to the bars of his cell. Wham! between the steel bars low down against his shins.

Suddenly Sargeant realized that he really was in jail. He wasn't on no train. The blood of the night before had dried on his face, his head hurt terribly, and a cop outside in the corridor was hitting him across the knuckles for holding onto the door, yelling and shaking the cell door.

"They musta took me to jail for breaking down the door last night," Sargeant thought, "that church door."

Sargeant went over and sat on a wooden bench against the cold stone wall. He was emptier than ever. His clothes were wet, clammy cold wet, and shoes sloppy with snow water. It was just about dawn. There he was, locked up behind a cell door, nursing his bruised fingers.

The bruised fingers were his, but not the *door.*

Not the *club,* but the fingers.

"You wait," mumbled Sargeant, black against the jail wall. "I'm gonna break down this door, too."

"Shut up—or I'll paste you one," said the cop.

"I'm gonna break down this door," yelled Sargeant as he stood up in his cell.

Then he must have been talking to himself because he said, "I wonder where Christ's gone? I wonder if he's gone to Kansas City?"

QUESTIONS

1 Snow is white. List the other things in the story described as white.

2 If you substitute the word "whites" for "snow" throughout, you will discover a pattern of Sargeant's race consciousness as the story progresses. In the opening paragraph we are told not only that Sargeant was not interested in the snow but also that he does not notice it. In the second paragraph we learn that the Reverend Dorset does notice the snow. Comment on the symbolic meaning of this contrast.

3 Why does Sargeant see the snow only after he is turned away? When does he first see it? What event makes him see?

4 Why does the church have two doors, but the parsonage and jail cell only one?

5 Analyze the imagery surrounding Christ, and comment on its relevance to the story, both literal and symbolic.

6 What is the symbolic significance of Sargeant grabbing for the pillar?

7 Discuss the symbolic meaning of Sargeant's fantasy, commencing with "And then the church fell down" and ending in the jail.

8 The literal story (including the fantasy in Sargeant's mind) is about a black man trying to get shelter in a snowstorm and ending up in jail. But the story is also about racism and about charity among all men. Explain the symbolic meaning of Sargeant yelling in his cell at the end, "I'm gonna break down this door."

9 Perhaps the pun, with its double meaning, is symbolism on its simplest level. A pun is a play on words. What is the pun in the name Reverend Dorset? Look up "sergeant" in the dictionary. What is its Latin root? Is there a pun in Sargeant's name? Is there a pun—or extended meaning—in Christ's answer to Sargeant's question: "Where you goin'?" "God knows."? What about the story's title, "On the Road"? Can you find more than one symbolic meaning for it?

10 In both "The Lightning-Rod Man" and "On the Road," a character appears who may be thought of as a personification of certain potentials inherent in man. Symbolically, what does it mean that each of these characters is left roaming abroad at the end?

11 Write your own answer to the general question "I wonder where Christ's gone?" as Sargeant asked it.

12 Stories like this one may seem to have an obvious theme. But be wary. Any statement of theme that sounds like a proverb or a trite moral should be reexamined carefully. It is probably an oversimplification. The conscious ambiguity of this story's title has already alerted the reader to expect complexity. What do you find the theme of this story to be? Check your answer against the operation of all the elements of fiction to which you have been introduced so far—words, images, comparisons, irony, and symbolism. All of these "spokes" must radiate from and point back to the same "hub"; otherwise you have not found a verifiable theme. Richly symbolic stories may have more than one interpretation. When this is true, the best statement of theme is the one that illuminates the greatest number of the story's details without contradicting any of them, and does so in the most economical way.

7
PLOT

things	conflict
action	revelation

Thus far these lessons in fiction have dealt with elements that are equally the concern of poetry: words, imagery, comparisons, irony, and symbol. The careful use of these elements enriches the *texture* of the essay and of spoken drama, as well as of poetry and fiction, giving these art forms more meaning, unity, and compression.

There are, however, other elements of particular importance to the *structure* of prose fiction. These elements have to do not with nuances, as do figures of speech or ironic overtones, but rather with the larger raw materials of fiction, and the way these materials are woven together.

It is obvious that fiction, being in part a rendition of real life, draws upon real life for its raw materials. What do we find in real life? Our senses tell us that our world is full of persons, places, and things, and that these interact. In terms of grammar, nouns describe the *things* in our environment; verbs describe their *action.*

Some authors let nouns do much of the work, and others depend more upon verbs. This variation explains why some fiction leaves the reader with a clear pictorial impression, whereas other fiction, though harder to picture later, leaves a strong sense of movement or restlessness. Underlining all the nouns in the opening paragraphs of a story and reading them off aloud, then doing the same with the verbs, will give you a vivid illustration of how a particular author achieves his effect.

Having noted that the raw materials of fiction are *things* and *action,* we can discuss one of the most important aspects of fiction, which is *plot.* A plot is a story with values: it is a series of actions that have some significant connection with each other. "The King died, and then the Queen died," is a story. "The King died, and then the Queen died of grief," is a plot. A reader comprehends a plot by remembering details as the story unfolds and anticipating that those details will be put to good use before the story has ended. In the simple story of the King and Queen (invented by the British author E. M. Forster), we remember the death of the King, because we plan to use this information. And we are not disappointed, for we put this memory to work when we discover the Queen died "of grief." A *conflict* has led to a *revelation.*

Sometimes you remember many incidents in a story, waiting to put them to good use, but the story seems to end abruptly. Here you are, remembering all these things, but they appear not to have been put to full account in the story and, therefore, you are left with a distinct impression that the story has not been resolved.

You are responding to a need for "plot." You remember that the King died and that the Queen died, but no significant connection between the events has been indicated. The story lacks the sophisticated conflict you are used to, and you are dissatisfied with it. Here the difficulty is with the story. In other instances the difficulty may lie with you. You may have missed a crucial detail in the first reading, and a second reading may make the resolution clear. Or, as we have seen in "The Lightning-Rod Man," the plot might be symbolic instead of literal.

No stories in this book are without plot, though mere physical interaction does not always hold the key to the plot. Often a changed mental attitude, as in Pirandello's "War" in Chapter 5, or a seemingly chance action, like a cloud obscuring the fourth star in "The Portable Phonograph" in Chapter 4, is intended to tell the reader that some significant interconnection, or revelation, has occurred. To say this revelation is "significant" means that we have placed a value judgment upon it. What seems "significant" to one reader might not seem so to another, but despite our varied backgrounds, we are all human beings, and the plots of the best stories are significant to almost everyone. For example, all human beings are affected by love and by death in one form or another, so it is not surprising that a preponderance of literature is concerned with these two subjects.

The plots of some stories are not difficult to describe. In "The Portable Phonograph," for example, the conflict pits the overwhelming forces of barbarism against the shattered remnants of civilization, best represented by Dr. Jenkins, and the revelation occurs, after the proper suspense, when Dr. Jenkins discovers that barbarism, represented by the aroused passions of the tubercular musician, is still present and is still murderous. We are not bothered that the story ends with this revelation, for everything significant has been disclosed. We can state the plot by naming the conflict—that is, the opposing forces—and the moment of revelation.

A story like "War," however, places a greater demand on our perceptions, since the action involves mental attitudes rather than physical forces. Nonetheless, in determining the plot, the same method of analysis applies. The conflict is shown in the debate among the several occupants of the railway carriage over the proper attitude of parents whose sons have been drafted to fight a war. Having recognized this, we look for the moment of revelation, and discover that it comes in two stages. The first occurs when the grief-stricken mother is moved by the fat man's rhetoric to reconsider her attitude of inconsolable grief. The second stage occurs when, in response to her blurted "Is your son really dead?" the fat man breaks into uncontrollable sobs, showing his own sudden, unexpected shift in attitude. Even though the story's plot has to do with changed attitudes, rather than physical actions, fiction dramatizes these conflicts in a world of things and actions. Having realized this, we are able to discuss the plot in terms of conflict and revelation.

Typically, this conflict emerges either between persons or values or, more commonly, between both simultaneously. Once the reader recognizes who or what is in conflict, he grasps the story's plot. Not only does he recognize the obvious struggle between Walter Mitty and his nagging wife but also the more interesting conflict between romantic escapism and everyday reality; not only does he recognize the struggle between Sargeant and the policeman but also the conflict between the depths of true charity and the shallows of institutional law and order; not only does he recognize the struggle between Sammy and the grocery store manager but also the conflict between uncompromising youth and compromised adults.

Or, there may appear less obvious conflicts, such as that between Crane's rational young lieutenant and the irrational forces of war, or the inner conflict of the boy in "Araby," between a romantic view of love lighted by his idealized vision of Mangan's sister and a realistic view darkened by the banal flirtation between the salesgirl and the two young men at the bazaar.

A story's conflict and revelation seldom come as a total surprise, since the reader is usually given some clues as to what will be revealed. For example, the boy's disillusion in "Araby" is well prepared for by the story's imagery, in which idealism and brightness are contrasted with the darker reality. We as readers object to a revelation that we have not been prepared for, or a revelation that does not grow naturally from the conflict. Such trick endings may startle us, but our interest in them is seldom sustained.

Of much greater interest is the suspense generated as we read a carefully plotted story like "The Piece of String," encountering its successive conflicts and wondering how these conflicts will be resolved through the revelation.

Perhaps the most sophisticated of all plots are those that use not only suspense but also dramatic irony for effect. Dramatic irony is present when the reader knows more than the characters themselves (see Chapter 5). Often he knows everything, including the way things will end. In this full knowledge, the reader enjoys something of a godlike view of the scene below. This dramatic irony explains the peculiar pleasure of rereading a book whose plot we know, or reseeing a movie whose conflict and revelation we remember. Through dramatic irony, suspense has been transferred to the pleasure derived not from how the story comes out, but from anticipating how the author will handle the revelation. We become more collaborators in, than spectators of, the action.

These three—surprise, suspense, and dramatic irony—describe three progressively sophisticated ways by which the plot can reveal significant connections of events to the reader.

William Carlos Williams

THE USE OF FORCE

They were new patients to me, all I had was the name, Olson. Please come down as soon as you can, my daughter is very sick.

When I arrived I was met by the mother, a big startled looking woman, very clean and apologetic who merely said, Is this the doctor? and let me in. In the back, she added. You must excuse us, doctor, we have her in the kitchen where it is warm. It is very damp here sometimes.

The child was fully dressed and sitting on her father's lap near the kitchen table. He tried to get up, but I motioned for him not to bother, took off my overcoat and started to look things over. I could see that they were all very nervous, eyeing me up and down distrustfully. As often, in such cases, they weren't telling me more than they had to, it was up to me to tell them; that's why they were spending three dollars on me.

The child was fairly eating me up with her cold, steady eyes, and no expression to her face whatever. She did not move and seemed, inwardly, quiet; an unusually attractive little thing, and as strong as a heifer in appearance. But her face was flushed, she was breathing rapidly, and I realized that she had a high fever. She had magnificent blonde hair, in profusion. One of those picture children often reproduced in advertising leaflets and the photogravure sections of the Sunday papers.

She's had a fever for three days, began the father and we don't know what it comes from. My wife has given her things, you know, like people do, but it don't do no good. And there's been a lot of sickness around. So we tho't you'd better look her over and tell us what is the matter.

As doctors often do I took a trial shot at it as a point of departure. Had she had a sore throat?

Both parents answered me together, No . . . No, she says her throat don't hurt her.

Does your throat hurt you? added the mother to the child. But the little girl's expression didn't change nor did she move her eyes from my face.

Have you looked?

I tried to, said the mother, but I couldn't see.

As it happens we had been having a number of cases of diphtheria in the school to which this child went during that month and we were all, quite apparently, thinking of that, though no one had as yet spoken of the thing.

Well, I said, suppose we take a look at the throat first. I smiled in my best professional manner and asking for the child's first name I said, come on, Mathilda, open your mouth and let's take a look at your throat.

Nothing doing.

Aw, come on, I coaxed, just open your mouth wide and let me take a look. Look, I said opening both hands wide, I haven't anything in my hands. Just open up and let me see.

Such a nice man, put in the mother. Look how kind he is to you. Come on, do what he tells you to. He won't hurt you.

At that I ground my teeth in disgust. If only they wouldn't use the word "hurt" I might be able to get somewhere. But I did not allow myself to be hurried or disturbed but speaking quietly and slowly I approached the child again.

As I moved my chair a little nearer suddenly with one cat-like movement both her hands clawed instinctively for my eyes and she almost reached them too. In fact she knocked my glasses flying and they fell, though unbroken, several feet away from me on the kitchen floor.

Both the mother and father almost turned themselves inside out in embarrassment and apology. You bad girl, said the mother, taking her and shaking her by one arm. Look what you've done. The nice man . . .

For heaven's sake, I broke in. Don't call me a nice man to her. I'm here to look at her throat on the chance that she might have diphtheria and possibly die of it. But that's nothing to her. Look here, I said to the child, we're going to look at your throat. You're old enough to understand what I'm saying. Will you open it now by yourself or shall we have to open it for you?

Not a move. Even her expression hadn't changed. Her breaths however were coming faster and faster. Then the battle began. I had to do it. I had to have a throat culture for her own protection. But first I told the parents that it was entirely up to them. I explained the danger but said that I would not insist on a throat examination so long as they would take the responsibility.

If you don't do what the doctor says you'll have to go to the hospital, the mother admonished her severely.

Oh yeah? I had to smile to myself. After all, I had already fallen in love with the savage brat, the parents were contemptible to me. In the ensuing struggle they grew more and more abject, crushed, exhausted while she surely rose to magnificent heights of insane fury of effort bred of her terror of me.

The father tried his best, and he was a big man but the fact that she was his daughter, his shame at her behavior and his dread of hurting her made him release her just at the critical moment several times when I had almost achieved success, till I wanted to kill him. But his dread also that she might have diphtheria made him tell me to go on, go on though he himself was almost fainting, while the mother moved back and forth behind us raising and lowering her hands in an agony of apprehension.

Put her in front of you on your lap, I ordered, and hold both her wrists.

But as soon as he did the child let out a scream. Don't, you're hurting me. Let go of my hands. Let them go I tell you. Then she shrieked terrifyingly, hysterically. Stop it! Stop it! You're killing me!

Do you think she can stand it, doctor! said the mother.

You get out, said the husband to his wife. Do you want her to die of diphtheria?

Come on now, hold her, I said.

Then I grasped the child's head with my left hand and tried to get the wooden tongue depressor between her teeth. She fought, with clenched teeth, desperately! But now I also had grown furious —at a child. I tried to hold myself down but I couldn't. I know how to expose a throat for inspection. And I did my best. When finally I got the wooden spatula behind the last teeth and just the point of it into the mouth cavity, she opened up for an instant but before I could see anything she came down again and gripping the wooden blade between her molars she reduced it to splinters before I could get it out again.

Aren't you ashamed, the mother yelled at her. Aren't you ashamed to act like that in front of the doctor?

Get me a smooth-handled spoon of some sort, I told the mother. We're going through with this. The child's mouth was already bleeding. Her tongue was cut and she was screaming in wild hysterical shrieks. Perhaps I should have desisted and come back in an hour or more. No doubt it would have been better. But I have seen at least two children lying dead in bed of neglect in such cases, and feeling that I must get a diagnosis now or never I went at it again. But the worst of it was that I too had got beyond reason. I could have torn the child apart in my own fury and enjoyed it. It was a pleasure to attack her. My face was burning with it.

The damned little brat must be protected against her own idiocy, one says to one's self at such times. Others must be protected against her. It is a social necessity. And all these things are true. But a blind fury, a feeling of adult shame, bred of a longing for muscular release are the operatives. One goes on to the end.

In a final unreasoning assault I overpowered the child's neck and jaws. I forced the heavy silver spoon back of her teeth and down her throat till she gagged. And there it was—both tonsils covered with membrane. She had fought valiantly to keep me from knowing her secret. She had been hiding that sore throat for three days at least and lying to her parents in order to escape just such an outcome as this.

Now truly she *was* furious. She had been on the defensive before but now she attacked. Tried to get off her father's lap and fly at me while tears of defeat blinded her eyes.

QUESTIONS

1 To test the use of this story's raw materials—*things* and *action*—do the following: Underline the nouns in the last two paragraphs. Read them aloud. Underline the verbs. Read them aloud. Do the same with the opening two paragraphs of "The Portable Phonograph." Make a statement about the use of nouns for pictures, and verbs for action, in these two examples.

2 We have said that a plot is a story with values. What conflict of values is operating between the doctor and the parents? The doctor and the girl?

3 What conflict of values is operating within the doctor? Is he conscious of this conflict? How does it complicate his task? Does he achieve a revelation? If so, what is it?

4 Is a conflict of values operating within the girl? Does she achieve any revelation? Do you, the reader, achieve a revelation that is larger and more complex than that attained by either the girl or the doctor? Does the story's final paragraph contribute to a larger insight? If so, how?

5 An understanding of *paradox* is helpful in analyzing this story. Paradox may be defined as the successful reconciliation of seemingly irreconcilable ideas. In this story it is possible to discover the paradoxical truth that there may be victory in defeat and defeat in victory. The girl's life is saved, but what has she lost in the struggle? The doctor wins the physical conflict, but what has he lost? Has he won something greater than the physical victory?

6 Is this a story of surprise, suspense, or dramatic irony?

7 Explain the possible symbolic meaning of "It was a pleasure to attack her. My face was burning with it." Support your explanation with other suggestive images and actions earlier in the story.

John Steinbeck

THE CHRYSANTHEMUMS

The high grey-flannel fog of winter closed off the Salinas Valley from the sky and from all the rest of the world. On every side it sat like a lid on the mountains and made of the great valley a closed pot. On the broad, level land floor the gang plows bit deep and left the black earth shining like metal where the shares had cut. On the foothill ranches across the Salinas River, the yellow stubble fields seemed to be bathed in pale cold sunshine, but there was no sunshine in the valley now in December. The thick willow scrub along the river flamed with sharp and positive yellow leaves.

It was a time of quiet and of waiting. The air was cold and tender. A light wind blew up from the southwest so that the farmers were mildly hopeful of a good rain before long; but fog and rain do not go together.

Across the river, on Henry Allen's foothill ranch there was little work to be done, for the hay was cut and stored and the orchards were plowed up to receive the rain deeply when it should come. The cattle on the higher slopes were becoming shaggy and rough-coated.

Elisa Allen, working in her flower garden, looked down across the yard and saw Henry, her husband, talking to two men in business suits. The three of them stood by the tractor shed, each man with one foot on the side of the little Fordson. They smoked cigarettes and studied the machine as they talked.

Elisa watched them for a moment and then went back to her work. She was thirty-five. Her face was lean and strong and her eyes were as clear as water. Her figure looked blocked and heavy in her gardening costume, a man's black hat pulled low down over her eyes, clod-hopper shoes, a figured print dress almost completely covered by a big corduroy apron with four big pockets to hold the snips, the trowel and scratcher, the seeds and the knife she worked with. She wore heavy leather gloves to protect her hands while she worked.

She was cutting down the old year's chrysanthemum stalks with a pair of short and powerful scissors. She looked down toward the men by the tractor shed now and then. Her face was eager and mature and handsome; even her work with the scissors was over-eager, over-powerful. The chrysanthemum stems seemed too small and easy for her energy.

She brushed a cloud of hair out of her eyes with the back of her glove, and left a smudge of earth on her cheek in doing it. Behind her stood the neat white farm house with red geraniums close-banked around it as high as the windows. It was a hard-swept looking little house, with hard-polished windows, and a clean mud-mat on the front steps.

Elisa cast another glance toward the tractor shed. The strangers were getting into their Ford coupe. She took off a glove and put her strong fingers down into the forest of new green chrysanthemum sprouts that were growing around the old roots. She spread the leaves and looked down among the close-growing stems. No aphids were there, no sowbugs or snails or cutworms. Her terrier fingers destroyed such pests before they could get started.

Elisa started at the sound of her husband's voice. He had come near quietly, and he leaned over the wire fence that protected her flower garden from cattle and dogs and chickens.

"At it again," he said. "You've got a strong new crop coming."

Elisa straightened her back and pulled on the gardening glove again. "Yes. They'll be strong this coming year." In her tone and on her face there was a little smugness.

"You've got a gift with things," Henry observed. "Some of those yellow chrysanthemums you had this year were ten inches across. I wish you'd work out in the orchard and raise some apples that big."

Her eyes sharpened. "Maybe I could do it, too. I've a gift with things, all right. My mother had it. She could stick anything in the ground and make it grow. She said it was having planters' hands that knew how to do it."

"Well, it sure works with flowers," he said.

"Henry, who were those men you were talking to?"

"Why, sure, that's what I came to tell you. They were from the Western Meat Company. I sold those thirty head of three-year-old steers. Got nearly my own price, too."

"Good," she said. "Good for you."

"And I thought," he continued, "I thought how it's Saturday afternoon, and we might go into Salinas for dinner at a restaurant, and then to a picture show—to celebrate, you see."

"Good," she repeated. "Oh, yes. That will be good."

Henry put on his joking tone. "There's fights tonight. How'd you like to go to the fights?"

"Oh, no," she said breathlessly. "No, I wouldn't like fights."

"Just fooling, Elisa. We'll go to a movie. Let's see. It's two now. I'm going to take Scotty and bring down those steers from the hill. It'll take us maybe two hours. We'll go in town about five and have dinner at the Cominos Hotel. Like that?"

"Of course I'll like it. It's good to eat away from home."

"All right, then. I'll go get up a couple of horses."

She said, "I'll have plenty of time to transplant some of these sets, I guess."

She heard her husband calling Scotty down by the barn. And a little later she saw the two men ride up the pale yellow hillside in search of the steers.

There was a little square sandy bed kept for rooting the chrysanthemums. With her trowel she turned the soil over and over, and smoothed it and patted it firm. Then she dug ten parallel trenches to receive the sets. Back at the chrysanthemum bed she pulled out the little crisp shoots, trimmed off the leaves of each one with her scissors and laid it on a small orderly pile.

A squeak of wheels and plod of hoofs came from the road. Elisa looked up. The country road ran along the dense bank of willows and cottonwoods that bordered the river, and up this road came a curious vehicle, curiously drawn. It was an old spring-wagon, with a round canvas top on it like the cover of a prairie schooner. It was drawn by an old bay horse and a little grey-and-white burro. A big stubble-bearded man sat between the cover flaps and drove the crawling team. Underneath the wagon, between the hind wheels, a lean and rangy mongrel dog walked sedately. Words were painted on the canvas in clumsy, crooked letters. "Pots, pans, knives, sisors, lawn mores. Fixed." Two rows of articles and the triumphantly definitive "Fixed" below. The black paint had run down in little sharp points beneath each letter.

Elisa, squatting on the ground, watched to see the crazy, loose-jointed wagon pass by. But it didn't pass. It turned into the farm road in front of her house, crooked old wheels skirling and squeaking. The rangy dog darted from between the wheels and ran ahead. Instantly the two ranch shepherds flew out at him. Then all three stopped, and with stiff and quivering tails, with taut straight legs, with ambassadorial dignity, they slowly circled, sniffing daintily. The caravan pulled up to Elisa's wire fence and stopped. Now the newcomer dog, feeling outnumbered, lowered his tail and retired under the wagon with raised hackles and bared teeth.

The man on the wagon seat called out, "That's a bad dog in a fight when he gets started."

Elisa laughed. "I see he is. How soon does he generally get started?"

The man caught up her laughter and echoed it heartily. "Sometimes not for weeks and weeks," he said. He climbed stiffly down, over the wheel. The horse and the donkey drooped like unwatered flowers.

Elisa saw that he was a very big man. Although his hair and

beard were greying, he did not look old. His worn black suit was wrinkled and spotted with grease. The laughter had disappeared from his face and eyes the moment his laughing voice ceased. His eyes were dark, and they were full of the brooding that gets in the eyes of teamsters and of sailors. The calloused hands he rested on the wire fence were cracked, and every crack was a black line. He took off his battered hat.

"I'm off my general road, ma'am," he said. "Does this dirt road cut over across the river to the Los Angeles highway?"

Elisa stood up and shoved the thick scissors in her apron pocket. "Well, yes, it does, but it winds around and then fords the river. I don't think your team could pull through the sand."

He replied with some asperity, "It might surprise you what them beasts can pull through."

"When they get started?" she asked.

He smiled for a second. "Yes. When they get started."

"Well," said Elisa, "I think you'll save time if you go back to the Salinas road and pick up the highway there."

He drew a big finger down the chicken wire and made it sing. "I ain't in any hurry, ma'am. I go from Seattle to San Diego and back every year. Takes all my time. About six months each way. I aim to follow nice weather."

Elisa took off her gloves and stuffed them in the apron pocket with the scissors. She touched the under edge of her man's hat, searching for fugitive hairs. "That sounds like a nice kind of a way to live," she said.

He leaned confidentially over the fence. "Maybe you noticed the writing on my wagon. I mend pots and sharpen knives and scissors. You got any of them things to do?"

"Oh, no," she said quickly. "Nothing like that." Her eyes hardened with resistance.

"Scissors is the worst thing," he explained. "Most people just ruin scissors trying to sharpen 'em, but I know how. I got a special tool. It's a little bobbit kind of thing, and patented. But it sure does the trick."

"No. My scissors are all sharp."

"All right, then. Take a pot," he continued earnestly, "a bent pot, or a pot with a hole. I can make it like new so you don't have to buy no new ones. That's a saving for you."

"No," she said shortly. "I tell you I have nothing like that for you to do."

His face fell to an exaggerated sadness. His voice took on a whining undertone. "I ain't had a thing to do today. Maybe I won't have no supper tonight. You see I'm off my regular road. I know folks on the highway clear from Seattle to San Diego. They save their things for me to sharpen up because they know I do it so good and save them money."

"I'm sorry," Elisa said irritably. "I haven't anything for you to do."

His eyes left her face and fell to searching the ground. They roamed about until they came to the chrysanthemum bed where she had been working. "What's them plants, ma'am?"

The irritation and resistance melted from Elisa's face. "Oh, those are chrysanthemums, giant whites and yellows. I raise them every year, bigger than anybody around here."

"Kind of a long-stemmed flower? Looks like a quick puff of colored smoke?" he asked.

"That's it. What a nice way to describe them."

"They smell kind of nasty till you get used to them," he said.

"It's a good bitter smell," she retorted, "not nasty at all."

He changed his tone quickly. "I like the smell myself."

"I had ten-inch blooms this year," she said.

The man leaned farther over the fence. "Look. I know a lady down the road a piece, has got the nicest garden you ever seen. Got nearly every kind of flower but no chrysanthemums. Last time I was mending a copper-bottom washtub for her (that's a hard job but I do it good), she said to me, 'If you ever run acrost some nice chrysanthemums I wish you'd try to get me a few seeds.' That's what she told me."

Elisa's eyes grew alert and eager. "She couldn't have known much about chrysanthemums. You can raise them from seed, but it's much easier to root the little sprouts you see there."

"Oh," he said. "I s'pose I can't take none to her, then."

"Why yes you can," Elisa cried. "I can put some in damp sand, and you can carry them right along with you. They'll take root in the pot if you keep them damp. And then she can transplant them."

"She'd sure like to have some, ma'am. You say they're nice ones?"

"Beautiful," she said. "Oh, beautiful." Her eyes shone. She tore off the battered hat and shook out her dark pretty hair. "I'll put them in a flower pot, and you can take them right with you. Come into the yard."

While the man came through the picket gate Elisa ran excitedly along the geranium-bordered path to the back of the house. And she returned carrying a big red flower pot. The gloves were forgotten now. She kneeled on the ground by the starting bed and dug up the sandy soil with her fingers and scooped it into the bright new flower pot. Then she picked up the little pile of shoots she had prepared. With her strong fingers she pressed them into the sand and tamped around them with her knuckles. The man stood over her. "I'll tell you what to do," she said. "You remember so you can tell the lady."

"Yes, I'll try to remember."

"Well, look. These will take root in about a month. Then she must set them out, about a foot apart in good rich earth like this, see?" She lifted a handful of dark soil for him to look at. "They'll grow fast and tall. Now remember this: In July tell her to cut them down, about eight inches from the ground."

"Before they bloom?" he asked.

"Yes, before they bloom." Her face was tight with eagerness. "They'll grow right up again. About the last of September the buds will start."

She stopped and seemed perplexed. "It's the budding that takes the most care," she said hesitantly. "I don't know how to tell you." She looked deep into his eyes, searchingly. Her mouth opened a little, and she seemed to be listening. "I'll try to tell you," she said. "Did you ever hear of planting hands?"

"Can't say I have, ma'am."

"Well, I can only tell you what it feels like. It's when you're picking off the buds you don't want. Everything goes right down into your finger-tips. You watch your fingers work. They do it themselves. You can feel how it is. They pick and pick the buds. They never make a mistake. They're with the plant. Do you see? Your fingers and the plant. You can feel that, right up your arm. They know. They never make a mistake. You can feel it. When you're like that you can't do anything wrong. Do you see that? Can you understand that?"

She was kneeling on the ground looking up at him. Her breast swelled passionately.

The man's eyes narrowed. He looked away self-consciously. "Maybe I know," he said. "Sometimes in the night in the wagon there——"

Elisa's voice grew husky. She broke in on him. "I've never lived as you do, but I know what you mean. When the night is dark—why, the stars are sharp-pointed, and there's quiet. Why, you rise up and up! Every pointed star gets driven into your body. It's like that. Hot and sharp and—lovely."

Kneeling there, her hand went out toward his legs in the greasy black trousers. Her hesitant fingers almost touched the cloth. Then her hand dropped to the ground. She crouched low like a fawning dog.

He said, "It's nice, just like you say. Only when you don't have no dinner, it ain't."

She stood up then, very straight, and her face was ashamed. She held the flower pot out to him and placed it gently in his arms. "Here. Put it in your wagon, on the seat, where you can watch it. Maybe I can find something for you to do."

At the back of the house she dug in the can pile and found two old and battered aluminum saucepans. She carried them back and gave them to him. "Here, maybe you can fix these."

His manner changed. He became professional. "Good as new I can fix them." At the back of his wagon he set a little anvil, and out of an oily tool box dug a small machine hammer. Elisa came through the gate to watch him while he pounded out the dents in the kettles. His mouth grew sure and knowing. At a difficult part of the work he sucked his under-lip.

"You sleep right in the wagon?" Elisa asked.

"Right in the wagon, ma'am. Rain or shine I'm dry as a cow in there."

"It must be nice," she said. "It must be very nice. I wish women could do such things."

"It ain't the right kind of a life for a woman."

Her upper lip raised a little, showing her teeth. "How do you know? How can you tell?" she said.

"I don't know, ma'am," he protested. "Of course I don't know. Now here's your kettles, done. You don't have to buy no new ones."

"How much?"

"Oh, fifty cent'll do. I keep my prices down and my work good. That's why I have all them satisfied customers up and down the highway."

Elisa brought him a fifty-cent piece from the house and dropped it in his hand. "You might be surprised to have a rival some time.

I can sharpen scissors, too. And I can beat the dents out of little pots. I could show you what a woman might do."

He put his hammer back in the oily box and shoved the little anvil out of sight. "It would be a lonely life for a woman, ma'am, and a scarey life, too, with animals creeping under the wagon all night." He climbed over the single-tree, steadying himself with a hand on the burro's white rump. He settled himself in the seat, picked up the lines. "Thank you kindly, ma'am," he said. "I'll do like you told me; I'll go back and catch the Salinas road."

"Mind," she called, "if you're long in getting there, keep the sand damp."

"Sand, ma'am? . . . Sand? Oh, sure. You mean around the chrysanthemums. Sure I will." He clucked his tongue. The beasts leaned luxuriously into their collars. The mongrel dog took his place between the back wheels. The wagon turned and crawled out the entrance road and back the way it had come, along the river.

Elisa stood in front of her wire fence watching the slow progress of the caravan. Her shoulders were straight, her head thrown back, her eyes half-closed, so that the scene came vaguely into them. Her lips moved silently, forming the words "Good-bye—good-bye." Then she whispered, "That's a bright direction. There's a glowing there." The sound of her whisper startled her. She shook herself free and looked about to see whether anyone had been listening. Only the dogs had heard. They lifted their heads toward her from their sleeping in the dust, and then stretched out their chins and settled asleep again. Elisa turned and ran hurriedly into the house.

In the kitchen she reached behind the stove and felt the water tank. It was full of hot water from the noonday cooking. In the bathroom she tore off her soiled clothes and flung them into the corner. And then she scrubbed herself with a little block of pumice, legs and thighs, loins and chest and arms, until her skin was scratched and red. When she had dried herself she stood in front of a mirror in her bedroom and looked at her body. She tightened her stomach and threw out her chest. She turned and looked over her shoulder at her back.

After a while she began to dress, slowly. She put on her newest underclothing and her nicest stockings and the dress which was the symbol of her prettiness. She worked carefully on her hair, pencilled her eyebrows and rouged her lips.

Before she was finished she heard the little thunder of hoofs and the shouts of Henry and his helper as they drove the red steers into the corral. She heard the gate bang shut and set herself for Henry's arrival.

His step sounded on the porch. He entered the house calling, "Elisa, where are you?"

"In my room, dressing. I'm not ready. There's hot water for your bath. Hurry up. It's getting late."

When she heard him splashing in the tub, Elisa laid his dark suit on the bed, and shirt and socks and tie beside it. She stood his polished shoes on the floor beside the bed. Then she went to the porch and sat primly and stiffly down. She looked toward the river road where the willow-line was still yellow with frosted leaves so that under the high grey fog they seemed a thin band of sunshine. This was the only color in the grey afternoon. She sat unmoving for a long time. Her eyes blinked rarely.

Henry came banging out of the door, shoving his tie inside his vest as he came. Elisa stiffened and her face grew tight. Henry stopped short and looked at her. "Why—why, Elisa. You look so nice!"

"Nice? You think I look nice? What do you mean by 'nice'?"

Henry blundered on. "I don't know. I mean you look different, strong and happy."

"I am strong? Yes, strong. What do you mean 'strong'?"

He looked bewildered. "You're playing some kind of a game," he said helplessly. "It's a kind of a play. You look strong enough to break a calf over your knee, happy enough to eat it like a watermelon."

For a second she lost her rigidity. "Henry! Don't talk like that. You didn't know what you said." She grew complete again. "I'm strong," she boasted. "I never knew before how strong."

Henry looked down toward the tractor shed, and when he brought his eyes back to her, they were his own again. "I'll get out the car. You can put on your coat while I'm starting."

Elisa went into the house. She heard him drive to the gate and idle down his motor, and then she took a long time to put on her hat. She pulled it here and pressed it there. When Henry turned the motor off she slipped into her coat and went out.

The little roadster bounced along on the dirt road by the river, raising the birds and driving the rabbits into the brush. Two cranes flapped heavily over the willow-line and dropped into the river-bed.

Far ahead on the road Elisa saw a dark speck. She knew.

She tried not to look as they passed it, but her eyes would not obey. She whispered to herself sadly, "He might have thrown them off the road. That wouldn't have been much trouble, not very much. But he kept the pot," she explained. "He had to keep the pot. That's why he couldn't get them off the road."

The roadster turned a bend and she saw the caravan ahead. She swung full around toward her husband so she could not see the little covered wagon and the mismatched team as the car passed them.

In a moment it was over. The thing was done. She did not look back. She said loudly, to be heard above the motor, "It will be good, tonight, a good dinner."

"Now you're changed again," Henry complained. He took one hand from the wheel and patted her knee. "I ought to take you in to dinner oftener. It would be good for both of us. We get so heavy out on the ranch."

"Henry," she asked, "could we have wine at dinner?"

"Sure we could. Say! That will be fine."

She was silent for a while; then she said, "Henry, at those prize fights, do the men hurt each other very much?"

"Sometimes a little, not often. Why?"

"Well, I've read how they break noses, and blood runs down their chests. I've read how the fighting gloves get heavy and soggy with blood."

He looked around at her. "What's the matter, Elisa? I didn't know you read things like that." He brought the car to a stop, then turned to the right over the Salinas River bridge.

"Do any women ever go to the fights?" she asked.

"Oh, sure, some. What's the matter, Elisa? Do you want to go? I don't think you'd like it, but I'll take you if you really want to go."

She relaxed limply in the seat. "Oh, no. No. I don't want to go. I'm sure I don't." Her face was turned away from him. "It will be enough if we can have wine. It will be plenty." She turned up her coat collar so he could not see that she was crying weakly—like an old woman.

QUESTIONS

1 Vocabulary: *skirling:* shrieking.

2 Underline the nouns in the first three paragraphs. Read them aloud. Underline the verbs. Read them aloud. Would you say that at the beginning of this story Steinbeck is more interested in creating a static picture or in giving the impression of action?

3 The French author Gustave Flaubert said that nothing comes alive in a story unless it acts upon, or is acted upon by, something else in the story. Analyze any three paragraphs in this story. Does Steinbeck follow Flaubert's advice? Now turn to Chapter 1 and analyze the excerpt from Jack London's *The Scarlet Plague.* Does London follow it?

4 Is this a story of surprise, suspense, or dramatic irony?

5 Your responses to the previous question will depend to a great extent on the amount of experience you have had in interpreting fiction. Those of you who answered "surprise" will discover on closer examination that the author has carefully supplied more than one clue indicating the peddler's feigned interest in the chrysanthemums; so you should not have been surprised by his callous emptying of the flower pot on the road. Nor, given the many indications of Elisa's behavior, should you have been surprised by her later actions when she discovers the deception. Those who answered "suspense" were probably reading more than was justified into Steinbeck's description of Elisa's warm reaction to the peddler. A thoughtful reconsideration of all the details should persuade you that any sexually melodramatic act on Elisa's part would have been false to both her character and the story. There remains, then, this question: did Steinbeck allow you to know all the facts—more facts than Elisa herself knew—and, therefore, provide you with a chance to anticipate the ending?

6 Throughout this book we have shown how all the elements of fiction work together to achieve the artistic unity that characterizes good fiction. Reread the first paragraph in this story. How do the contrasts in the imagery contribute to the story's effect?

7 The controlling "thing" in this story is named in the title. Is this "thing" also a symbol? If so, what does it symbolize?

8 Reread the final nine paragraphs of the story, beginning with " 'Henry,' she asked, 'could we have wine at dinner?' " What is the symbolic meaning of the juxtaposition here of wine and blood? How does this juxtaposition help to reveal the full meaning of Elisa's final words to her husband?

8
PACE

summary method | scenic method | syntax

In the preceding chapter, we noted that the raw materials of fiction are persons, places, things, and their interactions. When these interactions create a conflict, leading to a revelation, we have what we call plot.

Within this basic pattern, a writer may vary his way of putting the story together. One variation is the speed, or *pace,* he uses. He can pace his story fast, in *summary method* (as in the opening paragraphs of "The Masque of the Red Death"), condensing actions that have taken place over months or even years. He can pace the story slow, in *scenic method* (as in the conversation between the two waiters that begins with the second paragraph of "A Clean, Well-Lighted Place"), so that the events and the dialogue take nearly as much time to read as they took to occur. Or he can use both the summary and the scenic methods, creating rhythms of alternately fast and slow movement, sometimes bridging these with general, representative statements of what has happened in the past, attached only loosely to the time-sequence.

The effect of a fast pace in the summary method is to speed the action by covering a long span of time in a short span of writing. This method also widens the field of vision to panoramic dimensions, just as the cinema records long distance shots, showing more, but showing it less precisely.

The effects of a slow pace in the scenic method are to refine the focus upon specific imagery and detail, thus giving the reader a stronger sense of immediacy, of "being there." Scenic method is like a close-up camera shot that gives the audience a closer-than-life perspective. With this panoramic and close-up focusing, fiction and cinema can do something that live drama, always seen from a set distance by the audience, cannot. Both fiction and cinema have, as it were, a zoom lens. But in fiction, the author often varies not only his story's scope in space, but also its pace in time—a technique occasionally employed in the cinema by such devices as calendar leaves falling away, or changing seasons, or quick montages of action giving the impression of speeded narration.

Pace is also affected by *syntax*. Syntax is the arrangement of words into sentences. As a writer shapes his sentences, he achieves different effects: short sentences and single syllable words tend to suggest crisp action with sharp focus on the present moment; longer sentences, with internal punctuation and dependent clauses, and longer words tend to suggest a more meditative and thoughtful pace in which the future and the past are given a large consideration. Sometimes syntax is used for ironic contrast between thought and style, as we observed in the chapter on irony. More often, though, syntax adds to the meaning of a story by pacing the language appropriately to the events. When asked the secret of writing, Ernest Hemingway said, "All you have to do is write one true sentence. Write the truest sentence that you know." In the language of literature, truth and pace cannot be divorced.

Sherwood Anderson

THE STRENGTH OF GOD

The Reverend Curtis Hartman was pastor of the Presbyterian Church of Winesburg, and had been in that position ten years. He was forty years old, and by his nature very silent and reticent. To preach, standing in the pulpit before the people, was always a hardship for him and from Wednesday morning until Saturday evening he thought of nothing but the two sermons that must be preached on Sunday. Early on Sunday morning he went into a little room called a study in the bell tower of the church and prayed. In his prayers there was one note that always predominated. "Give me strength and courage for Thy work, O Lord!" he pleaded, kneeling on the bare floor and bowing his head in the presence of the task that lay before him.

The Reverend Hartman was a tall man with a brown beard. His wife, a stout, nervous woman, was the daughter of a manufacturer of underwear at Cleveland, Ohio. The minister himself was rather a favorite in the town. The elders of the church liked him because he was quiet and unpretentious and Mrs. White, the banker's wife, thought him scholarly and refined.

The Presbyterian Church held itself somewhat aloof from the other churches of Winesburg. It was larger and more imposing and its minister was better paid. He even had a carriage of his own and on summer evenings sometimes drove about town with his wife. Through Main Street and up and down Buckeye Street he went, bowing gravely to the people, while his wife, afire with secret pride, looked at him out of the corners of her eyes and worried lest the horse become frightened and run away.

For a good many years after he came to Winesburg things went well with Curtis Hartman. He was not one to arouse keen enthusiasm among the worshippers in his church but on the other hand he made no enemies. In reality he was much in earnest and sometimes suffered prolonged periods of remorse because he could not go crying the word of God in the highways and byways of the town. He wondered if the flame of the spirit really burned in him and dreamed of a day when a strong sweet new current of power would come like a great wind into his voice and his soul and the people would tremble before the spirit of God made manifest in him. "I am a poor stick and that will never really happen to me," he mused dejectedly, and then a patient smile lit up his features. "Oh well, I suppose I'm doing well enough," he added philosophically.

The room in the bell tower of the church, where on Sunday mornings the minister prayed for an increase in him of the power of God, had but one window. It was long and narrow and swung outward on a hinge like a door. On the window, made of little leaded panes, was a design showing the Christ laying his hand upon the head of a child. One Sunday morning in the summer as he sat by his desk in the room with a large Bible opened before him, and the sheets of his sermon scattered about, the minister was shocked to see, in the upper room of the house next door, a woman lying in her bed and smoking a cigarette while she read a book. Curtis Hartman went on tiptoe to the window and closed it softly. He was horror stricken at the thought of a woman smoking and trembled also to think that his eyes, just raised from the pages of the book of God, had looked upon the bare shoulders and white throat of a woman. With his brain in a whirl he went down into the pulpit and preached a long sermon without once thinking of his gestures or his voice. The sermon attracted unusual attention because of its power and clearness. "I wonder if she is listening, if my voice is carrying a message into her soul," he thought and began to hope that on future Sunday mornings he might be able to say words that would touch and awaken the woman apparently far gone in secret sin.

The house next door to the Presbyterian Church, through the windows of which the minister had seen the sight that had so upset him, was occupied by two women. Aunt Elizabeth Swift, a grey competent-looking widow with money in the Winesburg National Bank, lived there with her daughter Kate Swift, a school teacher. The school teacher was thirty years old and had a neat trim-looking figure. She had few friends and bore a reputation of having a sharp tongue. When he began to think about her, Curtis Hartman remembered that she had been to Europe and had lived for two years in New York City. "Perhaps after all her smoking means nothing," he thought. He began to remember that when he was a student in college and occasionally read novels, good although somewhat worldly women, had smoked through the pages of a book that had once fallen into his hands. With a rush of new determination he worked on his sermons all through the week and forgot, in his zeal to reach the ears and the soul of this new listener, both his embarrassment in the pulpit and the necessity of prayer in the study on Sunday mornings.

Reverend Hartman's experience with women had been somewhat limited. He was the son of a wagon maker from Muncie, Indiana, and had worked his way through college. The daughter of the underwear manufacturer had boarded in a house where he lived during his school days and he had married her after a formal and prolonged courtship, carried on for the most part by the girl herself. On his marriage day the underwear manufacturer had given his daughter five thousand dollars and he promised to leave her at least twice that amount in his will. The minister had thought himself fortunate in marriage and had never permitted himself to think of other women. He did not want to think of other women. What he wanted was to do the work of God quietly and earnestly.

In the soul of the minister a struggle awoke. From wanting to reach the ears of Kate Swift, and through his sermons to delve into her soul, he began to want also to look again at the figure lying white and quiet in the bed. On a Sunday morning when he could not sleep because of his thoughts he arose and went to walk in the streets. When he had gone along Main Street almost to the old Richmond place he stopped and picking up a stone rushed off to the room in the bell tower. With the stone he broke out a corner of the window and then locked the door and sat down at the desk before the open Bible to wait. When the shade of the window to Kate Swift's room was raised he could see, through the hole, directly into her bed, but she was not there. She also had arisen and had gone for a walk and the hand that raised the shade was the hand of Aunt Elizabeth Swift.

The minister almost wept with joy at this deliverance from the carnal desire to "peep" and went back to his own house praising God. In an ill moment he forgot, however, to stop the hole in the window. The piece of glass broken out at the corner of the window just nipped off the bare heel of the boy standing motionless and looking with rapt eyes into the face of the Christ.

Curtis Hartman forgot his sermon on that Sunday morning. He talked to his congregation and in his talk said that it was a mistake for people to think of their minister as a man set aside and intended by nature to lead a blameless life. "Out of my own experience I know that we, who are the ministers of God's word, are beset by the same temptations that assail you," he declared. "I have been tempted and have surrendered to temptation. It is only the hand of God, placed beneath my head, that has raised me up. As he has raised me so also will he raise you. Do not despair. In your hour of sin raise your eyes to the skies and you will be again and again saved."

Resolutely the minister put the thoughts of the woman in the bed out of his mind and began to be something like a lover in the presence of his wife. One evening when they drove out together he turned the horse out of Buckeye Street and in the darkness on

Gospel Hill, above Waterworks Pond, put his arm about Sarah Hartman's waist. When he had eaten breakfast in the morning and was ready to retire to his study at the back of his house he went around the table and kissed his wife on the cheek. When thoughts of Kate Swift came into his head, he smiled and raised his eyes to the skies. "Intercede for me, Master," he muttered, "keep me in the narrow path intent on Thy work."

And now began the real struggle in the soul of the brown-bearded minister. By chance he discovered that Kate Swift was in the habit of lying in her bed in the evenings and reading a book. A lamp stood on a table by the side of the bed and the light streamed down upon her white shoulders and bare throat. On the evening when he made the discovery the minister sat at the desk in the study from nine until after eleven and when her light was put out stumbled out of the church to spend two more hours walking and praying in the streets. He did not want to kiss the shoulders and the throat of Kate Swift and had not allowed his mind to dwell on such thoughts. He did not know what he wanted. "I am God's child and he must save me from myself," he cried, in the darkness under the trees as he wandered in the streets. By a tree he stood and looked at the sky that was covered with hurrying clouds. He began to talk to God intimately and closely. "Please, Father, do not forget me. Give me power to go tomorrow and repair the hole in the window. Lift my eyes again to the skies. Stay with me, Thy servant, in his hour of need."

Up and down through the silent streets walked the minister and for days and weeks his soul was troubled. He could not understand the temptation that had come to him nor could he fathom the reason for its coming. In a way he began to blame God, saying to himself that he had tried to keep his feet in the true path and had not run about seeking sin. "Through my days as a young man and all through my life here I have gone quietly about my work," he declared. "Why now should I be tempted? What have I done that this burden should be laid on me?"

Three times during the early fall and winter of that year Curtis Hartman crept out of his house to the room in the bell tower to sit in the darkness looking at the figure of Kate Swift lying in her bed and later went to walk and pray in the streets. He could not understand himself. For weeks he would go along scarcely thinking of the school teacher and telling himself that he had conquered the carnal desire to look at her body. And then something would happen. As he sat in the study of his own house, hard at work on a sermon, he would become nervous and begin to walk up and down the room. "I will go out into the streets," he told himself and even as he let himself in at the church door he persistently denied to himself the cause of his being there. "I will not repair the hole in the window and I will train myself to come here at night and sit in the presence of this woman without raising my eyes. I will not be defeated in this thing. The Lord has devised this temptation as a test of my soul and I will grope my way out of darkness into the light of righteousness."

One night in January when it was bitter cold and snow lay deep on the streets of Winesburg Curtis Hartman paid his last visit to the room in the bell tower of the church. It was past nine o'clock when he left his own house and he set out so hurriedly that he forgot to put on his overshoes. In Main Street no one was abroad but Hop Higgins the night watchman and in the whole town no one was awake but the watchman and young George Willard, who sat in the office of the *Winesburg Eagle* trying to write a story. Along the street to the church went the minister, plowing through the drifts and thinking that this time he would utterly give way to sin. "I want to look at the woman and to think of kissing her shoulders and I am going to let myself think what I choose," he declared bitterly and tears came into his eyes. He began to think that he would get out of the ministry and try some other way of life. "I shall go to some city and get into business," he declared. "If my nature is such that I cannot resist sin, I shall give myself over to sin. At least I shall not be a hypocrite, preaching the word of God with my mind thinking of the shoulders and neck of a woman who does not belong to me."

It was cold in the room of the bell tower of the church on that January night and almost as soon as he came into the room Curtis Hartman knew that if he stayed he would be ill. His feet were wet from tramping in the snow and there was no fire. In the room in the house next door Kate Swift had not yet appeared. With grim determination the man sat down to wait. Sitting in the chair and gripping the edge of the desk on which lay the Bible he stared into the darkness thinking the blackest thoughts of his life. He thought of his wife and for the moment almost hated her. "She has always been ashamed of passion and has cheated me," he thought. "Man has a right to expect living passion and beauty in a woman. He has no right to forget that he is an animal and in me there is something that is Greek. I will throw off the woman of my bosom and seek other women. I will besiege this school teacher. I will fly in the face of all men and if I am a creature of carnal lusts I will live then for my lusts."

The distracted man trembled from head to foot, partly from cold, partly from the struggle in which he was engaged. Hours passed and a fever assailed his body. His throat began to hurt and his teeth chattered. His feet on the study floor felt like two cakes of ice. Still he would not give up. "I will see this woman and will think the thoughts I have never dared to think," he told himself, gripping the edge of the desk and waiting.

Curtis Hartman came near dying from the effects of that night of waiting in the church, and also he found in the thing that happened what he took to be the way of life for him. On other evenings when he had waited he had not been able to see, through the little hole in the glass, any part of the school teacher's room except that occupied by her bed. In the darkness he had waited until the woman suddenly appeared sitting in the bed in her white night-robe. When the light was turned up she propped herself up among the pillows and read a book. Sometimes she smoked one of the cigarettes. Only her bare shoulders and throat were visible.

On the January night, after he had come near dying with cold and after his mind had two or three times actually slipped away into an odd land of fantasy so that he had by an exercise of will power to force himself back into consciousness, Kate Swift appeared. In the room next door a lamp was lighted and the waiting man stared into an empty bed. Then upon the bed before his eyes a naked woman threw herself. Lying face downward she wept and beat with her fists upon the pillow. With a final outburst of weeping she half arose, and in the presence of the man who had waited to look and to think thoughts the woman of sin began to pray. In the lamplight her figure, slim and strong, looked like the figure of the boy in the presence of the Christ on the leaded window.

Curtis Hartman never remembered how he got out of the church. With a cry he arose, dragging the heavy desk along the floor. The Bible fell, making a great clatter in the silence. When the light in the house next door went out he stumbled down the stairway and into the street. Along the street he went and ran in at the door of the *Winesburg Eagle.* To George Willard, who was tramping up and down in the office undergoing a struggle of his own, he began to talk half incoherently. "The ways of God are beyond human understanding," he cried, running in quickly and closing the door. He began to advance upon the young man, his eyes glowing and his voice ringing with fervor. "I have found the light," he cried. "After ten years in this town, God has manifested himself to me in the body of a woman." His voice dropped and he began to whisper. "I did not understand," he said. "What I took to be a trial of my soul was only a preparation for a new and more beautiful fervor of the spirit. God has appeared to me in the person of Kate Swift, the school teacher, kneeling naked on a bed. Do you know Kate Swift? Although she may not be aware of it, she is an instrument of God, bearing the message of truth."

Reverend Curtis Hartman turned and ran out of the office. At the door he stopped, and after looking up and down the deserted street, turned again to George Willard. "I am delivered. Have no fear." He held up a bleeding fist for the young man to see. "I smashed the glass of the window," he cried. "Now it will have to be wholly replaced. The strength of God was in me and I broke it with my fist."

QUESTIONS

1 What elements of time are specified in the first paragraph? Can you tell precisely when the story begins?

2 The paragraph that begins, "Reverend Hartman's experience with women had been somewhat limited," is a summary paragraph. Roughly, how much time is spanned in this paragraph?

3 How much time is spanned in the ensuing *three* paragraphs? Are these essentially summary or scenic in method?

4 Divide the story into those parts that are essentially summary in method and those essentially scenic. Remember that the presence of dialogue and specific imagery usually indicates the scenic method. What percentage of the story is devoted to summary method? to scenic method? How much elapsed time is spanned in the summary sections? how much in the scenic sections?

5 Typically, the most crucial events in a story are presented scenically. Is "The Strength of God" typical in this regard? Point out what you believe to be the moment of revelation. Is this presented in summary or in scenic method?

6 Write a brief chronological biography of Reverend Hartman from birth to his present age. Comment on the amount of space the story gives to his early years, months, days, and hours compared with his later ones.

James Baldwin

EXODUS

I

She had always seemed to Florence the oldest woman in the world —for she often spoke of Florence and Gabriel as the children of her old age; and she had been born, innumerable years ago, during slavery, on a plantation in another state. On this plantation she had grown up, one of the field workers, for she was very tall and strong; and by-and-by she had married, and raised children, all of whom had been taken from her, one by sickness, and two by auction, and one whom she had not been allowed to call her own, who had been raised in the master's house. When she was a woman grown, well past thirty as she reckoned it, with one husband buried —but the master had given her another—armies, plundering and burning, had come from the North to set them free. This was in answer to the prayers of the faithful, who had never ceased, both day and night, to cry out for deliverance.

For it had been the will of God that they should hear, and pass it, thereafter, one to another, the story of the Hebrew children, who had been held in bondage in the land of Egypt; and how the Lord had heard their groaning, and how His heart was moved; and how He bid them wait but a little season till He should send deliverance. She had known this story, so it seemed, from the day that she was born. And while life ran, rising in the morning before the sun came up, standing and bending in the fields when the sun was high, crossing the fields homeward while the sun went down at the gates of heaven far away—hearing the whistle of the foreman, and his eerie cry across the fields; in the whiteness of winter when hogs and turkeys and geese were slaughtered, and lights burned bright in the big house, and Bathsheba, the cook, sent over in a napkin bits of ham and chicken and cakes left over by the white folks; in all that befell, in her joys—her pipe in the evening, her man at night, the children she suckled, and guided on their first short steps—and in her tribulations, death, and parting, and the lash; she did not forget that deliverance was promised, and would surely come. She had only to endure and trust in God. She knew that the big house, the house of pride where the white folks lived, would come down: it was written in the Word of God. And they, who walked so proudly now, yet had not fashioned, for themselves, or their children, so sure a foundation as was hers. They walked on the edge of a steep place and their eyes were sightless—God would cause them to rush down, as the herd of swine had once rushed down, into the sea. For all that they were so beautiful, and took their ease, she knew them, and she pitied them, who would have no covering in the great day of His wrath.

Yet, she told her children, God was just, and He struck no people without first giving many warnings. God gave men time, but all the times were in His hand, and, one day, the time to forsake evil and do good would all be finished: then only the whirlwind, death riding on the whirlwind, awaited those people who had forgotten God. In all the days that she was growing up, signs failed not, but none heeded. *Slaves done riz,* was whispered in the cabin, and at the master's gate: slaves in another county had fired the master's house and fields, and dashed their children to death against the stones. *Another slave in hell,* Bathsheba might say one morning, shooing the pickaninnies away from the great porch: a slave had killed his master, or his overseer, and had gone down to hell to pay for it. *I ain't got long to stay here,* someone crooned beside her in the fields: who would be gone by morning on his journey North. All these signs, like the plagues with which the Lord had afflicted Egypt, only hardened the hearts of these people against the Lord. They thought the lash would save them, and they used the lash; or the knife, or the gallows, or the auction block; they thought that kindness would save them, and the master and mistress came down, smiling, to the cabins, making much of the pickaninnies, and bearing gifts. These were great days, and they all, black and white, seemed happy together. But when the Word has gone forth from the mouth of God nothing can turn it back.

The word was fulfilled one morning before she was awake. Many of the stories her mother told meant nothing to Florence, she knew them for what they were, tales by an old black woman in a cabin in the evening to distract her children from their cold and hunger. But the story of this day she was never to forget, it was a day like the day for which she lived. There was a great running and shouting, said her mother, everywhere outside, and, as she opened her eyes to the light of that day, so bright, she said, and cold, she was certain that the judgment trump had sounded. While she still sat, amazed, and wondering what, on the judgment day, would be the best behavior, in rushed Bathsheba, and behind her many tumbling children, and field hands, and house niggers, all together, and Bathsheba shouted, "Rise up, rise up, Sister Rachel, and see the Lord's deliverance! He done brought us out of Egypt, just like He promised, and we's free at last!"

Bathsheba grabbed her, tears running down her face; she, dressed in the clothes in which she had slept, walked to the door to look out on the new day God had given them.

On that day she saw the proud house humbled, green silk and velvet blowing out of windows, and the garden trampled by many horsemen, and the big gates open. The master and mistress, and their kin, and one child she had borne were in that house—which she did not enter. Soon it occurred to her that there was no reason any more to tarry here. She tied her things in a cloth, which she put on her head, and walked out through the big gate, never to see that country any more.

And this, as Florence grew, became her deep ambition: to walk out one morning through the cabin door, never to return. . . .

II

In 1900, when she was twenty-six, Florence walked out through the cabin door. She had thought to wait until her mother, who was so ill now that she no longer stirred out of bed, should be buried—but suddenly she knew that she would wait no longer, the time had come. She had been working as cook and serving girl for a large white family in town, and it was on the day that her master proposed that she become his concubine that she knew that her life among these wretched had come to its destined end. She left her employment that same day (leaving behind her a most vehement conjugal bitterness) and with part of the money which, with cunning, cruelty, and sacrifice, she had saved over a period of years, bought a railroad ticket to New York. When she bought it, in a kind of scarlet rage, she held, like a talisman at the back of her mind, the thought: "I can give it back, I can sell it. This don't mean I got to go." But she knew that nothing could stop her.

And it was this leave-taking which came to stand, in Florence's latter days, and with many another witness, at her bedside. Gray clouds obscured the sun that day, and outside the cabin window she saw that mist still covered the ground. Her mother lay in bed, awake; she was pleading with Gabriel, who had been out drinking the night before, and who was not really sober now, to mend his ways and come to the Lord. And Gabriel, full of the confusion, and pain, and guilt which were his whenever he thought of how he made his mother suffer, but which became nearly insupportable when she taxed him with it, stood before the mirror, head bowed, buttoning his shirt. Florence knew that he could not unlock his lips to speak; he could not say Yes to his mother, and to the Lord; and he could not say No.

"Honey," their mother was saying, "don't you *let* your old mother die without you look her in the eye and tell her she going to see you in glory. You hear me, boy?"

In a moment, Florence thought with scorn, tears would fill his eyes, and he would promise to "do better." He had been promising to "do better" since the day he had been baptized.

She put down her bag in the center of the hateful room.

"Ma," she said, "I'm going. I'm a-going this morning."

Now that she had said it, she was angry with herself for not having said it the night before, so that they would have had time to be finished with their weeping and their arguments. She had not trusted herself to withstand, the night before; but now there was almost no time left. The center of her mind was filled with the image of the great, white clock at the railway station, on which the hands did not cease to move.

"You going where?" her mother asked, sharply. But she knew that her mother had understood, had, indeed, long before this moment, known that this moment would come. The astonishment with which she stared at Florence's bag was not altogether astonishment, but a startled, wary attention. A danger imagined had become present and real, and her mother was already searching for a way to break Florence's will. All this Florence, in a moment, knew, and it made her stronger. She watched her mother, waiting.

But at the tone of his mother's voice, Gabriel, who had scarcely heard Florence's announcement, so grateful had he been that something had occurred to distract from him his mother's attention, dropped his eyes, and saw Florence's traveling bag. And he repeated his mother's question in a stunned, angry voice, understanding it only as the words hit the air:

"Yes, girl. Where you think you going?"

"I'm going," she said, "to New York. I got my ticket."

And her mother watched her. For a moment no one said a word. Then, Gabriel, in a changed and frightened voice, asked:

"And when you done decide that?"

She did not look at him, nor answer his question. She continued to watch her mother. "I got my ticket," she repeated. "I'm going on the morning train."

"Girl," asked her mother, quietly, "is you sure you know what you's doing?"

She stiffened, seeing in her mother's eyes a mocking pity. "I'm a woman grown," she said. "I know what I'm doing."

"And you going," cried Gabriel, "this morning—just like that? And you going to walk off and leave your mother—just like that?"

"You hush," she said, turning to him for the first time; "she got you, ain't she?"

This was indeed, she realized, as he dropped his eyes, the bitter, troubling point. He could not endure the thought of being left alone with his mother, with nothing whatever to put between himself and his guilty love. With Florence gone, time would have swallowed up all his mother's children, except himself; and *he,* then, must make amends for all the pain that she had borne, and sweeten her last moments with all his proofs of love. And his mother required of him one proof only, that he tarry no longer in sin. With Florence gone, his stammering time, his playing time, contracted with a bound to the sparest interrogative second; when he must stiffen himself, and answer to his mother, and all the host of heaven, Yes, or No.

Florence smiled inwardly a small, malicious smile, watching his slow bafflement, and panic, and rage; and she looked at her mother again. "She got you," she repeated. "She don't need me."

"You going North," her mother said, then. "And when you reckon on coming back?"

"I don't reckon on coming back," she said.

"You come crying back soon enough," said Gabriel, with malevolence, "soon as they whip your butt up there four or five times."

She looked at him again. "Just don't you try to hold your breath till then, you hear?"

"Girl," said her mother, "you mean to tell me the devil's done made your heart so hard you can just leave your mother on her dying bed, and you don't care if you don't never see her in this world no more? Honey, you can't tell me you done got so evil as all that?"

She felt Gabriel watching her to see how she would take this question—the question, which, for all her determination, she had dreaded most to hear. She looked away from her mother, and straightened, catching her breath, looking outward through the small, cracked window. There, outside, beyond the slowly rising mist, and farther off than her eyes could see, her life awaited her. The woman on the bed was old, her life was fading as the mist rose. She thought of her mother as already in the grave; and she would not let herself be strangled by the hands of the dead.

"I'm going, Ma," she said. "I got to go."

Her mother leaned back, face upward to the light, and began to cry. Gabriel moved to Florence's side and grabbed her arm. She looked up into his face and saw that his eyes were full of tears.

"You can't go," he said. "You can't go. You can't go and leave your mother thisaway. She need a woman, Florence, to help look after her. What she going to do here, all alone with me?"

She pushed him from her and moved to stand over her mother's bed.

"Ma," she said, "don't be like that. Ain't a blessed thing for you to cry about so. Ain't a thing can happen to me up North can't happen to me here. God's everywhere, Ma. Ain't no need to worry."

She knew that she was mouthing words; and she realized suddenly that her mother scorned to dignify these words with her attention. She had granted Florence the victory—with a promptness which had the effect of making Florence, however dimly and unwillingly, wonder if her victory was real; and she was not weeping for her daughter's future; she was weeping for the past, and weeping in an anguish in which Florence had no part. And all of this filled Florence with a terrible fear, which was immediately transformed into anger.

"Gabriel can take care of you," she said, her voice shaking with malice; "Gabriel ain't never going to leave you. Is you, boy?" and she looked at him. He stood, stupid with bewilderment and grief, a few inches from the bed. "But me," she said, "I got to go." She walked to the center of the room again, and picked up her bag.

"Girl," Gabriel whispered, "ain't you got no feelings at *all?*"

"Lord!" her mother cried; and at the sound her heart turned over; she and Gabriel, arrested, stared at the bed. "Lord, Lord, Lord! Lord, have mercy on my sinful daughter! Stretch out your hand and hold her back from the lake that burns forever! Oh, my Lord, my Lord!" and her voice dropped, and broke, and tears ran down her face. "Lord, I done my best with all the children what you give me. Lord, have mercy on my children, and my children's children."

"Florence," said Gabriel, "please don't go. Please don't go. You ain't really fixing to go and leave her like this?"

Tears stood suddenly in her own eyes, though she could not have said what she was crying for. "Leave me be," she said to Gabriel, and picked up her bag again. She opened the door; the cold morning air came in. "Good-by," she said. And then to Gabriel: "Tell her I said good-by." She walked through the cabin door and down the short steps into the frosty yard. Gabriel watched her, standing magnetized between the door and the weeping bed. Then, as her hand was on the gate, he ran before her, and slammed the gate shut.

"Girl, where you going? What you doing? You reckon on finding some men up North to dress you in pearls and diamonds?"

Violently, she opened the gate and moved out into the road. He watched her with his jaw hanging, until the dust and the distance swallowed her up.

QUESTIONS

1 When did Florence's exodus occur, and how old was she?

2 Another exodus occurred before Florence's. About when did it happen, and to whom?

3 How many years, approximately, are spanned in the opening three paragraphs of part I?

4 How much time is spanned in the three paragraphs immediately following these first three?

5 How much time is spanned during the entire part II?

6 Do you find any use of scenic method in part I? any use of summary method in part II?

7 The above answers show a wide variation in the author's handling of time. Mark the portions of the story told primarily in summary method. Mark the portions told primarily in scenic method. What percentage of the story is devoted to each? How much time is spanned in each?

8 In "Exodus" does Baldwin follow the usual pattern of presenting the most crucial events scenically? Point out what you think is the moment of revelation. Is this presented in summary or in scenic method?

9 Count the number of words and the number of sentences, and determine the average sentence length for the first two paragraphs in this story. Do the same for the final two paragraphs. State for each whether its effect is one of immediate action or primarily one of reflection. Explain the contribution the syntax makes to the effect of each paragraph.

10 Analyze the syntax of several passages from both "Exodus" and "A Clean, Well-Lighted Place" (Chapter 2). Do this by calculating the average sentence length, the average length of words, the amount of internal punctuation, and the percentage of complex sentences with dependent clauses, as compared with the number of simple sentences. (Treat compound sentences as two simple sentences.) Comment on the syntax of each story as appropriate, or inappropriate, to the subject. Is any irony of style at work?

11 In our discussion of the literal-minded reader in Chapter 6, we warned against the indiscriminate pursuit of symbols and supplied a series of four tests to which you should submit any image that you think is symbolic. Consider the image of "the great, white clock at the railway station" (p. 137), and apply the tests outlined in Chapter 6 to this image. Does the image meet the tests—is it a symbol?

12 The title of this story contains an allusion. What is it?

9
IMPRESSION

narrator's mind | private world | public world

We come now to an aspect of fiction that is its greatest strength: fiction not only dramatizes particular events but also presents these events to us through the eyes and the mind of a narrator. This narrator can provide us with a view of the story's events directly and dramatically, when he chooses, or he can filter them to us through his own *mind,* with all sorts of personal comments about them as they unfold. What is more, the author can enter the *private world* of any character he chooses, and show us that character's whole personality. He can make us receive one strong impression, many different impressions, or purposely ambiguous impressions as the story unfolds. Thus the reader's *impression* of the characters, the events, and the narrator can be deliberately formed by the author's method of presentation.

Some stories, like "A Clean, Well-Lighted Place," are told almost as pure drama, with access to the characters' private worlds kept to a minimum. But few authors choose to create fiction composed exclusively of this *public world,* because to become purely dramatic is to lose the private quality of fiction. More typically, fiction is a mixture of public and private experience. For example, in "Exodus," most of the first part is told through Florence's memory, and most of the second part is told in dramatic dialogue.

In part II we see Florence in the public world, after we have been admitted to her private world and to that of her mother in part I.

When the author of a story not only describes and dramatizes events but also comments on them by entering the private world of a character like Florence in "Exodus" or the private world of a narrator like the boy in "Araby," fiction comes closest to simulating the way life really is. In real life, we not only experience events with others just as fictional characters do but, like characters in fiction, we also have a private world and private thoughts of our own that others never know. This unique ability of fiction to simulate the experiences of real life probably explains why readers frequently identify with characters in fiction.

Fiction can create an impression more vivid than life itself. When an author decides to reveal the private worlds of his characters, he goes beyond what we can experience with others in real life. For, as E. M. Forster pointed out in *Aspects of the Novel,* there is a "fundamental difference between people in daily life and people in books." Forster noted that in daily life we never fully understand each other—we only know each other approximately, by external signs, and this knowledge serves well enough as the basis for society. But characters in fiction can be understood completely by the reader. This, Forster observed, is why fictional characters often seem more real than historical characters or may seem more familiar than some of our own friends: we have been told everything about these characters that can be told.

The writer of fiction may select any of these strategies to create the impression he wishes to leave with his reader, or he may use them all, as we are about to see in the story by Washington Irving. Here we are given three sources of information from which we form our impression—the public world of a character (as in drama), the private world of this character, and, finally, the mind of the narrator.

The more the narrator controls the story with his private comments, instead of letting the events enact themselves dramatically, the more he exposes himself as a personality distinct and separate from his story. If this narrator's presence becomes obvious, he must impress his audience with a dazzling picture, a very sharp wit, or a highly refined philosophy to convince the reader that his version of the drama is more lively and attractive than the drama itself. Or the author must give his narrator sentiments to express that he has reason to believe his readers already hold. Authors traditionally are good at creating persuasive narrators; readers, more often than not, are attracted as much to the mind of the narrator * as they are to the drama he tells about.

In this chapter, Washington Irving's "Adventure of the German Student" displays a mixture of the private and the public worlds of its characters, plus the intervention of the narrator's mind. As you read, notice which parts of the story are public property—that is, accessible to all characters. Notice, also, which parts are the private property of the individual characters, and, just as importantly, which parts the narrator's controlling mind gives to us directly.

The second story in this chapter, "The Valiant Woman," illustrates how rich and varied the "gluing together" by a skillful writer can be. Here we enter the private world of one of the characters by a less obvious means than Irving's—a means that does not call attention to itself. After you read J. F. Powers' story, compare it with "Adventure of the German Student," which is relatively simple in structure. By contrasting the two stories' techniques of pace and impression (especially the role played by the narrators), you may draw some important conclusions about the relationship between a story's structure and its effect.

Washington Irving

ADVENTURE OF THE GERMAN STUDENT

On a stormy night, in the tempestuous times of the French revolution, a young German was returning to his lodgings, at a late hour, across the old part of Paris. The lightning gleamed, and the loud claps of thunder rattled through the lofty narrow streets—but I should first tell you something about this young German.

Gottfried Wolfgang was a young man of good family. He had studied for some time at Göttingen, but being of a visionary and enthusiastic character, he had wandered into those wild and speculative doctrines which have so often bewildered German students. His secluded life, his intense application, and the singular nature

* For a discussion of the deliberately "unreliable narrator" that authors sometimes employ, see Chapter 10.

of his studies, had an effect on both mind and body. His health was impaired; his imagination diseased. He had been indulging in fanciful speculations on spiritual essences, until, like Swedenborg, he had an ideal world of his own around him. He took up a notion, I do not know from what cause, that there was an evil influence hanging over him; an evil genius or spirit seeking to ensnare him and ensure his perdition. Such an idea working on his melancholy temperament, produced the most gloomy effects. He became haggard and desponding. His friends discovered the mental malady preying upon him, and determined that the best cure was a change of scene; he was sent, therefore, to finish his studies amidst the splendors and gayeties of Paris.

Wolfgang arrived at Paris at the breaking out of the revolution. The popular delirium at first caught his enthusiastic mind, and he was captivated by the political and philosophical theories of the day: but the scenes of blood which followed shocked his sensitive nature, disgusted him with society and the world, and made him more than ever a recluse. He shut himself up in a solitary apartment in the *Pays Latin,* the quarter of students. There, in a gloomy street not far from the monastic walls of the Sorbonne, he pursued his favorite speculations. Sometimes he spent hours together in the great libraries of Paris, those catacombs of departed authors, rummaging among their hoards of dusty and obsolete works in quest of food for his unhealthy appetite. He was, in a manner, a literary ghoul, feeding in the charnel-house of decayed literature.

Wolfgang, though solitary and recluse, was of an ardent temperament, but for a time it operated merely upon his imagination. He was too shy and ignorant of the world to make any advances to the fair, but he was a passionate admirer of female beauty, and in his lonely chamber would often lose himself in reveries on forms and faces which he had seen, and his fancy would deck out images of loveliness far surpassing the reality.

While his mind was in this excited and sublimated state, a dream produced an extraordinary effect upon him. It was of a female face of transcendent beauty. So strong was the impression made, that he dreamt of it again and again. It haunted his thoughts by day, his slumbers by night; in fine, he became passionately enamoured of this shadow of a dream. This lasted so long that it became one of those fixed ideas which haunt the minds of melancholy men, and are at times mistaken for madness.

Such was Gottfried Wolfgang, and such his situation at the

time I mentioned. He was returning home late one stormy night, through some of the old and gloomy streets of the *Marais,* the ancient part of Paris. The loud claps of thunder rattled among the high houses of the narrow streets. He came to the Place de Grève, the square where public executions are performed. The lightning quivered about the pinnacles of the ancient Hôtel de Ville, and shed flickering gleams over the open space in front. As Wolfgang was crossing the square, he shrank back with horror at finding himself close by the guillotine. It was the height of the reign of terror, when this dreadful instrument of death stood ever ready, and its scaffold was continually running with the blood of the virtuous and the brave. It had that very day been actively employed in the work of carnage, and there it stood in grim array, amidst a silent and sleeping city, waiting for fresh victims.

Wolfgang's heart sickened within him, and he was turning shuddering from the horrible engine, when he beheld a shadowy form, cowering as it were at the foot of the steps which led up to the scaffold. A succession of vivid flashes of lightning revealed it more distinctly. It was a female figure, dressed in black. She was seated on one of the lower steps of the scaffold, leaning forward, her face hid in her lap; and her long dishevelled tresses hanging to the ground, streaming with the rain which fell in torrents. Wolfgang paused. There was something awful in this solitary monument of woe. The female had the appearance of being above the common order. He knew the times to be full of vicissitude, and that many a fair head, which had once been pillowed on down, now wandered houseless. Perhaps this was some poor mourner whom the dreadful axe had rendered desolate, and who sat here heart-broken on the strand of existence, from which all that was dear to her had been launched into eternity.

He approached, and addressed her in the accents of sympathy. She raised her head and gazed wildly at him. What was his astonishment at beholding, by the bright glare of the lightning, the very face which had haunted him in his dreams. It was pale and disconsolate, but ravishingly beautiful.

Trembling with violent and conflicting emotions, Wolfgang again accosted her. He spoke something of her being exposed at such an hour of the night, and to the fury of such a storm, and offered to conduct her to her friends. She pointed to the guillotine with a gesture of dreadful signification.

"I have no friend on earth!" said she.

"But you have a home," said Wolfgang.

"Yes—in the grave!"

The heart of the student melted at the words.

"If a stranger dare make an offer," said he, "without danger of being misunderstood, I would offer my humble dwelling as a shelter; myself as a devoted friend. I am friendless myself in Paris, and a stranger in the land; but if my life could be of service, it is at your disposal, and should be sacrificed before harm or indignity should come to you."

There was an honest earnestness in the young man's manner that had its effect. His foreign accent, too, was in his favor; it showed him not to be a hackneyed inhabitant of Paris. Indeed, there is an eloquence in true enthusiasm that is not to be doubted. The homeless stranger confided herself implicitly to the protection of the student.

He supported her faltering steps across the Pont Neuf, and by the place where the statue of Henry the Fourth had been overthrown by the populace. The storm had abated, and the thunder rumbled at a distance. All Paris was quiet; that great volcano of human passion slumbered for a while, to gather fresh strength for the next day's eruption. The student conducted his charge through the ancient streets of the *Pays Latin,* and by the dusky walls of the Sorbonne, to the great dingy hotel which he inhabited. The old portress who admitted them stared with surprise at the unusual sight of the melancholy Wolfgang with a female companion.

On entering his apartment, the student, for the first time, blushed at the scantiness and indifference of his dwelling. He had but one chamber, an old fashioned saloon heavily carved, and fantastically furnished with the remains of former magnificence, for it was one of those hotels in the quarter of the Luxembourg palace, which had once belonged to nobility. It was lumbered with books and papers, and all the usual apparatus of a student, and his bed stood in a recess at one end.

When lights were brought, and Wolfgang had a better opportunity of contemplating the stranger, he was more than ever intoxicated by her beauty. Her face was pale, but of a dazzling fairness, set off by a profusion of raven hair that hung clustering about it. Her eyes were large and brilliant, with a singular expression approaching almost to wildness. As far as her black dress permitted her shape to be seen, it was of perfect symmetry. Her whole appearance was highly striking, though she was dressed in the simplest style. The only thing approaching to an ornament which she wore, was a broad black band round her neck, clasped by diamonds.

The perplexity now commenced with the student how to dispose of the helpless being thus thrown upon his protection. He thought of abandoning his chamber to her, and seeking shelter for himself elsewhere. Still he was so fascinated by her charms, there seemed to be such a spell upon his thoughts and senses, that he could not tear himself from her presence. Her manner, too, was singular and unaccountable. She spoke no more of the guillotine. Her grief had abated. The attentions of the student had first won her confidence, and then, apparently, her heart. She was evidently an enthusiast like himself, and enthusiasts soon understand each other.

In the infatuation of the moment, Wolfgang avowed his passion for her. He told her the story of his mysterious dream, and how she had possessed his heart before he had even seen her. She was strangely affected by his recital, and acknowledged to have felt an impulse towards him equally unaccountable. It was the time for wild theory and wild actions. Old prejudices and superstitions were done away; everything was under the sway of the "Goddess of Reason." Among other rubbish of the old times, the forms and ceremonies of marriage began to be considered superfluous bonds for honorable minds. Social compacts were the vogue. Wolfgang was too much of a theorist not to be tainted by the liberal doctrines of the day.

"Why should we separate?" said he: "our hearts are united; in the eye of reason and honor we are as one. What need is there of sordid forms to bind high souls together?"

The stranger listened with emotion: she had evidently received illumination at the same school.

"You have no home nor family," continued he; "let me be everything to you, or rather let us be everything to one another. If form is necessary, form shall be observed—there is my hand. I pledge myself to you forever."

"Forever?" said the stranger, solemnly.

"Forever!" repeated Wolfgang.

The stranger clasped the hand extended to her: "Then I am yours," murmured she, and sank upon his bosom.

The next morning the student left his bride sleeping, and sallied forth at an early hour to seek more spacious apartments suitable to the change in his situation. When he returned, he found the stranger lying with her head hanging over the bed, and one arm thrown over it. He spoke to her, but received no reply. He advanced to awaken her from her uneasy posture. On taking her hand, it was cold—there was no pulsation—her face was pallid and ghastly. In a word, she was a corpse.

Horrified and frantic, he alarmed the house. A scene of confusion ensued. The police was summoned. As the officer of police entered the room, he started back on beholding the corpse.

"Great heaven!" cried he, "how did this woman come here?"

"Do you know anything about her?" said Wolfgang eagerly.

"Do I?" exclaimed the officer: "she was guillotined yesterday."

He stepped forward; undid the black collar round the neck of the corpse, and the head rolled on the floor!

The student burst into a frenzy. "The fiend! the fiend has gained possession of me!" shrieked he: "I am lost forever."

They tried to soothe him, but in vain. He was possessed with the frightful belief that an evil spirit had reanimated the dead body to ensnare him. He went distracted, and died in a madhouse.

QUESTIONS

1 Could the first paragraph of this story be filmed successfully? Could the second paragraph be filmed as easily? Which paragraph is rendered (1) in the public world, (2) in the private world? Is this private world colored by the mind of the narrator? If so, cite examples.

2 In his book *Tales of a Traveller,* in which this story first appeared, Irving created a narrator who told these stories with a little preface and conclusion to each. Sometimes this narrator clearly intrudes himself into the stories. With what phrase does he do this in "Adventure of the German Student"?

3 Upon the withdrawal of the narrator's controlling mind, several paragraphs show the public world mixed with Wolfgang's private world. Identify these paragraphs.

4 Suppose you were a film producer. Discuss the ease or difficulty with which you could film the first half of this story, ending with "from which all that was dear to her had been launched into eternity." Comment on whether this part of the story comes primarily from the public world, the private world, or the narrator's mind.

5 Answer question 4 using the second half of the story, beginning with "He approached, and addressed her in the accents of sympathy."

6 We noted that to be persuasive and effective, the intrusive narrator's mind must impress you with a dazzling picture, with a sharp wit, or with a sage philosophy. Comment on Irving's success at this.

7 It has often been said that syntax has become somewhat less complicated in modern stories. This story was first published in 1824. Analyze the sentence length and the number of dependent clauses in the first two paragraphs. Compare these with the first two paragraphs of Baldwin's "Exodus" (Chapter 8), written in 1952. What are the principal differences?

J. F. Powers

THE VALIANT WOMAN

They had come to the dessert in a dinner that was a shambles. "Well, John," Father Nulty said, turning away from Mrs. Stoner and to Father Firman, long gone silent at his own table. "You've got the bishop coming for confirmations next week."

"Yes," Mrs. Stoner cut in, "and for dinner. And if he don't eat any more than he did last year—"

Father Firman, in a rare moment, faced it. "Mrs. Stoner, the bishop is not well. You know that."

"And after I fixed that fine dinner and all." Mrs. Stoner pouted in Father Nulty's direction.

"I wouldn't feel bad about it, Mrs. Stoner," Father Nulty said. "He never eats much anywhere."

"It's funny. And that new Mrs. Allers said he ate just fine when he was there," Mrs. Stoner argued, and then spit out, "but she's a damned liar!"

Father Nulty, unsettled but trying not to show it, said, "Who's Mrs. Allers?"

"She's at Holy Cross," Mrs. Stoner said.

"She's the housekeeper," Father Firman added, thinking Mrs. Stoner made it sound as though Mrs. Allers were the pastor there.

"I swear I don't know what to do about the dinner this year," Mrs. Stoner said.

Father Firman moaned. "Just do as you've always done, Mrs. Stoner."

"Huh! And have it all to throw out! Is that any way to do?"

"Is there any dessert?" Father Firman asked coldly.

Mrs. Stoner leaped up from the table and bolted into the kitchen, mumbling. She came back with a birthday cake. She plunged it in the center of the table. She found a big wooden match in her apron pocket and thrust it at Father Firman.

"I don't like this bishop," she said. "I never did. And the way he went and cut poor Ellen Kennedy out of Father Doolin's will!"

She went back into the kitchen.

"Didn't they talk a lot of filth about Doolin and the housekeeper?" Father Nulty asked.

"I should think they did," Father Firman said. "All because he took her to the movies on Sunday night. After he died and the bishop cut her out of the will, though I hear he gives her a pension privately, they talked about the bishop."

"I don't like this bishop at all," Mrs. Stoner said, appearing with a cake knife. "Bishop Doran—there was the man!"

"We know," Father Firman said. "All man and all priest."

"He did know real estate," Father Nulty said.

Father Firman struck the match.

"Not on the chair!" Mrs. Stoner cried, too late.

Father Firman set the candle burning—it was suspiciously large and yellow, like a blessed one, but he could not be sure. They watched the fluttering flame.

"I'm forgetting the lights!" Mrs. Stoner said, and got up to turn them off. She went into the kitchen again.

The priests had a moment of silence in the candle-light.

"Happy birthday, John," Father Nulty said softly. "Is it fifty-nine you are?"

"As if you didn't know, Frank," Father Firman said, "and you the same but one."

Father Nulty smiled, the old gold of his incisors shining in the flickering light, his collar whiter in the dark, and raised his glass of water, which would have been wine or better in the bygone days, and toasted Father Firman.

"Many of 'em, John."

"Blow it out," Mrs. Stoner said, returning to the room. She waited by the light switch for Father Firman to blow out the candle.

Mrs. Stoner, who ate no desserts, began to clear the dishes into the kitchen, and the priests, finishing their cake and coffee in a hurry, went to sit in the study.

Father Nulty offered a cigar.

"John?"

"My ulcers, Frank."

"Ah, well, you're better off." Father Nulty lit the cigar and crossed his long black legs. "Fish Frawley has got him a Filipino, John. Did you hear?"

Father Firman leaned forward, interested. "He got rid of the woman he had?"

"He did. It seems she snooped."

"Snooped, eh?"

"She did. And gossiped. Fish introduced two town boys to her, said, 'Would you think these boys were my nephews?' That's all, and the next week the paper had it that his two nephews were visiting him from Erie. After that, he let her believe he was going East to see his parents, though both are dead. The paper carried the story. Fish returned and made a sermon out of it. Then he got the Filipino."

Father Firman squirmed with pleasure in his chair. "That's like Fish, Frank. He can do that." He stared at the tips of his fingers bleakly. "You could never get a Filipino to come to a place like this."

"Probably not," Father Nulty said. "Fish is pretty close to Minneapolis. Ah, say, do you remember the trick he played on us all in Marmion Hall!"

"That I'll not forget!" Father Firman's eyes remembered. "Getting up New Year's morning and finding the toilet seats all painted!"

"*Happy Circumcision!* Hah!" Father Nulty had a coughing fit.

When he had got himself together again, a mosquito came and sat on his wrist. He watched it a moment before bringing his heavy hand down. He raised his hand slowly, viewed the dead mosquito, and sent it spinning with a plunk of his middle finger.

"Only the female bites," he said.

"I didn't know that," Father Firman said.

"Ah, yes . . ."

Mrs. Stoner entered the study and sat down with some sewing—Father Firman's black socks.

She smiled pleasantly at Father Nulty. "And what do you think of the atom bomb, Father?"

"Not much," Father Nulty said.

Mrs. Stoner had stopped smiling. Father Firman yawned.

Mrs. Stoner served up another: "Did you read about this communist convert, Father?"

"He's been in the Church before," Father Nulty said, "and so it's not a conversion, Mrs. Stoner."

"No? Well, I already got him down on my list of Monsignor's converts."

"It's better than a conversion, Mrs. Stoner, for there is more rejoicing in heaven over the return of . . . uh, he that was lost, Mrs. Stoner, is found."

"And that congresswoman, Father?"

"Yes. A convert—she."

"And Henry Ford's grandson, Father. I got him down."

"Yes, to be sure."

Father Firman yawned, this time audibly, and held his jaw.

"But he's one only by marriage, Father," Mrs. Stoner said. "I always say you got to watch those kind."

"Indeed you do, but a convert nonetheless, Mrs. Stoner. Remember, Cardinal Newman himself was one."

Mrs. Stoner was unimpressed. "I see where Henry Ford's making steering wheels out of soybeans, Father."

"I didn't see that."

"I read it in the *Reader's Digest* or some place."

"Yes, well . . ." Father Nulty rose and held his hand out to Father Firman. "John," he said. "It's been good."

"I heard Hirohito's next," Mrs. Stoner said, returning to converts.

"Let's wait and see, Mrs. Stoner," Father Nulty said.

The priests walked to the door.

"You know where I live, John."

"Yes. Come again, Frank. Good night."

Father Firman watched Father Nulty go down the walk to his car at the curb. He hooked the screen door and turned off the porch light. He hesitated at the foot of the stairs, suddenly moved to go to bed. But he went back into the study.

"Phew!" Mrs. Stoner said. "I thought he'd never go. Here it is after eight o'clock."

Father Firman sat down in his rocking chair. "I don't see him often," he said.

"I give up!" Mrs. Stoner exclaimed, flinging the holey socks upon the horsehair sofa. "I'd swear you had a nail in your shoe."

"I told you I looked."

"Well, you ought to look again. And cut your toenails, why don't you? Haven't I got enough to do?"

Father Firman scratched in his coat pocket for a pill, found one, swallowed it. He let his head sink back against the chair and closed his eyes. He could hear her moving about the room, making the preparations; and how he knew them—the fumbling in the drawer for a pencil with a point, the rip of the page from his daily calendar, and finally the leg of the card table sliding up against his leg.

He opened his eyes. She yanked the floor lamp alongside the table, setting the bead fringe tinkling on the shade, and pulled up her chair on the other side. She sat down and smiled at him for the first time that day. Now she was happy.

She swept up the cards and began to shuffle with the abandoned virtuosity of an old riverboat gambler, standing them on end, fanning them out, whirling them through her fingers, dancing them halfway up her arms, cracking the whip over them. At last they lay before him tamed into a neat deck.

"Cut?"

"Go ahead," he said. She liked to go first.

She gave him her faint, avenging smile and drew a card, cast it aside for another which he thought must be an ace from the way she clutched it face down.

She was getting all the cards, as usual, and would have been invincible if she had possessed his restraint and if her cunning had been of a higher order. He knew a few things about leading and lying back that she would never learn. Her strategy was attack, forever attack, with one baffling departure: she might sacrifice certain tricks as expendable if only she could have the last ones, the heartbreaking ones, if she could slap them down one after another, shatteringly.

She played for blood, no bones about it, but for her there was no other way; it was her nature, as it was the lion's, and for this reason he found her ferocity pardonable, more a defect of the flesh, venial, while his own trouble was all in the will, mortal. He did not sweat and pray over each card as she must, but he did keep an eye out for reneging and demanded a cut now and then just to aggravate her, and he was always secretly hoping for aces.

With one card left in her hand, the telltale trick coming next, she delayed playing it, showing him first the smile, the preview of defeat. She laid it on the table—so! She held one more trump than he had reasoned possible. Had she palmed it from somewhere? No, she would not go that far; that would not be fair, was worse than reneging, which so easily and often happened accidentally, and she believed in being fair. Besides he had been watching her.

God smote the vines with hail, the sycamore trees with frost, and offered up the flocks to the lightning—but Mrs. Stoner! What a cross Father Firman had from God in Mrs. Stoner! There were other housekeepers as bad, no doubt, walking the rectories of the world, yes, but . . . yes. He could name one and maybe two priests who were worse off. One, maybe two. Cronin. His scraggly blonde of sixty—take her, with her everlasting banging on the grand piano, the gift of the pastor; her proud talk about the goiter operation at the Mayo Brothers', also a gift; her honking the parish Buick at passing strange priests because they were all in the game together. She was worse. She was something to keep the home fires burning. Yes sir. And Cronin said she was not a bad person really, but what was he? He was quite a freak himself.

For that matter, could anyone say that Mrs. Stoner was a bad person? No. He could not say it himself, and he was no freak. She had her points, Mrs. Stoner. She was clean. And though she cooked poorly, could not play the organ, would not take up the collection in an emergency, and went to card parties, and told all—even so, she was clean. She washed everything. Sometimes her underwear hung down beneath her dress like a paratrooper's pants, but it and everything she touched was clean. She washed constantly. She was clean.

She had her other points, to be sure—her faults, you might say. She snooped—no mistake about it—but it was not snooping for snooping's sake; she had a reason. She did other things, always with a reason. She overcharged on rosaries and prayer books, but that was for the sake of the poor. She censored the pamphlet rack, but that was to prevent scandal. She pried into the baptismal and matrimonial records, but there was no other way if Father was out, and in this way she had once uncovered a bastard and flushed him out of the rectory, but that was the perverted decency of the times. She held her nose over bad marriages in the presence of the victims, but that was her sorrow and came from having her husband buried in a mine. And he had caught her telling a bewildered young couple that there was only one good reason for their wanting to enter into a mixed marriage—the child had to have a name, and that—that was what?

She hid his books, kept him from smoking, picked his friends (usually the pastors of her colleagues), bawled out people for calling after dark, had no humor, except at cards, and then it was grim, very grim, and she sat hatchet-faced every morning at Mass. But she went to Mass, which was all that kept the church from being empty some mornings. She did annoying things all day long. She said annoying things into the night. She said she had given him the best years of her life. Had she? Perhaps—for the miner had her only a year. It was too bad, sinfully bad, when he thought of it like that. But all talk of best years and life was nonsense. He had to consider the heart of the matter, the essence. The essence was that housekeepers were hard to get, harder to get than ushers, than willing workers, than organists, than secretaries—yes, harder to get than assistants or vocations.

And she was a *saver*—saved money, saved electricity, saved string, bags, sugar, saved—him. That's what she did. That's what she said she did, and she was right, in a way. In a way, she was usually right. In fact, she was always right—in a way. And you could never get a Filipino to come way out here and live. Not a young one anyway, and he had never seen an old one. Not a Filipino. They liked to dress up and live.

Should he let it drop about Fish having one, just to throw a scare into her, let her know he was doing some thinking? No. It would be a perfect cue for the one about a man needing a woman to look after him. He was not up to that again, not tonight.

Now she was doing what she liked most of all. She was making a grand slam, playing it out card for card, though it was in the bag, prolonging what would have been cut short out of mercy in gentle company. Father Firman knew the agony of losing.

She slashed down the last card, a miserable deuce trump, and did in the hapless king of hearts he had been saving.

"Skunked you!"

She was awful in victory. Here was the bitter end of their long day together, the final murderous hour in which all they wanted to say—all he wouldn't and all she couldn't—came out in the cards. Whoever won at honeymoon won the day, slept on the other's scalp, and God alone had to help the loser.

"We've been at it long enough, Mrs. Stoner," he said, seeing her assembling the cards for another round.

"Had enough, huh!"

Father Firman grumbled something.

"No?"

"Yes."

She pulled the table away and left it against the wall for the next time. She went out of the study carrying the socks, content and clucking. He closed his eyes after her and began to get under way in the rocking chair, the nightly trip to nowhere. He could hear her brewing a cup of tea in the kitchen and conversing with the cat. She made her way up the stairs, carrying the tea, followed by the cat, purring.

He waited, rocking out to sea, until she would be sure to be through in the bathroom. Then he got up and locked the front door (she looked after the back door) and loosened his collar going upstairs.

In the bathroom he mixed a glass of antiseptic, always afraid of pyorrhea, and gargled to ward off pharyngitis.

When he turned on the light in his room, the moths and beetles began to batter against the screens, the lighter insects humming. . . .

Yes, and she had the guest room. How did she come to get that? Why wasn't she in the back room, in her proper place? He knew, if he cared to remember. The screen in the back room—it let in mosquitoes, and if it didn't do that she'd love to sleep back there, Father, looking out at the steeple and the blessed cross on top, Father, if it just weren't for the screen, Father. Very well, Mrs. Stoner, I'll get it fixed or fix it myself. Oh, could you now, Father? I could, Mrs. Stoner, and I will. In the meantime you take the guest room. Yes, Father, and thank you, Father, the house ringing with amenities then. Years ago, all that. She was a pie-faced girl then, not really a girl perhaps, but not too old to marry again. But she never had. In fact, he could not remember that she had even tried for a husband since coming to the rectory, but, of course, he could be wrong, not knowing how they went about it. God! God save us! Had she got her wires crossed and mistaken him all these years for *that? That!* Him! Suffering God! No. That was going too far. That was getting morbid. No. He must not think of that again, ever. No.

But just the same she had got the guest room and she had it yet. Well, did it matter? Nobody ever came to see him any more, nobody to stay overnight anyway, nobody to stay very long . . . not any more. He knew how they laughed at him. He had heard Frank humming all right—before he saw how serious and sad the situation was and took pity—humming, "Wedding Bells Are Breaking Up That Old Gang of Mine." But then they'd always laughed at him for something—for not being an athlete, for wearing glasses, for having kidney trouble . . . and mail coming addressed to Rev. and Mrs. Stoner.

Removing his shirt, he bent over the table to read the volume left open from last night. He read, translating easily, "Eisdem licet cum illis . . . Clerics are allowed to reside only with women about whom there can be no suspicion, either because of a natural bond (as mother, sister, aunt) or of advanced age, combined in both cases with good repute."

Last night he had read it, and many nights before, each time as though this time to find what was missing, to find what obviously was not in the paragraph, his problem considered, a way out. She was not mother, not sister, not aunt, and *advanced age* was a relative term (why, she was younger than he was) and so, eureka, she did not meet the letter of the law—but, alas, how she fulfilled the spirit! And besides it would be a slimy way of handling it after all her years of service. He could not afford to pension her off, either.

He slammed the book shut. He slapped himself fiercely on the back, missing the wily mosquito, and whirled to find it. He took a magazine and folded it into a swatter. Then he saw it—oh, the preternatural cunning of it!—poised in the beard of St. Joseph on the bookcase. He could not hit it there. He teased it away, wanting it to light on the wall, but it knew his thoughts and flew high away. He swung wildly, hoping to stun it, missed, swung back, catching St. Joseph across the neck. The statue fell to the floor and broke.

Mrs. Stoner was panting in the hall outside his door.

"What is it!"

"Mosquitoes!"

"What is it, Father? Are you hurt?"

"Mosquitoes—damn it! And only the female bites!"

Mrs. Stoner, after a moment, said, "Shame on you, Father. She needs the blood for her eggs."

He dropped the magazine and lunged at the mosquito with his bare hand.

She went back to her room, saying, "Pshaw, I thought it was burglars murdering you in your bed."

He lunged again.

QUESTIONS

1 In Irving's story "Adventure of the German Student," which is taken from a book told by a rambling narrator created by Irving, we saw this narrator intrude with "—but I should first tell you something about this young German." Does the narrator in "The Valiant Woman" similarly intrude himself?

2 Is this story told entirely through one impression, or are parts of it told in the public world as well as the private world? Identify any such parts.

3 Whose private world is entered—that of one person, or of more than one?

4 In questions 4 and 5 following Irving's story, you were asked to divide the story in half to determine which part would film with the greatest ease. Do this with "The Valiant Woman." The story's second half begins with the paragraph, "She was getting all the cards, as usual." Discuss the ease or difficulty with which you could film (1) the first half of this story, (2) the second half of the story.

5 Use your answers to question 4 to compare Powers' handling of public and private worlds with Irving's.

6 Stories containing fantastic events often are made more believable by removing these events from the reader in time and in place, and by having them told by one or more narrators (see, for example, "Amy Foster" in Part Two). The farther we get from a fantasy in space, time, and impression, the fewer objections we raise to it's implausibility. Comment on the appropriateness of the time, the place, and the way the narrators' intrusions are handled, in relation to the events, in each of these two stories.

7 Unlike "The Strength of God" in Chapter 8, "The Valiant Woman" is entirely focused within the span of two or three hours. This time span suggests the story is mainly scenic. Is any summary method employed? If so, where?

8 What plays on words are lurking in the names Father Firman and Mrs. Stoner?

9 Good authors make every detail count. When Father Firman swings wildly at the mosquito, he knocks over and smashes a statue. What irony lurks behind the fact that this is a statue of Saint Joseph and not some other saint? How is this action of Father Firman's symbolic?

10
POINT OF VIEW

dramatic distance

We saw in the preceding chapter that parts of most stories are told publicly like a play, with neither the narrator's mind nor the private world of the characters revealed. Other parts of stories yield a different impression, when, for example, an author comments on a character's private life as Irving does about his German student, or, more subtly, when an author lets these comments emerge directly from the character's private world, as Powers does with Father Firman. We call *point of view* all the possible ways the author can reveal—or conceal—himself and his characters. Point of view has little to do with the author's attitudes or beliefs. Point of view in fiction means, quite precisely, the role the mind of the author plays in the story, and how he chooses to reveal or conceal the private world of the characters.

It is not necessary to consider all the possible variations of point of view, although it may be useful to review some of them to see how many choices a writer has at hand to achieve his desired effect.

Some stories are told in the first person, "I." The teller is either the principal character, as in "Araby," or somebody completely outside the story, as in "Adventure of the German Student," or a minor character, as in "A Story" by Dylan Thomas in Chapter 11.

A story may be told in the third person, where no "I" narrates, but where everyone is referred to by his name, or by "he" or "she."

Sometimes the private worlds in such a story are limited to one character, and the reader sees, hears, and thinks only what this one character sees, hears, and thinks. This point of view is called *central intelligence;* it is used in "The Valiant Woman."

Other third-person stories are written so that the private worlds of several characters are open to the reader, who, at the will of the all-knowing narrator, can skip from character to character, place to place, time to time, experiencing many inner worlds; this all-knowing point of view is called *omniscient.* The omniscient point of view is clearly demonstrated in D. H. Lawrence's "The Horse Dealer's Daughter" in Part Two of this book. Lawrence as narrator enters the private worlds of several characters. An omniscient point of view is also suggested in Maupassant's "The Piece of String," but because of a somewhat reduced access, the point of view in this story should be considered *limited omniscience.*

These variations may be further complicated by using several points of view in the same story. Joseph Conrad, whose story "Amy Foster" appears in Part Two, was plagued by point of view; he never felt confident in telling a story from inside a character's mind, yet the inner experience interested him most. Therefore, we have in "Amy Foster" not only the relating of a typical "inner" experience of Amy and her lover Yanko but also the disclosure of this experience by a narrator who in turn is only the friend of the story's narrator. Often in Conrad's fiction, the "I" narrator drops completely from the action of the story after the first few paragraphs. Or, as in Poe's "The Masque of the Red Death," the "I" may appear only now and again in the story.

Another variation that alters the point of view is produced when the author chooses to tell the story with a sense of remembering from the distant past, as in Joyce's "Araby." Or he may choose to let the events unfold along with the telling, as in Updike's "A & P," in which the narrator shares the unfolding suspense with the reader.

In general, the wider the point of view and the more distant a story is from us in time, the more room there is for the controlling mind of the narrator to comment on the drama. Conversely, the narrower the focus and the more immediate the events seem in time, the less appropriate it is for the narrator to intrude and the more the reader must rely on his own inference of what the events signify.

What is often more important than naming the precise point of view used by an author is recognizing how reliable the narrator of the story is. One of the favorite techniques of authors who employ irony is to create a narrator who tells the story, but whose word must be doubted, and who is thus distinct and separate from the author. By creating such an unreliable narrator, the author is able not only to tell the story, but also to create an ironic tension between reader and narrator. This ironic tension between what the narrator thinks are the facts, and what we can infer are the facts, we may call *dramatic distance,* because it creates a discernible distance in knowledge between the author or the reader on the one hand, and the narrator on the other. When dramatic distance is present, we discover that dramatic irony is at work against the narrator. Dramatic irony, you recall, is present when the reader knows something that is unknown to a character. Often that unknowing character is the narrator himself. For example, in "A & P," Updike deliberately limits the vision of his youthful narrator. The opening paragraphs depend for effect largely on dramatic irony. From the very beginning we understand that Sammy is reporting things from a limited attitude. We are aware of the dramatic distance that exists between the author and the boy who tells the story.

If you are asked to analyze the point of view, you can usually find it by considering the following questions:

1. Is the story told in the first person or in the third person?
2. Is it recalled action somewhat distant in time, or continuing action with the events brought into a more immediate focus?
3. Is it omniscient or restricted in private knowledge; that is, is it told from a wider or from a more narrow point of view?
4. Is the narrator intended to be reliable or unreliable?

Thomas Wolfe

ONLY THE DEAD KNOW BROOKLYN

Dere's no guy livin' dat knows Brooklyn t'roo an' t'roo, because it'd take a guy a lifetime just to find his way aroun' duh f—— town.

So like I say, I'm waitin' for my train t' come when I sees dis big guy standin' deh—dis is duh foist I eveh see of him. Well, he's lookin' wild, y'know, an' I can see dat he's had plenty, but still he's holdin' it; he talks good an' is walkin' straight enough. So den, dis big guy steps up to a little guy dat's standin' deh, an' says, "How d'yuh get t' Eighteent' Avenoo an' Sixty-sevent' Street?" he says.

"Jesus! Yuh got me, chief," duh little guy says to him. "I ain't been heah long myself. Where is duh place?" he says. "Out in duh Flatbush section somewhere?"

"Nah," duh big guys says. "It's out in Bensonhoist. But I was neveh deh befoeh. How d'yuh get deh?"

"Jesus," duh little guy says, scratchin' his head, y'know—yuh could see duh little guy didn't know his way about—"yuh got me, chief. I neveh hoid of it. Do any of youse guys know where it is?" he says to me.

"Sure," I says. "It's out in Bensonhoist. Yuh take duh Fourt' Avenoo express, get off at Fifty-nint' Street, change to a Sea Beach local deh, get off at Eighteent' Avenoo an' Sixty-toid, an' den walk down foeh blocks. Dat's all yuh got to do," I says.

"G'wan!" some wise guy dat I neveh seen befoeh pipes up. "Whatcha talkin' about?" he says—oh, he was wise, y'know. "Duh guy is crazy! I tell yuh what yuh do," he says to duh big guy. "Yuh change to duh West End line at Toity-sixt'," he tells him. "Get off at Noo Utrecht an' Sixteent' Avenoo," he says. "Walk two blocks oveh, foeh blocks up," he says, "an' you'll be right deh." Oh, a *wise* guy, y'know.

"Oh, yeah?" I says. "Who told *you* so much?" He got me sore because he was so wise about it. "How long you been livin' heah?" I says.

"All my life," he says. "I was bawn in Williamsboig," he says. "An' I can tell you t'ings about dis town you neveh hoid of," he says.

"Yeah?" I says.

"Yeah," he says.

"Well, den, you can tell me t'ings about dis town dat nobody else has eveh hoid of, either. Maybe you make it all up yoehself at night," I says, "befoeh you go to sleep—like cuttin' out papeh dolls, or somp'n."

"Oh, yeah?" he says. "You're pretty wise, ain't yuh?"

"Oh, I don't know," I says. "Duh boids ain't usin' my head for Lincoln's statue yet," I says. "But I'm wise enough to know a phony when I see one."

"Yeah?" he says. "A wise guy, huh? Well, you're so wise dat some one's goin' t'bust yuh one right on duh snoot some day," he says. "Dat's how wise *you* are."

Well, my train was comin', or I'da smacked him den and dere, but when I seen duh train was comin', all I said was, "All right, mugg! I'm sorry I can't stay to take keh of you, but I'll be seein' yuh sometime, I hope, out in duh cemetery." So den I says to duh big guy, who'd been standin' deh all duh time, "You come wit me," I says. So when we gets onto duh train I says to him, "Where yuh goin' out in Bensonhoist?" I says. "What numbeh are yuh lookin' for?" I says. *You* know—I t'ought if he told me duh address I might be able to help him out.

"Oh," he says, "I'm not lookin' for no one. I don't know no one out deh."

"Then whatcha goin' out deh for?" I says.

"Oh," duh guy says, "I'm just goin' out to see duh place," he says. "I like duh sound of duh name—Bensonhoist, y'know—so I t'ought I'd go out an' have a look at it."

"Whatcha tryin' t'hand me?" I says. "Whatcha tryin' t'do—kid me?" *You* know, I t'ought duh guy was bein' wise wit me.

"No," he says, "I'm tellin' yuh duh troot. I like to go out an' take a look at places wit nice names like dat. I like to go out an' look at all kinds of places," he says.

"How'd yuh know deh was such a place," I says, "if yuh neveh been deh befoeh?"

"Oh," he says, "I got a map."

"A *map?*" I says.

"Sure," he says, "I got a map dat tells me about all dese places. I take it wit me every time I come out heah," he says.

And Jesus! Wit dat, he pulls it out of his pocket, an' so help me, but he's *got* it—he's tellin' duh troot—a big map of duh whole f—— place with all duh different pahts mahked out. You know—

Canarsie an' East Noo Yawk an' Flatbush, Bensonhoist, Sout' Brooklyn, duh Heights, Bay Ridge, Greenpernt—duh whole goddam layout, he's got it right deh on duh map.

"You been to any of dose places?" I says.

"Sure," he says, "I been to most of 'em. I was down in Red Hook just last night," he says.

"Jesus! Red Hook!" I says. "Whatcha do down deh?"

"Oh," he says, "nuttin' much. I just walked aroun'. I went into a coupla places an' had a drink," he says, "but most of the time I just walked aroun'."

"Just walked aroun'?" I says.

"Sure," he says, "just lookin' at t'ings, y'know."

"Where'd yuh go?" I asts him.

"Oh," he says, "I don't know duh name of duh place, but I could find it on my map," he says. "One time I was walkin' across some big fields where deh ain't no houses," he says, "but I could see ships oveh deh all lighted up. Dey was loadin'. So I walks across duh fields," he says, "to where duh ships are."

"Sure," I says, "I know where you was. You was down to duh Erie Basin."

"Yeah," he says, "I guess dat was it. Dey had some of dose big elevators an' cranes an' dey was loadin' ships, an' I could see some ships in drydock all lighted up, so I walks across duh fields to where dey are," he says.

"Den what did yuh do?" I says.

"Oh," he says, "nuttin' much. I came on back across duh fields after a while an' went into a coupla places an' had a drink."

"Didn't nuttin' happen while yuh was in dere?" I says.

"No," he says. "Nuttin' much. A coupla guys was drunk in one of duh places an' started a fight, but dey bounced 'em out," he says, "an' den one of duh guys stahted to come back again, but duh bartender gets his baseball bat out from under duh counteh, so duh guy goes on."

"Jesus!" I said. "Red Hook!"

"Sure," he says. "Dat's where it was, all right."

"Well, you keep outa deh," I says. "You stay away from deh."

"Why?" he says. "What's wrong wit it?"

"Oh," I says, "It's a good place to stay away from, dat's all. It's a good place to keep out of."

"Why?" he says. "Why is it?"

Jesus! Whatcha gonna do wit a guy as dumb as dat? I saw it

wasn't no use to try to tell him nuttin', he wouldn't know what I was talkin' about, so I just says to him, "Oh, nuttin'. Yuh might get lost down deh, dat's all."

"Lost?" he says. "No, I wouldn't get lost. I got a map," he says.

A map! Red Hook! Jesus!

So den duh guy begins to ast me all kinds of nutty questions: how big was Brooklyn an' could I find my way aroun' in it, an' how long would it take a guy to know duh place.

"Listen!" I says. "You get dat idea outa yoeh head right now," I says. "You ain't neveh gonna get to know Brooklyn," I says. "Not in a hunderd yeahs. I been livin' heah all my life," I says, "an' I don't even know all deh is to know about it, so how do you expect to know duh town," I says, "when you don't even live heah?"

"Yes," he says, "but I got a map to help me find my way about."

"Map or no map," I says, "yuh ain't gonna get to know Brooklyn wit no map," I says.

"Can you swim?" he says, just like dat. Jesus! By dat time, y'know, I begun to see dat duh guy was some kind of nut. He'd had plenty to drink, of course, but he had dat crazy look in his eye I didn't like. "Can you swim?" he says.

"Sure," I says. "Can't you?"

"No," he says. "Not more'n a stroke or two. I neveh loined good."

"Well, it's easy," I says. "All yuh need is a little confidence. Duh way I loined, me older bruddeh pitched me off duh dock one day when I was eight yeahs old, cloes an' all. 'You'll swim,' he says. 'You'll swim all right—or drown.' An', believe me, I *swam!* When yuh know yuh got to, you'll do it. Duh only t'ing yuh need is confidence. An' once you've loined," I says, "you've got nuttin' else to worry about. You'll neveh forget it. It's somp'n dat stays wit yuh as long as yuh live."

"Can yuh swim good?" he says.

"Like a fish," I tells him. "I'm a regulah fish in duh wateh," I says. "I loined to swim right off duh docks wit all duh oddeh kids," I says.

"What would you do if yuh saw a man drownin'?" duh guy says.

"Do? Why, I'd jump in an' pull him out," I says. "Dat's what I'd do."

"Did yuh eveh see a man drown?" he says.

"Sure," I says. "I see two guys—bot' times at Coney Island. Dey got out too far, an' neider one could swim. Dey drowned befoeh any one could get to 'em."

"What becomes of people after dey've drowned out heah?" he says.

"Drowned out where?" I says.

"Out heah in Brooklyn."

"I don't know whatcha mean," I says. "Neveh hoid of no one drownin' heah in Brooklyn, unless you mean a swimmin' pool. Yuh can't drown in Brooklyn," I says. "Yuh gotta drown somewhere else—in duh ocean, where dere's wateh."

"Drownin'," duh guy says, lookin' at his map. "Drownin'." Jesus! I could see by den he was some kind of nut, he had dat crazy expression in his eyes when he looked at you, an' I didn't know what he might do. So we was comin' to a station, an' it wasn't my stop, but I got off anyway, an' waited for duh next train.

"Well, so long, chief," I says. "Take it easy, now."

"Drownin'," duh guy says, lookin' at his map. "Drownin'."

Jesus! I've t'ought about dat guy a t'ousand times since den an' wondered what eveh happened to 'm goin' out to look at Bensonhoist because he liked duh name! Walkin' aroun' t'roo Red Hook by himself at night an' lookin' at his map! How many people did I see get drowned out heah in Brooklyn! How long would it take a guy wit a good map to know all deh was to know about Brooklyn!

Jesus! What a nut *he* was! I wondeh what eveh happened to 'im, anyway! I wondeh if some one knocked him on duh head, or if he's still wanderin' aroun' in duh subway in duh middle of duh night wit his little map! Duh poor guy! Say, I've got to laugh, at dat, when I t'ink about him! Maybe he's found out by now dat he'll neveh live long enough to know duh whole of Brooklyn. It'd take a guy a lifetime to know Brooklyn t'roo an' t'roo. An' even den, yuh wouldn't know it all.

QUESTIONS

1 Is this story told in the first or third person?

2 Is the narrator omniscient or restricted in private knowledge?

3 Is the narrator intended to be reliable or unreliable? How do you know?

4 Has the author created dramatic distance between himself and his narrator? Point out evidence of dramatic irony at work in this story.

5 The author, Thomas Wolfe, projected an image of himself as "the big guy" in this story. Does "the big guy" come on as a sensible, sensitive character? Comment on the presence or absence of dramatic distance between the author and "the big guy."

6 Cite several examples in the story where the narrator's mind is revealed. Assuming that the intrusion of the mind of the narrator contributes to the story, state what you think this contribution is.

7 In what ways does the narrator reveal himself to be literal-minded? What metaphor is carried by the word "Drownin' "?

8 Toward whom is the irony in the title pointed?

9 The final words of the story come almost as a refrain. The narrator means them literally, but the reader is aware that they have taken on a richer significance by now even though the speaker does not realize it. What is that significance? How does this illustrate irony at work?

Ralph Ellison

KING OF THE BINGO GAME

The woman in front of him was eating roasted peanuts that smelled so good that he could barely contain his hunger. He could not even sleep and wished they'd hurry and begin the bingo game. There, on his right, two fellows were drinking wine out of a bottle wrapped in a paper bag, and he could hear soft gurgling in the dark. His stomach gave a low, gnawing growl. "If this was down South," he thought, "all I'd have to do is lean over and say, 'Lady, gimme a few of those peanuts, please ma'm,' and she'd pass me the bag and never think nothing of it." Or he could ask the fellows for a drink in the same way. Folks down South stuck together that way; they didn't even have to know you. But up here it was different. Ask somebody for something, and they'd think you were crazy. Well, I ain't crazy. I'm just broke, 'cause I got no birth certificate to get a job, and Laura 'bout to die 'cause we got no money for a doctor. But I ain't crazy. And yet a pinpoint of doubt was focused in his mind as he glanced toward the screen and saw the hero stealthily entering a dark room and sending the beam of a flashlight along a wall of bookcases. This is where he finds the trapdoor, he remembered. The man would pass abruptly through the wall and find the girl tied to a bed, her legs and arms spread wide, and her clothing torn to rags. He laughed softly to himself. He had seen the picture three times, and this was one of the best scenes.

On his right the fellow whispered wide-eyed to his companion, "Man, look a-yonder!"

"Damn!"

"Wouldn't I like to have her tied up like that . . ."

"Hey! That fool's letting her loose!"

"Aw, man, he loves her."

"Love or no love!"

The man moved impatiently beside him, and he tried to involve himself in the scene. But Laura was on his mind. Tiring quickly of watching the picture he looked back to where the white beam filtered from the projection room above the balcony. It started small and grew large, specks of dust dancing in its whiteness as it reached the screen. It was strange how the beam always landed right on the screen and didn't mess up and fall somewhere else. But they had it all fixed. Everything was fixed. Now suppose when they showed that girl with her dress torn the girl started taking off the rest of her clothes, and when the guy came in he didn't untie her but kept her there and went to taking off his own clothes? *That* would be something to see. If a picture got out of hand like that those guys up there would go nuts. Yeah, and there'd be so many folks in here you couldn't find a seat for nine months! A strange sensation played over his skin. He shuddered. Yesterday he'd seen a bedbug on a woman's neck as they walked out into the bright street. But exploring his thigh through a hole in his pocket he found only goose pimples and old scars.

The bottle gurgled again. He closed his eyes. Now a dreamy music was accompanying the film and train whistles were sounding in the distance, and he was a boy again walking along a railroad trestle down South, and seeing the train coming, and running back as fast as he could go, and hearing the whistle blowing, and getting off the trestle to solid ground just in time, with the earth trembling beneath his feet, and feeling relieved as he ran down the cinder-strewn embankment onto the highway, and looking back and seeing with terror that the train had left the track and was following him right down the middle of the street, and all the white people laughing as he ran screaming . . .

"Wake up there, buddy! What the hell do you mean hollering like that? Can't you see we trying to enjoy this here picture?"

He stared at the man with gratitude.

"I'm sorry, old man," he said. "I musta been dreaming."

"Well, here, have a drink. And don't be making no noise like that, damn!"

His hands trembled as he tilted his head. It was not wine, but whiskey. Cold rye whiskey. He took a deep swoller, decided it was better not to take another, and handed the bottle back to its owner.

"Thanks, old man," he said.

Now he felt the cold whiskey breaking a warm path straight through the middle of him, growing hotter and sharper as it moved. He had not eaten all day, and it made him light-headed. The smell of the peanuts stabbed him like a knife, and he got up and found a seat in the middle aisle. But no sooner did he sit than he saw a row of intense-faced young girls, and got up again, thinking, "You chicks musta been Lindy-hopping somewhere." He found a seat several rows ahead as the lights came on, and he saw the screen disappear behind a heavy red and gold curtain; then the curtain rising, and the man with the microphone and a uniformed attendant coming on the stage.

He felt for his bingo cards, smiling. The guy at the door wouldn't like it if he knew about his having *five* cards. Well, not everyone played the bingo game; and even with five cards he didn't have much of a chance. For Laura, though, he had to have faith. He studied the cards, each with its different numerals, punching the free center hole in each and spreading them neatly across his lap; and when the lights faded he sat slouched in his seat so that he could look from his cards to the bingo wheel with but a quick shifting of his eyes.

Ahead, at the end of the darkness, the man with the microphone was pressing a button attached to a long cord and spinning the bingo wheel and calling out the number each time the wheel came to rest. And each time the voice rang out his finger raced over the cards for the number. With five cards he had to move fast. He became nervous; there were too many cards, and the man went too fast with his grating voice. Perhaps he should just select one and throw the others away. But he was afraid. He became warm. Wonder how much Laura's doctor would cost? Damn that, watch the cards! And with despair he heard the man call three in a row which he missed on all five cards. This way he'd never win . . .

When he saw the row of holes punched across the third card, he sat paralyzed and heard the man call three more numbers before he stumbled forward, screaming,

"Bingo! Bingo!"

"Let that fool up there," someone called.

"Get up there, man!"

He stumbled down the aisle and up the steps to the stage into a light so sharp and bright that for a moment it blinded him, and he felt that he had moved into the spell of some strange, mysterious power. Yet it was as familiar as the sun, and he knew it was the perfectly familiar bingo.

The man with the microphone was saying something to the audience as he held out his card. A cold light flashed from the man's finger as the card left his hand. His knees trembled. The man stepped closer, checking the card against the numbers chalked on the board. Suppose he had made a mistake? The pomade on the man's hair made him feel faint, and he backed away. But the man was checking the card over the microphone now, and he had to stay. He stood tense, listening.

"Under the O, forty-four," the man chanted. "Under the I, seven. Under the G, three. Under the B, ninety-six. Under the N, thirteen!"

His breath came easier as the man smiled at the audience.

"Yessir, ladies and gentlemen, he's one of the chosen people!"

The audience rippled with laughter and applause.

"Step right up to the front of the stage."

He moved slowly forward, wishing that the light was not so bright.

"To win tonight's jackpot of $36.90 the wheel must stop between the double zero, understand?"

He nodded, knowing the ritual from the many days and nights he had watched the winners march across the stage to press the button that controlled the spinning wheel and receive the prizes. And now he followed the instructions as though he'd crossed the slippery stage a million prize-winning times.

The man was making some kind of a joke, and he nodded vacantly. So tense had he become that he felt a sudden desire to cry and shook it away. He felt vaguely that his whole life was determined by the bingo wheel; not only that which would happen now that he was at last before it, but all that had gone before, since his birth, and his mother's birth and the birth of his father. It had always been there, even though he had not been aware of it, handing out the unlucky cards and numbers of his days. The feeling persisted, and he started quickly away. I better get down from here before I make a fool of myself, he thought.

"Here, boy," the man called. "You haven't started yet."

Someone laughed as he went hesitantly back.

"Are you all reet?"

He grinned at the man's jive talk, but no words would come, and he knew it was not a convincing grin. For suddenly he knew that he stood on the slippery brink of some terrible embarrassment.

"Where are you from, boy?" the man asked.

"Down South."

"He's from down South, ladies and gentlemen," the man said. "Where from? Speak right into the mike."

"Rocky Mont," he said. "Rock' Mont, North Car'lina."

"So you decided to come down off that mountain to the U.S.," the man laughed. He felt that the man was making a fool of him, but then something cold was placed in his hand, and the lights were no longer behind him.

Standing before the wheel he felt alone, but that was somehow right, and he remembered his plan. He would give the wheel a short quick twirl. Just a touch of the button. He had watched it many times, and always it came close to double zero when it was short and quick. He steeled himself; the fear had left, and he felt a profound sense of promise, as though he were about to be repaid for all the things he'd suffered all his life. Trembling, he pressed the button. There was a whirl of lights, and in a second he realized with finality that though he wanted to, he could not stop. It was as though he held a high-powered line in his naked hand. His nerves tightened. As the wheel increased its speed it seemed to draw him more and more into its power, as though it held his fate; and with it came a deep need to submit, to whirl, to lose himself in its swirl of color. He could not stop it now, he knew. So let it be.

The button rested snuggly in his palm where the man had placed it. And now he became aware of the man beside him, advising him through the microphone, while behind the shadowy audience hummed with noisy voices. He shifted his feet. There was still that feeling of helplessness within him, making part of him desire to turn back, even now that the jackpot was right in his hand. He squeezed the button until his fist ached. Then, like the sudden shriek of a subway whistle, a doubt tore through his head. Suppose he did not spin the wheel long enough? What could he do, and how could he tell? And then he knew, even as he wondered, that as long as he pressed the button, he could control the jackpot. He and only he could determine whether or not it was to be his. Not even the man with the microphone could do anything about it now. He felt drunk. Then, as though he had come down from a high hill into a valley of people, he heard the audience yelling.

"Come down from there, you jerk!"

"Let somebody else have a chance . . ."

"Ole Jack thinks he done found the end of the rainbow . . ."

The last voice was not unfriendly, and he turned and smiled dreamily into the yelling mouths. Then he turned his back squarely on them.

"Don't take too long, boy," a voice said.

He nodded. They were yelling behind him. Those folks did not understand what had happened to him. They had been playing the bingo game day in and night out for years, trying to win rent money or hamburger change. But not one of those wise guys had discovered this wonderful thing. He watched the wheel whirling past the numbers and experienced a burst of exaltation: This is God! This is the really truly God! He said it aloud, "This is God!"

He said it with such absolute conviction that he feared he would fall fainting into the footlights. But the crowd yelled so loud that they could not hear. Those fools, he thought. I'm here trying to tell them the most wonderful secret in the world, and they're yelling like they gone crazy. A hand fell upon his shoulder.

"You'll have to make a choice now, boy. You've taken too long."

He brushed the hand violently away.

"Leave me alone, man. I know what I'm doing!"

The man looked surprised and held on to the microphone for support. And because he did not wish to hurt the man's feelings he smiled, realizing with a sudden pang that there was no way of explaining to the man just why he had to stand there pressing the button forever.

"Come here," he called tiredly.

The man approached, rolling the heavy microphone across the stage.

"Anybody can play this bingo game, right?" he said.

"Sure, but . . ."

He smiled, feeling inclined to be patient with this slick looking white man with his blue sport shirt and his sharp gabardine suit.

"That's what I thought," he said. "Anybody can win the jackpot as long as they get the lucky number, right?"

"That's the rule, but after all . . ."

"That's what I thought," he said. "And the big prize goes to the man who knows how to win it?"

The man nodded speechlessly.

"Well then, go on over there and watch me win like I want to. I ain't going to hurt nobody," he said "and I'll show you how to win. I mean to show the whole world how it's got to be done."

And because he understood, he smiled again to let the man know that he held nothing against him for being white and impatient. Then he refused to see the man any longer and stood pressing the button, the voices of the crowd reaching him like sounds in distant streets. Let them yell. All the Negroes down there were just ashamed because he was black like them. He smiled inwardly, knowing how it was. Most of the time he was ashamed of what Negroes did himself. Well, let them be ashamed for something this time. Like him. He was like a long thin black wire that was being stretched and wound upon the bingo wheel; wound until he wanted to scream; wound, but this time himself controlling the winding and the sadness and the shame, and because he did, Laura would be all right. Suddenly the lights flickered. He staggered backwards. Had something gone wrong? All this noise. Didn't they know that although he controlled the wheel, it also controlled him, and unless he pressed the button forever and forever and ever it would stop, leaving him high and dry, dry and high on this hard high slippery hill and Laura dead? There was only one chance; he had to do whatever the wheel demanded. And gripping the button in despair, he discovered with surprise that it imparted a nervous energy. His spine tingled. He felt a certain power.

Now he faced the raging crowd with defiance, its screams penetrating his eardrums like trumpets shrieking from a jukebox. The vague faces glowing in the bingo lights gave him a sense of himself that he had never known before. He was running the show, by God! They had to react to him, for he was their luck. This is *me,* he thought. Let the bastards yell. Then someone was laughing inside him, and he realized that somehow he had forgotten his own name. It was a sad, lost feeling to lose your name, and a crazy thing to do. That name had been given him by the white man who had owned his grandfather a long lost time ago down South. But maybe those wise guys knew his name.

"Who am I?" he screamed.

"Hurry up and bingo, you jerk!"

They didn't know either, he thought sadly. They didn't even know their own names, they were all poor nameless bastards. Well, he didn't need that old name; he was reborn. For as long as he pressed the button he was The-man-who-pressed-the-button-who-held-the-prize-who-was-the-King-of-Bingo. That was the way it was, and he'd have to press the button even if nobody understood, even though Laura did not understand.

"Live!" he shouted.

The audience quieted like the dying of a huge fan.

"Live, Laura, baby. I got holt of it now, sugar. Live!"

He screamed it, tears streaming down his face. "I got nobody but YOU!"

The screams tore from his very guts. He felt as though the rush of blood to his head would burst out in baseball seams of small red droplets, like a head beaten by police clubs. Bending over he saw a trickle of blood splashing the toe of his shoe. With his free hand he searched his head. It was his nose. God, suppose something has gone wrong? He felt that the whole audience had somehow entered him and was stamping its feet in his stomach, and he was unable to throw them out. They wanted the prize, that was it. They wanted the secret for themselves. But they'd never get it; he would keep the bingo wheel whirling forever, and Laura would be safe in the wheel. But would she? It had to be, because if she were not safe the wheel would cease to turn; it could not go on. He had to get away, *vomit* all, and his mind formed an image of himself running with Laura in his arms down the tracks of the subway just ahead of an A train, running desperately *vomit* with people screaming for him to come out but knowing no way of leaving the tracks because to stop would bring the train crushing down upon him and to attempt to leave across the other tracks would mean to run into a hot third rail as high as his waist which threw blue sparks that blinded his eyes until he could hardly see.

He heard singing and the audience was clapping its hands.

Shoot the liquor to him, Jim, boy!
Clap-clap-clap
Well a-calla the cop
He's blowing his top!
Shoot the liquor to him, Jim, boy!

Bitter anger grew within him at the singing. They think I'm crazy. Well let 'em laugh. I'll do what I got to do.

He was standing in an attitude of intense listening when he saw that they were watching something on the stage behind him. He felt weak. But when he turned he saw no one. If only his thumb did not ache so. Now they were applauding. And for a moment he thought that the wheel had stopped. But that was impossible, his thumb still pressed the button. Then he saw them. Two men in uniform beckoned from the end of the stage. They were coming toward him, walking in step, slowly, like a tap-dance team returning for a third encore. But their shoulders shot forward, and he backed away, looking wildly about. There was nothing to fight them with. He had only the long black cord which led to a plug somewhere back stage, and he couldn't use that because it operated the bingo wheel. He backed slowly, fixing the men with his eyes as his lips stretched over his teeth in a tight, fixed grin; moved toward the end of the stage and realizing that he couldn't go much further, for suddenly the cord became taut and he couldn't afford to break the cord. But he had to do something. The audience was howling. Suddenly he stopped dead, seeing the men halt, their legs lifted as in an interrupted step of a slow-motion dance. There was nothing to do but run in the other direction and he dashed forward, slipping and sliding. The men fell back, surprised. He struck out violently going past.

"Grab him!"

He ran, but all too quickly the cord tightened, resistingly, and he turned and ran back again. This time he slipped them, and discovered by running in a circle before the wheel he could keep the cord from tightening. But this way he had to flail his arms to keep the men away. Why couldn't they leave a man alone? He ran, circling.

"Ring down the curtain," someone yelled. But they couldn't do that. If they did the wheel flashing from the projection room would be cut off. But they had him before he could tell them so, trying to pry open his fist, and he was wrestling and trying to bring his knees into the fight and holding on to the button, for it was his life. And now he was down, seeing a foot coming down, crushing his wrist cruelly, down, as he saw the wheel whirling serenely above.

"I can't give it up," he screamed. Then quietly, in a confidential tone, "Boys, I really can't give it up."

It landed hard against his head. And in the blank moment they had it away from him, completely now. He fought them trying to pull him up from the stage as he watched the wheel spin slowly to a stop. Without surprise he saw it rest at double zero.

"You see," he pointed bitterly.

"Sure, boy, sure, it's O. K.," one of the men said smiling.

And seeing the man bow his head to someone he could not see, he felt very, very happy; he would receive what all the winners received.

But as he warmed in the justice of the man's tight smile he did not see the man's slow wink, nor see the bow-legged man behind him step clear of the swiftly descending curtain and set himself for a blow. He only felt the dull pain exploding in his skull, and he knew even as it slipped out of him that his luck had run out on the stage.

QUESTIONS

1 Vocabulary: *Lindy-hopping:* a popular dance step of the thirties.

2 Is this story told in the first person or third person?

3 Is the action recalled from the past or presented as a continuing experience?

4 Is there a "central intelligence" point of view? If so, whose?

5 Does the story reveal a point of view that is "omniscient" or of "limited omniscience"?

6 The story reveals both a public world and a private world. Identify each. Which predominates?

7 Does the narrator's mind enter the story?

8 Given your answers to the previous questions and given also the subject of this story, comment on the appropriateness of the author's choice of point of view.

9 In Chapter 6 we noted that *literary symbolism* has four characteristics. Review these characteristics. Now test Ellison's story "King of the Bingo Game" against the title "King of the Jews." Compare it with the story of Christ as told in the gospels, especially the Transfiguration and the Crucifixion. (In Matthew, these appear in Chapters 17 and 27.) Pay particular attention to the following passages from Ellison's story:

(a) He stumbled down the aisle and up the steps to the stage into a light so sharp and bright that for a moment it blinded him, and he felt that he had moved into the spell of some strange, mysterious power. Yet it was as familiar as the sun, and he knew it was the perfectly familiar bingo.

(b) "Yessir, ladies and gentlemen, he's one of the chosen people!"

(c) He felt vaguely that his whole life was determined by the bingo wheel; not only that which would happen now that he was at last before it, but all that had gone before, since his birth, and his mother's birth and the birth of his father.

(d) "Where from? Speak right into the mike."
"Rocky Mont," he said. "Rock' Mont, North Car'lina."
"So you decided to come down off that mountain to the U.S.," the man laughed.

(e) Then, as though he had come down from a high hill into a valley of people, he heard the audience yelling.

(f) "This is God!"

(g) "I mean to show the whole world how it's got to be done."

(h) . . . unless he pressed the button forever and forever and ever it would stop, leaving him high and dry, dry and high on this hard high slippery hill. . . .
(i) Well, he didn't need that old name; he was reborn.
(j) He felt as though the rush of blood to his head would burst out in baseball seams of small red droplets. . . .
(k) *Shoot the liquor to him, Jim, boy!*

10 Is this symbolic situation revealed to the principal character?

11
ATTITUDE

thesis | theme

We observed in Chapter 1 that a story has two aspects (1) the reality recognizable from the everyday world, and (2) the artificial shaping by which the author has heightened reality through art. To these we may now add, as an aspect of fiction, (3) the author's apparent view of the world.

Often authors wish to persuade readers to share their view. If you wish to persuade someone, you usually try to do so by presenting an argument. Frequently this argument takes the form of an example, and when it does, you are using the same form of persuasion used in the earliest short fiction. The Leo Tolstoy story that follows illustrates this simple form. Its title, "Little Girls Wiser Than Old Men," states the author's attitude, and the story concludes with two forthright statements of the same attitude, one made by a character, and one made directly by the author as an attached moral, or thesis sentence.

When a story explicitly states a belief that the author wishes the reader to share, it is a story with a *thesis*. Often we can pick a sentence from such a story intact, and put the words "I believe" in front of it to express clearly the author's attitude. For example, in "The Lightning-Rod Man" the narrator says in response to a symbolic situation, "I read in the rainbow, that the Deity will not, of purpose, make war on man's earth." We feel sure that Melville shares this attitude because his narrator appears to be a fair and reliable spokesman, and there seems to be no dramatic distance between Melville and the narrator. Remember, we are now concerned only with the *author's* attitude, not the characters' attitudes.

In this chapter you will read two stories that are at opposite ends of the spectrum in the way they express their author's attitudes. The first, by Tolstoy, separates the events from the thesis sentence decisively. The second, by Dylan Thomas, is the kind of story in which the sheer continuing experience seems to overwhelm any particular belief the author wants us to share. Most stories fall somewhere between these two extremes.

Tolstoy obviously has a purpose beyond entertainment, and he states it as a thesis. Like Tolstoy, storytellers are often teachers. They want to entertain and to instruct. However, the greatest storytellers, like the greatest orators, know that the strength of their persuasion lies not in their statement of thesis, but in the story itself—in their "argument." They have such faith in their stories that they omit any thesis sentence. They seldom reveal their purposes openly, satisfied that if the reader temporarily experiences the world as seen through the author's eyes he will come to share this vision, and will forever after be affected by it. Such a gentle and unobtrusive persuasion in which the thesis is not explicit is the author's way of commenting about life. When this comment is implicit in the story, and when the author's purpose is thus concealed, it is called the story's *theme*. Fused with the action, resting at the center of all the story's elements like the hub in a wheel, this implicit "comment" is inextricably part of the story's experience.

Discussions of theme can be unsatisfactory and even misleading. No statement of theme can recreate the experience of the story; therefore, such a statement always seems limited and not quite right. We should not expect too much from it. A statement of theme is not equivalent to the story, but it is a way of helping us return to the story with a greater appreciation and understanding of its comment on human life. Hunting for the theme is merely a way of getting to know a story, not an end in itself, just as an acquaintance develops into a friendship not by our discovering what a person "means," but rather by discovering what he is.

Thematic statements cannot be mathematically precise. Each of us will interpret a story a little differently, depending upon the vision we bring to it. And we may well keep in mind the words of Joseph Conrad, who said, "a work of art is very seldom limited to one exclusive meaning and not necessarily tending to a definite conclusion."

This latitude does not mean that one interpretation of a story's theme is as good as another, or that "anything goes." As we have said, a story's theme is a unifying device—the hub in the wheel. The poet Robert Frost was referring to this unifying function of theme when he said, "Theme steadies us." This was his way of saying that all the elements in a work reflect it and illuminate it. Therefore, since theme is central to a story, no statement of theme that ignores or contradicts one of the story's elements is adequate.

The best stories do not "mean"; they exist as experiences. Unlike real life in which each experience slips away uncaptured, stories preserve experiences so that we can return to them again and again. As the author's vision makes itself felt, we become aware of his theme. The philosopher George Santayana said, "To turn events into ideas is the function of literature."

Leo Tolstoy

LITTLE GIRLS WISER THAN OLD MEN

Easter was early that year. People had just stopped riding sleighs, snow lay around in barnyards, and rivulets were running. A whole puddle from a thawing manure pile had collected in an alleyway between two yards, and two little girls from different houses, one smaller and the other a little older, had gathered by that puddle to play. Both girls had been dressed by their mothers in new jumpers, the little one in dark blue, the bigger one in a yellow print, and both had red kerchiefs wrapped around their heads. They had come out to the puddle right after the noon service, had shown each other their finery, and then begun to play. They thought it would be fun to splash around in the water. The younger one began to wade into the water with her shoes on, but the older one stopped her, saying, "Don't, Malasha, mother will scold. Look, I'll take off my shoes. You take yours off, too."

The girls took off their shoes, pulled up their skirts, and started wading toward each other. Malasha was in up to her ankles when she said, "It's deep, Akulyushka, I'm afraid."

"Go on! It won't get any deeper. Come straight toward me."

When they got close to each other Akulka said, "You, Malasha, don't splash me. Walk carefully."

But no sooner had she said this than Malasha plopped her foot into the water and spattered Akulka's jumper. Not only spattered the jumper, but water got into Akulka's eyes and nose. Akulka saw the spots on her clothes, got mad, swore at Malasha, and ran after her trying to hit her. Frightened, Malasha saw that she had done something bad; she tore from the puddle and ran off for home. Akulka's mother came by just then, saw that her daughter's jumper was spattered and her blouse muddy. "Wretch," she screamed, "where've you been mucking around?"

"Malasha spattered me, on purpose."

Akulka's mother then seized Malasha and swatted her on the back of her head. Malasha let out a howl that the whole street could hear, and then *her* mother came running up.

"What are you hitting my child for?" And she began to scream at her neighbor. Strong words followed strong words and the women were soon swearing at each other in earnest. Now the menfolk came running up and in no time a whole crowd had gathered, everyone screaming and swearing and no one listening to what the other said.

They shouted and swore, someone pushed someone else and a good fight was in the making when an old woman, Akulka's grandmother, stepped up. She made her way into the midst of the muzhiks and tried to calm them.

"What's got into you, brothers? Is this the time for fighting? You should be happy on a day like today, and look at the wickedness you've started."

But no one paid any attention to the old woman. They nearly knocked her off her feet and she wouldn't have had any effect on the crowd at all if it hadn't been for Akulka and Malasha. While the women were upbraiding each other Akulka wiped her jumper clean and went back to the puddle. She picked up a stone and began gouging the earth, to make a channel so that the water would run off into the street. While she was scratching away,

Malasha came up and began to help her, making a little ditch with a piece of wood. The muzhiks were just about at each other's throats, but the girls had each made a little ditch so that the water ran off into the gutter. They threw a chip into the running water and it floated away toward where the grandmother was trying to separate the men. The girls came running along after the chip, one on one side, the other on the other.

"Grab it, Malasha, grab it," shouted Akulka. Malasha tried to say something, but couldn't, she was laughing so hard.

And the girls ran along, laughing at the chip as it bobbed in the water, and they ran right into the midst of the muzhiks. The grandmother saw them and turned to the men:

"You folks should fear God. Look, you've started a fight because of these two little girls, but they've made up long ago—look at the darlings, out of the goodness of their hearts they're playing again. They are wiser than you are."

The muzhiks looked at the girls—and they were ashamed. Then they laughed at themselves and broke up, each to his house.

Unless you turn and become like children, you will never enter the Kingdom of Heaven.

QUESTIONS

1 Vocabulary: *Akulyushka* and *Akulka* are different forms of the same name. *muzhik:* Russian peasant.

2 The "things" in this story begin with "Easter." Explain the significance of "Easter" as an opening noun.

3 What is the story's complication?

4 The revelation, instead of being implied by the plot itself, is explicity stated, first in the grandmother's last sentence, and then by the narrator himself in the final thesis sentence. Reread the story, omitting the title and everything after "they ran right into the midst of the men." Comment on whether the story to this point is sufficiently self-contained to include a revelation for the reader.

5 An author's attitude is closely related to the degree of dramatic distance he maintains. Question 5 following Thomas Wolfe's story, "Only the Dead Know Brooklyn," asks whether dramatic distance exists between the narrator and the author. We noted that Wolfe projected an image of himself as "the big guy." State the relationship of Wolfe's *attitude,* or belief, to the following statement in his final paragraph; "Jesus! What a nut *he* was."

6 In Ralph Ellison's "King of the Bingo Game," does dramatic distance exist between the main character and the author? State the relationship of Ellison's *attitude* to the following: " 'I can't give it up,' he screamed. Then, quietly, in a confidential tone, 'Boys, I really can't give it up.' "

Dylan Thomas

A STORY

If you can call it a story. There's no real beginning or end and there's very little in the middle. It is all about a day's outing, by charabanc, to Porthcawl, which, of course, the charabanc never reached, and it happened when I was so high and much nicer.

I was staying at the time with my uncle and his wife. Although she was my aunt, I never thought of her as anything but the wife of my uncle, partly because he was so big and trumpeting and red-hairy and used to fill every inch of the hot little house like an old buffalo squeezed into an airing cupboard, and partly because she was so small and silk and quick and made no noise at all as she whisked about on padded paws, dusting the china dogs, feeding the buffalo, setting the mouse-traps that never caught her; and once she sleaked out of the room, to squeak in a nook or nibble in the hayloft, you forgot she had ever been there.

But there he was, always, a steaming hulk of an uncle, his braces straining like hawsers, crammed behind the counter of the tiny shop at the front of the house, and breathing like a brass band; or guzzling and blustery in the kitchen over his gutsy supper, too big for everything except the great black boats of his boots. As he ate, the house grew smaller; he billowed out over the furniture, the loud check meadow of his waistcoat littered, as though after a picnic, with cigarette ends, peelings, cabbage stalks, birds' bones, gravy; and the forest fire of his hair crackled among the hooked hams from the ceiling. She was so small she could hit him only if she stood on a chair; and every Saturday night at half-past ten he would lift her up, under his arm, onto a chair in the kitchen so that she could hit him on the head with whatever was handy, which was always a china dog. On Sundays, and when pickled, he sang high tenor, and had won many cups.

The first I heard of the annual outing was when I was sitting one evening on a bag of rice behind the counter, under one of my uncle's stomachs, reading an advertisement for sheep-dip, which was all there was to read. The shop was full of my uncle, and when Mr. Benjamin Franklyn, Mr. Weazley, Noah Bowen, and Will Sentry came in, I thought it would burst. It was like all being together in a drawer that smelled of cheese and turps, and twist tobacco and sweet biscuits and snuff and waistcoat. Mr. Benjamin Franklyn said that he had collected enough money for the charabanc and twenty cases of pale ale and a pound apiece over that he would distribute among the members of the outing when they first stopped for refreshment, and he was about sick and tired, he said, of being followed by Will Sentry.

"All day long, wherever I go," he said, "he's after me like a collie with one eye. I got a shadow of my own *and* a dog. I don't need no Tom, Dick or Harry pursuing me with his dirty muffler on."

Will Sentry blushed, and said, "It's only oily. I got a bicycle."

"A man has no privacy at all," Mr. Franklyn went on. "I tell you he sticks so close I'm afraid to go out the back in case I sit in his lap. It's a wonder to me," he said, "he don't follow me into bed at night."

"Wife won't let," Will Sentry said.

And that started Mr. Franklyn off again, and they tried to soothe him down by saying, "Don't you mind Will Sentry." "No harm in old Will." "He's only keeping an eye on the money, Benjie."

"Aren't I honest?" asked Mr. Franklyn in surprise. There was no answer for some time; then Noah Bowen said, "You know what the committee is. Ever since Bob the Fiddle they don't feel safe with a new treasurer."

"Do you think *I'm* going to drink the outing funds, like Bob the Fiddle did?" said Mr. Franklyn.

"You *might,*" said my uncle, slowly.

"I resign," said Mr. Franklyn.

"Not with our money you won't," Will Sentry said.

"Who put the dynamite in the salmon pool?" said Mr. Weazley, but nobody took any notice of him. And, after a time, they all began to play cards in the thickening dusk of the hot, cheesy shop, and my uncle blew and bugled whenever he won, and Mr. Weazley grumbled like a dredger, and I fell to sleep on the gravy-scented mountain meadow of uncle's waistcoat.

On Sunday evening, after Bethesda, Mr. Franklyn walked into the kitchen where my uncle and I were eating sardines from the tin with spoons because it was Sunday and his wife would not let us play draughts. She was somewhere in the kitchen, too. Perhaps she was inside the grandmother clock, hanging from the weights and breathing. Then, a second later, the door opened again and Will Sentry edged into the room, twiddling his hard, round hat. He and Mr. Franklyn sat down on the settee, stiff and mothballed and black in their chapel and funeral suits.

"I brought the list," said Mr. Franklyn. "Every member fully paid. You ask Will Sentry."

My uncle put on his spectacles, wiped his whiskery mouth with a handkerchief big as a Union Jack, laid down his spoon of sardines, took Mr. Franklyn's list of names, removed the spectacles so that he could read, and then ticked the names off one by one.

"Enoch Davies. Aye. He's good with his fists. You never know. Little Gerwain. Very melodious bass. Mr. Cadwalladwr. That's right. He can tell opening time better than my watch. Mr. Weazley. Of course. He's been to Paris. Pity he suffers so much in the chara-banc. Stopped us nine times last year between the Beehive and the Red Dragon. Noah Bowen. Ah, very peaceable. He's got a tongue like a turtledove. Never a argument with Noah Bowen. Jenkins Loughor. Keep him off economics. It cost us a plateglass window. And ten pints for the Sergeant. Mr. Jervis. Very tidy."

"He tried to put a pig in the charra," Will Sentry said.

"Live and let live," said my uncle.

Will Sentry blushed.

"Sinbad the Sailor's Arms. Got to keep in with him. Old O. Jones."

"Why old O. Jones?" said Will Sentry.

"Old O. Jones always goes," said my uncle.

I looked down at the kitchen table. The tin of sardines was gone. By gee, I said to myself, Uncle's wife is quick as a flash.

"Cuthbert Johnny Fortnight. Now there's a card," said my uncle.

"He whistles after women," Will Sentry said.

"So do you," said Mr. Benjamin Franklyn, "in your mind."

My uncle at last approved the whole list, pausing only to say, when he came across one name, "If we weren't a Christian community, we'd chuck that Bob the Fiddle in the sea."

"We can do that in Porthcawl," said Mr. Franklyn, and soon after that he went, Will Sentry no more than an inch behind him, their Sundaybright boots squeaking on the kitchen cobbles.

And then, suddenly, there was my uncle's wife standing in front of the dresser, with a china dog in one hand. By gee, I said to myself again, did you ever see such a woman, if that's what she is.

The lamps were not lit yet in the kitchen and she stood in a wood of shadows, with the plates on the dresser behind her shining—like pink and white eyes.

"If you go on that outing on Saturday, Mr. Thomas," she said to my uncle in her small, silk voice, "I'm going home to my mother's."

Holy Mo, I thought, she's got a mother. Now that's one old bald mouse of a hundred and five I won't be wanting to meet in a dark lane.

"It's me or the outing, Mr. Thomas."

I would have made my choice at once, but it was almost half a minute before my uncle said, "Well, then, Sarah, it's the outing, my love." He lifted her up, under his arm, onto a chair in the kitchen, and she hit him on the head with the china dog. Then he lifted her down again, and then I said good night.

For the rest of the week my uncle's wife whisked quiet and quick round the house with her darting duster, my uncle blew and bugled and swole, and I kept myself busy all the time being up to no good. And then at breakfast time on Saturday morning, the morning of the outing, I found a note on the kitchen table. It said, "There's some eggs in the pantry. Take your boots off before you go to bed." My uncle's wife had gone, as quick as a flash.

When my uncle saw the note, he tugged out the flag of his handkerchief and blew such a hubbub of trumpets that the plates on the dresser shook. "It's the same every year," he said. And then he looked at me. "But this year it's different. *You'll* have to come on the outing, too, and what the members will say I dare not think."

The charabanc drew up outside, and when the members of the outing saw my uncle and me squeeze out of the shop together, both of us catlicked and brushed in our Sunday best, they snarled like a zoo.

"Are you bringing a *boy?*" asked Mr. Benjamin Franklyn as we climbed into the charabanc. He looked at me with horror.

"Boys is nasty," said Mr. Weazley.

"He hasn't paid his contributions," Will Sentry said.

"No room for boys. Boys get sick in charabancs."

"So do you, Enoch Davies," said my uncle.

"Might as well bring *women.*"

The way they said it, women were worse than boys.

"Better than bringing grandfathers."

"Grandfathers is nasty, too," said Mr. Weazley.

"What can we do with him when we stop for refreshments?"

"I'm a grandfather," said Mr. Weazley.

"Twenty-six minutes to opening time," shouted an old man in a panama hat, not looking at a watch. They forgot me at once.

"Good old Mr. Cadwalladwr," they cried, and the charabanc started off down the village street.

A few cold women stood at their doorways, grimly watching us go. A very small boy waved goodbye, and his mother boxed his ears. It was a beautiful August morning.

We were out of the village, and over the bridge, and up the hill toward Steeplehat Wood when Mr. Franklyn, with his list of names in his hand, called out loud, "Where's old O. Jones?"

"Where's old O.?"

"We've left old O. behind."

"Can't go without old O."

And though Mr. Weazley hissed all the way, we turned and drove back to the village, where, outside the Prince of Wales, old O. Jones was waiting patiently and alone with a canvas bag.

"I didn't want to come at all," old O. Jones said as they hoisted him on a seat and stuck a bottle in his hand, "but I always go." And over the bridge and up the hill and under the deep green wood and along the dusty road we wove, slow cows and ducks flying by, until "Stop the bus!" Mr. Weazley cried, "I left my teeth on the mantelpiece."

"Never you mind," they said, "you're not going to bite nobody," and they gave him a bottle with a straw.

"I might want to smile," he said.

"Not you," they said.

"What's the time, Mr. Cadwalladwr?"

"Twelve minutes to go" shouted back the old man in the panama, and they all began to curse him.

The charabanc pulled up outside the Mountain Sheep, a small, unhappy public house with a thatched roof like a wig with ringworm. From a flagpole by the Gents fluttered the flag of Siam. I knew it was the flag of Siam because of cigarette cards. The landlord stood at the door to welcome us, simpering like a wolf. He was a long, lean, blackfanged man with a greased love-curl and pouncing eyes. "What a beautiful August day!" he said, and touched his love-curl with a claw. That was the way he must have welcomed the Mountain Sheep before he ate it, I said to myself. The members rushed out, bleating, and into the bar.

"You keep an eye on the charra," my uncle said, "see nobody steals it now."

"There's nobody to steal it," I said, "except some cows," but my uncle was gustily blowing his bugle in the bar. I looked at the cows opposite, and they looked at me. There was nothing else for us to do. Forty-five minutes passed, like a very slow cloud. The sun shone on the lonely road, the lost, unwanted boy, and the lake-eyed cows. In the dark bar they were so happy they were breaking glasses. A Shoni-Onion Breton man, with a beret and a necklace of onions, bicycled down the road and stopped at the door.

"Quelle un grand matin, monsieur," I said.

"There's French, boy bach!" he said.

I followed him down the passage, and peered into the bar. I could hardly recognize the members of the outing. They had all changed color. Beetroot, rhubarb and puce, they hollered and rollicked in that dark, damp hole like enormous ancient bad boys, and my uncle surged in the middle, all red whiskers and bellies. On the floor was broken glass and Mr. Weazley.

"Drinks all round," cried Bob the Fiddle, a small, absconding man with bright blue eyes and a plump smile.

"Who's been robbing the orphans?"

"Who sold his little babby to the gyppoes?"

"Trust old Bob, he'll let you down."

"You will have your little joke," said Bob the Fiddle, smiling like a razor, "but I forgive you, boys."

Out of the fug and babel I heard: "Where's old O. Jones?" "Where are you, old O.?" "He's in the kitchen cooking his dinner." "He never forgets his dinner time." "Good old O. Jones." "Come out and fight." "No, not now, later." "No, now when I'm in a temper." "Look at Will Sentry, he's proper snobbled." "Look at his willful feet." "Look at Mr. Weazley lording it on the floor."

Mr. Weazley got up, hissing like a gander. "That boy pushed me down deliberate," he said, pointing to me at the door, and I slunk away down the passage and out to the mild, good cows.

Time clouded over, the cows wondered, I threw a stone at them and they wandered, wondering, away. Then out blew my uncle, ballooning, and one by one the members lumbered after him in a grizzle. They had drunk the Mountain Sheep dry. Mr. Weazley had won a string of onions that the Shoni-Onion man had raffled in the bar.

"What's the good of onions if you left your teeth on the mantelpiece?" he said. And when I looked through the back window of the thundering charabanc, I saw the pub grow smaller in the distance. And the flag of Siam, from the flagpole by the Gents, fluttered now at half mast.

The Blue Bull, the Dragon, the Star of Wales, the Twll in the Wall, the Sour Grapes, the Shepherd's Arms, the Bells of Aberdovey: I had nothing to do in the whole wild August world but remember the names where the outing stopped and keep an eye on the charabanc. And whenever it passed a public house, Mr. Weazley would cough like a billy goat and cry, "Stop the bus, I'm dying of breath." And back we would all have to go.

Closing time meant nothing to the members of that outing. Behind locked doors, they hymned and rumpused all the beautiful afternoon. And, when a policeman entered the Druid's Tap by the back door, and found them all choral with beer, "Sssh!" said Noah Bowen, "the pub is shut."

"Where do you come from?" he said in his buttoned, blue voice.

They told him.

"I got a auntie there," the policeman said. And very soon he was singing "Asleep in the Deep."

Off we drove again at last, the charabanc bouncing with tenors and flagons, and came to a river that rushed along among willows.

"Water!" they shouted.

"Porthcawl!" sang my uncle.

"Where's the donkeys?" said Mr. Weazley.

And out they lurched, to paddle and whoop in the cool, white, winding water. Mr. Franklyn, trying to polka on the slippery stones, fell in twice. "Nothing is simple," he said with dignity as he oozed up the bank.

"It's cold!" they cried.

"It's lovely!"

"It's smooth as a moth's nose!"

"It's *better* than Porthcawl!"

And dusk came down warm and gentle on thirty wild, wet, pickled, splashing men without a care in the world at the end of the world in the west of Wales. And, "Who goes there?" called Will Sentry to a wild duck flying.

They stopped at the Hermit's Nest for a rum to keep out the

cold. "I played for Aberavon in 1898," said a stranger to Enoch Davies.

"Liar," said Enoch Davies.

"I can show the photos," said the stranger.

"Forged," said Enoch Davies.

"And I'll show you my cap at home."

"Stolen."

"I got friends to prove it," the stranger said in a fury.

"Bribed," said Enoch Davies.

On the way home, through the simmering moonsplashed dark, old O. Jones began to cook his supper on a primus stove in the middle of the charabanc. Mr. Weazley coughed himself blue in the smoke. "Stop the bus!" he cried, "I'm dying of breath." We all climbed down into the moonlight. There was not a public house in sight. So they carried out the remaining cases, and the primus stove, and old O. Jones himself, and took them into a field, and sat down in a circle in the field and drank and sang while old O. Jones cooked sausage and mash and the moon flew above us. And there I drifted to sleep against my uncle's mountainous waistcoat, and, as I slept, "Who goes there?" called out Will Sentry to the flying moon.

QUESTIONS

1 Vocabulary: *charabanc:* a sightseeing bus. *airing cupboard:* a cooler or storage area for food. *turps:* turpentine. *Bethesda:* chapel. "*Quelle un grand matin, monsieur*": What a great morning, sir. *bach:* bachelor. *fug:* stuffiness. *in a grizzle:* grumbling.

2 The story's first two sentences could be misleading. Does the narrator really doubt that this is a story? Can you discover a conflict, complications, a resolution, and a revelation—in short, a plot?

3 The narrator, as an adult, tells about an experience he had as a boy. What comment is Thomas making about adults when he has his narrator say "it happened when I was so high and much nicer"? Is this ironic?

4 Who is the most important adult character in the story? Does he have some of the qualities of a legendary figure? What are they? Is he a symbol? If so, of what? Are the other male adults in some sense a projection of this principal character?

5 The narrator speaks figuratively of his uncle as "an old buffalo squeezed into an airing cupboard." Find other examples of figurative language. Does this language suit the action in this story?

6 Find examples of ironic overstatement. Do they suit the action of the story?

7 Find examples of musical devices, such as alliteration, rhyme, cacophony, euphony. Does this language suit the action of the story?

8 Find examples of highly connotative words, or words with unusual denotations such as "sleaked," which seems to be made up from "sneaked" and "slid." Do these words suit the action of the story?

9 What proportion of the story is told in the scenic method? in summary method? Is this ratio appropriate here?

10 Does the narrator's tone, through the techniques noted above, come across as essentially positive and rollicking, or balanced and neutral, or negative and unhappy? Might this tonal effect imply the *author's* attitude toward the events?

11 Is the narrator's attitude at the end the same as at the beginning? Does the story's technique affect your answer?

12 If, as we have said, a story's theme is the attitude the author expresses in his story, and if he makes no explicit thesis sentence, the "attitude" emerges from the story's technique. Based on the tone of the story, state Thomas' attitude toward wives and husbands and freedom.

13 Themes add to our understanding of life, but most authors (unlike Tolstoy in the previous story) let us build our own rules of conduct. What is your attitude toward the uncle and his friends? toward the aunt? toward male outings in general? Has the story in any way altered your attitude toward such things?

14 Tolstoy makes his own attitude explicit by his title, by the old woman's final statement, and by his thesis statement at the end. Thomas chooses to let his readers infer his attitude from the experience he recounts. Do you prefer one method to the other? If you have a preference, defend your answer by reference to the specific techniques each author uses. If you have no preference, indicate the extent to which each author's technique seems to suit the attitude he reveals.

12
TECHNIQUE

It is usually easy to decide *whether* you think a story is good, but it is often not so easy to explain *why* you think so. Sometimes special reasons affect your opinion. Certain subjects may be inherently boring or repugnant to you, while other subjects may be far more interesting to you than to other readers because of something you have experienced. But the more you can develop an interest in fiction, not for special but for general reasons, the wider your horizons will be. Since appreciation depends on knowledge, the reader who understands the elements of prose fiction will greatly extend the range of stories he can enjoy or admire. Moreover, he will have a better chance of deciding *whether* he thinks a story is good and understanding *why.* For the difference between good fiction and bad may be determined by analyzing the author's technique—how well he has made the "artificial" aspects of fiction work in his story. Some great fiction, created by minds of rare quality, departs from standard techniques. Happily, exceptions will always exist to any "rules" that attempt to constrict a creation of the mind. But these exceptions are few, and their discovery is usually a reward of careful analysis. We can safely assume that analysis of technique will lead to a valid judgment of the literary worth of most stories.

The purpose of this chapter is to help you sharpen your developing powers of analysis by inviting you to decide which of the next two stories you think is better—and why. Preceding the stories is a summary list of questions on the techniques of fiction that may be asked about these two stories, or about any work of fiction. To people not skilled in literary criticism this list may seem formidable indeed, for to answer any one of these questions thoughtfully is a considerable undertaking. And to answer all the questions about any one story would be not only exhaustive but exhausting. Yet, when the skilled literary critic approaches a work of fiction, he must first consider all the questions. Then he quickly sifts out those questions that his experience tells him will not be fruitful for that particular story, and he answers the rest with painstaking thoroughness.

Of course there is no guarantee that any single question will lead to an important understanding. But if each of a group of readers—skilled or not—answers one or two questions, their cumulative insights and discoveries can sometimes match in quality as well as quantity the single effort of an experienced literary critic.

In the list below the figures in parentheses refer to the chapters in which the elements of fiction covered by a particular question are explained.

Questions for the Analysis of Fiction

1. What does the title of the story denote? What does it connote? Is it ambiguous? Is it ironic? Does it contain an allusion, and if so, what does its source suggest? (2, 4, 5)
2. In the author's selection of words, what use does he make of careful denotation, deliberate ambiguity, or evocative connotation? Does he employ musical devices such as rhythm and repetition for specific effect? For a given passage, does this effect support the passage's topic or ironically set up a tension contrary to it? (2, 5)
3. After listing the separate images in the story, can you discover relationships among some of these images that strongly suggest a pattern or several different patterns? Do any of these clusters of related images point to the story's theme? (3)
4. Can you explain the story's allusions? What contribution do they make to the story's effect? Is figurative language used? Why did the author use the figurative imagery and details

that he chose? How do they relate to a principal character, to the story's action, to its theme, or to a combination of these? Are clichés employed for ironic effect? (4)

5. Is irony of situation present in the story? Is irony of style present? Does dramatic irony appear? If more than one type of irony is used, does the author use these types in an evenly balanced way, or does he emphasize one type more than the others? To what purpose does the author employ overstatement, understatement, opposite statement? If the story is humorous, what irony or set of ironies underlies the humor? (5)

6. Does the author make deliberate use of literary symbolism? Can otherwise obscure aspects of the story be explained through symbolic interpretation? Does the story employ allegory or personification? (6)

7. Is there a predominance of either nouns or verbs? Is the story's effect primarily a visual one carried by nouns, a fluid one carried by verbs, or a combination? Are *certain* parts of the story dominated by nouns or by verbs? What is the story's principal conflict or set of conflicts? What values are opposed in this conflict? What events or details contribute to the story's complication? What is its revelation? To whom does the revelation come—to any character? to the reader only? What needs to be remembered and what needs to be anticipated for the plot to be intelligible? (7)

8. Is the story told primarily in summary or scenic method? Approximately what percentage of the story is devoted to each? What is the story's most important moment? Is this rendered in summary or scenic method? Does pace of language contribute to the story's effect? Why did the author pace his story as he did? (8)

9. Which part of the story is dramatized for public view? Which characters have their private worlds revealed to the reader? Does the mind of the narrator, as distinct from the other characters, enter into the story? Why did the writer choose this particular mixture of public and private impression? (9)

10. Is the point of view of the story revealed by a first- or third-person narrator? Does the point of view emphasize recalled

action or continuing experience? Is the narrator limited or omniscient? Is the point of view consistent throughout? Why did the author choose this point of view, or this particular combination? Can you discern the presence of dramatic distance? If so, why did the author employ dramatic distance? (10)

11. Does the story have an explicitly stated thesis? If so, what is it? Does the story have an implicit theme? If it does, what is that theme, stated as a full sentence? How do all the various elements used in the story contribute to the revelation of the theme? (11)

Read both of the stories, then turn to the questions that appear after the second one.

Samuel Clemens

LUCK

It was at a banquet in London in honor of one of the two or three conspicuously illustrious English military names of this generation. For reasons which will presently appear, I will withhold his real name and titles and call him Lieutenant-General Lord Arthur Scoresby, Y.C., K.C.B., etc, etc, etc. What a fascination there is in a renowned name! There sat the man, in actual flesh, whom I had heard of so many thousands of times since that day, thirty years before, when his name shot suddenly to the zenith from a Crimean battlefield, to remain forever celebrated. It was food and drink to me to look, and look, and look at that demigod; scanning, searching, noting: the quietness, the reserve, the noble gravity of his countenance; the simple honesty that expressed itself all over him; the sweet unconsciousness of his greatness—unconsciousness of the hundreds of admiring eyes fastened upon him, unconsciousness of the deep, loving, sincere worship welling out of the breasts of those people and flowing toward him.

The clergyman at my left was an old acquaintance of mine—clergyman now, but had spent the first half of his life in the camp and field and as an instructor in the military school at Woolwich. Just at the moment I have been talking about a veiled and singular light glimmered in his eyes and he leaned down and muttered confidentially to me—indicating the hero of the banquet with a gesture:

"Privately—he's an absolute fool."

This verdict was a great surprise to me. If its subject had been Napoleon, or Socrates, or Solomon, my astonishment could not have been greater. Two things I was well aware of: that the Reverend was a man of strict veracity and that his judgment of men was good. Therefore I knew, beyond doubt or question, that the world was mistaken about this hero: he *was* a fool. So I meant to find out, at a convenient moment, how the Reverend, all solitary and alone, had discovered the secret.

Some days later the opportunity came, and this is what the Reverend told me:

About forty years ago I was an instructor in the military academy at Woolwich. I was present in one of the sections when young Scoresby underwent his preliminary examination. I was touched to the quick with pity, for the rest of the class answered up brightly and handsomely, while he—why, dear me, he didn't know anything, so to speak. He was evidently good, and sweet, and lovable, and guileless; and so it was exceedingly painful to see him stand there, as serene as a graven image, and deliver himself of answers which were verily miraculous for stupidity and ignorance. All the compassion in me was aroused in his behalf. I said to myself, when he comes to be examined again he will be flung over, of course; so it will be simply a harmless act of charity to ease his fall as much as I can. I took him aside and found that he knew a little of Caesar's history; and as he didn't know anything else, I went to work and drilled him like a galley-slave on a certain line of stock questions concerning Caesar which I knew would be used. If you'll believe me, he went through with flying colors on examination day! He went through on that purely superficial "cram," and got compliments too, while others, who knew a thousand times more than he, got plucked. By some strangely lucky accident—an accident not likely to happen twice in a century—he was asked no question outside of the narrow limits of his drill.

It was stupefying. Well, all through his course I stood by him, with something of the sentiment which a mother feels for a crippled child; and he always saved himself, just by miracle apparently.

Now, of course, the thing that would expose him and kill him at last was mathematics. I resolved to make his death as easy as I could; so I drilled him and crammed him, and crammed him and drilled him, just on the line of questions which the examiners would be most likely to use, and then launched him on his fate. Well, sir, try to conceive of the result: to my consternation, he took the first prize! And with it he got a perfect ovation in the way of compliments.

Sleep? There was no more sleep for me for a week. My conscience tortured me day and night. What I had done I had done purely through charity, and only to ease the poor youth's fall. I never had dreamed of any such preposterous results as the thing that had happened. I felt as guilty and miserable as Frankenstein. Here was a wooden-head whom I had put in the way of glittering promotions and prodigious responsibilities, and but one thing could happen: he and his responsibilities would all go to ruin together at the first opportunity.

The Crimean War had just broken out. Of course there had to be a war, I say to myself. We could have peace and give this donkey a chance to die before he is found out. I waited for the earthquake. It came. And it made me reel when it did come. He was actually gazetted to a captaincy in a marching regiment! Better men grow old and gray in the service before they climb to a sublimity like that. And who could ever have foreseen that they would go and put such a load of responsibility on such green and inadequate shoulders? I could just barely have stood it if they had made him a cornet; but a captain—think of it! I thought my hair would turn white.

Consider what I did—I who so loved repose and inaction. I said to myself, I am responsible to the country for this, and I must go along with him and protect the country against him as far as I can. So I took my poor little capital and went with a sigh and bought a cornetcy in his regiment, and away we went to the field.

And there—oh, dear, it was awful. Blunders?—why, he never did anything *but* blunder. But, you see, nobody was in the fellow's secret. Everybody had him focused wrong, and necessarily misinterpreted his performance every time. Consequently they took his idiotic blunders for inspirations of genius. They did, honestly! His mildest blunders were enough to make a man in his right mind cry;

and they did make me cry—and rage and rave, too, privately. And the thing that kept me always in a sweat of apprehension was the fact that every fresh blunder he made always increased the luster of his reputation! I kept saying to myself, he'll get so high that when discovery does finally come it will be like the sun falling out of the sky.

He went right along up, from grade to grade, over the dead bodies of his superiors, until at last, in the hottest moment of the battle of —— down went our colonel, and my heart jumped into my mouth, for Scoresby was next in rank! Now for it, said I; we'll all land in Sheol in ten minutes, sure.

The battle was awfully hot; the allies were steadily giving way all over the field. Our regiment occupied a position that was vital; a blunder now must be destruction. At this crucial moment, what does this immortal fool do but detach the regiment from its place and order a charge over a neighboring hill where there wasn't a suggestion of an enemy! "There you go!" I said to myself; "this *is* the end at last."

And away we did go, and were over the shoulder of the hill before the insane movement could be discovered and stopped. And what did we find? An entire and unsuspected Russian army in reserve! And what happened? We were eaten up? That is necessarily what would have happened in ninety-nine cases out of a hundred. But no; those Russians argued that no single regiment would come browsing around there at such a time. It must be the entire English army, and that the sly Russian game was detected and blocked; so they turned tail, and away they went, pell-mell, over the hill and down into the field, in wild confusion, and we after them; they themselves broke the solid Russian center in the field, and tore through, and in no time there was the most tremendous rout you ever saw, and the defeat of the allies was turned into a sweeping and splendid victory! Marshal Canrobert looked on, dizzy with astonishment, admiration, and delight; and sent right off for Scoresby, and hugged him, and decorated him on the field in presence of all the armies!

And what was Scoresby's blunder that time? Merely the mistaking his right hand for his left—that was all. An order had come to him to fall back and support our right; and instead, he fell *forward* and went over the hill to the left. But the name he won that day as a marvelous military genius filled the world with his glory, and that glory will never fade while history books last.

He is just as good and sweet and lovable and unpretending as a man can be, but he doesn't know enough to come in when it rains. Now that is absolutely true. He is the supremest ass in the universe; and until half an hour ago nobody knew it but himself and me. He has been pursued, day by day and year by year, by a most phenomenal and astonishing luckiness. He has been a shining soldier in all our wars for a generation; he has littered his whole military life with blunders, and yet has never committed one that didn't make him a knight or a baronet or a lord or something. Look at his breast; why, he is just clothed in domestic and foreign decorations. Well, sir, every one of them is the record of some shouting stupidity or other; and, taken together, they are proof that the very best thing in all this world that can befall a man is to be born lucky. I say again, as I said at the banquet, Scoresby's an absolute fool.

Frank O'Connor

MY OEDIPUS COMPLEX

Father was in the army all through the war—the first war, I mean—so, up to the age of five, I never saw much of him, and what I saw did not worry me. Sometimes I woke and there was a big figure in khaki peering down at me in the candlelight. Sometimes in the early morning I heard the slamming of the front door and the clatter of nailed boots down the cobbles of the lane. These were Father's entrances and exits. Like Santa Claus he came and went mysteriously.

In fact, I rather liked his visits, though it was an uncomfortable squeeze between Mother and him when I got into the big bed in the early morning. He smoked, which gave him a pleasant musty smell, and shaved, an operation of astounding interest. Each time he left a trail of souvenirs—model tanks and Gurkha knives with handles made of bullet cases, and German helmets and cap badges and button-sticks, and all sorts of military equipment—carefully stowed away in a long box on top of the wardrobe, in case they ever came in handy. There was a bit of the magpie about Father; he expected everything to come in handy. When his back was turned, Mother let me get a chair and rummage through his treasures. She didn't seem to think so highly of them as he did.

The war was the most peaceful period of my life. The window of my attic faced southeast. My mother had curtained it, but that had small effect. I always woke with the first light and, with all the responsibilities of the previous day melted, feeling myself rather like the sun, ready to illumine and rejoice. Life never seemed so simple and clear and full of possibilities as then. I put my feet out from under the clothes—I called them Mrs. Left and Mrs. Right—and invented dramatic situations for them in which they discussed the problems of the day. At least Mrs. Right did; she was very demonstrative, but I hadn't the same control of Mrs. Left, so she mostly contented herself with nodding agreement.

They discussed what Mother and I should do during the day, what Santa Claus should give a fellow for Christmas, and what steps should be taken to brighten the home. There was that little matter of the baby, for instance. Mother and I could never agree about that. Ours was the only house in the terrace without a new baby, and Mother said we couldn't afford one till Father came back from the war because they cost seventeen and six. That showed how simple she was. The Geneys up the road had a baby, and everyone knew they couldn't afford seventeen and six. It was probably a cheap baby, and Mother wanted something really good, but I felt she was too exclusive. The Geneys' baby would have done us fine.

Having settled my plans for the day, I got up, put a chair under the attic window, and lifted the frame high enough to stick out my head. The window overlooked the front gardens of the terrace behind ours, and beyond these it looked over a deep valley to the tall, red-brick houses terraced up the opposite hillside, which were all still in shadow, while those at our side of the valley were all lit up, though with long strange shadows that made them seem unfamiliar; rigid and painted.

After that I went into Mother's room and climbed into the big bed. She woke and I began to tell her of my schemes. By this time, though I never seem to have noticed it, I was petrified in my nightshirt, and I thawed as I talked until, the last frost melted, I fell asleep beside her and woke again only when I heard her below in the kitchen, making the breakfast.

After breakfast we went into town; heard Mass at St. Augustine's and said a prayer for Father, and did the shopping. If the afternoon was fine we either went for a walk in the country or a visit to Mother's great friend in the convent, Mother St. Dominic. Mother had them all praying for Father, and every night, going to bed, I asked God to send him back safe from the war to us. Little, indeed, did I know what I was praying for!

One morning, I got into the big bed, and there, sure enough, was Father in his usual Santa Claus manner, but later, instead of uniform, he put on his best blue suit, and Mother was as pleased as anything. I saw nothing to be pleased about, because, out of uniform, Father was altogether less interesting, but she only beamed, and explained that our prayers had been answered, and off we went to Mass to thank God for having brought Father safely home.

The irony of it! That very day when he came in to dinner he took off his boots and put on his slippers, donned the dirty old cap he wore about the house to save him from colds, crossed his legs, and began to talk gravely to Mother, who looked anxious. Naturally, I disliked her looking anxious, because it destroyed her good looks, so I interrupted him.

"Just a moment, Larry!" she said gently.

This was only what she said when we had boring visitors, so I attached no importance to it and went on talking.

"Do be quiet, Larry!" she said impatiently. "Don't you hear me talking to Daddy?"

This was the first time I had heard those ominous words, "talking to Daddy," and I couldn't help feeling that if this was how God answered prayers, he couldn't listen to them very attentively.

"Why are you talking to Daddy?" I asked with as great a show of indifference as I could muster.

"Because Daddy and I have business to discuss. Now, don't interrupt again!"

In the afternoon, at Mother's request, Father took me for a walk. This time we went into town instead of out to the country, and I thought at first, in my usual optimistic way, that it might be an improvement. It was nothing of the sort. Father and I had quite different notions of a walk in town. He had no proper interest in trams, ships, and horses, and the only thing that seemed to divert him was talking to fellows as old as himself. When I wanted to stop he simply went on, dragging me behind him by the hand; when he wanted to stop I had no alternative but to do the same.

I noticed that it seemed to be a sign that he wanted to stop for a long time whenever he leaned against a wall. The second time I saw him do it I got wild. He seemed to be settling himself forever. I pulled him by the coat and trousers, but, unlike Mother who, if you were too persistent, got into a wax and said: "Larry, if you don't behave yourself, I'll give you a good slap," Father had an extraordinary capacity for amiable inattention. I sized him up and wondered would I cry, but he seemed to be too remote to be annoyed even by that. Really, it was like going for a walk with a mountain! He either ignored the wrenching and pummeling entirely, or else glanced down with a grin of amusement from his peak. I had never met anyone so absorbed in himself as he seemed.

At teatime, "talking to Daddy" began again, complicated this time by the fact that he had an evening paper, and every few minutes he put it down and told Mother something new out of it. I felt this was foul play. Man for man, I was prepared to compete with him any time for Mother's attention, but when he had it all made up for him by other people it left me no chance. Several times I tried to change the subject without success.

"You must be quiet while Daddy is reading, Larry," Mother said impatiently.

It was clear that she either genuinely liked talking to Father better than talking to me, or else that he had some terrible hold on her which made her afraid to admit the truth.

"Mummy," I said that night when she was tucking me up, "do you think if I prayed hard God would send Daddy back to the war?"

She seemed to think about that for a moment.

"No, dear," she said with a smile. "I don't think he would."

"Why wouldn't he, Mummy?"

"Because there isn't a war any longer, dear."

"But, Mummy, couldn't God make another war, if he liked?"

"He wouldn't like to, dear. It's not God who makes wars, but bad people."

"Oh!" I said.

I was disappointed about that. I began to think that God wasn't quite what he was cracked up to be.

Next morning I woke at my usual hour, feeling like a bottle of champagne. I put out my feet and invented a long conversation in which Mrs. Right talked of the trouble she had with her own father till she put him in the Home. I didn't quite know what the

Home was but it sounded the right place for Father. Then I got my chair and stuck my head out of the attic window. Dawn was just breaking, with a guilty air that made me feel I had caught it in the act. My head bursting with stories and schemes, I stumbled in next door, and in the half-darkness scrambled into the big bed. There was no room at Mother's side so I had to get between her and Father. For the time being I had forgotten about him, and for several minutes I sat bolt upright, racking my brains to know what I could do with him. He was taking up more than his fair share of the bed, and I couldn't get comfortable, so I gave him several kicks that made him grunt and stretch. He made room all right, though. Mother waked and felt for me. I settled back comfortably in the warmth of the bed with my thumb in my mouth.

"Mummy!" I hummed, loudly and contentedly.

"Sssh! dear," she whispered. "Don't wake Daddy!"

This was a new development, which threatened to be even more serious than "talking to Daddy." Life without my early-morning conferences was unthinkable.

"Why?" I asked severely.

"Because poor Daddy is tired."

This seemed to me a quite inadequate reason, and I was sickened by the sentimentality of her "poor Daddy." I never liked that sort of gush; it always struck me as insincere.

"Oh!" I said lightly. Then in my most winning tone: "Do you know where I want to go with you today, Mummy?"

"No, dear," she sighed.

"I want to go down the Glen and fish for thornybacks with my new net, and then I want to go out to the Fox and Hounds, and—"

"Don't-wake-Daddy!" she hissed angrily, clapping her hand across my mouth.

But it was too late. He was awake, or nearly so. He grunted and reached for the matches. Then he stared incredulously at his watch.

"Like a cup of tea, dear?" asked Mother in a meek, hushed voice I had never heard her use before. It sounded almost as though she were afraid.

"Tea?" he exclaimed indignantly. "Do you know what the time is?"

"And after that I want to go up the Rathcooney Road," I said loudly, afraid I'd forget something in all those interruptions.

"Go to sleep at once, Larry!" she said sharply.

I began to snivel. I couldn't concentrate, the way that pair went on, and smothering my early-morning schemes was like burying a family from the cradle.

Father said nothing, but lit his pipe and sucked it, looking out into the shadows without minding Mother or me. I knew he was mad. Every time I made a remark Mother hushed me irritably. I was mortified. I felt it wasn't fair; there was even something sinister in it. Every time I had pointed out to her the waste of making two beds when we could both sleep in one, she had told me it was healthier like that, and now here was this man, this stranger, sleeping with her without the least regard for her health!

He got up early and made tea, but though he brought Mother a cup he brought none for me.

"Mummy," I shouted, "I want a cup of tea, too."

"Yes, dear," she said patiently. "You can drink from Mummy's saucer."

That settled it. Either Father or I would have to leave the house. I didn't want to drink from Mother's saucer; I wanted to be treated as an equal in my own home, so, just to spite her, I drank it all and left none for her. She took that quietly, too.

But that night when she was putting me to bed she said gently: "Larry, I want you to promise me something."

"What is it?" I asked.

"Not to come in and disturb poor Daddy in the morning. Promise?"

"Poor Daddy" again! I was becoming suspicious of everything involving that quite impossible man.

"Why?" I asked.

"Because poor Daddy is worried and tired and he doesn't sleep well."

"Why doesn't he, Mummy?"

"Well, you know, don't you, that while he was at the war Mummy got the pennies from the Post Office?"

"From Miss MacCarthy?"

"That's right. But now, you see, Miss MacCarthy hasn't any more pennies, so Daddy must go out and find us some. You know what would happen if he couldn't?"

"No," I said, "tell us."

"Well, I think we might have to go out and beg for them like the poor old woman on Fridays. We wouldn't like that, would we?"

"No," I agreed. "We wouldn't."

"So you'll promise not to come in and wake him?"

"Promise."

Mind you, I meant that. I knew pennies were a serious matter, and I was all against having to go out and beg like the old woman on Fridays. Mother laid out all my toys in a complete ring round the bed so that, whatever way I got out, I was bound to fall over one of them.

When I woke I remembered my promise all right. I got up and sat on the floor and played—for hours, it seemed to me. Then I got my chair and looked out the attic window for more hours. I wished it was time for Father to wake; I wished someone would make me a cup of tea. I didn't feel in the least like the sun; instead, I was bored and so very, very cold! I simply longed for the warmth and depth of the big featherbed.

At last I could stand it no longer. I went into the next room. As there was still no room at Mother's side I climbed over her and she woke with a start.

"Larry," she whispered, gripping my arm very tightly, "what did you promise?"

"But I did, Mummy," I wailed, caught in the very act. "I was quiet for ever so long."

"Oh, dear, and you're perished!" she said sadly, feeling me all over. "Now, if I let you stay will you promise not to talk?"

"But I want to talk, Mummy," I wailed.

"That has nothing to do with it," she said with a firmness that was new to me. "Daddy wants to sleep. Now, do you understand that?"

I understood it only too well. I wanted to talk, he wanted to sleep—whose house was it, anyway?

"Mummy," I said with equal firmness, "I think it would be healthier for Daddy to sleep in his own bed."

That seemed to stagger her, because she said nothing for a while.

"Now, once for all," she went on, "you're to be perfectly quiet or go back to your own bed. Which is it to be?"

The injustice of it got me down. I had convicted her out of her own mouth of inconsistency and unreasonableness, and she hadn't even attempted to reply. Full of spite, I gave Father a kick, which she didn't notice but which made him grunt and open his eyes in alarm.

"What time is it?" he asked in a panic-stricken voice, not looking at Mother but the door, as if he saw someone there.

"It's early yet," she replied soothingly. "It's only the child. Go to sleep again. . . . Now, Larry," she added, getting out of bed, "you've wakened Daddy and you must go back."

This time, for all her quiet air, I knew she meant it, and knew that my principal rights and privileges were as good as lost unless I asserted them at once. As she lifted me, I gave a screech, enough to wake the dead, not to mind Father. He groaned.

"That damn child! Doesn't he ever sleep?"

"It's only a habit, dear," she said quietly, though I could see she was vexed.

"Well, it's time he got out of it," shouted Father, beginning to heave in the bed. He suddenly gathered all the bedclothes about him, turned to the wall, and then looked back over his shoulder with nothing showing only two small, spiteful, dark eyes. The man looked very wicked.

To open the bedroom door, Mother had to let me down, and I broke free and dashed for the farthest corner, screeching. Father sat bolt upright in bed.

"Shut up, you little puppy!" he said in a choking voice.

I was so astonished that I stopped screeching. Never, never had anyone spoken to me in that tone before. I looked at him incredulously and saw his face convulsed with rage. It was only then that I fully realized how God had codded me, listening to my prayers for the safe return of this monster.

"Shut up, you!" I bawled, beside myself.

"What's that you said?" shouted Father, making a wild leap out of bed.

"Mick, Mick!" cried Mother. "Don't you see the child isn't used to you?"

"I see he's better fed than taught," snarled Father, waving his arms wildly. "He wants his bottom smacked."

All his previous shouting was as nothing to these obscene words referring to my person. They really made my blood boil.

"Smack your own!" I screamed hysterically. "Smack your own! Shut up! Shut up!"

At this he lost his patience and let fly at me. He did it with the lack of conviction you'd expect of a man under Mother's horrified eyes, and it ended up as a mere tap, but the sheer indignity of being struck at all by a stranger, a total stranger who had cajoled his way back from the war into our big bed as a result of my innocent intercession, made me completely dotty. I shrieked and shrieked, and danced in my bare feet, and Father, looking awkward and hairy in nothing but a short grey army shirt, glared down at me like a mountain out for murder. I think it must have been then that I realized he was jealous too. And there stood Mother in her nightdress, looking as if her heart was broken between us. I hoped she felt as she looked. It seemed to me that she deserved it all.

From that morning out my life was a hell. Father and I were enemies, open and avowed. We conducted a series of skirmishes against one another, he trying to steal my time with Mother and I his. When she was sitting on my bed, telling me a story, he took to looking for some pair of old boots which he alleged he had left behind him at the beginning of the war. While he talked to Mother I played loudly with my toys to show my total lack of concern. He created a terrible scene one evening when he came in from work and found me at his box, playing with his regimental badges, Gurkha knives and button-sticks. Mother got up and took the box from me.

"You mustn't play with Daddy's toys unless he lets you, Larry," she said severely. "Daddy doesn't play with yours."

For some reason Father looked at her as if she had struck him and then turned away with a scowl.

"Those are not toys," he growled, taking down the box again to see had I lifted anything. "Some of those curios are very rare and valuable."

But as time went on I saw more and more how he managed to alienate Mother and me. What made it worse was that I couldn't grasp his method or see what attraction he had for Mother. In every possible way he was less winning than I. He had a common accent and made noises at his tea. I thought for a while that it might be the newspapers she was interested in, so I made up bits of news of my own to read to her. Then I thought it might be the smoking, which I personally thought attractive, and took his pipes and went round the house dribbling into them till he caught me. I even made noises at my tea, but Mother only told me I was disgusting. It all seemed to hinge round that unhealthy habit of sleeping together, so I made a point of dropping into their bedroom and nosing round, talking to myself, so that they wouldn't know I was watching them, but they were never up to anything that I could see. In the end it beat me. It seemed to depend on being grown-up and giving people rings, and I realized I'd have to wait.

But at the same time I wanted him to see that I was only waiting, not giving up the fight. One evening when he was being particularly obnoxious, chattering away well above my head, I let him have it.

"Mummy," I said, "do you know what I'm going to do when I grow up?"

"No, dear," she replied. "What?"

"I'm going to marry you," I said quietly.

Father gave a great guffaw out of him, but he didn't take me in. I knew it must only be pretense. And Mother, in spite of everything, was pleased. I felt she was probably relieved to know that one day Father's hold on her would be broken.

"Won't that be nice?" she said with a smile.

"It'll be very nice," I said confidently. "Because we're going to have lots and lots of babies."

"That's right, dear," she said placidly. "I think we'll have one soon, and then you'll have plenty of company."

I was no end pleased about that because it showed that in spite of the way she gave in to Father she still considered my wishes. Besides, it would put the Geneys in their place.

It didn't turn out like that, though. To begin with, she was very preoccupied—I supposed about where she would get the seventeen and six—and though Father took to staying out late in the evenings it did me no particular good. She stopped taking me for walks, became as touchy as blazes, and smacked me for nothing at all. Sometimes I wished I'd never mentioned the confounded baby—I seemed to have a genius for bringing calamity on myself.

And calamity it was! Sonny arrived in the most appalling hullabaloo—even that much he couldn't do without a fuss—and from the first moment I disliked him. He was a difficult child—so far as I was concerned he was always difficult—and demanded far too much attention. Mother was simply silly about him, and couldn't see when he was only showing off. As company he was worse than useless. He slept all day, and I had to go round the house on tiptoe to avoid waking him. It wasn't any longer a question of not waking Father. The slogan now was "Don't-wake-Sonny!" I couldn't understand why the child wouldn't sleep at the proper time, so whenever Mother's back was turned I woke him. Sometimes to keep him awake I pinched him as well. Mother caught me at it one day and gave me a most unmerciful flaking.

One evening, when Father was coming in from work, I was playing trains in the front garden. I let on not to notice him; instead, I pretended to be talking to myself, and said in a loud voice: "If another bloody baby comes into this house, I'm going out."

Father stopped dead and looked at me over his shoulder.

"What's that you said?" he asked sternly.

"I was only talking to myself," I replied, trying to conceal my panic. "It's private."

He turned and went in without a word. Mind you, I intended it as a solemn warning, but its effect was quite different. Father started being quite nice to me. I could understand that, of course. Mother was quite sickening about Sonny. Even at mealtimes she'd get up and gawk at him in the cradle with an idiotic smile, and tell Father to do the same. He was always polite about it, but he looked so puzzled you could see he didn't know what she was talking about. He complained of the way Sonny cried at night, but she only got cross and said that Sonny never cried except when there was something up with him—which was a flaming lie, because Sonny never had anything up with him, and only cried for attention. It was really painful to see how simple-minded she was. Father wasn't attractive, but he had a fine intelligence. He saw through Sonny, and now he knew that I saw through him as well.

One night I woke with a start. There was someone beside me in the bed. For one wild moment I felt sure it must be Mother, having come to her senses and left Father for good, but then I heard Sonny in convulsions in the next room, and Mother saying: "There! There! There!" and I knew it wasn't she. It was Father. He was lying beside me, wide awake, breathing hard and apparently as mad as hell.

After a while it came to me what he was mad about. It was his turn now. After turning me out of the big bed, he had been turned out himself. Mother had no consideration now for anyone but that poisonous pup, Sonny. I couldn't help feeling sorry for Father. I had been through it all myself, and even at that age I was magnanimous. I began to stroke him down and say: "There! There!" He wasn't exactly responsive.

"Aren't you asleep either?" he snarled.

"Ah, come on and put your arm around us, can't you?" I said, and he did, in a sort of way. Gingerly, I suppose, is how you'd describe it. He was very bony but better than nothing.

At Christmas he went out of his way to buy me a really nice model railway.

QUESTIONS

1 Vocabulary for "Luck": *Y.C., K.C.B.:* abbreviations of British honorary titles. *Frankenstein:* the title character—in a novel by Mary W. Shelley—who created a monster that destroyed him. *gazetted:* announced in an official British publication listing military and other appointments. *cornet:* British cavalry officer of the lowest rank. *Sheol:* in the Old Testament, a place in the depths of the earth where the dead go.

Vocabulary for "My Oedipus Complex": *Gurkha:* one of a warlike people of Hindu faith living in the mountains of Nepal. *wax:* a fit of temper. *codded:* hoaxed or kidded. *flaking:* spanking; compare with *hiding, skinning. flaming:* a slang way of saying flagrant.

2 Using the "Questions for the Analysis of Fiction" presented in this chapter, compare Samuel Clemens' technique in "Luck" with that used by Frank O'Connor in "My Oedipus Complex." Which story do you find richer in the variety of elements used? What references from the two stories can you cite to support your judgment?

3 Which story do you think affords the deeper insight into human behavior? Is this the story with the more complex technique?

4 Which story did you like more? Why? Was your choice a result of personal reasons or of objective reasons of artistry? If it was for personal reasons, state precisely what experiences in your life led you to this special preference. If it was for objective reasons of artistry, support your choice with specific references from the story you prefer.

13 VISION

Throughout these chapters we have said that literature is distinguished from nonliterature because its words must carry a greater burden of meaning, and in so doing, give a richer reward to the reader. The poet Ezra Pound said, "Great literature is simply language charged with meaning to the utmost possible degree." To this we should add the observation of the American philosopher William James who said, "The difference between first- and second-best things in art absolutely seems to escape verbal definition—it is a matter of a hair, a shade, an inward quiver of some kind—yet what miles away."

These miles of difference that separate great fiction from the near great do seem to elude definition, but they are deeply felt. Despite his reservations, James did catch this feeling when he spoke of "an inward quiver of some kind." Pound, too, caught this feeling when he spoke of "language *charged* with meaning." Both James's "inward quiver" and Pound's "charged" refer to the emotional pressure that great fiction exerts and to the intensity of our response to this pressure.

This emotional pressure seems to be more than a matter of technique. It is technique used to reveal a clear *vision* of what it means to be human. To writers possessing such a vision we surrender our feelings. Their generosity of spirit calls forth a like response from us. Moreover, this vision transcends the technique that gives it expression. For example, one may find faults in William Faulkner's experimental technique, yet he is regarded as a great American author, in part because of his deep and enduring faith in the ability of man to survive, and to survive with dignity, under the most difficult and trying circumstances. It is this faith that receives such moving expression in "Barn Burning," reprinted in Part Two of this book. Even when an author's technique appears to be flawless, it is his moral vision that invests it with greatness. For example, behind the consummate style for which Ernest Hemingway has become celebrated, lies an intensity that tells his readers he was aware of the brutally complicated decisions that life poses for most men. His stories, like "A Clean, Well-Lighted Place," show men facing these decisions with silent dignity and accepting defeat with unconscious grace.

Like all great art, the best prose fiction acknowledges how complex the human condition is. It suggests that even in defeat, man can assert a victory. The very act of writing demonstrates the author's belief in the importance of human creativity and thus signals his faith in the worth of mankind. But the greatest moral vision is never simplistic. It wrestles with questions and poses problems; it rarely supplies answers or proposes solutions. The finest fiction-writers share a common recognition of the complexity of life. The engrossing stories they tell reflect their awareness of this complexity. These stories stand as monuments of what it means to be a man. They link humanity, as Herman Melville understood when, speaking of great authors and their works, he said "one shock of recognition runs the whole circle round." Communication of such intensity is an act of love; these authors are lovers of mankind whose oaths of allegiance are the very works they create.

In this chapter you will find two stories that acknowledge how difficult man's circumstances are. In both, the principal characters are pitted against massed forces of evil too great to overcome. Both authors present evil in the form of witchcraft. Both preserve dramatic distance from their struggling mortals. And neither offers solutions to the terrifying problems their stories pose. Their moral vision is at once comprehensive, penetrating, disturbing, and complex.

But these stories, standing side by side, present a special problem. They are divided in time by nearly one hundred years. This fact, in itself, suggests the universality of their moral concern. The unanswered question—why is there evil for men to do?—had relevance for Hawthorne in 1835 and for Porter in 1930, as it has for us today. But universality of moral concern and similarity of subject do not guarantee that both stories are equally easy to understand. Hawthorne's more leisurely pace, his more elaborate style, the setting of his story in early colonial America, and his habitual use of allegory may erect barriers between his story and today's reader.

Nevertheless, it should be possible for the reader to breach these barriers. In this book we have tried to help him do so. We have attempted to display clearly the techniques of fiction used by the best authors. And it has been our premise throughout that a reader's pleasure grows in proportion to his understanding of an author's craft.

These two stories provide a test of this premise and of your understanding. Both stories are accomplished in technique. Both are informed by a powerful vision. But between you and one of them stands the barrier of an additional one hundred years. Can you, armed with knowledge of the elements of fiction, find the key to the mystery of both stories with equal confidence?

Katherine Anne Porter

MAGIC

And, Madame Blanchard, believe that I am happy to be here with you and your family because it is so serene, everything, and before this I worked for a long time in a fancy house—maybe you don't know what is a fancy house? Naturally . . . everyone must have heard sometime or other. Well, Madame, I work always where there is work to be had, and so in this place I worked very hard all hours, and saw too many things, things you wouldn't believe, and I wouldn't think of telling you, only maybe it will rest you while I brush your hair. You'll excuse me too but I could not help hearing you say to the laundress maybe someone had bewitched your linens, they fall away so fast in the wash. Well, there was a girl there in that house, a poor thing, thin, but well-liked by all the men who called, and you understand she could not get along with the woman who ran the house. They quarreled, the madam cheated her on her checks: you know, the girl got a check, a brass one, every time, and at the week's end she gave those back to the madam, yes, that was the way, and got her percentage, a very small little of her earnings: it is a business, you see, like any other—and the madam used to pretend the girl had given back only so many checks, you see, and really she had given many more, but after they were out of her hands, what could she do? So she would say, I will get out of this place, and curse and cry. Then the madam would hit her over the head. She always hit people over the head with bottles, it was the way she fought. My good heavens, Madame Blanchard, what confusion there would be sometimes with a girl running raving downstairs, and the madam pulling her back by the hair and smashing a bottle on her forehead.

It was nearly always about the money, the girls got in debt so, and if they wished to go they could not without paying every sou marqué. The madam had full understanding with the police; the girls must come back with them or go to the jails. Well, they always came back with the policemen or with another kind of man friend of the madam: she could make men work for her too, but she paid them very well for all, let me tell you: and so the girls stayed on unless they were sick; if so, if they got too sick, she sent them away again.

Madame Blanchard said, "You are pulling a little here," and eased a strand of hair: "and then what?"

Pardon—but this girl, there was a true hatred between her and the madam. She would say many times, I make more money than anybody else in the house, and every week were scenes. So at last she said one morning, Now I will leave this place, and she took out forty dollars from under her pillow and said, Here's your money! The madam began to shout, Where did you get all that, you ——? and accused her of robbing the men who came to visit her. The girl said, Keep your hands off or I'll brain you: and at that the madam took hold of her shoulders, and began to lift her knee and kick this girl most terribly in the stomach, and even in her most secret place, Madame Blanchard, and then she beat her in the face with a bottle, and the girl fell back again into her room where I was making clean. I helped her to the bed, and she sat there holding her sides with her head hanging down, and when she got up again there was blood everywhere she had sat. So then the madam came in once more and screamed, Now you can get out, you are no good for me any more: I don't repeat all, you understand it is too much. But she took all the money she could find, and at the door she gave the girl a great push in the back with her knee, so that she fell again in the street, and then got up and went away with the dress barely on her.

After this the men who knew this girl kept saying, Where is Ninette? And they kept asking this in the next days, so that the madam could not say any longer, I put her out because she is a thief. No, she began to see she was wrong to send this Ninette away, and then she said, She will be back in a few days, don't trouble yourself.

And now, Madame Blanchard, if you wish to hear, I come to the strange part, the thing recalled to me when you said your linens were bewitched. For the cook in that place was a woman, colored like myself, like myself with much French blood just the same, like myself living always among people who worked spells. But she had a very hard heart, she helped the madam in everything, she liked to watch all that happened, and she gave away tales on the girls. The madam trusted her above everything, and she said, Well, where can I find that slut? because she had gone altogether out of Basin Street before the madam began to ask the police to bring her again. Well, the cook said, I know a charm that works here in New Orleans, colored women do it to bring back their men: in seven days they come again very happy to stay and they cannot say why: even your enemy will come back to you believing you are his friend. It is a New Orleans charm for sure, for certain, they say it does not work even across the river. . . . And then they did it just as the cook said. They took the chamber pot of this girl from under her bed, and in it they mixed with water and milk all the relics of her they found there: the hair from her brush, and the face powder from the puff, and even little bits of her nails they found about the edges of the carpet where she sat by habit to cut her finger- and toe-nails; and they dipped the sheets with her blood into the water, and all the time the cook said something over it in a low voice; I could not hear all, but at last she said to the madam, Now spit in it: and the madam spat, and the cook said, When she comes back she will be dirt under your feet.

Madame Blanchard closed her perfume bottle with a thin click: "Yes, and then?"

Then in seven nights the girl came back and she looked very sick, the same clothes and all, but happy to be there. One of the men said, Welcome home, Ninette! and when she started to speak to the madam, the madam said, Shut up and get upstairs and dress yourself. So Ninette, this girl, she said, I'll be down in just a minute. And after that she lived there quietly.

QUESTIONS

1 Vocabulary: *sou marqué:* literally, "marked sou," which means formally, "legal (or recorded) penny"; colloquially, "every last cent."

2 We are immediately struck by the shortness of this story. Is there a connection between its brevity and its methods of narration? What portions of the story are told by the scenic method? What portions are told by the summary method?

3 Is the narrator unreliable? How do you know? To whom does this story's revelation come?

4 Identify some verbal ironies found in the words the narrator uses to describe certain places, persons, or things to Mrs. Blanchard. What irony is concealed in Mrs. Blanchard's name? Mrs. Blanchard speaks only twice, and each time her words are accompanied by a single action. Do these two instances form a pattern? If so, does this pattern contribute to the story's irony?

5 What is the central irony in this story? How does the point of view contribute to that irony? Is this irony implicit in the title?

6 To what extent is this story a conscious comment on white racism? Does this story carry a message for our times? How does the part played by the cook affect your answers to the previous questions? How does it complicate the story's theme?

7 What do you think is the author's attitude toward the experience narrated here? Dramatic distance exists between the author and the narrator. What does the author gain by preserving such dramatic distance? Does she lose anything by doing so?

8 How much do you really know about Ninette? How does your meager knowledge universalize the figure of Ninette? How does it contribute to the theme of the story?

Nathaniel Hawthorne

YOUNG GOODMAN BROWN

Young Goodman Brown came forth at sunset into the street at Salem village, but put his head back, after crossing the threshold, to exchange a parting kiss with his young wife. And Faith, as the wife was aptly named, thrust her own pretty head into the street, letting the wind play with the pink ribbons of her cap while she called to Goodman Brown.

"Dearest heart," whispered she, softly and rather sadly, when her lips were close to his ear, "prithee put off your journey until sunrise and sleep in your own bed tonight. A lone woman is troubled with such dreams and such thoughts that she's afeard of herself sometimes. Pray tarry with me this night, dear husband, of all nights in the year."

"My love and my Faith," replied young Goodman Brown, "of all nights in the year, this one night must I tarry away from thee. My journey, as thou callest it, forth and back again, must needs be done 'twixt now and sunrise. What, my sweet, pretty wife, dost thou doubt me already, and we but three months married?"

"Then God bless you!" said Faith, with the pink ribbons, "and may you find all well when you come back."

"Amen!" cried Goodman Brown. "Say thy prayers, dear Faith, and go to bed at dusk, and no harm will come to thee."

So they parted; and the young man pursued his way until, being about to turn the corner by the meeting-house, he looked back and saw the head of Faith still peeping after him with a melancholy air, in spite of her pink ribbons.

"Poor little Faith!" thought he, for his heart smote him. "What a wretch am I to leave her on such an errand! She talks of dreams, too. Methought as she spoke there was trouble in her face, as if a dream had warned her what work is to be done tonight. But no, no; 't would kill her to think it. Well, she's a blessed angel on earth; and after this one night I'll cling to her skirts and follow her to heaven."

With this excellent resolve for the future, Goodman Brown felt himself justified in making more haste on his present evil purpose. He had taken a dreary road, darkened by all the gloomiest trees of the forest, which barely stood aside to let the narrow path creep through and closed immediately behind. It was all as lonely as could be; and there is this peculiarity in such a solitude, that the traveller knows not who may be concealed by the innumerable trunks and the thick boughs overhead; so that with lonely footsteps he may yet be passing through an unseen multitude.

"There may be a devilish Indian behind every tree," said Goodman Brown to himself; and he glanced fearfully behind him as he added, "What if the devil himself should be at my very elbow!"

His head being turned back, he passed a crook of the road and, looking forward again, beheld the figure of a man, in grave and decent attire, seated at the foot of an old tree. He arose at Goodman Brown's approach and walked onward side by side with him.

"You are late, Goodman Brown," said he. "The clock of the Old South was striking as I came through Boston, and that is full fifteen minutes agone."

"Faith kept me back a while," replied the young man, with a tremor in his voice caused by the sudden appearance of his companion, though not wholly unexpected.

It was now deep dusk in the forest, and deepest in that part of it where these two were journeying. As nearly as could be discerned, the second traveller was about fifty years old, apparently in the same rank of life as Goodman Brown, and bearing a considerable resemblance to him, though perhaps more in expression than features. Still they might have been taken for father and son. And yet, though the elder person was as simply clad as the younger, and as simple in manner too, he had an indescribable air of one who knew the world and who would not have felt abashed at the governor's dinner table or in King William's court, were it possible that his affairs should call him thither. But the only thing about him that could be fixed upon as remarkable was his staff, which bore the likeness of a great black snake, so curiously wrought that it might almost be seen to twist and wriggle itself like a living serpent. This, of course, must have been an ocular deception, assisted by the uncertain light.

"Come, Goodman Brown," cried his fellow traveller, "this is a dull pace for the beginning of a journey. Take my staff, if you are so soon weary."

"Friend," said the other, exchanging his slow pace for a full stop, "having kept covenant by meeting thee here, it is my purpose now to return whence I came. I have scruples touching the matter thou wot'st of."

"Sayest thou so?" replied he of the serpent, smiling apart. "Let us walk on, nevertheless, reasoning as we go; and if I convince thee not thou shalt turn back. We are but a little way in the forest yet."

"Too far! too far!" exclaimed the goodman, unconsciously resuming his walk. "My father never went into the woods on such an errand, nor his father before him. We have been a race of honest men and good Christians since the days of the martyrs; and shall I be the first of the name of Brown that ever took this path and kept. . . ."

"Such company, thou wouldst say," observed the elder person, interpreting his pause. "Well said, Goodman Brown! I have been as well acquainted with your family as with ever a one among the Puritans; and that's no trifle to say. I helped your grandfather, the constable, when he lashed the Quaker woman so smartly through the streets of Salem; and it was I that brought your father a pitch-pine knot, kindled at my own hearth, to set fire to an Indian village, in King Philip's war. They were my good friends, both; and many a pleasant walk have we had along this path, and returned merrily after midnight. I would fain be friends with you for their sake."

"If it be as thou sayest," replied Goodman Brown, "I marvel they never spoke of these matters; or, verily, I marvel not, seeing that the least rumor of the sort would have driven them from New England. We are a people of prayer, and good works to boot, and abide no such wickedness."

"Wickedness or not," said the traveller with the twisted staff, "I have a very general acquaintance here in New England. The deacons of many a church have drunk the communion wine with me; the selectmen of divers towns make me their chairman; and a majority of the Great and General Court are firm supporters of my interest. The governor and I, too—But these are state secrets."

"Can this be so?" cried Goodman Brown, with a stare of amazement at his undisturbed companion. "Howbeit, I have nothing to do with the governor and council; they have their own ways and are no rule for a simple husbandman like me. But, were I to go on with thee, how should I meet the eye of that good old man, our minister, at Salem village? Oh, his voice would make me tremble both Sabbath day and lecture day."

Thus far the elder traveller had listened with due gravity; but now burst into a fit of irrepressible mirth, shaking himself so violently that his snakelike staff actually seemed to wriggle in sympathy.

"Ha! ha! ha!" shouted he again and again; then composing himself, "Well, go on, Goodman Brown, go on; but, prithee, don't kill me with laughing."

"Well, then, to end the matter at once," said Goodman Brown, considerably nettled, "there is my wife, Faith. It would break her dear little heart; and I'd rather break my own."

"Nay, if that be the case," he answered the other, "e'en go thy ways, Goodman Brown. I would not for twenty old women like the one hobbling before us that Faith should come to any harm."

As he spoke he pointed his staff at a female figure on the path, in whom Goodman Brown recognized a very pious and exemplary dame, who had taught him his catechism in youth and was still his moral and spiritual adviser, jointly with the minister and Deacon Gookin.

"A marvel, truly, that Goody Cloyse should be so far in the wilderness at nightfall," said he. "But with your leave, friend, I shall take a cut through the woods until we have left this Christian woman behind. Being a stranger to you, she might ask whom I was consorting with and whither I was going."

"Be it so," said his fellow traveller. "Betake you to the woods, and let me keep the path."

Accordingly the young man turned aside, but took care to watch his companion, who advanced softly along the road until he had come within a staff's length of the old dame. She, meanwhile, was making the best of her way, with singular speed for so aged a woman, and mumbling some indistinct words—a prayer, doubtless—as she went. The traveller put forth his staff and touched her withered neck with what seemed the serpent's tail.

"The devil!" screamed the pious old lady.

"Then Goody Cloyse knows her old friend?" observed the traveller, confronting her and leaning on his writhing stick.

"Ah, forsooth, and is it your worship indeed?" cried the good dame. "Yea, truly is it, and in the very image of my old gossip, Goodman Brown, the grandfather of the silly fellow that now is. But—would your worship believe it?—my broomstick hath strangely disappeared, stolen, as I suspect, by that unhanged witch, Goody Cory, and that, too, when I was all anointed with the juice of smallage, and cinquefoil, and wolf's bane—"

"Mingled with fine wheat and the fat of a newborn babe," said the shape of old Goodman Brown.

"Ah, your worship knows the recipe," cried the old lady, cackling aloud. "So, as I was saying, being all ready for the meeting, and no horse to ride on, I made up my mind to foot it; for they tell me there is a nice young man to be taken into communion tonight. But now your good worship will lend me your arm, and we shall be there in a twinkling."

"That can hardly be," answered her friend. "I may not spare you my arm, Goody Cloyse; but here is my staff, if you will."

So saying, he threw it down at her feet, where, perhaps, it assumed life, being one of the rods which its owner had formerly lent to the Egyptian magi. Of this fact, however, Goodman Brown could not take cognizance. He had cast up his eyes in astonishment and, looking down again, beheld neither Goody Cloyse nor the serpentine staff, but his fellow traveller alone, who waited for him as calmly as if nothing had happened.

"That old woman taught me my catechism," said the young man; and there was a world of meaning in this simple comment.

They continued to walk onward, while the elder traveller exhorted his companion to make good speed and persevere in the path, discoursing so aptly that his arguments seemed rather to spring up in the bosom of his auditor than to be suggested by himself. As they went, he plucked a branch of maple to serve for a walking stick, and began to strip it of the twigs and little boughs, which were wet with evening dew. The moment his fingers touched them they became strangely withered and dried up as with a week's sunshine. Thus the pair proceeded at a good free pace, until suddenly, in a gloomy hollow of the road, Goodman Brown sat himself down on the stump of a tree and refused to go any farther.

"Friend," said he stubbornly, "my mind is made up. Not another step will I budge on this errand. What if a wretched old woman do choose to go to the devil when I thought she was going to heaven: is that any reason why I should quit my dear Faith and go after her?"

"You will think better of this by and by," said his acquaintance composedly. "Sit here and rest yourself a while; and when you feel like moving again, there is my staff to help you along."

Without more words, he threw his companion the maple stick, and was as speedily out of sight as if he had vanished into the deepening gloom. The young man sat a few moments by the roadside, applauding himself greatly and thinking with how clear a conscience he should meet the minister in his morning walk, nor shrink from the eye of good old Deacon Gookin. And what calm sleep would be his that very night, which was to have been spent so wickedly, but so purely and sweetly now, in the arms of Faith! Amidst these pleasant and praiseworthy meditations, Goodman Brown heard the tramp of horses along the road and deemed it advisable to conceal himself within the verge of the forest, conscious of the guilty purpose that had brought him thither, though now so happily turned from it.

On came the hoof tramps and the voices of the riders, two grave old voices, conversing soberly as they drew near. These mingled sounds appeared to pass along the road, within a few yards of the young man's hiding-place; but, owing doubtless to the depth of the gloom at that particular spot, neither the travellers nor their steeds were visible. Though their figures brushed the small boughs by the wayside, it could not be seen that they intercepted, even for a moment, the faint gleam from the strip of bright sky athwart which they must have passed. Goodman Brown alternately crouched and stood on tiptoe, pulling aside the branches and thrusting forth his head as far as he durst, without discerning so much as a shadow. It vexed him the more, because he could have sworn, were such a thing possible, that he recognized the voices of the minister and Deacon Gookin, jogging along quietly, as they were wont to do, when bound to some ordination or ecclesiastical council. While yet within hearing, one of the riders stopped to pluck a switch.

"Of the two, reverend sir," said the voice like the deacon's, "I had rather miss an ordination dinner than tonight's meeting. They tell me that some of our community are to be here from Falmouth and beyond, and others from Connecticut and Rhode Island, besides several of the Indian powwows, who, after their fashion, know almost as much deviltry as the best of us. Moreover, there is a goodly young woman to be taken into communion."

"Mighty well, Deacon Gookin!" replied the solemn old tones of the minister. "Spur up, or we shall be late. Nothing can be done, you know, until I get on the ground."

The hoofs clattered again; and the voices, talking so strangely in the empty air, passed on through the forest, where no church had ever been gathered or solitary Christian prayed. Whither, then, could these holy men be journeying so deep into the heathen wilderness? Young Goodman Brown caught hold of a tree for support, being ready to sink down on the ground, faint and overburdened with the heavy sickness of his heart. He looked up to the sky, doubting whether there really was a heaven above him. Yet there was the blue arch, and the stars brightening in it.

"With heaven above and Faith below, I will yet stand firm against the devil!" cried Goodman Brown.

While he still gazed upward into the deep arch of the firmament and had lifted his hands to pray, a cloud, though no wind was stirring, hurried across the zenith and hid the brightening stars. The blue sky was still visible, except directly overhead, where this black mass of cloud was sweeping swiftly northward. Aloft in the air, as if from the depths of the cloud, came a confused and doubtful sound of voices. Once the listener fancied that he could distinguish the accents of townspeople of his own, men and women, both pious and ungodly, many of whom he had met at the communion table, and had seen others rioting at the tavern. The next moment, so indistinct were the sounds, he doubted whether he had heard aught but the murmur of the old forest, whispering without a wind. Then came a stronger swell of those familiar tones, heard daily in the sunshine at Salem village but never until now from a cloud of night. There was one voice of a young woman uttering lamentations, yet with an uncertain sorrow, and entreating for some favor which, perhaps, it would grieve her to obtain; and all the unseen multitude, both saints and sinners, seemed to encourage her onward.

"Faith!" shouted Goodman Brown, in a voice of agony and desperation; and the echoes of the forest mocked him, crying, "Faith! Faith!" as if bewildered wretches were seeking her all through the wilderness.

The cry of grief, rage, and terror was yet piercing the night, when the unhappy husband held his breath for a response. There was a scream, drowned immediately in a louder murmur of voices, fading into far-off laughter as the dark cloud swept away, leaving the clear and silent sky above Goodman Brown. But something fluttered lightly down through the air and caught on the branch of a tree. The young man seized it and beheld a pink ribbon.

"My Faith is gone!" cried he after one stupefied moment. "There is no good on earth, and sin is but a name. Come, devil, for to thee is this world given."

And maddened with despair, so that he laughed loud and long, did Goodman Brown grasp his staff and set forth again, at such a rate that he seemed to fly along the forest path rather than to walk or run. The road grew wilder and drearier and more faintly traced, and vanished at length, leaving him in the heart of the dark wilderness, still rushing onward with the instinct that guides mortal men to evil. The whole forest was peopled with frightful sounds—the creaking of the trees, the howling of wild beasts, and the yell of Indians; while sometimes the wind tolled like a distant church bell, and sometimes gave a broad roar around the traveller, as if all nature were laughing him to scorn. But he was himself the chief horror of the scene, and shrank not from its other horrors.

"Ha! ha! ha!" roared Goodman Brown when the wind laughed at him. "Let us hear which will laugh loudest. Think not to frighten me with your deviltry. Come witch, come wizard, come Indian powwow, come devil himself, and here comes Goodman Brown. You may as well fear him as he fear you."

In truth, all through the haunted forest there could be nothing more frightful than the figure of Goodman Brown. On he flew among the black pines, brandishing his staff with frenzied gestures, now giving vent to an inspiration of horrid blasphemy and now shouting forth such laughter as set all the echoes of the forest laughing like demons around him. The fiend in his own shape is less hideous than when he rages in the breast of man. Thus sped the demoniac on his course, until, quivering among the trees, he saw a red light before him, as when the felled trunks and branches of a clearing have been set on fire and throw up their lurid blaze against the sky, at the hour of midnight. He paused in a lull of the tempest that had driven him onward and heard the swell of what seemed a hymn, rolling solemnly from a distance with the weight of many voices. He knew the tune; it was a familiar one in the choir of the village meeting-house. The verse died heavily away and was lengthened by a chorus, not of human voices but of all the sounds of the benighted wilderness pealing in awful harmony together. Goodman Brown cried out, and his cry was lost to his own ear by its unison with the cry of the desert.

In the interval of silence he stole forward until the light glared full upon his eyes. At one extremity of an open space, hemmed in by the dark wall of the forest, arose a rock bearing some rude, natural resemblance either to an altar or a pulpit, and surrounded by four blazing pines, their tops aflame, their stems untouched, like candles at an evening meeting. The mass of foliage that had overgrown the summit of the rock was all on fire, blazing high into the night and fitfully illuminating the whole field. Each pendent twig and leafy festoon was in a blaze. As the red light arose and fell, a numerous congregation alternately shone forth, then disappeared in shadow, and again grew, as it were, out of the darkness, peopling the heart of the solitary woods at once.

"A grave and dark-clad company," quoth Goodman Brown.

In truth they were such. Among them, quivering to and fro between gloom and splendor, appeared faces that would be seen next day at the council board of the province, and others which, Sabbath after Sabbath, looked devoutly heavenward, and benignantly over the crowded pews, from the holiest pulpits in the land. Some affirm that the lady of the governor was there. At least there were high dames well known to her, and wives of honored husbands, and widows, a great multitude, and ancient maidens, all of excellent repute, and fair young girls, who trembled lest their mothers should espy them. Either the sudden gleams of light flashing over the obscure field bedazzled Goodman Brown, or he recognized a score of the church members of Salem village famous for their especial sanctity. Good old Deacon Gookin had arrived and waited at the skirts of that venerable saint, his revered pastor. But, irreverently consorting with these grave, reputable, and pious people, these elders of the church, these chaste dames and dewy virgins, there were men of dissolute lives and women of spotted fame, wretches given over to all mean and filthy vice, and suspected even of horrid crimes. It was strange to see that the good shrank not from the wicked, nor were the sinners abashed by the saints. Scattered also among their palefaced enemies were the Indian priests, or powwows, who had often scared their native forest with more hideous incantations than any known to English witchcraft.

"But where is Faith?" thought Goodman Brown; and, as hope came into his heart, he trembled.

Another verse of the hymn arose, a slow and mournful strain such as the pious love, but joined to words which expressed all that our nature can conceive of sin, and darkly hinted at far more. Unfathomable to mere mortals is the lore of fiends. Verse after verse was sung; and still the chorus of the desert swelled between like the deepest tone of a mighty organ; and with the final peal of that dreadful anthem there came a sound as if the roaring wind, the rushing streams, the howling beasts, and every other voice of the unconcerted wilderness were mingling and according with the voice of guilty man in homage to the prince of all. The four blazing pines threw up a loftier flame and obscurely discovered shapes and visages of horror on the smoke wreaths above the impious assembly. At the same moment the fire on the rock shot redly forth and formed a glowing arch above its base, where now appeared a figure. With reverence be it spoken, the figure bore no slight similitude both in garb and manner to some grave divine of the New England churches.

"Bring forth the converts!" cried a voice that echoed through the field and rolled into the forest.

At the word, Goodman Brown stepped forth from the shadow of the trees and approached the congregation, with whom he felt a loathful brotherhood by the sympathy of all that was wicked in his heart. He could have well-nigh sworn that the shape of his own dead father beckoned him to advance, looking downward from a smoke wreath, while a woman with dim features of despair threw out her hand to warn him back. Was it his mother? But he had no power to retreat one step, nor to resist, even in thought, when the minister and good old Deacon Gookin seized his arms and led him to the blazing rock. Thither came also the slender form of a veiled female led between Goody Cloyse, that pious teacher of the catechism, and Martha Carrier, who had received the devil's promise to be a queen of hell. A rampant hag was she. And there stood the proselytes beneath the canopy of fire.

"Welcome, my children," said the dark figure, "to the communion of your race. Ye have found thus young your nature and your destiny. My children, look behind you!"

They turned; and flashing forth, as it were, in a sheet of flame, the fiend worshippers were seen; the smile of welcome gleamed darkly on every visage.

"There," resumed the sable form, "are all whom ye have reverenced from youth. Ye deemed them holier than yourselves and shrank from your own sin, contrasting it with their lives of righteousness and prayerful aspirations heavenward. Yet here are they all in my worshipping assembly. This night it shall be granted you to know their secret deeds: how hoary-bearded elders of the church have whispered wanton words to the young maids of their households; how many a woman, eager for widows' weeds, has given her husband a drink at bedtime and let him sleep his last sleep in her bosom; how beardless youths have made haste to inherit their fathers' wealth; and how fair damsels—blush not, sweet ones—have dug little graves in the garden, and bidden me, the sole guest, to an infant's funeral. By the sympathy of your human hearts for sin ye shall scent out all the places—whether in church, bed-chamber, street, field, or forest—where crime has been committed, and shall exult to behold the whole earth one stain of guilt, one mighty blood spot. Far more than this. It shall be yours to penetrate, in every bosom, the deep mystery of sin, the fountain of all wicked arts, and which inexhaustibly supplies more evil impulses than human power—than my power at its utmost—can make manifest in deeds. And now, my children, look upon each other."

They did so; and by the blaze of the hell-kindled torches the wretched man beheld his Faith, and the wife her husband, trembling before that unhallowed altar.

"Lo, there ye stand, my children," said the figure in a deep and solemn tone, almost sad with its despairing awfulness, as if his once angelic nature could yet mourn for our miserable race. "Depending upon one another's hearts, ye had still hoped that virtue were not all a dream. Now are ye undeceived. Evil is the nature of mankind. Evil must be your only happiness. Welcome again, my children, to the communion of your race."

"Welcome," repeated the fiend worshippers, in one cry of despair and triumph.

And there they stood, the only pair, as it seemed, who were yet hesitating on the verge of wickedness in this dark world. A basin was hollowed, naturally, in the rock. Did it contain water, reddened by the lurid light? or was it blood? or, perchance, a liquid flame? Herein did the shape of evil dip his hand and prepare to lay the mark of baptism upon their foreheads, that they might be partakers of the mystery of sin, more conscious of the secret guilt of others, both in deed and thought, than they could now be of their own. The husband cast one look at his pale wife, and Faith at him. What polluted wretches would the next glance show them to each other, shuddering alike at what they disclosed and what they saw!

"Faith! Faith!" cried the husband, "look up to heaven, and resist the wicked one."

Whether Faith obeyed he knew not. Hardly had he spoken when he found himself amid calm night and solitude, listening to a roar of the wind which died heavily away through the forest. He staggered against the rock and felt it chill and damp; while a hanging twig that had been all on fire besprinkled his cheek with the coldest dew.

The next morning young Goodman Brown came slowly into the

street of Salem village, staring around him like a bewildered man. The good old minister was taking a walk along the graveyard to get an appetite for breakfast and meditate his sermon, and bestowed a blessing as he passed on Goodman Brown. He shrank from the venerable saint as if to avoid an anathema. Old Deacon Gookin was at domestic worship, and the holy words of his prayer were heard through the open window. "What God doth the wizard pray to?" quoth Goodman Brown. Goody Cloyse, that excellent old Christian, stood in the early sunshine at her own lattice, catechizing a little girl who had brought her a pint of morning's milk. Goodman Brown snatched away the child as from the grasp of the fiend himself. Turning the corner by the meeting-house, he spied the head of Faith, with the pink ribbons, gazing anxiously forth and bursting into such joy at sight of him that she skipped along the street and almost kissed her husband before the whole village. But Goodman Brown looked sternly and sadly into her face and passed on without a greeting.

Had Goodman Brown fallen alseep in the forest and only dreamed a wild dream of a witch meeting?

Be it so if you will; but, alas! it was a dream of evil omen for young Goodman Brown. A stern, a sad, a darkly meditative, a distrustful if not a desperate man did he become from the night of that fearful dream. On the Sabbath day, when the congregation were singing a holy psalm, he could not listen because an anthem of sin rushed loudly upon his ear and drowned all the blessed strain. When the minister spoke from the pulpit with power and fervid eloquence, and, with his hand on the open Bible, of the sacred truths of our religion, and of saintlike lives and triumphant deaths, and of future bliss or misery unutterable, then did Goodman Brown turn pale, dreading lest the roof should thunder down upon the gray blasphemer and his hearers. Often, waking suddenly at midnight, he shrank from the bosom of Faith; and at morning or eventide, when the family knelt down at prayer, he scowled and muttered to himself, and gazed sternly at his wife, and turned away. And when he had lived long, and was borne to his grave a hoary corpse, followed by Faith, an aged woman, and children and grandchildren, a goodly procession, besides neighbors not a few, they carved no hopeful verse upon his tombstone, for his dying hour was gloom.

QUESTIONS

1 Vocabulary: The *Old South:* the church or meeting house built in Boston in 1729. *King William:* William III was King of England (1689–1702). *King Philip's war:* King Philip was an American Indian chief who led a war against the New England colonists (1675–76). *The Great and General Court:* the governing body of the Massachusetts Colony. *Egyptian magi:* Pharaoh's magicians referred to in Exodus 7:12.

2 Hawthorne uses a favorite convention of storytellers: the journey. Is this journey a real one, or is it symbolic? Why is it significant that the journey leads into a dark forest and that it is undertaken at night?

3 This story has some of the properties of allegory. Hawthorne makes explicitly clear that the "second traveller" is the personification of the devil. What does Young Goodman Brown personify? What does his wife personify? May we say that all the other persons Brown encounters in the forest represent a "collective personification" of something? If so, what?

4 Things, as well as people, take on symbolic significance in this story. What is symbolized by: the pink ribbons on Faith's cap; the second traveller's snakelike staff; the cloud moving without the aid of wind to blot out the stars directly over Brown's head?

5 Certain actions described or details supplied in this story are full of symbolic meaning. How do you interpret: the fire that cast a red light, as it rose and fell, on the faces of the congregation surrounding the pulpitlike rock in the forest; the withering of the maple branch used as a walking stick by the second traveller; the seemingly hysterical laugh of Brown as he hurried to the forest meeting place; Brown's twice concealing himself when he and the devil encountered first Goody Cloyse, and then the minister and Deacon Gookin on their journey?

6 Hawthorne was fascinated by what people of his day called "the sin of pride." He seems to have meant by that phrase anyone's manifestation of too-great confidence in his own wisdom or the rightness of his own conduct. Does Brown display this sin of pride at the beginning of the story? If so, in what human attribute is he too confident? Does he display the same sin at the end of the story? In what human attribute is he too deficient? What has he really learned, if anything, from his journey? What has he failed to learn? Do the answers to these questions point toward Hawthorne's theme—his attitude toward the fictional experience he has recounted?

7 You can find many examples, running through the story like a musical motif, of one of Hawthorne's favorite devices—deliberate ambiguity—as illustrated by the question asked in the next-to-last paragraph. Why do you think he uses this device so often? Does it have anything to do with the "real" and "artificial" aspects of fiction mentioned in the first chapter of this book? Might it have something to do with the way an author views the great moral dilemmas that underlie all human behavior?

8 By now you have grown accustomed to casting a wary eye on the titles of short stories. Examine every word of the title, "Young Goodman Brown." Is there a pun in this title? Is irony lurking in every word? If so, what is the irony in each case? Could you argue that the theme of this story is distilled in its title?

QUESTIONS
comparing "Magic" and "Young Goodman Brown"

1 Both stories are studies in evil. In what sense does the face of evil that is presented in each story differ? How is it the same? Does the author's view of evil seem more comprehensive in one story than in the other? Explain your answer.

2 Both stories are also studies in violence. What different kinds of violence are involved? Does your answer help you to determine the moral concerns of each author?

3 In which story does the author's style (choice of words and sentence structure) seem to parallel or "fit" the subject matter? In which story does the style appear to be in "tension" or in ironic contrast with the subject matter? How does this difference relate to the choice of a narrator in each instance? What does it have to do with the moral vision of the respective authors? Does it depend upon the period of time in which these stories were written?

4 Both stories contain dramatic irony: in one story the reader knows more than the narrator; in the other, the reader knows more than the title character. Is the revelation achieved by the reader more shocking in one story than in the other? Explain your answer.

5 Hawthorne's story has a much larger cast of characters than Porter's story has. What important idea in Hawthorne's story made such a large cast essential? Conversely, why was it essential for Porter to keep her cast of characters scaled down? Would you explain this difference in the number of characters as a difference in moral vision between Hawthorne and Porter, or as a difference in their fictional techniques?

6 State the theme of each story. Is this easier to do for one story than for the other? If one was easier for you, do you think it was so because one story has a more recognizable set of techniques than the other, or because one story has a more complex moral vision than the other, or both?

7 If you were required to write an essay comparing these two stories, which question would you rather answer: (1) Why do you think one story is better than the other? or (2) How do these stories achieve their different effects through the use of different techniques? Explain your choice.

14
TRANSLATION

Many aspects of fiction can be translated from one language to another; some cannot. Obviously the sound of a translation is very different from the sound of the original. Hence certain musical devices, such as alliteration and rhyme, or effects, like cacophony and euphony, will often not come through in a literal translation, though a clever translator can sometimes simulate such effects. Homonyms, puns, suggestive word sounds, and deliberate ambiguities are usually sacrificed in favor of accuracy of meaning.

The story in this chapter by the well-known Colombian writer Hernando Téllez is printed in English, and also in its original Spanish, on facing pages. Even to someone not familiar with both languages, a quick glance shows certain variations. For example, the first paragraph in the original Spanish version has been broken into several paragraphs in the English version. A further look at the translation will reveal some changes in punctuation—like the use of dashes for commas, as in "peacefully—alive and shaved," which heightens the stress of the Spanish original "tranquilamente, vivo y afeitado."

If you know a little Spanish, you will find many variations that the translator employs. Note, for example, the alliteration in English, "proud of the preciseness of my profession," that creates a very different sound-and-rhythm pattern than the original, "orgulloso de la pulcritud en su oficio." In the next sentence a rhyme in Spanish, "una buena faena," is lost in the English translation, "a fitting challenge." These examples suggest the problems, the possibilities, and the limitations of translation in prose fiction. This chapter should make you aware of the problems and limitations a student must face when trying to analyze a translated story, knowing that some parts of the translation may not be the author's own.

Hernando Téllez

ESPUMA Y NADA MÁS

No saludó al entrar. Yo estaba repasando sobre una badana la mejor de mis navajas. Y cuando lo reconocí me puse a temblar. Pero él no se dio cuenta. Para disimular continué repasando la hoja. La probé luego sobre la yema del dedo gordo y volví a mirarla, contra la luz. En ese instante se quitaba el cinturón ribeteado de balas de donde pendía la funda de la pistola. La colgó de uno de los clavos del ropero y encima colocó el kepis. Volvió completamente el cuerpo para hablarme y deshaciendo el nudo de la corbata, me dijo: "Hace un calor de todos los demonios. Aféiteme". Y se sentó en la silla. Le calculé cuatro días de barba. Los cuatro días de la última excursión en busca de los nuestros. El rostro aparecía quemado, curtido por el sol. Me puse a preparar minuciosamente el jabón. Corté unas rebanadas de la pasta, dejándolas caer en el recipiente, mezclé un poco de agua tibia y con la brocha empecé a revolver. Pronto subió la espuma. "Los muchachos de la tropa deben tener tanta barba como yo". Seguí batiendo la espuma. "Pero nos fue bien, ¿sabe? Pescamos a los principales. Unos vienen muertos y otros todavía viven. Pero pronto estarán todos muertos". "¿Cuántos cogieron?" pregunté. "Catorce. Tuvimos que internarnos bastante para dar con ellos. Pero ya la están pagando. Y no se salvarán ni uno, ni uno." Se echó para atrás en la silla al verme con la brocha en la mano, rebosante de espuma. Faltaba ponerle la sábana. Ciertamente yo estaba aturdido. Extraje del cajón una sábana y la anudé al cuello de mi cliente. Él no cesaba de hablar. Suponía que yo era uno de los partidarios del orden. "El pueblo habrá escarmentado con lo del otro día", dijo. "Sí," repuse mientras concluía de hacer el nudo sobre la oscura nuca, olorosa a sudor. "¿Estuvo bueno, verdad?" "Muy bueno", contesté mientras regresaba a la brocha. El hombre cerró los ojos con un gesto de fatiga y esperó así la fresca caricia del jabón. Jamás lo había tenido tan cerca de mí. El día en que ordenó que el pueblo desfilara por el patio de la Escuela para ver a los cuatro rebeldes allí colgados, me crucé con él un instante. Pero el espectáculo de los cuerpos mutilados me impedía fijarme en el rostro del hombre que lo dirigía todo y que ahora iba a tomar en mis manos. No era un rostro desagradable, ciertamente. Y la barba, envejeciéndolo un poco, no le caía mal. Se llamaba Torres. El

Hernando Téllez

JUST LATHER, THAT'S ALL

He said nothing when he entered. I was passing the best of my razors back and forth on a strop. When I recognized him I started to tremble. But he didn't notice. Hoping to conceal my emotion, I continued sharpening the razor. I tested it on the meat of my thumb, and then held it up to the light. At that moment he took off the bullet-studded belt that his gun holster dangled from. He hung it up on a wall hook and placed his military cap over it. Then he turned to me, loosening the knot of his tie, and said, "It's hot as hell. Give me a shave." He sat in the chair.

I estimated he had a four-day beard. The four days taken up by the latest expedition in search of our troops. His face seemed reddened, burned by the sun. Carefully, I began to prepare the soap. I cut off a few slices, dropped them into the cup, mixed in a bit of warm water, and began to stir with the brush. Immediately the foam began to rise. "The other boys in the group should have this much beard, too." I continued stirring the lather.

"But we did all right, you know. We got the main ones. We brought back some dead, and we've got some others still alive. But pretty soon they'll all be dead."

"How many did you catch?" I asked.

"Fourteen. We had to go pretty deep into the woods to find them. But we'll get even. Not one of them comes out of this alive, not one."

He leaned back on the chair when he saw me with the lather-covered brush in my hand. I still had to put the sheet on him. No doubt about it, I was upset. I took a sheet out of a drawer and knotted it around my customer's neck. He wouldn't stop talking. He probably thought I was in sympathy with his party.

"The town must have learned a lesson from what we did the other day," he said.

"Yes," I replied, securing the knot at the base of his dark, sweaty neck.

"That was a fine show, eh?"

"Very good," I answered, turning back for the brush. The man closed his eyes with a gesture of fatigue and sat waiting for the cool

capitán Torres. Un hombre con imaginación, porque ¿a quién se le había ocurrido antes colgar a los rebeldes desnudos y luego ensayar sobre determinados sitios del cuerpo una mutilación a bala? Empecé a extender la primera capa de jabón. Él seguía con los ojos cerrados. "De buena gana me iría a domir un poco", dijo, "pero esta tarde hay mucho que hacer". Retiré la brocha y pregunté con aire falsamente desinteresado: "¿Fusilamiento?" "Algo por el estilo, pero más lento", respondió. "¿Todos?" "No. Unos cuantos apenas". Reanudé de nuevo la tarea de enjabonarle la barba. Otra vez me temblaban las manos. El hombre no podía darse cuenta de ello y ésa era mi ventaja. Pero yo hubiera querido que él no viniera. Probablemente muchos de los nuestros lo habrían visto entrar. Y el enemigo en la casa impone condiciones. Yo tendría que afeitar esa barba como cualquiera otra, con cuidado, con esmero, como la de un buen parroquiano, cuidando de que ni por un solo poro fuese a brotar una gota de sangre. Cuidando de que en los pequeños remolinos no se desviara la hoja. Cuidando de que la piel quedara limpia, templada, pulida, y de que al pasar el dorso de mi mano por ella, sintiera la superficie sin un pelo. Sí. Yo era un revolucionario clandestino, pero era también un barbero de conciencia, orgulloso de la pulcritud en su oficio. Y esa barba de cuatro días se prestaba para una buena faena.

Tomé la navaja, levanté en ángulo oblicuo las dos cachas, dejé libre la hoja y empecé la tarea, de una de las patillas hacia abajo. La hoja respondía a la perfección. El pelo se presentaba indócil y duro, no muy crecido, pero compacto. La piel iba apareciendo poco a poco. Sonaba la hoja con su ruido característico, y sobre ella crecían los grumos de jabón mezclados con trocitos de pelo. Hice una pausa para limpiarla, tomé la badana de nuevo y me puse a asentar el acero, porque yo soy un barbero que hace bien sus cosas. El hombre que había mantenido los ojos cerrados, los abrió, sacó una de las manos por encima de la sábana, se palpó la zona del rostro que empezaba a quedar libre de jabón, y me dijo: "Venga usted a las seis, esta tarde, a la Escuela". "¿Lo mismo del otro día?", le pregunté horrorizado. "Puede que resulte mejor", respondió. "¿Qué piensa usted hacer?" "No sé todavía. Pero nos divertiremos". Otra vez se echó hacia atrás y cerró los ojos. Yo me acerqué con la navaja en alto. "¿Piensa castigarlos a todos?", aventuré tímidamente. "A todos". El jabón se secaba sobre la cara. Debía apresurarme. Por el espejo, miré hacia la calle. Lo mismo de siempre: la tienda de víveres y en ella dos o tres compradores. Luego miré el reloj: las

caress of the soap. I had never had him so close to me. The day he ordered the whole town to file into the patio of the school to see the four rebels hanging there, I came face to face with him for an instant. But the sight of the mutilated bodies kept me from noticing the face of the man who had directed it all, the face I was now about to take into my hands. It was not an unpleasant face, certainly. And the beard, which made him seem a bit older than he was, didn't suit him badly at all. His name was Torres. Captain Torres. A man of imagination, because who else would have thought of hanging the naked rebels and then holding target practice on certain parts of their bodies? I began to apply the first layer of soap. With his eyes closed, he continued. "Without any effort I could go straight to sleep," he said, "but there's plenty to do this afternoon." I stopped the lathering and asked with a feigned lack of interest: "A firing squad?" "Something like that, but a little slower." I got on with the job of lathering his beard. My hands started trembling again. The man could not possibly realize it, and this was in my favor. But I would have preferred that he hadn't come. It was likely that many of our faction had seen him enter. And an enemy under one's roof imposes certain conditions. I would be obliged to shave that beard like any other one, carefully, gently, like that of any customer, taking pains to see that no single pore emitted a drop of blood. Being careful to see that the little tufts of hair did not lead the blade astray. Seeing that his skin ended up clean, soft, and healthy, so that passing the back of my hand over it I couldn't feel a hair. Yes, I was secretly a rebel, but I was also a conscientious barber, and proud of the preciseness of my profession. And this four-days' growth of beard was a fitting challenge.

I took the razor, opened up the two protective arms, exposed the blade and began the job, from one of the sideburns downward. The razor responded beautifully. His beard was inflexible and hard, not too long, but thick. Bit by bit the skin emerged. The razor rasped along, making its customary sound as fluffs of lather mixed with bits of hair gathered along the blade. I paused a moment to clean it, then took up the strop again to sharpen the razor, because I'm a barber who does things properly. The man, who had kept his eyes closed, opened them now, removed one of his hands from under the sheet, felt the spot on his face where the soap had been cleared off, and said, "Come to the school today at six o'clock." "The same thing as the other day?" I asked horrified. "It could be better," he replied. "What do you plan to do?"

dos y veinte de la tarde. La navaja seguía descendiendo. Ahora de la otra patilla hacia abajo. Una barba azul, cerrada. Debía dejársela crecer como algunos poetas o como algunos sacerdotes. Le quedaría bien. Muchos no lo reconocerían. Y mejor para él, pensé, mientras trataba de pulir suavemente todo el sector del cuello. Porque allí sí que debía manejar con habilidad la hoja, pues el pelo, aunque en agraz, se enredaba en pequeños remolinos. Una barba crespa. Los poros podían abrirse, diminutos, y soltar su perla de sangre. Un buen barbero como yo finca su orgullo en que eso no ocurra a ningún cliente. Y éste era un cliente de calidad. ¿A cuántos de los nuestros había ordenado matar? ¿A cuántos de los nuestros había ordenado que los mutilaran?... Mejor no pensarlo. Torres no sabía que yo era su enemigo. No lo sabía él ni lo sabían los demás. Se trataba de un secreto entre muy pocos, precisamente para que yo pudiese informar a los revolucionarios de lo que Torres estaba haciendo en el pueblo y de lo que proyectaba hacer cada vez que emprendía una excursión para cazar revolucionarios. Iba a ser, pues, muy difícil explicar que yo lo tuve entre mis manos y lo dejé ir tranquilamente, vivo y afeitado.

La barba le había desaparecido casi completamente. Parecía más joven, con menos años de los que llevaba a cuestas cuando entró. Yo supongo que eso ocurre siempre con los hombres que entran y salen de las peluquerías. Bajo el golpe de mi navaja Torres rejuvenecía, sí, porque yo soy un buen barbero, el mejor de este pueblo, lo digo sin vanidad. Un poco más de jabón, aquí, bajo la barbilla, sobre la manzana, sobre esta gran vena. ¡Qué calor! Torres debe estar sudando como yo. Pero él no tiene miedo. Es un hombre sereno, que ni siquiera piensa en lo que ha de hacer esta tarde con los prisioneros. En cambio yo, con esta navaja entre las manos, puliendo y puliendo esta piel, evitando que brote sangre de estos poros, cuidando todo golpe, no puedo pensar serenamente. Maldita la hora en que vino, porque yo soy un revolucionario pero no soy un asesino. Y tan fácil como resultaría matarlo. Y lo merece. ¿Lo merece? No, ¡qué diablos! Nadie merece que los demás hagan el sacrificio de convertirse en asesinos. ¿Qué se gana con ello? Pues nada. Vienen otros y otros y los primeros matan a los segundos y éstos a los terceros y siguen hasta que todo es un mar de sangre. Yo podría cortar este cuello, así, ¡zas!, ¡zas! No le daría tiempo de quejarse y como tiene los ojos cerrados no vería ni el brillo de la navaja ni el brillo de mis ojos. Pero estoy temblando como un verdadero asesino. De ese cuello brotaría un chorro de sangre sobre la sábana, sobre la silla, sobre mis manos, sobre el suelo. Tendría que

"I don't know yet. But we'll amuse ourselves." Once more he leaned back and closed his eyes. I approached him with the razor poised. "Do you plan to punish them all?" I ventured timidly. "All." The soap was drying on his face. I had to hurry. In the mirror I looked toward the street. It was the same as ever: the grocery store with two or three customers in it. Then I glanced at the clock: two-twenty in the afternoon. The razor continued on its downward stroke. Now from the other sideburn down. A thick, blue beard. He should have let it grow like some poets or priests do. It would suit him well. A lot of people wouldn't recognize him. Much to his benefit, I thought, as I attempted to cover the neck area smoothly. There, for sure, the razor had to be handled masterfully, since the hair, although softer, grew into little swirls. A curly beard. One of the tiny pores could be opened up and issue forth its pearl of blood. A good barber such as I prides himself on never allowing this to happen to a client. And this was a first-class client. How many of us had he ordered shot? How many of us had he ordered mutilated? It was better not to think about it. Torres did not know that I was his enemy. He did not know it nor did the rest. It was a secret shared by very few, precisely so that I could inform the revolutionaries of what Torres was doing in the town and of what he was planning each time he undertook a rebel-hunting excursion. So it was going to be very difficult to explain that I had him right in my hands and let him go peacefully—alive and shaved.

The beard was now almost completely gone. He seemed younger, less burdened by years than when he had arrived. I suppose this always happens with men who visit barber shops. Under the stroke of my razor Torres was being rejuvenated—rejuvenated because I am a good barber, the best in the town, if I may say so. A little more lather here, under his chin, on his Adam's apple, on this big vein. How hot it is getting! Torres must be sweating as much as I. But he is not afraid. He is a calm man, who is not even thinking about what he is going to do with the prisoners this afternoon. On the other hand I, with this razor in my hands, stroking and re-stroking this skin, trying to keep blood from oozing from these pores, can't even think clearly. Damn him for coming, because I'm a revolutionary and not a murderer. And how easy it would be to kill him. And he deserves it. Does he? No! What the devil! No one deserves to have someone else make the sacrifice of becoming a murderer. What do you gain by it? Nothing. Others come along and still others, and the first ones kill the second ones and they the

cerrar la puerta. Y la sangre seguiría corriendo por el piso, tibia, imborrable, incontenible, hasta la calle, como un pequeño arroyo escarlata. Estoy seguro de que un golpe fuerte, una honda incisión, le evitaría todo dolor. No sufriría. ¿Y qué hacer con el cuerpo? ¿Dónde ocultarlo? Yo tendría que huir, dejar estas cosas, refugiarme lejos, bien lejos. Pero me perseguirían hasta dar conmigo. "El asesino del Capitán Torres. Lo degolló mientras le afeitaba la barba. Una cobardía". Y por otro lado: "El vengador de los nuestros. Un hombre para recordar (aquí mi nombre). Era el barbero del pueblo. Nadie sabía que él defendía nuestra causa..." ¿Y qué ¿Asesino, o héroe? Del filo de esta navaja depende mi destino. Puedo inclinar un poco más la mano, apoyar un poco más la hoja, y hundirla. La piel cederá como la seda, como el caucho, como la badana. No hay nada más tierno que la piel del hombre y la sangre siempre está ahí, lista a brotar. Una navaja como ésta no traiciona. Es la mejor de mis navajas. Pero yo no quiero ser un asesino, no señor. Usted vino para que yo lo afeitara. Y yo cumplo honradamente con mi trabajo... No quiero mancharme de sangre. De espuma y nada más. Usted es un verdugo y yo no soy más que un barbero. Y cada cual en su puesto. Esto es. Cada cual en su puesto.

La barba había quedado limpia, pulida y templada. El hombre se incorporó para mirarse en el espejo. Se pasó las manos por la piel y la sintió fresca y nuevecita.

"Gracias", dijo. Se dirigió al ropero en busca del cinturón, de la pistola y del kepis. Yo debía estar muy pálido y sentía la camisa empapada. Torres concluyó de ajustar la hebilla, rectificó la posición de la pistola en la funda y luego de alisarse maquinalmente los cabellos, se puso el kepis. Del bolsillo del pantalón extrajo unas monedas para pagarme el importe del servicio. Y empezó a caminar hacia la puerta. En el umbral se detuvo un segundo y volviéndose me dijo:

"Me habían dicho que usted me mataría. Vine para comprobarlo. Pero matar no es fácil. Yo sé por qué se lo digo". Yo siguió calle abajo.

next ones and it goes on like this until everything is a sea of blood. I could cut this throat just so, zip! zip! I wouldn't give him time to complain and since he has his eyes closed he wouldn't see the glistening knife blade or my glistening eyes. But I'm trembling like a real murderer. Out of his neck a gush of blood would spout onto the sheet, on the chair, on my hands, on the floor. I would have to close the door. And the blood would keep inching along the floor, warm, ineradicable, uncontainable, until it reached the street, like a little scarlet stream. I'm sure that one solid stroke, one deep incision, would prevent any pain. He wouldn't suffer. But what would I do with the body? Where would I hide it? I would have to flee, leaving all I have behind, and take refuge far away, far, far away. But they would follow until they found me. "Captain Torres' murderer. He slit his throat while he was shaving him—a coward." And then on the other side. "The avenger of us all. A name to remember. (And here they would mention my name.) He was the town barber. No one knew he was defending our cause."

And what of all this? Murderer or hero? My destiny depends on the edge of this blade. I can turn my hand a bit more, press a little harder on the razor, and sink it in. The skin would give way like silk, like rubber, like the strop. There is nothing more tender than human skin and the blood is always there, ready to pour forth. A blade like this doesn't fail. It is my best. But I don't want to be a murderer, no sir. You came to me for a shave. And I perform my work honorably. . . . I don't want blood on my hands. Just lather, that's all. You are an executioner and I am only a barber. Each person has his own place in the scheme of things. That's right. His own place.

Now his chin had been stroked clean and smooth. The man sat up and looked into the mirror. He rubbed his hands over his skin and felt it fresh, like new.

"Thanks," he said. He went to the hanger for his belt, pistol and cap. I must have been very pale; my shirt felt soaked. Torres finished adjusting the buckle, straightened his pistol in the holster and after automatically smoothing down his hair, he put on the cap. From his pants pocket he took out several coins to pay me for my services. And he began to head toward the door. In the doorway he paused for a moment, and turning to me he said:

"They told me that you'd kill me. I came to find out. But killing isn't easy. You can take my word for it." And he headed on down the street.

QUESTIONS

1 In the first paragraph of the English version we see the sentence " 'It's hot as hell.' " The Spanish version, " 'Hace un calor de todos los demonios,' " translates literally, "It's hot as all the devils," or to be exact, "It makes a heat like all the demons." Comment on the impact of the translator's version of this sentence compared with the literal translation from the Spanish. If you know some Spanish, you will be able to find other examples of free translation in which words are altered by the translator. Comment on their effect.

2 Note the sentence in the long central paragraph on page 245 of the English version: "There, for sure, the razor had to be handled masterfully, since the hair, though softer, grew in little swirls." The Spanish version reads, "Porque allí sí que debía manejar con habilidad la hoja, pues el pelo, aunque en agraz, se enredaba en pequeños remolinos." Discuss the effects in this sentence of alliteration, consonance, and assonance in the English translation compared with the Spanish version.

3 Discuss the effects of alliteration, consonance, and assonance in the two long sentences on page 245 beginning with, "He is a calm man. . . ." The Spanish version begins, "Es un hombre sereno. . . ."

4 In the fourth paragraph from the end, the narrator tells us, "Each person has his own place in the scheme of things." If you know some Spanish you will discover the original omits the phrase "in the scheme of things," leaving it simply "Y cada cual en su puesto." Why did the translator extend this sentence? Find and comment on other additions or omissions in the English version.

5 Based on the variations revealed by the answers to the questions above, write a short essay on the problems that a student faces when analyzing stories in translation.

PART TWO

William Faulkner

BARN BURNING

The store in which the Justice of the Peace's court was sitting smelled of cheese. The boy, crouched on his nail keg at the back of the crowded room, knew he smelled cheese, and more: from where he sat he could see the ranked shelves close-packed with the solid, squat, dynamic shapes of tin cans whose labels his stomach read, not from the lettering which meant nothing to his mind but from the scarlet devils and the silver curve of fish—this, the cheese which he knew he smelled and the hermetic meat which his intestines believed he smelled coming in intermittent gusts momentary and brief between the other constant one, the smell and sense just a little of fear because mostly of despair and grief, the old fierce pull of blood. He could not see the table where the Justice sat and before which his father and his father's enemy (*our enemy* he thought in that despair; *ourn! mine and hisn both! He's my father!*) stood, but he could hear them, the two of them that is, because his father had said no word yet:

"But what proof have you, Mr. Harris?"

"I told you. The hog got into my corn. I caught it up and sent it back to him. He had no fence that would hold it. I told him so, warned him. The next time I put the hog in my pen. When he came to get it I gave him enough wire to patch up his pen. The next time I put the hog up and kept it. I rode down to his house and saw the wire I gave him still rolled on to the spool in his yard. I told him he could have the hog when he paid me a dollar pound fee. That evening a nigger came with the dollar and got the hog. He was a strange nigger. He said, 'He say to tell you wood and hay kin burn.' I said, 'What?' 'That whut he say to tell you,' the nigger said. 'Wood and hay kin burn.' That night my barn burned. I got the stock out but I lost the barn."

"Where is the nigger? Have you got him?"

"He was a strange nigger, I tell you. I don't know what became of him."

"But that's not proof. Don't you see that's not proof?"

"Get that boy up here. He knows." For a moment the boy thought too that the man meant his older brother until Harris said, "Not him. The little one. The boy," and, crouching, small for his age, small and wiry like his father, in patched and faded jeans even too small for him, with straight, uncombed, brown hair and eyes gray and wild as storm scud, he saw the men between himself and the table part and become a lane of grim faces, at the end of which he saw the justice, a shabby, collarless, graying man in spectacles, beckoning him. He felt no floor under his bare feet; he seemed to walk beneath the palpable weight of the grim turning faces. His father, stiff in his black Sunday coat donned not for the trial but for the moving, did not even look at him. *He aims for me to lie,* he thought, again with that frantic grief and despair. *And I will have to do hit.*

"What's your name, boy?" the Justice said.

"Colonel Sartoris Snopes," the boy whispered.

"Hey?" the Justice said. "Talk louder. Colonel Sartoris? I reckon anybody named for Colonel Sartoris in this country can't help but tell the truth, can they?" The boy said nothing. *Enemy! Enemy!* he thought; for a moment he could not even see, could not see that the Justice's face was kindly nor discern that his voice was troubled when he spoke to the man named Harris: "Do you want me to question this boy?" But he could hear, and during those subsequent long seconds while there was absolutely no sound in the crowded little room save that of quiet and intent breathing it was as if he had swung outward at the end of a grape vine, over a ravine, and at the top of the swing had been caught in a prolonged instant of mesmerized gravity, weightless in time.

"No!" Harris said violently, explosively. "Damnation! Send

him out of here!" Now time, the fluid world, rushed beneath him again, the voices coming to him again through the smell of cheese and sealed meat, the fear and despair and the old grief of blood:

"This case is closed. I can't find against you, Snopes, but I can give you advice. Leave this country and don't come back to it."

His father spoke for the first time, his voice cold and harsh, level, without emphasis: "I aim to. I don't figure to stay in a country among people who . . ." he said something unprintable and vile, addressed to no one.

"That'll do," the Justice said. "Take your wagon and get out of this country before dark. Case dismissed."

His father turned, and he followed the stiff black coat, the wiry figure walking a little stiffly from where a Confederate provost's man's musket ball had taken him in the heel on a stolen horse thirty years ago, followed the two backs now, since his older brother had appeared from somewhere in the crowd, no taller than the father but thicker, chewing tobacco steadily, between the two lines of grim-faced men and out of the store and across the worn gallery and down the sagging steps and among the dogs and half-grown boys in the mild May dust, where as he passed a voice hissed:

"Barn burner!"

Again he could not see, whirling; there was a face in a red haze, moonlike, bigger than the full moon, the owner of it half again his size, he leaping in the red haze toward the face, feeling no blow, feeling no shock when his head struck the earth, scrabbling up and leaping again, feeling no blow this time either and tasting no blood, scrabbling up to see the other boy in full flight and himself already leaping into pursuit as his father's hand jerked him back, the harsh, cold voice speaking above him: "Go get in the wagon."

It stood in a grove of locusts and mulberries across the road. His two hulking sisters in their Sunday dresses and his mother and her sister in calico and sunbonnets were already in it, sitting on and among the sorry residue of the dozen and more movings which even the boy could remember—the battered stove, the broken beds and chairs, the clock inlaid with mother-of-pearl, which would not run, stopped at some fourteen minutes past two o'clock of a dead and forgotten day and time, which had been his mother's dowry. She was crying, though when she saw him she drew her sleeve across her face and began to descend from the wagon. "Get back," the father said.

"He's hurt. I got to get some water and wash his . . ."

"Get back in the wagon," his father said. He got in too, over the tail-gate. His father mounted to the seat where the older brother already sat and struck the gaunt mules two savage blows with the peeled willow, but without heat. It was not even sadistic; it was exactly that same quality which in later years would cause his descendants to over-run the engine before putting a motor car into motion, striking and reining back in the same movement. The wagon went on, the store with its quiet crowd of grimly watching men dropped behind; a curve in the road hid it. *Forever* he thought. *Maybe he's done satisfied now, now that he has* . . . stopping himself, not to say it aloud even to himself. His mother's hand touched his shoulder.

"Does hit hurt?" she said.

"Naw," he said. "Hit don't hurt. Lemme be."

"Can't you wipe some of the blood off before hit dries?"

"I'll wash to-night," he said. "Lemme be, I tell you."

The wagon went on. He did not know where they were going. None of them ever did or ever asked, because it was always somewhere, always a house of sorts waiting for them a day or two days or even three days away. Likely his father had already arranged to make a crop on another farm before he . . . Again he had to stop himself. He (the father) always did. There was something about his wolflike independence and even courage when the advantage was at least neutral which impressed strangers, as if they got from his latent ravening ferocity not so much a sense of dependability as a feeling that his ferocious conviction in the rightness of his own actions would be of advantage to all whose interest lay with his.

That night they camped, in a grove of oaks and beeches where a spring ran. The nights were still cool and they had a fire against it, of a rail lifted from a nearby fence and cut into lengths—a small fire, neat, niggard almost, a shrewd fire; such fires were his father's habit and custom always, even in freezing weather. Older, the boy might have remarked this and wondered why not a big one; why should not a man who had not only seen the waste and extravagance of war, but who had in his blood an inherent voracious prodigality with material not his own, have burned everything in sight? Then he might have gone a step farther and thought that that was the reason: that niggard blaze was the living fruit of nights passed during those four years in the woods hiding from all men, blue or gray, with his strings of horses (captured horses, he called them). And older still, he might have divined the true reason: that the element of fire spoke to some deep mainspring of his father's being, as the element of steel or of powder spoke to other men, as the one weapon for the preservation of integrity, else breath were not worth the breathing, and hence to be regarded with respect and used with discretion.

But he did not think this now and he had seen those same niggard blazes all his life. He merely ate his supper beside it and was already half asleep over his iron plate when his father called him, and once more he followed the stiff back, the stiff and ruthless limp, up the slope and on to the starlit road where, turning, he could see his father against the stars but without face or depth—a shape black, flat, and bloodless as though cut from tin in the iron folds of the frockcoat which had not been made for him, the voice harsh like tin and without heat like tin:

"You were fixing to tell them. You would have told him." He didn't answer. His father struck him with the flat of his hand on the side of the head, hard but without heat, exactly as he had struck the two mules at the store, exactly as he would strike either of them with any stick in order to kill a horse fly, his voice still without heat or anger: "You're getting to be a man. You got to learn. You got to learn to stick to your own blood or you ain't going to have any blood to stick to you. Do you think either of them, any man there this morning, would? Don't you know all they wanted was a chance to get at me because they knew I had them beat? Eh?" Later, twenty years later, he was to tell himself, "If I had said they wanted only truth, justice, he would have hit me again." But now he said nothing. He was not crying. He just stood there. "Answer me," his father said.

"Yes," he whispered. His father turned.

"Get on to bed. We'll be there tomorrow."

Tomorrow they were there. In the early afternoon the wagon stopped before a paintless two-room house identical almost with the dozen others it had stopped before even in the boy's ten years, and again, as on the other dozen occasions, his mother and aunt got down and began to unload the wagon, although his two sisters and his father and brother had not moved.

"Likely hit ain't fitten for hawgs," one of the sisters said.

"Nevertheless, fit it will and you'll hog it and like it," his father said. "Get out of them chairs and help your Ma unload."

The two sisters got down, big, bovine, in a flutter of cheap ribbons; one of them drew from the jumbled wagon bed a battered lantern, the other a worn broom. His father handed the reins to the older son and began to climb stiffly over the wheel. "When they get unloaded, take the team to the barn and feed them." Then he said, and at first the boy thought he was still speaking to his brother: "Come with me."

"Me?" he said.

"Yes," his father said. "You."

"Abner," his mother said. His father paused and looked back—the harsh level stare beneath the shaggy, graying, irascible brows.

"I reckon I'll have a word with the man that aims to begin tomorrow owning me body and soul for the next eight months."

They went back up the road. A week ago—or before last night, that is—he would have asked where they were going, but not now. His father had struck him before last night but never before had he paused afterward to explain why; it was as if the blow and the following calm, outrageous voice still rang, repercussed, divulging nothing to him save the terrible handicap of being young, the light weight of his few years, just heavy enough to prevent his soaring free of the world as it seemed to be ordered but not heavy enough to keep him footed solid in it, to resist it and try to change the course of its events.

Presently he could see the grove of oaks and cedars and the other flowering trees and shrubs where the house would be, though not the house yet. They walked beside a fence massed with honeysuckle and Cherokee roses and came to a gate swinging open between two brick pillars, and now, beyond a sweep of drive, he saw the house for the first time and at that instant he forgot his father and the terror and despair both, and even when he remembered his father again (who had not stopped) the terror and despair did not return. Because, for all the twelve movings, they had sojurned until now in a poor country, a land of small farms and fields and houses, and he had never seen a house like this before. *Hit's big as a courthouse* he thought quietly, with a surge of peace and joy whose reason he could not have thought into words, being too young for that: *They are safe from him. People whose lives are a part of this peace and dignity are beyond his touch, he no more to them than a buzzing wasp: capable of stinging for a little moment but that's all; the spell of this peace and dignity rendering even the barns and stable and cribs which belong to it impervious to the puny flames he might contrive* . . . this, the peace and joy, ebbing for an instant as he looked again at the stiff black back, the stiff and implacable limp of the figure which was not dwarfed by the house, for the reason that it had never looked big anywhere and which now, against the serene columned backdrop, had more than ever that impervious quality of something cut ruthlessly from tin, depthless, as though, sidewise to the sun, it would cast no shadow. Watching him, the boy remarked the absolutely undeviating course which his father held and saw the stiff foot come squarely down in a pile of fresh droppings where a horse had stood in the drive and which his father could have avoided by a simple change of stride. But it ebbed only for a moment, though he could not have thought this into words either, walking on in the spell of the house, which he could even want but without envy, without sorrow, certainly never with that ravening and jealous rage which unknown to him walked in the ironlike black coat before him: *Maybe he will feel it too. Maybe it will even change him now from what maybe he couldn't help but be.*

They crossed the portico. Now he could hear his father's stiff foot as it came down on the boards with clocklike finality, a sound out of all proportion to the displacement of the body it bore and which was not dwarfed either by the white door before it, as though it had attained to a sort of vicious and ravening minimum not to be dwarfed by anything—the flat, wide, black hat, the formal coat of broadcloth which had once been black but which had now that friction-glazed greenish cast of the bodies of old house flies, the lifted sleeve which was too large, the lifted hand like a curled claw. The door opened so promptly that the boy knew the Negro must have been watching them all the time, an old man with neat grizzled hair, in a linen jacket, who stood barring the door with his body, saying, "Wipe yo foots, white man, fo you come in here. Major ain't home nohow."

"Get out of my way, nigger," his father said, without heat too, flinging the door back and the Negro also and entering, his hat still on his head. And now the boy saw the prints of the stiff foot on the doorjamb and saw them appear on the pale rug behind the machine-like deliberation of the foot which seemed to bear (or transmit) twice the weight which the body compassed. The Negro was shouting "Miss Lula! Miss Lula!" somewhere behind them, then the boy, deluged as though by a warm wave by a suave turn of carpeted stair and a pendant glitter of chandeliers and a mute gleam of gold frames, heard the swift feet and saw her too, a lady—perhaps he had never seen her like before either—in a gray, smooth gown with lace at the throat and an apron tied at the waist and the sleeves turned back, wiping cake or biscuit dough from her hands with a towel as she came up the hall, looking not at his father at all but at the tracks on the blond rug with an expression of incredulous amazement.

"I tried," the Negro cried. "I tole him to . . ."

"Will you please go away?" she said in a shaking voice. "Major de Spain is not at home. Will you please go away?"

His father had not spoken again. He did not speak again. He did not even look at her. He just stood stiff in the center of the rug, in his hat, the shaggy iron-gray brows twitching slightly above the pebble-colored eyes as he appeared to examine the house with brief deliberation. Then with the same deliberation he turned; the boy watched him pivot on the good leg and saw the stiff foot drag round the arc of the turning, leaving a final long and fading smear. His father never looked at it, he never once looked down at the rug. The Negro held the door. It closed behind them, upon the hysteric and indistinguishable woman-wail. His father stopped at the top of the steps and scraped his boot clean on the edge of it. At the gate he stopped again. He stood for a moment, planted stiffly on the stiff foot, looking back at the house. "Pretty and white, ain't it?" he said. "That's sweat. Nigger sweat. Maybe it ain't white enough yet to suit him. Maybe he wants to mix some white sweat with it."

Two hours later the boy was chopping wood behind the house within which his mother and aunt and the two sisters (the mother and aunt, not the two girls, he knew that; even at this distance and muffled by walls the flat loud voices of the two girls emanated an incorrigible idle inertia) were setting up the stove to prepare a meal, when he heard the hooves and saw the linen-clad man on a fine sorrel mare, whom he recognized even before he saw the rolled rug in front of the Negro youth following on a fat bay carriage horse—a suffused, angry face vanishing, still at full gallop, beyond the corner of the house where his father and brother were sitting in the two tilted chairs; and a moment later, almost before he could have put the axe down, he heard the hooves again and watched the sorrel mare go back out of the yard, already galloping again. Then his father began to shout one of the sisters' names, who presently emerged backward from the kitchen door dragging the rolled rug along the ground by one end while the other sister walked behind it.

"If you ain't going to tote, go on and set up the wash pot," the first said.

"You, Sarty!" the second shouted. "Set up the wash pot!" His father appeared at the door, framed against that shabbiness, as he had been against that other bland perfection, impervious to either, the mother's anxious face at his shoulder.

"Go on," the father said. "Pick it up." The two sisters stooped, broad, lethargic; stooping, they presented an incredible expanse of pale cloth and a flutter of tawdry ribbons.

"If I thought enough of a rug to have to git hit all the way from France I wouldn't keep hit where folks coming in would have to tromp on hit," the first said. They raised the rug.

"Abner," the mother said. "Let me do it."

"You go back and git dinner," his father said. "I'll tend to this."

From the woodpile through the rest of the afternoon the boy watched them, the rug spread flat in the dust beside the bubbling wash pot, the two sisters stooping over it with that profound and lethargic reluctance, while the father stood over them in turn, implacable and grim, driving them though never raising his voice again. He could smell the harsh homemade lye they were using; he saw his mother come to the door once and look toward them with an expression not anxious now but very like despair; he saw his father turn, and he fell to with the axe and saw from the corner of his eye his father raise from the ground a flattish fragment of field stone and examine it and return to the pot, and this time his mother actually spoke: "Abner. Abner. Please don't. Please, Abner."

Then he was done too. It was dusk; the whippoorwills had already begun. He could smell coffee from the room where they would presently eat the cold food remaining from the mid-afternoon meal, though when he entered the house he realized they were having coffee again probably because there was a fire on the hearth, before which the rug now lay spread over the backs of two chairs. The tracks of his father's foot were gone. Where they had been were now long, water-cloudy scoriations resembling the sporadic course of a lilliputian mowing machine.

It still hung there while they ate the cold food and then went to bed, scattered without order or claim up and down the two rooms, his mother in one bed, where his father would later lie, the older brother in the other, himself, the aunt, and the two sisters on pallets on the floor. But his father was not in bed yet. The last thing the boy remembered was the depthless, harsh silhouette of the hat and coat bending over the rug and it seemed to him that he had not even closed his eyes when the silhouette was standing over him, the fire almost dead behind it, the stiff foot prodding him awake. "Catch up the mule," his father said.

When he returned with the mule his father was standing in the black door, the rolled rug over his shoulder. "Ain't you going to ride?" he said.

"No. Give me your foot."

He bent his knee into his father's hand, the wiry, surprising power flowed smoothly, rising, he rising with it, on to the mule's bare back (they had owned a saddle once; the boy could remember it though not when or where) and with the same effortlessness his father swung the rug up in front of him. Now in the starlight they retraced the afternoon's path, up the dusty road rife with honeysuckle, through the gate and up the black tunnel of the drive to the lightless house, where he sat on the mule and felt the rough warp of the rug drag across his thighs and vanish.

"Don't you want me to help?" he whispered. His father did not answer and now he heard again that stiff foot striking the hollow portico with that wooden and clocklike deliberation, that outrageous overstatement of the weight it carried. The rug, hunched, not flung (the boy could tell that even in the darkness) from his father's shoulder struck the angle of wall and floor with a sound unbelievably loud, thunderous, then the foot again, unhurried and enormous; a light came on in the house and the boy sat, tense, breathing steadily and quietly and just a little fast, though the foot itself did not increase its beat at all, descending the steps now; now the boy could see him.

"Don't you want to ride now?" he whispered. "We kin both ride now," the light within the house altering now, flaring up and sinking. *He's coming down the stairs now,* he thought. He had already ridden the mule up beside the horse block; presently his father was up behind him and he doubled the reins over and slashed the mule across the neck, but before the animal could begin to trot the hard, thin arm came round him, the hard, knotted hand jerking the mule back to a walk.

In the first red rays of the sun they were in the lot, putting plow gear on the mules. This time the sorrel mare was in the lot before he heard it at all, the rider collarless and even bareheaded, trembling, speaking in a shaking voice as the woman in the house had done, his father merely looking up once before stooping again to the hame he was buckling, so that the man on the mare spoke to his stooping back:

"You must realize you have ruined that rug. Wasn't there anybody here, any of your women . . ." he ceased, shaking, the boy watching him, the older brother leaning now in the stable door, chewing, blinking slowly and steadily at nothing apparently. "It cost a hundred dollars. But you never had a hundred dollars. You never will. So I'm going to charge you twenty bushels of corn against your crop. I'll add it in your contract and when you come to the commissary you can sign it. That won't keep Mrs. de Spain quiet but maybe it will teach you to wipe your feet off before you enter her house again."

Then he was gone. The boy looked at his father, who still had not spoken or even looked up again, who was now adjusting the loggerhead in the hame.

"Pap," he said. His father looked at him—the inscrutable face, the shaggy brows beneath which the gray eyes glinted coldly. Suddenly the boy went toward him, fast, stopping as suddenly. "You done the best you could!" he cried. "If he wanted hit done different why didn't he wait and tell you how? He won't git no twenty bushels! He won't git none! We'll gether hit and hide hit! I kin watch . . ."

"Did you put the cutter back in that straight stock like I told you?"

"No, sir," he said.

"Then go do it."

That was Wednesday. During the rest of that week he worked steadily, at what was within his scope and some which was beyond it, with an industry that did not need to be driven nor even commanded twice; he had this from his mother, with the difference that some at least of what he did he liked to do, such as splitting wood with the half-size axe which his mother and aunt had earned, or saved money somehow, to present him with at Christmas. In company with the two older women (and on one afternoon, even one of the sisters), he built pens for the shoat and the cow which were a part of his father's contract with the landlord, and one afternoon, his father being absent, gone somewhere on one of the mules, he went to the field.

They were running a middle buster now, his brother holding the plow straight while he handled the reins, and walking beside the straining mule, the rich black soil shearing cool and damp against his bare ankles, he thought *Maybe this is the end of it. Maybe even that twenty bushels that seems hard to have to pay for just a rug will be a cheap price for him to stop forever and always from being what he used to be;* thinking, dreaming now, so that his brother had to speak sharply to him to mind the mule: *Maybe he even won't collect the twenty bushels. Maybe it will all add up and balance and vanish—corn, rug, fire; the terror and grief, the being pulled two ways like between two teams of horses—gone, done with for ever and ever.*

Then it was Saturday; he looked up from beneath the mule he was harnessing and saw his father in the black coat and hat. "Not that," his father said. "The wagon gear." And then, two hours later, sitting in the wagon bed behind his father and brother on the seat, the wagon accomplished a final curve, and he saw the weathered paintless store with its tattered tobacco- and patent-medicine posters and the tethered wagons and saddle animals below the gallery. He mounted the gnawed steps behind his father and brother, and there again was the lane of quiet, watching faces for the three of them to walk through. He saw the man in spectacles sitting at the plank table and he did not need to be told this was a Justice of the Peace; he sent one glare of fierce, exultant, partisan defiance at the man in collar and cravat now, whom he had seen but twice before in his life, and that on a galloping horse, who now wore on his face an expression not of rage but of amazed unbelief which the boy could not have known was at the incredible circumstance of being sued by one of his own tenants, and came and stood against his father and cried at the Justice: "He ain't done it! He ain't burnt . . ."

"Go back to the wagon," his father said.

"Burnt?" the Justice said. "Do I understand this rug was burned too?"

"Does anybody here claim it was?" his father said. "Go back to the wagon." But he did not, he merely retreated to the rear of the room, crowded as that other had been, but not to sit down this time, instead, to stand pressing among the motionless bodies, listening to the voices:

"And you claim twenty bushels of corn is too high for the damage you did to the rug?"

"He brought the rug to me and said he wanted the tracks washed out of it. I washed the tracks out and took the rug back to him."

"But you didn't carry the rug back to him in the same condition it was in before you made the tracks on it."

His father did not answer, and now for perhaps half a minute there was no sound at all save that of breathing, the faint, steady suspiration of complete and intent listening.

"You decline to answer that, Mr. Snopes?" Again his father did not answer. "I'm going to find against you, Mr. Snopes. I'm going to find that you were responsible for the injury to Major de Spain's rug and hold you liable for it. But twenty bushels of corn seems a little high for a man in your circumstances to have to pay. Major de Spain claims it cost a hundred dollars. October corn will be worth about fifty cents. I figure that if Major de Spain can stand a ninety-five dollar loss on something he paid cash for, you can stand a five-dollar loss you haven't earned yet. I hold you in damages to Major de Spain to the amount of ten bushels of corn over and above your contract with him, to be paid to him out of your crop at gathering time. Court adjourned."

It had taken no time hardly, the morning was but half begun. He thought they would return home and perhaps back to the field, since they were late, far behind all other farmers. But instead his father passed on behind the wagon, merely indicating with his hand for the older brother to follow with it, and crossed the road toward the blacksmith shop opposite, pressing on after his father, overtaking him, speaking, whispering up at the harsh, calm face beneath the weathered hat. "He won't git no ten bushels neither. He won't git one. We'll . . ." until his father glanced for an instant down at him, the face absolutely calm, the grizzled eyebrows tangled above the cold eyes, the voice almost pleasant, almost gentle:

"You think so? Well, we'll wait till October anyway."

The matter of the wagon—the setting of a spoke or two and the tightening of the tires—did not take long either, the business of the tires accomplished by driving the wagon into the spring branch behind the shop and letting it stand there, the mules nuzzling into the water from time to time, and the boy on the seat with the idle reins, looking up the slope and through the sooty tunnel of the shed where the slow hammer rang and where his father sat on an upended cypress bolt, easily, either talking or listening, still sitting there when the boy brought the dripping wagon up out of the branch and halted it before the door.

"Take them on to the shade and hitch," his father said. He did so and returned. His father and the smith and a third man squatting on his heels inside the door were talking, about crops and animals; the boy, squatting too in the ammoniac dust and hoof-parings and scales of rust, heard his father tell a long and unhurried story out of the time before the birth of the older brother even when he had been a professional horsetrader. And then his father came up beside him where he stood before a tattered last year's circus poster on the other side of the store, gazing rapt and quiet at the scarlet horses, the incredible poisings and convolutions of tulle and tights and the painted leers of comedians, and said, "It's time to eat."

But not at home. Squatting beside his brother against the front wall, he watched his father emerge from the store and produce from a paper sack a segment of cheese and divide it carefully and deliberately into three with his pocket knife and produce crackers from the same sack. They all three squatted on the gallery and ate, slowly, without talking; then in the store again, they drank from a tin dipper tepid water smelling of the cedar bucket and of living beech trees. And still they did not go home. It was a horse lot this time, a tall rail fence upon and along which men stood and sat and out of which one by one horses were led, to be walked and trotted and then cantered back and forth along the road while the slow swapping and buying went on and the sun began to slant westward, they—the three of them—watching and listening, the older brother with his muddy eyes and his steady, inevitable tobacco, the father commenting now and then on certain of the animals, to no one in particular.

It was after sundown when they reached home. They ate supper by lamplight, then, sitting on the doorstep, the boy watched the night fully accomplish, listening to the whippoorwills and the frogs, when he heard his mother's voice: "Abner! No! No! Oh, God. Oh, God. Abner!" and he rose, whirled, and saw the altered light through the door where a candle stub now burned in a bottle neck on the table and his father, still in the hat and coat, at once formal and burlesque as though dressed carefully for some shabby and ceremonial violence, emptying the reservoir of the lamp back into the five-gallon kerosene can from which it had been filled, while the mother tugged at his arm until he shifted the lamp to the other hand and flung her back, not savagely or viciously, just hard, into the wall, her hands flung out against the wall for balance, her mouth open and in her face the same quality of hopeless despair as had been in her voice. Then his father saw him standing in the door.

"Go to the barn and get that can of oil we were oiling the wagon with," he said. The boy did not move. Then he could speak.

"What . . ." he cried. "What are you . . ."

"Go get that oil," his father said. "Go."

Then he was moving, running, outside the house, toward the stable: this the old habit, the old blood which he had not been permitted to choose for himself, which had been bequeathed him willy nilly and which had run for so long (and who knew where, battening on what of outrage and savagery and lust) before it came to him. *I could keep on,* he thought. *I could run on and on and never look back, never need to see his face again. Only I can't. I can't,* the rusted can in his hand now, the liquid sploshing in it as he ran back to the house and into it, into the sound of his mother's weeping in the next room, and handed the can to his father.

"Ain't you going to even send a nigger?" he cried. "At least you sent a nigger before!"

This time his father didn't strike him. The hand came even faster than the blow had, the same hand which had set the can on the table with almost excruciating care flashing from the can toward him too quick for him to follow it, gripping him by the back of his shirt and on to tiptoe before he had seen it quit the can, the face stooping at him in breathless and frozen ferocity, the cold, dead voice speaking over him to the older brother who leaned against the table, chewing with that steady, curious, sidewise motion of cows:

"Empty the can into the big one and go on. I'll catch up with you."

"Better tie him up to the bedpost," the brother said.

"Do like I told you," the father said. Then the boy was moving, his bunched shirt and the hard, bony hand between his shoulder-blades, his toes just touching the floor, across the room and into the other one, past the sisters sitting with spread heavy thighs in the two chairs over the cold hearth, and to where his mother and aunt sat side by side on the bed, the aunt's arms about his mother's shoulders.

"Hold him," the father said. The aunt made a startled movement. "Not you," the father said. "Lennie. Take hold of him. I want to see you do it." His mother took him by the wrist. "You'll hold him better than that. If he gets loose don't you know what he is going to do? He will go up yonder." He jerked his head toward the road. "Maybe I'd better tie him."

"I'll hold him," his mother whispered.

"See you do then." Then his father was gone, the stiff foot heavy and measured upon the boards, ceasing at last.

Then he began to struggle. His mother caught him in both arms, he jerking and wrenching at them. He would be stronger in the end, he knew that. But he had no time to wait for it. "Lemme go!" he cried. "I don't want to have to hit you!"

"Let him go!" the aunt said. "If he don't go, before God, I am going up there myself!"

"Don't you see I can't?" his mother cried. "Sarty! Sarty! No! No! Help me, Lizzie!"

Then he was free. His aunt grasped at him but it was too late. He whirled, running, his mother stumbled forward on to her knees behind him, crying to the nearer sister: "Catch him, Net! Catch him!" But that was too late too, the sister (the sisters were twins, born at the same time, yet either of them now gave the impression of being, encompassing as much living meat and volume and weight as any other two of the family) not yet having begun to rise from the chair, her head, face, alone merely turned, presenting to him in the flying instant an astonishing expanse of young female features untroubled by any surprise even, wearing only an expression of bovine interest. Then he was out of the room, out of the house, in the mild dust of the starlit road and the heavy rifeness of honeysuckle, the pale ribbon unspooling with terrific slowness under his running feet, reaching the gate at last and turning in, running, his heart and lungs drumming, on up the drive toward the lighted house, the lighted door. He did not knock, he burst in, sobbing for breath, incapable for the moment of speech; he saw the astonished face of the Negro in the linen jacket without knowing when the Negro had appeared.

"De Spain!" he cried, panted. "Where's . . ." then he saw the white man too emerging from a white door down the hall. "Barn!" he cried. "Barn!"

"What?" the white man said. "Barn?"

"Yes!" the boy cried. "Barn!"

"Catch him!" the white man shouted.

But it was too late this time too. The Negro grasped his shirt, but the entire sleeve, rotten with washing, carried away, and he was out that door too and in the drive again, and had actually never ceased to run even while he was screaming into the white man's face.

Behind him the white man was shouting, "My horse! Fetch my horse!" and he thought for an instant of cutting across the park and climbing the fence into the road, but he did not know the park nor how high the vine-massed fence might be and he dared not risk it. So he ran on down the drive, blood and breath roaring; presently he was in the road again though he could not see it. He could not hear either: the galloping mare was almost upon him before he heard her, and even then he held his course, as if the very urgency of his wild grief and need must in a moment more find him wings, waiting until the ultimate instant to hurl himself aside and into the weed-choked roadside ditch as the horse thundered past and on, for an instant in furious silhouette against the stars, the tranquil early summer night sky which, even before the shape of the horse and rider vanished, stained abruptly and violently upward: a long, swirling roar incredible and soundless, blotting the stars, and he springing up and into the road again, running again, knowing it was too late yet still running even after he heard the shot and, an instant later, two shots, pausing now without knowing he had ceased to run, crying "Pap! Pap!" running again before he knew he had begun to run, stumbling, tripping over something and scrabbling up again without ceasing to run, looking backward over his shoulder at the glare as he got up, running on among the invisible trees, panting, sobbing, "Father! Father!"

At midnight he was sitting on the crest of a hill. He did not know it was midnight and he did not know how far he had come. But there was no glare behind him now and he sat now, his back toward what he had called home for four days anyhow, his face toward the dark woods which he would enter when breath was strong again, small, shaking steadily in the chill darkness, hugging himself into the remainder of his thin, rotten shirt, the grief and despair now no longer terror and fear but just grief and despair. *Father. My father,* he thought. "He was brave!" he cried suddenly, aloud but not loud, no more than a whisper: "He was! He was in the war! He was in Colonel Sartoris' cav'ry!" not knowing that his father had gone to that war a private in the fine old European sense, wearing no uniform, admitting the authority of and giving fidelity to no man or army or flag, going to war as Malbrouck himself did: for booty—it meant nothing and less than nothing to him if it were enemy booty or his own.

The slow constellations wheeled on. It would be dawn and then sun-up after a while and he would be hungry. But that would be tomorrow and now he was only cold, and walking would cure that. His breathing was easier now and he decided to get up and go on, and then he found that he had been asleep because he knew it was almost dawn, the night almost over. He could tell that from the whippoorwills. They were everywhere now among the dark trees below him, constant and inflectioned and ceaseless, so that, as the instant for giving over to the day birds drew nearer and nearer, there was no interval at all between them. He got up. He was a little stiff, but walking would cure that too as it would the cold, and soon there would be the sun. He went on down the hill, toward the dark woods within which the liquid silver voices of the birds called unceasing—the rapid and urgent beating of the urgent and quiring heart of the late spring night. He did not look back.

D. H. Lawrence

THE HORSE DEALER'S DAUGHTER

"Well, Mabel, and what are you going to do with yourself?" asked Joe, with foolish flippancy. He felt quite safe himself. Without listening for an answer, he turned aside, worked a grain of tobacco to the tip of his tongue, and spat it out. He did not care about anything, since he felt safe himself.

The three brothers and the sister sat round the desolate breakfast table, attempting some sort of desultory consultation. The morning's post had given the final tap to the family fortune, and all was over. The dreary dining-room itself, with its heavy mahogany furniture, looked as if it were waiting to be done away with.

But the consultation amounted to nothing. There was a strange air of ineffectuality about the three men, as they sprawled at table, smoking and reflecting vaguely on their own condition. The girl was alone, a rather short, sullen-looking young woman of twenty-seven. She did not share the same life as her brothers. She would have been good-looking, save for the impassive fixity of her face, "bull-dog," as her brothers called it.

There was a confused tramping of horses' feet outside. The three men all sprawled round in their chairs to watch. Beyond the dark hollybushes that separated the strip of lawn from the high-road, they could see a cavalcade of shire horses swinging out of their own yard, being taken for exercise. This was the last time. These were the last horses that would go through their hands. The young men watched with critical, callous look. They were all frightened at the collapse of their lives, and the sense of disaster in which they were involved left them no inner freedom.

Yet they were three fine, well-set fellows enough. Joe, the eldest, was a man of thirty-three, broad and handsome in a hot, flushed way. His face was red, he twisted his black moustache over a thick finger, his eyes were shallow and restless. He had a sensual way of uncovering his teeth when he laughed, and his bearing was stupid. Now he watched the horses with a glazed look of helplessness in his eyes, a certain stupor of downfall.

The great draught-horses swung past. They were tied head to tail, four of them, and they heaved along to where a lane branched off from the highroad, planting their great hoofs floutingly in the fine black mud, swinging their great rounded haunches sumptuously, and trotting a few sudden steps as they were led into the lane, round the corner. Every movement showed a massive, slumbrous strength, and a stupidity which held them in subjection. The groom at the head looked back, jerking the leading rope. And the cavalcade moved out of sight up the lane, the tail of the last horse bobbed up tight and stiff, held out taut from the swinging great haunches as they rocked behind the hedges in a motion like sleep.

Joe watched with glazed hopeless eyes. The horses were almost like his own body to him. He felt he was done for now. Luckily he was engaged to a woman as old as himself, and therefore her father, who was steward of a neighbouring estate, would provide him with a job. He would marry and go into harness. His life was over, he would be a subject animal now.

He turned uneasily aside, the retreating steps of the horses echoing in his ears. Then, with foolish restlessness, he reached for the scraps of bacon-rind from the plates, and making a faint whistling sound, flung them to the terrier that lay against the fender. He watched the dog swallow them, and waited till the creature looked into his eyes. Then a faint grin came on his face, and in a high, foolish voice he said:

"You won't get much more bacon, shall you, you little bitch?"

The dog faintly and dismally wagged its tail, then lowered its haunches, circled round, and lay down again.

There was another helpless silence at the table. Joe sprawled uneasily in his seat, not willing to go till the family conclave was dissolved. Fred Henry, the second brother, was erect, clean-limbed, alert. He had watched the passing of the horses with more sang-froid. If he was an animal, like Joe, he was an animal which controls, not one which is controlled. He was master of any horse, and he carried himself with a well-tempered air of mastery. But he was not master of the situations of life. He pushed his coarse brown moustache upwards, off his lip, and glanced irritably at his sister, who sat impassive and inscrutable.

"You'll go and stop with Lucy for a bit, shan't you?" he asked. The girl did not answer.

"I don't see what else you can do," persisted Fred Henry.

"Go as a skivvy," Joe interpolated laconically.

The girl did not move a muscle.

"If I was her, I should go in for training for a nurse," said Malcolm, the youngest of them all. He was the baby of the family, a young man of twenty-two, with a fresh, jaunty *museau.*

But Mabel did not take any notice of him. They had talked at her and round her for so many years, that she hardly heard them at all.

The marble clock on the mantelpiece softly chimed the half-hour, the dog rose uneasily from the hearthrug and looked at the party at the breakfast table. But still they sat on in ineffectual conclave.

"Oh, all right," said Joe suddenly, apropos of nothing. "I'll get a move on."

He pushed back his chair, straddled his knees with a downward jerk, to get them free, in horsey fashion, and went to the fire. Still he did not go out of the room; he was curious to know what the others would do or say. He began to charge his pipe, looking down at the dog and saying, in a high, affected voice:

"Going wi' me? Going wi' me are ter? Tha'rt goin' further than tha counts on just now, dost hear?"

The dog faintly wagged its tail, the man stuck out his jaw and covered his pipe with his hands, and puffed intently, losing himself in the tobacco, looking down all the while at the dog with an absent brown eye. The dog looked up at him in mournful distrust. Joe stood with his knees stuck out, in real horsey fashion.

"Have you had a letter from Lucy?" Fred Henry asked of his sister.

"Last week," came the neutral reply.

"And what does she say?"

There was no answer.

"Does she *ask* you to go and stop there?" persisted Fred Henry.

"She says I can if I like."

"Well, then, you'd better. Tell her you'll come on Monday."

This was received in silence.

"That's what you'll do then, is it?" said Fred Henry, in some exasperation.

But she made no answer. There was a silence of futility and irritation in the room. Malcolm grinned fatuously.

"You'll have to make up your mind between now and next Wednesday," said Joe loudly, "or else find yourself lodgings on the kerbstone."

The face of the young woman darkened, but she sat on immutable.

"Here's Jack Fergusson!" exclaimed Malcolm, who was looking aimlessly out of the window.

"Where?" exclaimed Joe, loudly.

"Just gone past."

"Coming in?"

Malcolm craned his neck to see the gate.

"Yes," he said.

There was a silence. Mabel sat on like one condemned, at the head of the table. Then a whistle was heard from the kitchen. The dog got up and barked sharply. Joe opened the door and shouted:

"Come on."

After a moment a young man entered. He was muffled up in overcoat and a purple woollen scarf, and his tweed cap, which he did not remove, was pulled down on his head. He was of medium height, his face was rather long and pale, his eyes looked tired.

"Hello, Jack! Well, Jack!" exclaimed Malcolm and Joe. Fred Henry merely said, "Jack."

"What's doing?" asked the newcomer, evidently addressing Fred Henry.

"Same. We've got to be out by Wednesday. Got a cold?"

"I have—got it bad, too."

"Why don't you stop in?"

"*Me* stop in? When I can't stand on my legs, perhaps I shall have a chance." The young man spoke huskily. He had a slight Scotch accent.

"It's a knock-out, isn't it," said Joe, boisterously, "if a doctor goes round croaking with a cold. Looks bad for the patients, doesn't it?"

The young doctor looked at him slowly.

"Anything the matter with *you,* then?" he asked sarcastically.

"Not as I know of. Damn your eyes, I hope not. Why?"

"I thought you were very concerned about the patients, wondered if you might be one yourself."

"Damn it, no, I've never been patient to no flaming doctor, and hope I never shall be," returned Joe.

At this point Mabel rose from the table, and they all seemed to become aware of her existence. She began putting the dishes together. The young doctor looked at her, but did not address her. He had not greeted her. She went out of the room with the tray, her face impassive and unchanged.

"When are you off then, all of you?" asked the doctor.

"I'm catching the eleven-forty," replied Malcolm. "Are you goin' down wi' th' trap, Joe?"

"Yes, I've told you I am going down wi' th' trap, haven't I?"

"We'd better be getting her in then. So long, Jack, if I don't see you before I go," said Malcolm, shaking hands.

He went out, followed by Joe, who seemed to have his tail between his legs.

"Well, this is the devil's own," exclaimed the doctor, when he was left alone with Fred Henry. "Going before Wednesday, are you."

"That's the orders," replied the other.

"Where, to Northampton?"

"That's it."

"The devil!" exclaimed Fergusson, with quiet chagrin.

And there was silence between the two.

"All settled up, are you?" asked Fergusson.

"About."

There was another pause.

"Well, I shall miss yer, Freddy, boy," said the young doctor.

"And I shall miss thee, Jack," returned the other.

"Miss you like hell," mused the doctor.

Fred Henry turned aside. There was nothing to say. Mabel came in again, to finish clearing the table.

"What are *you* going to do, then, Miss Pervin?" asked Fergusson. "Going to your sister's, are you?"

Mabel looked at him with her steady, dangerous eyes, that always made him uncomfortable, unsettling his superficial ease.

"No," she said.

"Well, what in the name of fortune are *you* going to do? Say what you mean to do," cried Fred Henry, with futile intensity.

But she only averted her head, and continued her work. She folded the white table-cloth, and put on the chenille cloth.

"The sulkiest bitch that ever trod!" muttered her brother.

But she finished her task with perfectly impassive face, the young doctor watching her interestedly all the while. Then she went out.

Fred Henry stared after her, clenching his lips, his blue eyes fixing in sharp antagonism, as he made a grimace of sour exasperation.

"You could bray her into bits, and that's all you'd get out of her," he said in a small, narrowed tone.

The doctor smiled faintly.

"What's she *going* to do, then?" he asked.

"Strike me if *I* know!" returned the other.

There was a pause. Then the doctor stirred.

"I'll be seeing you to-night, shall I?" he said to his friend.

"Ay—where's it to be? Are we going over to Jessdale?"

"I don't know. I've got such a cold on me. I'll come round to the Moon and Stars, anyway."

"Let Lizzie and May miss their night for once, eh?"

"That's it—if I feel as I do now."

"All's one—"

The two young men went through the passage and down to the back door together. The house was large, but it was servantless now, and desolate. At the back was a small bricked house-yard, and beyond that a big square, gravelled fine and red, and having stables on two sides. Sloping, dank, winter-dark fields stretched away on the open sides.

But the stables were empty. Joseph Pervin, the father of the family, had been a man of no education, who had become a fairly large horse dealer. The stables had been full of horses, there was a great turmoil and come-and-go of horses and of dealers and grooms. Then the kitchen was full of servants. But of late things had declined. The old man had married a second time, to retrieve his fortunes. Now he was dead and everything was gone to the dogs, there was nothing but debt and threatening.

For months, Mabel had been servantless in the big house, keeping the home together in penury for her ineffectual brothers. She had kept house for ten years. But previously it was with unstinted means. Then, however brutal and coarse everything was, the sense of money had kept her proud, confident. The men might be foul-mouthed, the women in the kitchen might have bad reputations, her brothers might have illegitimate children. But so long as there was money, the girl felt herself established and brutally proud, reserved.

No company came to the house, save dealers and coarse men. Mabel had no associates of her own sex, after her sister went away. But she did not mind. She went regularly to church, she attended to her father. And she lived in the memory of her mother, who had died when she was fourteen, and whom she had loved. She had loved her father, too, in a different way, depending upon him, and feeling secure in him, until at the age of fifty-four he married again. And then she had set hard against him. Now he had died and left them all hopelessly in debt.

She had suffered badly during the period of poverty. Nothing, however, could shake the curious sullen, animal pride that dominated each member of the family. Now, for Mabel, the end had come. Still she would not cast about her. She would follow her own way just the same. She would always hold the keys of her own situation. Mindless and persistent, she endured from day to day. What should she think? Why should she answer anybody? It was enough that this was the end, and there was no way out. She need not pass any more darkly along the main street of the small town, avoiding every eye. She need not demean herself any more, going into the shops and buying the cheapest food. This was at an end. She thought of nobody, not even of herself. Mindless and persistent, she seemed in a sort of ecstasy to be coming nearer to her fulfilment, her own glorification, approaching her dead mother, who was glorified.

In the afternoon she took a little bag, with shears and sponge and a small scrubbing brush, and went out. It was a grey, wintry day, with saddened, dark green fields and an atmosphere blackened by the smoke of foundries not far off. She went quickly, darkly along the causeway, heeding nobody, through the town to the churchyard.

There she always felt secure, as if no one could see her, although as a matter of fact she was exposed to the stare of every one who passed along under the churchyard wall. Nevertheless, once under the shadow of the great looming church, among the graves, she felt immune from the world, reserved within the thick churchyard wall as in another country.

Carefully she clipped the grass from the grave, and arranged the pinky white, small chrysanthemums in the tin cross. When this was done, she took an empty jar from a neighbouring grave, brought water, and carefully, most scrupulously sponged the marble head-stone and the coping-stone.

It gave her sincere satisfaction to do this. She felt in immediate contact with the world of her mother. She took minute pains, went through the park in a state bordering on pure happiness, as if in performing this task she came into a subtle, intimate connection with her mother. For the life she followed here in the world was far less real than the world of death she inherited from her mother.

The doctor's house was just by the church. Fergusson, being a mere hired assistant, was slave to the country-side. As he hurried now to attend to the out-patients in the surgery, glancing across the graveyard with his quick eye, he saw the girl at her task at the grave. She seemed so intent and remote, it was like looking into another world. Some mystical element was touched in him. He slowed down as he walked, watching her as if spell-bound.

She lifted her eyes, feeling him looking. Their eyes met. And each looked away again at once, each feeling, in some way, found out by the other. He lifted his cap and passed on down the road. There remained distinct in his consciousness, like a vision, the memory of her face, lifted from the tombstone in the churchyard, and looking at him with slow, large, portentous eyes. It *was* portentous, her face. It seemed to mesmerize him. There was a heavy power in her eyes which laid hold of his whole being, as if he had drunk some powerful drug. He had been feeling weak and done before. Now the life came back into him, he felt delivered from his own fretted, daily self.

He finished his duties at the surgery as quickly as might be, hastily filling up the bottle of the waiting people with cheap drugs. Then, in perpetual haste, he set off again to visit several cases in another part of his round, before tea-time. At all times he preferred to walk if he could, but particularly when he was not well. He fancied the motion restored him.

The afternoon was falling. It was grey, deadened, and wintry, with a slow, moist, heavy coldness sinking in and deadening all the faculties. But why should he think or notice? He hastily climbed the hill and turned across the dark green fields, following the black cinder-track. In the distance, across a shallow dip in the country, the small town was clustered like smouldering ash, a tower, a spire, a heap of low, raw, extinct houses. And on the nearest fringe of the town, sloping into the dip, was Oldmeadow, the Pervins' house. He could see the stables and the outbuildings distinctly, as they lay towards him on the slope. Well, he would not go there many more times! Another resource would be lost to him, another place gone: the only company he cared for in the alien, ugly little town he was losing. Nothing but work, drudgery, constant hastening from dwelling to dwelling among the colliers and the iron-workers. It wore him out, but at the same time he had a craving for it. It was a stimulant to him to be in the homes of the working people, moving as it were through the innermost body of their life. His nerves were excited and gratified. He could come so near, into the very lives of the rough, inarticulate, powerfully emotional men and women. He grumbled, he said he hated the hellish hole. But as a matter of fact it excited him, the contact with the rough, strongly-feeling people was a stimulant applied direct to his nerves.

Below Oldmeadow, in the green, shallow, soddened hollow of fields lay a square, deep pond. Roving across the landscape, the doctor's quick eye detected a figure in black passing through the gate of the field, down towards the pond. He looked again. It would be Mabel Pervin. His mind suddenly became alive and attentive.

Why was she going down there? He pulled up on the path on the slope above, and stood staring. He could just make sure of the small black figure moving in the hollow of the failing day. He seemed to see her in the midst of such obscurity, that he was like a clairvoyant, seeing rather with the mind's eye than with ordinary sight. Yet he could see her positively enough, whilst he kept his eye attentive. He felt, if he looked away from her, in the thick, ugly falling dusk, he would lose her altogether.

He followed her minutely as she moved, direct and intent, like something transmitted rather than stirring in voluntary activity, straight down the field towards the pond. There she stood on the bank for a moment. She never raised her head. Then she waded slowly into the water.

He stood motionless as the small black figure walked slowly and deliberately towards the centre of the pond, very slowly, gradually moving deeper into the motionless water, and still moving forward as the water got up to her breast. Then he could see her no more in the dusk of the dead afternoon.

"There!" he exclaimed. "Would you believe it?"

And he hastened straight down, running over the wet, soddened fields, pushing through the hedges, down into the depression of callous wintry obscurity. It took him several minutes to come to the pond. He stood on the bank, breathing heavily. He could see nothing. His eyes seemed to penetrate the dead water. Yes, perhaps that was the dark shadow of her black clothing beneath the surface of the water.

He slowly ventured into the pond. The bottom was deep, soft clay, he sank in, and the water clasped dead cold round his legs. As he stirred he could smell the cold, rotten clay that fouled up into the water. It was objectionable in his lungs. Still, repelled and yet not heeding, he moved deeper into the pond. The cold water rose over his thighs, over his loins, upon his abdomen. The lower part of his body was all sunk in the hideous cold element. And the bottom was so deeply soft and uncertain, he was afraid of pitching with his mouth underneath. He could not swim, and was afraid.

He crouched a little, spreading his hands under the water and moving them round, trying to feel for her. The dead cold pond swayed upon his chest. He moved again, a little deeper, and again, with his hands underneath, he felt all around under the water. And he touched her clothing. But it evaded his fingers. He made a desperate effort to grasp it.

And so doing he lost his balance and went under, horribly, suffocating in the foul earthy water, struggling madly for a few moments. At last, after what seemed an eternity, he got his footing, rose again into the air and looked around. He gasped, and knew he was in the world. Then he looked at the water. She had risen near him. He grasped her clothing, and drawing her nearer, turned to take his way to land again.

He went very slowly, carefully, absorbed in the slow progress. He rose higher, climbing out of the pond. The water was now only about his legs; he was thankful, full of relief to be out of the clutches of the pond. He lifted her and staggered on to the bank, out of the horror of wet, grey clay.

He laid her down on the bank. She was quite unconscious and running with water. He made the water come from her mouth, he worked to restore her. He did not have to work very long before he could feel the breathing begin again in her; she was breathing naturally. He worked a little longer. He could feel her live beneath his hands; she was coming back. He wiped her face, wrapped her in his overcoat, looked round into the dim, dark grey world, then lifted her and staggered down the bank and across the fields.

It seemed an unthinkably long way, and his burden so heavy he felt he would never get to the house. But at last he was in the stable-yard, and then in the house-yard. He opened the door and went into the house. In the kitchen he laid her down on the hearth-rug, and called. The house was empty. But the fire was burning in the grate.

Then again he kneeled to attend to her. She was breathing regularly, her eyes were wide open and as if conscious, but there seemed something missing in her look. She was conscious in herself, but unconscious of her surroundings.

He ran upstairs, took blankets from a bed, and put them before the fire to warm. Then he removed her saturated, earthy-smelling clothing, rubbed her dry with a towel, and wrapped her naked in the blankets. Then he went into the dining-room, to look for spirits. There was a little whisky. He drank a gulp himself, and put some into her mouth.

The effect was instantaneous. She looked full into his face, as if she had been seeing him for some time, and yet had only just become conscious of him.

"Dr. Fergusson?" she said.

"What?" he answered.

He was divesting himself of his coat, intending to find some dry clothing upstairs. He could not bear the smell of the dead, clayey water, and he was mortally afraid for his own health.

"What did I do?" she asked.

"Walked into the pond," he replied. He had begun to shudder like one sick, and could hardly attend to her. Her eyes remained full on him, he seemed to be going dark in his mind, looking back at her helplessly. The shuddering became quieter in him, his life came back in him, dark and unknowing, but strong again.

"Was I out of my mind?" she asked, while her eyes were fixed on him all the time.

"Maybe, for the moment," he replied. He felt quiet, because his strength had come back. The strange fretful strain had left him.

"Am I out of my mind now?" she asked.

"Are you?" he reflected a moment. "No," he answered truthfully. "I don't see that you are." He turned his face aside. He was afraid now, because he felt dazed, and felt dimly that her power was stronger than his, in this issue. And she continued to look at him fixedly all the time. "Can you tell me where I shall find some dry things to put on?" he asked.

"Did you dive into the pond for me?" she asked.

"No," he answered. "I walked in. But I went in overhead as well."

There was silence for a moment. He hesitated. He very much wanted to go upstairs to get into dry clothing. But there was another desire in him. And she seemed to hold him. His will seemed to have gone to sleep, and left him, standing there slack before her. But he felt warm inside himself. He did not shudder at all, though his clothes were sodden on him.

"Why did you?" she asked.

"Because I didn't want you to do such a foolish thing," he said.

"It wasn't foolish," she said, still gazing at him as she lay on the floor, with a sofa cushion under her head. "It was the right thing to do. *I* knew best, then."

"I'll go and shift these wet things," he said. But still he had not the power to move out of her presence, until she sent him. It was as if she had the life of his body in her hands, and he could not extricate himself. Or perhaps he did not want to.

Suddenly she sat up. Then she became aware of her own immediate condition. She felt the blankets about her, she knew her own limbs. For a moment it seemed as if her reason were going. She looked round, with wild eye, as if seeking something. He stood still with fear. She saw her clothing lying scattered.

"Who undressed me?" she asked, her eyes resting full and inevitable on his face.

"I did," he replied, "to bring you round."

For some moments she sat and gazed at him awfully, her lips parted.

"Do you love me, then?" she asked.

He only stood and stared at her, fascinated. His soul seemed to melt.

She shuffled forward on her knees, and put her arms round him, round his legs, as he stood there, pressing her breasts against his knees and thighs, clutching him with strange, convulsive certainty, pressing his thighs against her, drawing him to her face, her throat, as she looked up at him with flaring, humble eyes of transfiguration, triumphant in first possession.

"You love me," she murmured, in strange transport, yearning and triumphant and confident. "You love me. I know you love me, I know."

And she was passionately kissing his knees, through the wet

clothing, passionately and indiscriminately kissing his knees, his legs, as if unaware of everything.

He looked down at the tangled wet hair, the wild, bare, animal shoulders. He was amazed, bewildered, and afraid. He had never thought of loving her. He had never wanted to love her. When he rescued her and restored her, he was a doctor, and she was a patient. He had had no single personal thought of her. Nay, this introduction of the personal element was very distasteful to him, a violation of his professional honour. It was horrible to have her there embracing his knees. It was horrible. He revolted from it, violently. And yet—and yet—he had not the power to break away.

She looked at him again, with the same supplication of powerful love, and that same transcendent, frightening light of triumph. In view of the delicate flame which seemed to come from her face like a light, he was powerless. And yet he had never intended to love her. He had never intended. And something stubborn in him could not give way.

"You love me," she repeated, in a murmur of deep rhapsodic assurance. "You love me."

Her hands were drawing him, drawing him down to her. He was afraid, even a little horrified. For he had, really, no intention of loving her. Yet her hands were drawing him towards her. He put out his hand quickly to steady himself, and grasped her bare shoulder. A flame seemed to burn the hand that grasped her soft shoulder. He had no intention of loving her: his whole will was against his yielding. It was horrible. And yet wonderful was the touch of her shoulders, beautiful the shining of her face. Was she perhaps mad? He had a horror of yielding to her. Yet something in him ached also.

He had been staring away at the door, away from her. But his hand remained on her shoulder. She had gone suddenly very still. He looked down at her. Her eyes were now wide with fear, with doubt, the light was dying from her face, a shadow of terrible greyness was returning. He could not bear the touch of her eyes' question upon him, and the look of death behind the question.

With an inward groan he gave way, and let his heart yield towards her. A sudden gentle smile came on his face. And her eyes, which never left his face, slowly, slowly filled with tears. He watched the strange water rise in her eyes, like some slow fountain coming up. And his heart seemed to burn and melt away in his breast.

He could not bear to look at her any more. He dropped on his knees and caught her head with his arms and pressed her face against his throat. She was very still. His heart, which seemed to have broken, was burning with a kind of agony in his breast. And he felt her slow, hot tears wetting his throat. But he could not move.

He felt the hot tears wet his neck and the hollows of his neck, and he remained motionless, suspended through one of man's eternities. Only now it had become indispensable to him to have her face pressed close to him; he could never let her go again. He could never let her head go away from the close clutch of his arm. He wanted to remain like that for ever, with his heart hurting him in a pain that was also life to him. Without knowing, he was looking down on her damp, soft brown hair.

Then, as it were suddenly, he smelt the horrid stagnant smell of that water. And at the same moment she drew away from him and looked at him. Her eyes were wistful and unfathomable. He was afraid of them, and he fell to kissing her, not knowing what he was doing. He wanted her eyes not to have that terrible, wistful, unfathomable look.

When she turned her face to him again, a faint delicate flush was glowing, and there was again dawning that terrible shining of joy in her eyes, which really terrified him, and yet which he now wanted to see, because he feared the look of doubt still more.

"You love me?" she said, rather faltering.

"Yes." The word cost him a painful effort. Not because it wasn't true. But because it was too newly true, the *saying* seemed to tear open again his newly-torn heart. And he hardly wanted it to be true, even now.

She lifted her face to him, and he bent forward and kissed her on the mouth, gently, with the one kiss that is an eternal pledge. And as he kissed her his heart strained again in his breast. He never intended to love her. But now it was over. He had crossed over the gulf to her, and all that he had left behind had shrivelled and become void.

After the kiss, her eyes again slowly filled with tears. She sat still, away from him, with her face drooped aside, and her hands folded in her lap. The tears fell very slowly. There was complete silence. He too sat there motionless and silent on the hearthrug. The strange pain of his heart that was broken seemed to consume him. That he should love her? That this was love! That he should be ripped open in this way! Him, a doctor! How they would all jeer if they knew! It was agony to him to think they might know.

In the curious naked pain of the thought he looked again to her. She was sitting there drooped into a muse. He saw a tear fall, and his heart flared hot. He saw for the first time that one of her shoulders was quite uncovered, one arm bare, he could see one of her small breasts; dimly, because it had become almost dark in the room.

"Why are you crying?" he asked, in an altered voice.

She looked up at him, and behind her tears the consciousness of her situation for the first time brought a dark look of shame to her eyes.

"I'm not crying, really," she said, watching him half frightened.

He reached his hand, and softly closed it on her bare arm.

"I love you! I love you!" he said in a soft, low vibrating voice, unlike himself.

She shrank, and dropped her head. The soft, penetrating grip of his hand on her arm distressed her. She looked up at him.

"I want to go," she said. "I want to go and get you some dry things."

"Why?" he said. "I'm all right."

"But I want to go," she said. "And I want you to change your things."

He released her arm, and she wrapped herself in the blanket, looking at him rather frightened. And still she did not rise.

"Kiss me," she said wistfully.

He kissed her, but briefly, half in anger.

Then, after a second, she rose nervously, all mixed up in the blanket. He watched her in her confusion, as she tried to extricate herself and wrap herself up so that she could walk. He watched her relentlessly, as she knew. And as she went, the blanket trailing, and as he saw a glimpse of her feet and her white leg, he tried to remember her as she was when he had wrapped her in the blanket. But then he didn't want to remember, because she had been nothing to him then, and his nature revolted from remembering her as she was when she was nothing to him.

A tumbling, muffled noise from within the dark house startled him. Then he heard her voice:—"There are clothes." He rose and went to the foot of the stairs, and gathered up the garments she had thrown down. Then he came back to the fire, to rub himself down and dress. He grinned at his own appearance when he had finished.

The fire was sinking, so he put on coal. The house was now quite dark, save for the light of a street-lamp that shone in faintly from beyond the holly trees. He lit the gas with matches he found on the mantelpiece. Then he emptied the pockets of his own clothes, and threw all his wet things in a heap into the scullery. After which he gathered up her sodden clothes, gently, and put them in a separate heap on the copper-top in the scullery.

It was six o'clock on the clock. His own watch had stopped. He ought to go back to the surgery. He waited, and still she did not come down. So he went to the foot of the stairs and called:

"I shall have to go."

Almost immediately he heard her coming down. She had on her best dress of black voile, and her hair was tidy, but still damp. She looked at him—and in spite of herself, smiled.

"I don't like you in those clothes," she said.

"Do I look a sight?" he answered.

They were shy of one another.

"I'll make you some tea," she said.

"No, I must go."

"Must you?" And she looked at him again with the wide, strained, doubtful eyes. And again, from the pain of his breast, he knew how he loved her. He went and bent to kiss her, gently, passionately, with his heart's painful kiss.

"And my hair smells so horrible," she murmured in distraction. "And I'm so awful, I'm so awful! Oh, no, I'm too awful." And she broke into bitter, heart-broken sobbing. "You can't want to love me, I'm horrible."

"Don't be silly, don't be silly," he said, trying to comfort her, kissing her, holding her in his arms. "I want you, I want to marry you, we're going to be married, quickly, quickly—tomorrow if I can."

But she only sobbed terribly, and cried:

"I feel awful. I feel awful. I feel I'm horrible to you."

"No, I want you, I want you," was all he answered, blindly, with that terrible intonation which frightened her almost more than her horror lest he should *not* want her.

Albert Camus

THE GUEST

The schoolmaster was watching the two men climb toward him. One was on horseback, the other on foot. They had not yet tackled the abrupt rise leading to the schoolhouse built on the hillside. They were toiling onward, making slow progress in the snow, among the stones, on the vast expanse of the high, deserted plateau. From time to time the horse stumbled. He could not be heard yet but the breath issuing from his nostrils could be seen. The schoolmaster calculated that it would take them a half hour to get onto the hill. It was cold; he went back into the school to get a sweater.

He crossed the empty, frigid classroom. On the blackboard the four rivers of France, drawn with four different colored chalks, had been flowing toward their estuaries for the past three days. Snow had suddenly fallen in mid-October after eight months of drought without the transition of rain, and the twenty pupils, more or less, who lived in the villages scattered over the plateau had stopped coming. With fair weather they would return. Daru now heated only the single room that was his lodging, adjoining the classroom. One of the windows faced, like the classroom windows, the south. On that side the school was a few kilometers from the point where the plateau began to slope toward the south. In clear weather the purple mass of the mountain range where the gap opened onto the desert could be seen.

Somewhat warmed, Daru returned to the window from which he had first noticed the two men. They were no longer visible. Hence they must have tackled the rise. The sky was not so dark, for the snow had stopped falling during the night. The morning had dawned with a dirty light which had scarcely become brighter as the ceiling of clouds lifted. At two in the afternoon it seemed as if the day were merely beginning. But still this was better than those three days when the thick snow was falling amidst unbroken darkness with little gusts of wind that rattled the double door of the classroom. Then Daru had spent long hours in his room, leaving it only to go to the shed and feed the chickens or get some coal. Fortunately the delivery truck from Tadjid, the nearest village to the north, had brought his supplies two days before the blizzard. It would return in forty-eight hours.

Besides, he had enough to resist a siege, for the little room was cluttered with bags of wheat that the administration had left as a supply to distribute to those of his pupils whose families had suffered from the drought. Actually they had all been victims because they were all poor. Every day Daru would distribute a ration to the children. They had missed it, he knew, during these bad days. Possibly one of the fathers or big brothers would come this afternoon and he could supply them with grain. It was just a matter of carrying them over to the next harvest. Now shiploads of wheat were arriving from France and the worst was over. But it would be hard to forget that poverty, that army of ragged ghosts wandering in the sunlight, the plateaus burned to a cinder month after month, the earth shriveled up little by little, literally scorched, every stone bursting into dust under one's foot. The sheep had died then by thousands, and even a few men, here and there, sometimes without anyone's knowing.

In contrast with such poverty, he who lived almost like a monk, in his remote schoolhouse, had felt like a lord with his whitewashed walls, his narrow couch, his unpainted shelves, his well, and his weekly provisioning with water and food. And suddenly this snow, without warning, without the foretaste of rain. This is the way the region was, cruel to live in, even without men, who didn't help matters either. But Daru had been born here. Everywhere else, he felt exiled.

He went out and stepped forward on the terrace in front of the schoolhouse. The two men were now halfway up the slope. He recognized the horseman to be Balducci, the old gendarme he had known for a long time. Balducci was holding at the end of a rope an Arab walking behind him with hands bound and head lowered. The gendarme waved a greeting to which Daru did not reply, lost as he was in contemplation of the Arab dressed in a faded blue *jellaba,* his feet in sandals but covered with socks of heavy raw wool, his head crowned with a narrow, short *chèche.* Balducci was holding back his horse in order not to hurt the Arab, and the group was advancing slowly.

Within earshot, Balducci shouted, "One hour to do the three kilometers from El Ameur!" Daru did not answer. Short and square in his thick sweater, he watched them climb. Not once had the Arab raised his head. "Hello," said Daru when they got up onto the terrace. "Come in and warm up." Balducci painfully got down from his horse without letting go of the rope. He smiled at the schoolmaster from under his bristling mustache. His little dark eyes, deepset under a tanned forehead, and his mouth surrounded with wrinkles made him look attentive and studious. Daru took the bridle, led the horse to the shed, and came back to the two men who were now waiting for him in the school. He led them into his room. "I am going to heat up the classroom," he said. "We'll be more comfortable there."

When he entered the room again, Balducci was on the couch. He had undone the rope tying him to the Arab, who had squatted near the stove. His hands still bound, the *chèche* pushed back on his head, the Arab was looking toward the window. At first Daru noticed only his huge lips, fat, smooth, almost Negroid; yet his nose was straight, his eyes dark and full of fever. The *chèche* uncovered an obstinate forehead and, under the weathered skin now rather discolored by the cold, the whole face had a restless and rebellious look. "Go into the other room," said the schoolmaster, "and I'll make you some mint tea." "Thanks," Balducci said. "What a chore! How I long for retirement." And addressing his prisoner in Arabic, he said, "Come on, you." The Arab got up and, slowly, holding his bound wrists in front of him, went into the classroom.

With the tea, Daru brought a chair. But Balducci was already sitting in state at the nearest pupil's desk, and the Arab had squatted against the teacher's platform facing the stove, which stood between the desk and the window. When he held out the glass of tea to the prisoner, Daru hesitated at the sight of his bound hands. "He might perhaps be untied." "Sure," said Balducci. "That was for the trip." He started to get to his feet. But Daru, setting the glass on the floor, had knelt beside the Arab. Without saying anything, the Arab watched him with his feverish eyes. Once his hands were free, he rubbed his swollen wrists against each other, took the glass of tea and sucked up the burning liquid in swift little sips.

"Good," said Daru. "And where are you headed?"

Balducci withdrew his mustache from the tea. "Here, son."

"Odd pupils! And you're spending the night?"

"No. I'm going back to El Ameur. And you will deliver this fellow to Tinguit. He is expected at police headquarters."

Balducci was looking at Daru with a friendly little smile.

"What's this story?" asked the schoolmaster. "Are you pulling my leg?"

"No, son. Those are the orders."

"The orders? I'm not . . ." Daru hesitated, not wanting to hurt the old Corsican. "I mean, that's not my job."

"What! What's the meaning of that? In wartime people do all kinds of jobs."

"Then I'll wait for the declaration of war!"

Balducci nodded. "O.K. But the orders exist and they concern you too. Things are bubbling, it appears. There is talk of a forthcoming revolt. We are mobilized, in a way."

Daru still had his obstinate look.

"Listen, son," Balducci said. "I like you and you've got to understand. There's only a dozen of us at El Ameur to patrol the whole territory of a small department and I must be back in a hurry. He couldn't be kept there. His village was beginning to stir; they wanted to take him back. You must take him to Tinguit tomorrow before the day is over. Twenty kilometers shouldn't faze a husky fellow like you. After that, all will be over. You'll come back to your pupils and your comfortable life."

Behind the wall the horse could be heard snorting and pawing the earth. Daru was looking out the window. Decidedly the weather was clearing and the light was increasing over the snowy plateau. When all the snow was melted, the sun would take over again and once more would burn the fields of stone. For days still, the unchanging sky would shed its dry light on the solitary expanse where nothing had any connection with man.

"After all," he said, turning around toward Balducci, "what

did he do?" And, before the gendarme had opened his mouth, he asked, "Does he speak French?"

"No, not a word. We had been looking for him for a month, but they were hiding him. He killed his cousin."

"Is he against us?"

"I don't think so. But you can never be sure."

"Why did he kill?"

"A family squabble, I think. One owed grain to the other, it seems. It's not at all clear. In short, he killed his cousin with a billhook. You know, like a sheep, *kreezk!*"

Balducci made the gesture of drawing a blade across his throat, and the Arab, his attention attracted, watched him with a sort of anxiety. Daru felt a sudden wrath against the man, against all men with their rotten spite, their tireless hates, their blood lust.

But the kettle was singing on the stove. He served Balducci more tea, hesitated, then served the Arab again, who drank avidly a second time. His raised arms made the *jellaba* fall open, and the schoolmaster saw his thin, muscular chest.

"Thanks, son," Balducci said. "And now I'm off."

He got up and went toward the Arab, taking a small rope from his pocket.

"What are you doing?" Daru asked dryly.

Balducci, disconcerted, showed him the rope.

"Don't bother."

The old gendarme hesitated. "It's up to you. Of course, you are armed?"

"I have my shotgun."

"Where?"

"In the trunk."

"You ought to have it near your bed."

"Why? I have nothing to fear."

"You're crazy, son. If there's an uprising, no one is safe; we're all in the same boat."

"I'll defend myself. I'll have time to see them coming."

Balducci began to laugh, then suddenly the mustache covered the white teeth. "You'll have time? O.K. That's just what I was saying. You always have been a little cracked. That's why I like you; my son was like that."

At the same time he took out his revolver and put it on the desk. "Keep it; I don't need two weapons from here to El Ameur."

The revolver shone against the black paint of the table. When the gendarme turned toward him, the schoolmaster caught his smell of leather and horseflesh.

"Listen, Balducci," Daru said suddenly, "all this disgusts me, beginning with your fellow here. But I won't hand him over. Fight, yes, if I have to. But not that."

The old gendarme stood in front of him and looked at him severely.

"You're being a fool," he said slowly. "I don't like it either. You don't get used to putting a rope on a man even after years of it, and you're even ashamed—yes, ashamed. But you can't let them have their way."

"I won't hand him over," Daru said again.

"It's an order, son, and I repeat it."

"That's right. Repeat to them what I've said to you: I won't hand him over."

Balducci made a visible effort to reflect. He looked at the Arab and at Daru. At last he decided.

"No, I won't tell them anything. If you want to drop us, go ahead; I'll not denounce you. I have an order to deliver the prisoner and I'm doing so. And now you'll just sign this paper for me."

"There's no need. I'll not deny that you left him with me."

"Don't be mean with me. I know you'll tell the truth. You're from around these parts and you are a man. But you must sign; that's the rule."

Daru opened his drawer, took out a little square bottle of purple ink, the red wooden penholder with the "sergeant-major" pen he used for models of handwriting, and signed. The gendarme carefully folded the paper and put it into his wallet. Then he moved toward the door.

"I'll see you off," Daru said.

"No," said Balducci. "There's no use being polite. You insulted me."

He looked at the Arab, motionless in the same spot, sniffed peevishly, and turned away toward the door. "Good-by, son," he said. The door slammed behind him. His footsteps were muffled by the snow. The horse stirred on the other side of the wall and several chickens fluttered in fright. A moment later Balducci reappeared outside the window leading the horse by the bridle. He walked toward the little rise without turning around and disappeared from sight with the horse following him.

Daru walked back toward the prisoner, who, without stirring, never took his eyes off him. "Wait," the schoolmaster said in Arabic and went toward the bedroom. As he was going through the door, he had a second thought, went to the desk, took the revolver, and stuck in in his pocket. Then, without looking back, he went into his room.

For some time he lay on his couch watching the sky gradually close over, listening to the silence. It was this silence that had seemed painful to him during the first days here, after the war. He had requested a post in the little town at the base of the foothills separating the upper plateaus from the desert. There, rocky walls, green and black to the north, pink and lavender to the south, marked the frontier of eternal summer. He had been named to a post farther north, on the plateau itself. In the beginning, the solitude and the silence had been hard for him on these wastelands peopled only by stones. Occasionally, furrows suggested cultivation, but they had been dug to uncover a certain kind of stone good for building. The only plowing here was to harvest rocks. Elsewhere a thin layer of soil accumulated in the hollows would be scraped out to enrich paltry village gardens. This is the way it was: bare rock covered three quarters of the region. Towns sprang up, flourished, then disappeared; men came by, loved one another or fought bitterly, then died. No one in this desert, neither he nor his guest, mattered. And yet, outside this desert neither of them, Daru knew, could have really lived.

When he got up, no noise came from the classroom. He was amazed at the unmixed joy he derived from the mere thought that the Arab might have fled and that he would be alone with no decision to make. But the prisoner was there. He had merely stretched out between the stove and the desk and he was staring at the ceiling. In that position, his thick lips were particularly noticeable, giving him a pouting look. "Come," said Daru. The Arab got up and followed him. In the bedroom the schoolmaster pointed to a chair near the table under the window. The Arab sat down without ceasing to watch Daru.

"Are you hungry?"

"Yes," the prisoner said.

Daru set the table for two. He took flour and oil, shaped a cake in a frying pan, and lighted the little stove that functioned on bottled gas. While the cake was cooking, he went out to the shed to get cheese, eggs, dates, and condensed milk. When the cake was done he set it on the window sill to cool, heated some condensed milk diluted with water, and beat up the eggs into an omelette. In one of his motions he bumped into the revolver stuck in his right pocket. He set the bowl down, went into the classroom, and put the revolver in his desk drawer. When he came back to the room, night was falling. He put on the light and served the Arab. "Eat," he said. The Arab took a piece of the cake, lifted it eagerly to his mouth, and stopped short.

"And you?" he asked.

"After you. I'll eat too."

The thick lips opened slightly. The Arab hesitated, then bit into the cake determinedly.

The meal over, the Arab looked at the schoolmaster. "Are you the judge?"

"No, I'm simply keeping you until tomorrow."

"Why do you eat with me?"

"I'm hungry."

The Arab fell silent. Daru got up and went out. He brought back a camp cot from the shed and set it up between the table and the stove, at right angles to his own bed. From a large suitcase which, upright in a corner, served as a shelf for papers, he took two blankets and arranged them on the cot. Then he stopped, felt useless, and sat down on his bed. There was nothing more to do or to get ready. He had to look at this man. He looked at him, therefore, trying to imagine his face bursting with rage. He couldn't do so. He could see nothing but the dark yet shining eyes and the animal mouth.

"Why did you kill him?" he asked in a voice whose hostile tone surprised him.

The Arab looked away. "He ran away. I ran after him."

He raised his eyes to Daru again and they were full of a sort of woeful interrogation. "Now what will they do to me?"

"Are you afraid?"

The Arab stiffened, turning his eyes away.

"Are you sorry?"

The Arab stared at him openmouthed. Obviously he did not understand. Daru's annoyance was growing. At the same time he felt awkward and self-conscious with his big body wedged between the two beds.

"Lie down there," he said impatiently. "That's your bed."

The Arab didn't move. He cried out, "Tell me!"

The schoolmaster looked at him.

"Is the gendarme coming back tomorrow?"

"I don't know."

"Are you coming with us?"

"I don't know. Why?"

The prisoner got up and stretched out on top of the blankets, his feet toward the window. The light from the electric bulb shone straight into his eyes and he closed them at once.

"Why?" Daru repeated, standing beside the bed.

The Arab opened his eyes under the blinding light and looked at him, trying not to blink. "Come with us," he said.

In the middle of the night, Daru was still not asleep. He had gone to bed after undressing completely; he generally slept naked. But when he suddenly realized that he had nothing on, he wondered. He felt vulnerable and the temptation came to him to put his clothes back on. Then he shrugged his shoulders; after all, he wasn't a child and, if it came to that, he could break his adversary in two. From his bed, he could observe him lying on his back, still motionless, his eyes closed under the harsh light. When Daru turned out the light, the darkness seemed to congeal all of a sudden. Little by little, the night came back to life in the window where the starless sky was stirring gently. The schoolmaster soon made out the body lying at his feet. The Arab was still motionless but his eyes seemed open. A faint wind was prowling about the schoolhouse. Perhaps it would drive away the clouds and the sun would reappear.

During the night the wind increased. The hens fluttered a little and then were silent. The Arab turned over on his side with his back to Daru, who thought he heard him moan. Then he listened for his guest's breathing, which had become heavier and more regular. He listened to that breathing so close to him and mused without being able to go to sleep. In the room where he had been sleeping alone for a year, this presence bothered him. But it bothered him also because it imposed on him a sort of brotherhood he refused to accept in the present circumstances; yet he was familiar with it. Men who share the same rooms, soldiers or prisoners, develop a strange alliance as if, having cast off their armor with their clothing, they fraternized every evening, over and above their differences, in the ancient community of dream and fatigue. But Daru shook himself; he didn't like such musings, and it was essential for him to sleep.

A little later, however, when the Arab stirred slightly, the schoolmaster was still not asleep. When the prisoner made a second move, he stiffened, on the alert. The Arab was lifting himself slowly on his arms with almost the motion of a sleepwalker. Seated upright in bed, he waited motionless without turning his head toward Daru, as if he were listening attentively. Daru did not stir; it had just occurred to him that the revolver was still in the drawer of his desk. It was better to act at once. Yet he continued to observe the prisoner, who, with the same slithery motion, put his feet on the ground, waited again, then stood up slowly. Daru was about to call out to him when the Arab began to walk, in a quite natural but extraordinarily silent way. He was heading toward the door at the end of the room that opened into the shed. He lifted the latch with precaution and went out, pushing the door behind him but without shutting it.

Daru had not stirred. "He is running away," he merely thought. "Good riddance!" Yet he listened attentively. The hens were not fluttering; the guest must be on the plateau. A faint sound of water reached him, and he didn't know what it was until the Arab again stood framed in the doorway, closed the door carefully, and came back to bed without a sound. Then Daru turned his back on him and fell asleep. Still later he seemed, from the depths of his sleep, to hear furtive steps around the schoolhouse. "I'm dreaming! I'm dreaming!" he repeated to himself. And he went on sleeping.

When he awoke, the sky was clear; the loose window let in a cold, pure air. The Arab was asleep, hunched up under the blankets now, his mouth open, utterly relaxed. But when Daru shook him he started dreadfully, staring at Daru with wild eyes as if he had never seen him and with such a frightened expression that the schoolmaster stepped back. "Don't be afraid. It is I. You must eat." The Arab nodded his head and said yes. Calm had returned to his face, but his expression was vacant and listless.

The coffee was ready. They drank it seated together on the cot as they munched their pieces of the cake. Then Daru led the Arab under the shed and showed him the faucet where he washed. He went back into the room, folded the blankets on the cot, made his own bed, and put the room in order. Then he went through the classroom and out onto the terrace. The sun was already rising in the blue sky; a soft, bright light enveloped the deserted plateau.

On the ridge the snow was melting in spots. The stones were about to reappear. Crouched on the edge of the plateau, the schoolmaster looked at the deserted expanse. He thought of Balducci. He had hurt him, for he had sent him off as though he didn't want to be associated with him. He could still hear the gendarme's farewell and, without knowing why, he felt strangely empty and vulnerable.

At that moment, from the other side of the schoolhouse, the prisoner coughed. Daru listened to him almost despite himself and then, furious, threw a pebble that whistled through the air before sinking into the snow. That man's stupid crime revolted him, but to hand him over was contrary to honor; just thinking of it made him boil with humiliation. He simultaneously cursed his own people who had sent him this Arab and the Arab who had dared to kill and not managed to get away. Daru got up, walked in a circle on the terrace, waited motionless, and then went back into the schoolhouse.

The Arab, leaning over the cement floor of the shed, was washing his teeth with two fingers. Daru looked at him and said, "Come." He went back into the room ahead of the prisoner. He slipped a hunting jacket on over his sweater and put on walking shoes. Standing, he waited until the Arab had put on his *chèche* and sandals. They went into the classroom, and the schoolmaster pointed to the exit saying, "Go ahead." The fellow didn't budge. "I'm coming," said Daru. The Arab went out. Daru went back into the room and made a package with pieces of rusk, dates, and sugar in it. In the classroom, before going out, he hesitated a second in front of his desk, then crossed the threshold and locked the door. "That's the way," he said. He started toward the east, followed by the prisoner. But a short distance from the schoolhouse he thought he heard a slight sound behind him. He retraced his steps and examined the surroundings of the house; there was no one there. The Arab watched him without seeming to understand. "Come on," said Daru.

They walked for an hour and rested beside a sharp needle of limestone. The snow was melting faster and faster and the sun was drinking up the puddles just as quickly, rapidly cleaning the plateau, which gradually dried and vibrated like the air itself. When they resumed walking, the ground rang under their feet. From time to time a bird rent the space in front of them with a joyful cry. Daru felt a sort of rapture before the vast familiar expanse, now almost entirely yellow under its dome of blue sky. They walked an hour more, descending toward the south. They reached a sort of flattened elevation made up of crumbly rocks. From there on, the plateau sloped down—eastward toward a low plain on which could be made out a few spindly trees, and to the south toward outcroppings of rock that gave the landscape a chaotic look.

Daru surveyed the two directions. Not a man could be seen. He turned toward the Arab, who was looking at him blankly. Daru offered the package to him. "Take it," he said. "There are dates, bread, and sugar. You can hold out for two days. Here are a thousand francs too."

The Arab took the package and the money but kept his full hands at chest level as if he didn't know what to do with what was being given him.

"Now look," the schoolmaster said as he pointed in the direction of the east, "there's the way to Tinguit. You have a two-hour walk. At Tinguit are the administration and the police. They are expecting you."

The Arab looked toward the east, still holding the package and the money against his chest. Daru took his elbow and turned him rather roughly toward the south. At the foot of the elevation on which they stood could be seen a faint path. "That's the trail across the plateau. In a day's walk from here you'll find pasturelands and the first nomads. They'll take you in and shelter you according to their law."

The Arab had now turned toward Daru, and a sort of panic was visible in his expression. "Listen," he said.

Daru shook his head. "No, be quiet. Now I'm leaving you." He turned his back on him, took two long steps in the direction of the school, looked hesitantly at the motionless Arab, and started off again. For a few minutes he heard nothing but his own step resounding on the cold ground, and he did not turn his head. A moment later, however, he turned around. The Arab was still there on the edge of the hill, his arms hanging now, and he was looking at the schoolmaster. Daru felt something rise in his throat. But he swore with impatience, waved vaguely, and started off again. He had already gone a distance when he again stopped and looked. There was no longer anyone on the hill.

Daru hesitated. The sun was now rather high in the sky and beginning to beat down on his head. The schoolmaster retraced his steps, at first somewhat uncertainly, then with decision. When he reached the little hill, he was bathed in sweat. He climbed it as fast as he could and stopped, out of breath, on the top. The rock fields to the south stood out sharply against the blue sky, but on the plain to the east a steamy heat was rising. And in that slight haze, Daru, with heavy heart, made out the Arab walking slowly on the road to prison.

A little later, standing before the window of the classroom, the schoolmaster was watching the clear light bathing the whole surface of the plateau. Behind him on the blackboard, among the winding French rivers, sprawled the clumsily chalked up words he had just read: "You handed over our brother. You will pay for this." Daru looked at the sky, the plateau, and, beyond, the invisible lands stretching all the way to the sea. In this vast landscape he had loved so much, he was alone.

Anton Chekhov

THE KISS

On the twentieth of May, at eight o'clock in the evening, six batteries of the N Artillery Brigade arrived at the village of Miestetchki to spend the night, before going to their camp.

The confusion was at its height—some officers at the guns, others in the church square with the quartermaster—when a civilian upon a remarkable horse rode from the rear of the church. The small cob with well-shaped neck wobbled along, all the time dancing on its legs as if someone were whipping them. Reaching the officers, the rider doffed his cap with ceremony and said—

"His Excellency, General von Rabbek, requests the honor of the officers' company at tea in his house near by . . ."

The horse shook its head, danced, and wobbled backwards; its rider again took off his cap, and turning around disappeared behind the church.

"The devil!" the general exclaimed, the officers dispersing to their quarters. "We are almost asleep, yet along comes this von Rabbek with his tea! That tea! I remember it!"

The officers of the six batteries had vivid recollections of a past invitation. During recent maneuvers they had been asked, with their Cossack comrades, to tea at the house of a local country gentleman, a Count, retired from military service; and this hearty old Count overwhelmed them with attentions, fed them like gourmands, poured vodka into them and made them stay the night. All this, of course, was fine. The trouble was that the old soldier entertained his guests too well. He kept them up till daybreak while he poured forth tales of past adventures and pointed out valuable paintings, engravings, arms, and letters from celebrated men. And the tired officers listened, perforce, until he ended, only to find out that the time for sleep had gone.

Was von Rabbek another old Count? It might easily be. But there was no neglecting his invitation. The officers washed and dressed, and set out for von Rabbek's house. At the church square they learnt that they must descend the hill to the river, and follow the bank till they reached the general's gardens, where they would find a path direct to the house. Or, if they chose to go uphill, they would reach the general's barns half a *verst* from Miestetchki. It was this route they chose.

"But who is this von Rabbek?" asked one. "The man who commanded the N Cavalry Division at Plevna?"

"No, that was not von Rabbek, but simply Rabbe—without the von."

"What glorious weather!"

At the first barn they came to, two roads diverged; one ran straight forward and faded in the dusk; the other, turning to the right, led to the general's house. As the officers drew near they talked less loudly. To right and to left stretched rows of red-roofed brick barns, in aspect heavy and morose as the barracks of provincial towns. In front gleamed the lighted windows of von Rabbek's house.

"A good omen, gentlemen!" cried a young officer. "Our setter runs in advance. There is game ahead!"

On the face of Lieutenant Lobuitko, the tall stout officer referred to, there was not one trace of hair though he was twenty-five years old. He was famed among comrades for the instinct which told him of the presence of women in the neighborhood. On hearing his comrade's remark, he turned his head and said—

"Yes. There are women there. My instinct tells me."

A handsome, well-preserved man of sixty, in mufti, came to the hall door to greet his guests. It was von Rabbek. As he pressed their hands, he explained that though he was delighted to see them, he must beg pardon for not asking them to spend the night; as guests he already had his two sisters, their children, his brother, and several neighbors—in fact, he had not one spare room. And though he shook their hands and apologized and smiled, it was plain that he was not half as glad to see them as was the last year's Count, and that he had invited them merely because good manners demanded it. The officers climbing the soft-carpeted steps and listening to their host understood this perfectly well; and realized that they carried into the house an atmosphere of intrusion and alarm. Would any man—they asked themselves—who had gathered his two sisters and their children, his brother and his neighbors, to celebrate, no doubt, some family festival, find pleasure in the invasion of nineteen officers whom he had never seen before?

A tall elderly lady, with a good figure, and a long face with black eyebrows, who resembled closely the ex-Empress Eugénie, greeted them at the drawing-room door. Smiling courteously and with dignity, she affirmed that she was delighted to see the officers, and only regretted that she could not ask them to stay the night. But the courteous, dignified smile disappeared when she turned away, and it was quite plain that she had seen many officers in her day, that they caused not the slightest interest, and that she had invited them merely because an invitation was dictated by good breeding and by her position in the world.

In a big dining room, at a big table, sat ten men and women, drinking tea. Behind them, veiled in cigar smoke, stood several young men, among them one, red-whiskered and extremely thin, who spoke English loudly with a lisp. Through an open door the officers saw into a brightly lighted room with blue wallpaper.

"You are too many to introduce singly, gentlemen!" said the general loudly, with affected joviality. "Make one another's acquaintance, please—without formalities!"

The visitors, some with serious, even severe faces, some smiling constrainedly, all with a feeling of awkwardness, bowed, and took their seats at the table. Most awkward of all felt Staff-Captain Riabovitch, a short, round-shouldered, spectacled officer, whiskered like a lynx. While his brother officers looked serious or smiled constrainedly, his face, his lynx whiskers, and his spectacles seemed to explain: "I am the most timid, modest, undistinguished officer in the whole brigade." For some time after he took his seat at the table he could not fix his attention on any single thing. Faces, dresses, the cut-glass cognac bottles, the steaming tumblers, the molded cornices—all merged in a single, overwhelming sentiment which caused him intense fright and made him wish to hide his head. Like an inexperienced lecturer he saw everything before him, but could distinguish nothing, and was in fact the victim of what men of science diagnose as "psychical blindness."

But, slowly conquering his diffidence, Riabovitch began to distinguish and observe. As became a man both timid and unsocial, he remarked first of all the amazing temerity of his new friends. Von Rabbek, his wife, two elderly ladies, a girl in lilac, and the red-whiskered youth (who, it appeared, was a young von Rabbek) sat down among the officers as unconcernedly as if they had held rehearsals, and at once plunged into various heated arguments in which they soon involved their guests. That artillerists have a much better time than cavalrymen or infantrymen was proved conclusively by the lilac girl, while von Rabbek and the elderly ladies affirmed the converse. The conversation became desultory. Riabovitch listened to the lilac girl fiercely debating themes she knew nothing about and took no interest in, and watched the insincere smiles which appeared on and disappeared from her face.

While the von Rabbek family with amazing strategy inveigled their guests into the dispute, they kept their eyes on every glass and mouth. Had everyone tea, was it sweet enough, why didn't one eat biscuits, was another fond of cognac? And the longer Riabovitch listened and looked, the more pleased he was with this disingenuous, disciplined family.

After tea the guests repaired to the drawing room. Instinct had not cheated Lobuitko. The room was packed with young women and girls, and ere a minute had passed the setter-lieutenant stood beside a very young, fair-haired girl in black, and, bending down as if resting on an invisible sword, shrugged his shoulders coquettishly. He was uttering, no doubt, most unentertaining nonsense, for the fair girl looked indulgently at his sated face, and exclaimed indifferently, "Indeed!" And this indifferent "Indeed!" might have quickly convinced the setter that he was on a wrong scent.

Music began. As the notes of a mournful valse throbbed out of the open window, through the heads of all flashed the feeling that outside that window it was springtime, a night of May. The air was odorous of young poplar leaves, of roses and lilacs—and the valse and the spring were sincere. Riabovitch, with valse and cognac mingling tipsily in his head, gazed at the window with a smile; then began to follow the movements of the women; and it seemed that the smell of roses, poplars, and lilacs came not from the gardens outside, but from the women's faces and dresses.

They began to dance. Young von Rabbek valsed twice round the room with a very thin girl; and Lobuitko, slipping on the parqueted floor, went up to the girl in lilac, and was granted a dance. But Riabovitch stood near the door with the wallflowers, and looked silently on. Amazed at the daring of men who in sight of a crowd could take unknown women by the waist, he tried in vain to picture himself doing the same. A time had been when he envied his comrades their courage and dash, suffered from painful heart-searchings, and was hurt by the knowledge that he was timid, round-shouldered, and undistinguished, that he had lynx whiskers, and that his waist was much too long. But with years he had grown reconciled to his own insignificance, and now looking at the dancers and loud talkers, he felt no envy, but only mournful emotions.

At the first quadrille von Rabbek junior approached and invited two nondancing officers to a game of billiards. The three left the room, and Riabovitch, who stood idle, and felt impelled to join in the general movement, followed. They passed the dining room, traversed a narrow glazed corridor and a room where three sleepy footmen jumped from a sofa with a start; and after walking, it seemed, through a whole houseful of rooms, entered a small billiard room.

Von Rabbek and the two officers began their game. Riabovitch, whose only game was cards, stood near the table and looked indifferently on, as the players, with unbuttoned coats, wielded their cues, moved about, joked, and shouted obscure technical terms. Riabovitch was ignored, save when one of the players jostled him or nudged him with the cue, and turning towards him said briefly, "Pardon!" so that before the game was over he was thoroughly bored, and, impressed by a sense of his superfluity, resolved to return to the drawing room and turned away.

It was on the way back that his adventure took place. Before he had gone far he saw that he had missed his way. He remembered distinctly the room with the three sleepy footmen; and after passing through five or six rooms entirely vacant, he saw his mistake. Retracing his steps, he turned to the left, and found himself in an almost dark room which he had not seen before; and after hesitating a minute, he boldly opened the first door he saw, and found himself in complete darkness. Through a chink of the door in front peered a bright light; from afar throbbed the dullest music of a mournful mazurka. Here, as in the drawing room, the windows were open wide, and the smell of poplars, lilacs, and roses flooded the air.

Riabovitch paused in irresolution. For a moment all was still. Then came the sound of hasty footsteps; then, without any warning of what was to come, a dress rustled, a woman's breathless voice whispered "At last!" and two soft, scented, unmistakably womanly arms met round his neck, a warm cheek impinged on his, and he received a sounding kiss. But hardly had the kiss echoed through the silence when the unknown shrieked loudly, and fled away—as it seemed to Riabovitch—in disgust. Riabovitch himself nearly screamed, and rushed headlong towards the bright beam in the door chink.

As he entered the drawing room his heart beat violently, and his hands trembled so perceptibly that he clasped them behind his back. His first emotion was shame, as if everyone in the room already knew that he had just been embraced and kissed. He retired into his shell, and looked fearfully around. But finding that hosts and guests were calmly dancing or talking, he regained courage, and surrendered himself to sensations experienced for the first time in his life. The unexampled had happened. His neck, fresh from the embrace of two soft, scented arms, seemed anointed with oil; near his left mustache, where the kiss had fallen, trembled a slight, delightful chill, as from peppermint drops; and from head to foot he was soaked in new and extraordinary sensations, which continued to grow and grow.

He felt that he must dance, talk, run into the garden, laugh unrestrainedly. He forgot altogether that he was round-shouldered, undistinguished, lynx-whiskered, that he had an "indefinite exterior"—a description from the lips of a woman he had happened to overhear. As Madame von Rabbek passed him he smiled so broadly and graciously that she came up and looked at him questioningly.

"What a charming house you have!" he said, straightening his spectacles.

And Madame von Rabbek smiled back, said that the house still belonged to her father, and asked were his parents still alive, how long he had been in the Army, and why he was so thin. After hearing his answers she departed. But though the conversation was over, he continued to smile benevolently, and think what charming people were his new acquaintances.

At supper Riabovitch ate and drank mechanically what was put before him, heard not a word of the conversation, and devoted all his powers to the unraveling of his mysterious, romantic adventure. What was the explanation? It was plain that one of the girls, he reasoned, had arranged a meeting in the dark room, and after waiting some time in vain had, in her nervous tension, mistaken Riabovitch for her hero. The mistake was likely enough, for on entering the dark room Riabovitch had stopped irresolutely as if he, too, were waiting for someone. So far the mystery was explained.

"But which of them was it?" he asked, searching the women's faces. She certainly was young, for old women do not indulge in such romances. Secondly, she was not a servant. That was proved unmistakably by the rustle of her dress, the scent, the voice . . .

When at first he looked at the girl in lilac she pleased him; she had pretty shoulders and arms, a clever face, a charming voice. Riabovitch piously prayed that it was she. But, smiling insincerely, she wrinkled her long nose, and that at once gave her an elderly air. So Riabovitch turned his eyes on the blonde in black. The blonde was younger, simpler, sincerer; she had charming kiss-curls, and drank from her tumbler with inexpressible grace. Riabovitch hoped it was she—but soon he noticed that her face was flat, and bent his eyes on her neighbor.

"It is a hopeless puzzle," he reflected. "If you take the arms and shoulders of the lilac girl, add the blonde's curls, and the eyes of the girl on Lobuitko's left, then—"

He composed a portrait of all these charms, and had a clear vision of the girl who had kissed him. But she was nowhere to be seen.

Supper over, the visitors, sated and tipsy, bade their entertainers good-by. Both host and hostess apologized for not asking them to spend the night.

"I am very glad, gentlemen!" said the general, and this time seemed to speak sincerely, no doubt because speeding the parting guest is a kindlier office than welcoming him unwelcomed. "I am very glad indeed! I hope you will visit me on your way back. Without ceremony, please! Which way will you go? Up the hill? No, go down the hill and through the garden. That way is shorter."

The officers took his advice. After the noise and glaring illumination within doors, the garden seemed dark and still. Until they reached the wicket gate all kept silence. Merry, half tipsy, and content as they were, the night's obscurity and stillness inspired pensive thought. Through their brains, as through Riabovitch's, sped probably the same question: "Will the time ever come when I, like von Rabbek, shall have a big house, a family, a garden, the chance of being gracious—even insincerely—to others, of making them sated, tipsy, and content?"

But once the garden lay behind them, all spoke at once, and burst into causeless laughter. The path they followed led straight to the river, and then ran beside it, winding around bushes, ravines, and overhanging willow trees. The track was barely visible; the other bank was lost entirely in gloom. Sometimes the black water imaged stars, and this was the only indication of the river's speed. From beyond it sighed a drowsy snipe, and beside them in a bush, heedless of the crowd, a nightingale chanted loudly. The officers gathered in a group and swayed the bush, but the nightingale continued his song.

"I like his cheek!" they echoed admiringly. "He doesn't care a *kopek!* The old rogue!"

Near their journey's end the path turned up the hill, and joined the road not far from the church enclosure; and there the officers, breathless from climbing, sat on the grass and smoked. Across the river gleamed a dull red light, and for want of a subject they argued the problem, whether it was a bonfire, a window light, or something else. Riabovitch looked also at the light, and felt that it smiled and winked at him as if it knew about the kiss.

On reaching home, he undressed without delay, and lay upon his bed. He shared the cabin with Lobuitko and a Lieutenant Merzliakoff, a staid, silent little man, by repute highly cultivated, who took with him everywhere *The Messenger of Europe* and read it eternally. Lobuitko undressed, tramped impatiently from corner to corner, and sent his servant for beer. Merzliakoff lay down, balanced the candle on his pillow, and hid his head behind *The Messenger of Europe.*

"Where is she now?" muttered Riabovitch, looking at the soot-blacked ceiling.

His neck still seemed anointed with oil, near his mouth still trembled the speck of peppermint chill. Through his brain twinkled successively the shoulders and arms of the lilac girl, the kiss-curls and honest eyes of the girl in black, the waists, dresses, brooches. But though he tried his best to fix these vagrant images, they glimmered, winked, and dissolved; and as they faded finally into the vast black curtain which hangs before the closed eyes of all men, he began to hear hurried footsteps, the rustle of petticoats, the sound of a kiss. A strong, causeless joy possessed him. But as he surrendered himself to this joy, Lobuitko's servant returned with the news that no beer was obtainable. The lieutenant resumed his impatient march up and down the room.

"The fellow's an idiot," he exclaimed, stopping first near Riabovitch and then near Merzliakoff. "Only the worst numbskull and blockhead can't get beer! *Canaille!*"

"Everyone knows there's no beer here," said Merzliakoff, without lifting his eyes from *The Messenger of Europe.*

"You believe that!" exclaimed Lobuitko. "Lord in heaven, drop me on the moon, and in five minutes I'll find both beer and women! I will find them myself! Call me a rascal if I don't!"

He dressed slowly, silently lighted a cigarette, and went out.

"Rabbek, Grabbek, Labbek," he muttered, stopping in the hall. "I won't go alone, devil take me! Riabovitch, come for a walk! What?"

As he got no answer, he returned, undressed slowly, and lay down. Merzliakoff sighed, dropped *The Messenger of Europe,* and put out the light. "Well?" muttered Lobuitko, puffing his cigarette in the dark.

Riabovitch pulled the bedclothes up to his chin, curled himself into a roll, and strained his imagination to join the twinkling images into one coherent whole. But the vision fled him. He soon fell asleep, and his last impression was that he had been caressed and gladdened, that into his life had crept something strange, and indeed ridiculous, but uncommonly good and radiant. And this thought did not forsake him even in his dreams.

When he awoke the feeling of anointment and peppermint chill was gone. But joy, as on the night before, filled every vein. He looked entranced at the windowpanes gilded by the rising sun, and listened to the noises outside. Someone spoke loudly under the very window. It was Lebedietsky, commander of his battery, who had just overtaken the brigade. He was talking to the sergeant-major, loudly, owing to lack of practice in soft speech.

"And what next?" he roared.

"During yesterday's shoeing, your honor, *Golubtchik* was picked. The regimental doctor ordered clay and vinegar. And last night, your honor, mechanic Artemieff was drunk, and the lieutenant ordered him to be put on the limber of the reserve gun carriage."

The sergeant-major added that Karpoff had forgotten the tent pegs and the new lanyards for the friction tubes, and that the officers had spent the evening at General von Rabbek's. But here at the window appeared Lebedietsky's red-bearded face. He blinked his short-sighted eyes at the drowsy men in bed, and greeted them.

"Is everything all right?"

"The saddle wheeler galled his withers with the new yoke," answered Lobuitko.

The commander sighed, mused a moment, and shouted—

"I am thinking of calling on Alexandra Yegorovna. I want to see her. Good-by! I will catch you up before night."

Fifteen minutes later the brigade resumed its march. As he passed von Rabbek's barns, Riabovitch turned his head and looked at the house. The Venetian blinds were down; evidently all still slept. And among them slept she—she who had kissed him but a few hours before. He tried to visualize her asleep. He projected the bedroom window opened wide with green branches peering in, the freshness of the morning air, the smell of poplars, lilacs, and roses, the bed, a chair, the dress which rustled last night, a pair of tiny slippers, a ticking watch on the table—all these came to him clearly with every detail. But the features, the kind, sleepy smile—all, in short, that was essential and characteristic—fled his imagination as quicksilver flees the hand. When he had covered half a *verst* he again turned back. The yellow church, the house, gardens, and river were bathed in light. Imaging an azure sky, the green-banked river specked with silver sunshine flakes was inexpressibly fair; and, looking at Miestetchki for the last time, Riabovitch felt sad, as if parting forever with something very near and dear.

By the road before him stretched familiar, uninteresting scenes; to the right and left, fields of young rye and buckwheat with hopping rooks; in front, dust and the napes of human necks; behind, the same dust and faces. Ahead of the column marched four soldiers with swords—that was the advance guard. Next came the bandsmen. Advance guard and bandsmen, like mutes in a funeral procession, ignored the regulation intervals and marched too far ahead. Riabovitch, with the first gun of Battery No. 5, could see four batteries ahead.

To a layman, the long, lumbering march of an artillery brigade is novel, interesting, inexplicable. It is hard to understand why a single gun needs so many men; why so many, such strangely harnessed horses are needed to drag it. But to Riabovitch, a master of all these things, it was profoundly dull. He had learned years ago why a solid sergeant-major rides beside the officer in front of each battery; why the sergeant-major is called the *unosni,* and why the drivers of leaders and wheelers ride behind him. Riabovitch knew why the near horses are called saddle horses, and why the off horses are called led horses—and all of this was uninteresting beyond words. On one of the wheelers rode a soldier still covered with yesterday's dust, and with a cumbersome, ridiculous guard on his right leg. But Riabovitch, knowing the use of this leg guard, found it in no way ridiculous. The drivers, mechanically and with occasional cries, flourished their whips. The guns in themselves were unimpressive. The limbers were packed with tarpaulin-covered sacks of oats; and the guns themselves, hung round with teapots and satchels, looked like harmless animals, guarded for some obscure reason by men and horses. In the lee of the gun tramped six gunners, swinging their arms, and behind each gun came more *unosniye,* leaders, wheelers; and yet more guns, each as ugly and uninspiring as the one in front. And as every one of the six batteries in the brigade had four guns, the procession stretched along the road at least half a *verst.* It ended with a wagon train, with which, its head bent in thought, walked the donkey Magar, brought from Turkey by a battery commander.

Dead to his surroundings, Riabovitch marched onward, looking at the napes ahead or at the faces behind. Had it not been for last night's event, he would have been half asleep. But now he was absorbed in novel, entrancing thoughts. When the brigade set out that morning he had tried to argue that the kiss had no significance save as a trivial though mysterious adventure; that it was without real import; and that to think of it seriously was to behave himself absurdly. But logic soon flew away and surrendered him to his vivid imaginings. At times he saw himself in von Rabbek's dining room, *tête-à-tête* with a composite being, formed of the girl in lilac and the blonde in black. At times he closed his eyes, and pictured himself with a different, this time quite an unknown, girl of cloudy feature; he spoke to her, caressed her, bent over her shoulders; he imagined war and parting . . . then reunion, the first supper together, children . . .

"To the brakes!" rang the command as they topped the brow of each hill.

Riabovitch also cried "To the brakes!" and each time dreaded that the cry would break the magic spell, and recall him to realities.

They passed a big country house. Riabovitch looked across the fence into the garden, and saw a long path, straight as a ruler, carpeted with yellow sand, and shaded by young birches. In an ecstasy of enchantment, he pictured little feminine feet treading the yellow sand; and, in a flash, imagination restored the woman who had kissed him, the woman he had visualized after supper the night before. The image settled in his brain and never afterward forsook him.

The spell reigned until midday, when a loud command came from the rear of the column.

"Attention! Eyes right! Officers!"

In a *calèche* drawn by a pair of white horses appeared the general of the brigade. He stopped at the second battery, and called out something which no one understood. Up galloped several officers, among them Riabovitch.

"Well, how goes it?" The general blinked his red eyes, and continued, "Are there any sick?"

Hearing the answer, the little skinny general mused a moment, turned to an officer, and said—

"The driver of your third-gun wheeler has taken off his leg guard and hung it on the limber. *Canaille!* Punish him!"

Then raising his eyes to Riabovitch, he added—

"And in your battery, I think, the harness is too loose."

Having made several other equally tiresome remarks, he looked at Lobuitko, and laughed.

"Why do you look so downcast, Lieutenant Lobuitko? You are sighing for Madame Lopukhoff, eh? Gentlemen, he is pining for Madame Lopukhoff!"

Madame Lopukhoff was a tall, stout lady, long past forty. Being partial to big women, regardless of age, the general ascribed the same taste to his subordinates. The officers smiled respectfully; and the general, pleased that he had said something caustic and laughable, touched the coachman's back and saluted. The *calèche* whirled away.

"All this, though it seems to me impossible and unearthly, is in reality very commonplace," thought Riabovitch, watching the clouds of dust raised by the general's carriage. "It is an everyday event, and within everyone's experience . . . This old general, for instance, must have loved in his day; he is married now, and has children. Captain Wachter is also married, and his wife loves him, though he has an ugly red neck and no waist . . . Salmanoff is coarse, and a typical Tartar, but he has had a romance ending in marriage . . . I, like the rest, must go through it all sooner or later."

And the thought that he was an ordinary man, and that his life was ordinary, rejoiced and consoled him. He boldly visualized *her* and his happiness, and let his imagination run mad.

Towards evening the brigade ended its march. While the other officers sprawled in their tents, Riabovitch, Merzliakoff, and Lobuitko sat round a packing case and supped. Merzliakoff ate slowly, and, resting *The Messenger of Europe* on his knees, read on steadily. Lobuitko, chattering without cease, poured beer into his glass. But Riabovitch, whose head was dizzy from uninterrupted daydreams, ate in silence. When he had drunk three glasses he felt tipsy and weak; and an overmastering impulse forced him to relate his adventure to his comrades.

"A most extraordinary thing happened to me at von Rabbek's," he began, doing his best to speak in an indifferent, ironical tone. "I was on my way, you understand, from the billiard room. . . ."

And he attempted to give a very detailed history of the kiss. But in a minute he had told the whole story. In that minute he had exhausted every detail; and it seemed to him terrible that the story required such a short time. It ought, he felt, to have lasted all the night. As he finished, Lobuitko, who as a liar himself believed in no one, laughed incredulously. Merzliakoff frowned, and, with his eyes still glued to *The Messenger of Europe,* said indifferently—

"God knows who it was! She threw herself on your neck, you say, and didn't cry out! Some lunatic, I expect!"

"It must have been a lunatic," agreed Riabovitch.

"I, too, have had adventures of that kind," began Lobuitko, making a frightful face. "I was on my way to Kovno. I traveled second-class. The carriage was packed, and I couldn't sleep. So I gave the guard a *rouble,* and he took my bag, and put me in a *coupé.* I lay down, and pulled my rug over me. It was pitch dark, you understand. Suddenly I felt someone tapping my shoulder and breathing in my face. I stretched out my hand, and felt an elbow. Then I opened my eyes. Imagine! A woman! Coal-black eyes, lips red as good coral, nostrils breathing passion, breasts—buffers!"

"Draw it mild!" interrupted Merzliakoff in his quiet voice. "I can believe about the breasts, but if it was pitch dark how could you see the lips?"

By laughing at Merzliakoff's lack of understanding, Lobuitko tried to shuffle out of the dilemma. The story annoyed Riabovitch.

He rose from the box, lay on his bed, and swore that he would never again take anyone into his confidence.

Life in camp passed without event. The days flew by, each like the one before. But on every one of these days Riabovitch felt, thought, and acted as a man in love. When at daybreak his servant brought him cold water, and poured it over his head, it flashed at once into his half-awakened brain that something good and warm and caressing had crept into his life.

At night when his comrades talked of love and of women, he drew in his chair, and his face was the face of an old soldier who talks of battles in which he has taken part. And when the rowdy officers, led by setter Lobuitko, made Don Juanesque raids upon the neighboring "suburb," Riabovitch, though he accompanied them, was morose and conscience-struck, and mentally asked *her* forgiveness. In free hours and sleepless nights, when his brain was obsessed by memories of childhood, of his father, his mother, of everything akin and dear, he remembered always Miestetchki, the dancing horse, von Rabbek, von Rabbek's wife, so like the ex-Empress Eugénie, the dark room, the chink in the door.

On the thirty-first of August he left camp, this time not with the whole brigade but with only two batteries. As an exile returning to his native land, he was agitated and enthralled by day-dreams. He longed passionately for the queer-looking horse, the church, the insincere von Rabbeks, the dark room; and that internal voice which so often cheats the lovelorn whispered an assurance that he should see *her* again. But doubt tortured him. How should he meet her? What must he say? Would she have forgotten the kiss? If it came to the worst—he consoled himself—if he never saw her again, he might walk once more through the dark room, and remember . . .

Towards evening the white barns and well-known church rose on the horizon. Riabovitch's heart beat wildly. He ignored the remark of an officer who rode by, he forgot the whole world, and he gazed greedily at the river glimmering afar, at the green roofs, at the dove-cote, over which fluttered birds dyed golden by the setting sun.

As he rode towards the church, and heard again the quartermaster's raucous voice, he expected every second a horseman to appear from behind the fence and invite the officers to tea. . . . But the quartermaster ended his harangue, the officers hastened to the village, and no horseman appeared.

"When von Rabbek hears from the peasants that we are back he will send for us," thought Riabovitch. And so assured was he of this, that when he entered the hut he failed to understand why his comrades had lighted a candle, and why the servants were preparing the samovar.

A painful agitation oppressed him. He lay on his bed. A moment later he rose to look for the horseman. But no horseman was in sight. Again he lay down; again he rose; and this time, impelled by restlessness, went into the street and walked towards the church. The square was dark and deserted. On the hill stood three silent soldiers. When they saw Riabovitch they started and saluted, and he, returning their salute, began to descend the well-remembered path.

Beyond the stream, in a sky stained with purple, the moon slowly rose. Two chattering peasant women walked in a kitchen garden and pulled cabbage leaves; behind them their log cabins stood out black against the sky. The river bank was as it had been in May; the bushes were the same; things differed only in that the nightingale no longer sang, that it smelt no longer of poplars and young grass.

When he reached von Rabbek's garden Riabovitch peered through the wicket gate. Silence and darkness reigned. Save only the white birch trunks and patches of pathway, the whole garden merged in a black, impenetrable shade. Riabovitch listened greedily, and gazed intent. For a quarter of an hour he loitered; then hearing no sound, and seeing no light, he walked wearily towards home.

He went down to the river. In front rose the general's bathing box; and white towels hung on the rail of the bridge. He climbed on to the bridge and stood still; then, for no reason whatever, touched a towel. It was clammy and cold. He looked down at the river which sped past swiftly, murmuring almost inaudibly against the bathing-box piles. Near the left bank glowed the moon's ruddy reflection, overrun by ripples which stretched it, tore it in two, and, it seemed, would sweep it away as twigs and shavings are swept.

"How stupid! How stupid!" thought Riabovitch, watching the hurrying ripples, "How stupid everything is!"

Now that hope was dead, the history of the kiss, his impatience, his ardor, his vague aspirations and disillusion appeared in a clear light. It no longer seemed strange that the general's horseman had not come, and that he would never again see *her* who had kissed him by accident instead of another. On the contrary, he felt, it would be strange if he did ever see her again . . .

The water flew past him, whither and why no one knew. It had flown past in May; it had sped a stream into a great river; a river, into the sea; it had floated on high in mist and fallen again in rain; it might be, the water of May was again speeding past under Riabovitch's eyes. For what purpose? Why?

And the whole world—life itself—seemed to Riabovitch an inscrutable, aimless mystification . . . Raising his eyes from the stream and gazing at the sky, he recalled how Fate in the shape of an unknown woman had once caressed him; he recalled his summer fantasies and images—and his whole life seemed to him unnaturally thin and colorless and wretched . . .

When he reached the cabin his comrades had disappeared. His servant informed him that all had set out to visit "General Fonrabbkin," who had sent a horseman to bring them . . . For a moment Riabovitch's heart thrilled with joy. But that joy he extinguished. He cast himself upon his bed, and wroth with his evil fate, as if he wished to spite it, ignored the invitation.

Henry James

THE TREE OF KNOWLEDGE

It was one of the secret opinions, such as we all have, of Peter Brench that his main success in life would have consisted in his never having committed himself about the work, as it was called, of his friend Morgan Mallow. This was a subject on which it was, to the best of his belief, impossible with veracity, to quote him, and it was nowhere on record that he had, in the connection, on any occasion and in any embarrassment, either lied or spoken the truth. Such a triumph had its honor even for a man of other triumphs—a man who had reached fifty, who had escaped marriage, who had lived within his means, who had been in love with Mrs. Mallow for years without breathing it, and who, last but not least, had judged himself once for all. He had so judged himself in fact that he felt an extreme and general humility to be his proper portion; yet there was nothing that made him think so well of his parts as the course he had steered so often through the shallows just mentioned. It became thus a real wonder that the friends in whom he had most confidence were just those with whom he had most reserves. He couldn't tell Mrs. Mallow—or at least he supposed, excellent man, he couldn't—that she was the one beautiful reason he had never married; any more than he could tell her husband that the sight of the multiplied marbles in that gentleman's studio was an affliction of which even time had never blunted the edge. His victory, however, as I have intimated, in regard to these productions, was not simply in his not having let it out that he deplored them; it was, remarkably, in his not having kept it in by anything else.

The whole situation, among these good people, was verily a marvel, and there was probably not such another for a long way from the spot that engages us—the point at which the soft declivity of Hampstead began at that time to confess in broken accents to Saint John's Wood. He despised Mallow's statues and adored Mallow's wife, and yet was distinctly fond of Mallow, to whom, in turn, he was equally dear. Mrs. Mallow rejoiced in the statues—though she preferred, when pressed, the busts; and if she was visibly attached to Peter Brench it was because of his affection for Morgan. Each loved the other moreover for the love borne in each case to Lancelot, whom the Mallows respectively cherished as their only child and whom the friend of their fireside identified as the third—but decidedly the handsomest—of his godsons. Already in the old years it had come to that—that no one, for such a relation, could possibly have occurred to any of them, even to the baby itself, but Peter. There was luckily a certain independence, of the pecuniary sort, all round: the Master could never otherwise have spent his solemn *Wanderjahre* in Florence and Rome, and continued by the Thames as well as by the Arno and the Tiber to add unpurchased group to group and model, for what was too apt to prove in the event mere love, fancy-heads of celebrities either too busy or too buried—too much of the age or too little of it—to sit. Neither could Peter, lounging in almost daily, have found time to keep the whole complicated tradition so alive by his presence. He was massive but mild, the depositary of these mysteries—large and loose and ruddy and curly, with deep tones, deep eyes, deep pockets, to say nothing of the habit of long pipes, soft hats and brownish greyish weather-faded clothes, apparently always the same.

He had "written," it was known, but had never spoken, never spoken in particular of that; and he had the air (since, as was believed, he continued to write) of keeping it up in order to have something more—as if he hadn't at the worst enough—to be silent about. Whatever his air, at any rate, Peter's occasional unmentioned prose and verse were quite truly the result of an impulse to maintain the purity of his taste by establishing still more firmly the right relation of fame to feebleness. The little green door of his domain was in a garden-wall on which the discolored stucco made patches, and in the small detached villa behind it everything was old, the furniture, the servants, the books, the prints, the immemorial habits and the new improvements. The Mallows, at Carrara Lodge, were within ten minutes, and the studio there was on their little land, to which they had added, in their happy faith, for building it. This was the good fortune, if it was not the ill, of her having brought him in marriage a portion that put them in a manner at their ease and enabled them thus, on their side, to keep it up. And they did keep it up—they always had—the infatuated sculptor and his wife, for whom nature had refined on the impossible by relieving them of the sense of the difficult. Morgan had at all events everything of the sculptor but the spirit of Phidias—the brown velvet, the becoming *beretto,* the "plastic" presence, the fine fingers, the beautiful accent in Italian and the old Italian factotum. He seemed to make up for everything when he addressed Egidio with the "tu" and waved him to turn one of the rotary pedestals of which the place was full. They were tremendous Italians at Carrara Lodge, and the secret of the part played by this fact in Peter's life was in a large degree that it gave him, sturdy Briton as he was, just the amount of "going abroad" he could bear. The Mallows were all his Italy, but it was in a measure for Italy he liked them. His one worry was that Lance—to which they had shortened his godson—was, in spite of a public school, perhaps a shade too Italian. Morgan meanwhile looked like somebody's flattering idea of somebody's own person as expressed in the great room provided at the Uffizi Museum for the general illustration of that idea by eminent hands. The Master's sole regret that he hadn't been born rather to the brush than to the chisel sprang from his wish that he might have contributed to that collection.

It appeared with time at any rate to be to the brush that Lance had been born; for Mrs. Mallow, one day when the boy was turning twenty, broke it to their friend, who shared, to the last delicate morsel, their problems and pains, that it seemed as if nothing would really do but that he should embrace the career. It had been impossible longer to remain blind to the fact that he was gaining no glory at Cambridge, where Brench's own college had for a year tempered its tone to him as for Brench's own sake. Therefore why renew the vain form of preparing him for the impossible? The impossible—it had become clear—was that he should be anything but an artist.

"Oh dear, dear!" said poor Peter.

"Don't you believe in it?" asked Mrs. Mallow, who still, at more than forty, had her violet velvet eyes, her creamy satin skin and her silken chestnut hair.

"Believe in what?"

"Why, in Lance's passion."

"I don't know what you mean by 'believing in it.' I've never been unaware, certainly, of his disposition, from his earliest time, to daub and draw; but I confess I've hoped it would burn out."

"But why should it," she sweetly smiled, "with his wonderful heredity? Passion is passion—though of course indeed *you,* dear Peter, know nothing of that. Has the Master's ever burned out?"

Peter looked off a little and, in his familiar formless way, kept up for a moment, a sound between a smothered whistle and a subdued hum. "Do you think he's going to be another Master?"

She seemed scarce prepared to go that length, yet she had on the whole a marvellous trust. "I know what you mean by that. Will it be a career to incur the jealousies and provoke the machinations that have been at times almost too much for his father? Well—say it may be, since nothing but clap-trap, in these dreadful days, *can,* it would seem, make its way, and since, with the curse of refinement and distinction, one may easily find one's self begging one's bread. Put it at the worst—say he *has* the misfortune to wing his flight further than the vulgar taste of his stupid countrymen can follow. Think, all the same, of the happiness—the same the Master has had. He'll *know.*"

Peter looked rueful. "Ah but *what* will he know?"

"Quiet joy!" cried Mrs. Mallow, quite impatient and turning away.

II

He had of course before long to meet the boy himself on it and to hear that practically everything was settled. Lance was not to go up again, but to go instead to Paris where, since the die was cast, he would find the best advantages. Peter had always felt he must be taken as he was, but had never perhaps found him so much of that pattern as on this occasion. "You chuck Cambridge then altogether? Doesn't that seem rather a pity?"

Lance would have been like his father, to his friend's sense, had he had less humor, and like his mother had he had more beauty. Yet it was a good middle way for Peter that, in the modern manner, he was, to the eye, rather the young stockbroker than the young artist. The youth reasoned that it was a question of time—there was such a mill to go through, such an awful lot to learn. He had talked with fellows and had judged. "One has got, today," he said, "don't you see? to know."

His interlocutor, at this, gave a groan. "Oh hang it, *don't* know!"

Lance wondered. " 'Don't'? Then what's the use—?"

"The use of what?"

"Why, of anything. Don't you think I've talent?"

Peter smoked away for a little in silence; then went on: "It isn't knowledge, it's ignorance that—as we've been beautifully told—is bliss."

"Don't you think I've talent?" Lance repeated.

Peter, with his trick of queer kind demonstrations, passed his arm round his godson and held him a moment. "How do I know?"

"Oh," said the boy, "if it's your own ignorance you're defending—!"

Again, for a pause, on the sofa, his godfather smoked. "It isn't. I've the misfortune to be omniscient."

"Oh well," Lance laughed again, "if you know *too* much—!"

"That's what I do, and it's why I'm so wretched."

Lance's gaiety grew. "Wretched? Come, I say!"

"But I forgot," his companion went on—"you're not to know about that. It would indeed, for you too, make the too much. Only I'll tell you what I'll do." And Peter got up from the sofa. "If you'll go up again I'll pay your way at Cambridge."

Lance stared, a little rueful in spite of being still more amused. "Oh Peter! You disapprove so of Paris?"

"Well, I'm afraid of it."

"Ah I see!"

"No, you don't see—yet. But you will—that is you would. And you mustn't."

The young man thought more gravely. "But one's innocence, already—!"

"Is considerably damaged? Ah, that won't matter," Peter persisted—"we'll patch it up here."

"Here? Then you want me to stay at home?"

Peter almost confessed to it. "Well, we're so right—we four together—just as we are. We're so safe. Come, don't spoil it."

The boy, who had turned to gravity, turned from this, on the real pressure in his friend's tone, to consternation. "Then what's a fellow to be?"

"My particular care. Come, old man"—and Peter now fairly pleaded—"*I'll* look out for you."

Lance, who had remained on the sofa with his legs out and his hands in his pockets, watched him with eyes that showed suspicion. Then he got up. "You think there's something the matter with me—that I can't make a success."

"Well, what do you call a success?"

Lance thought again. "Why, the best sort, I suppose, is to please one's self. Isn't that the sort that, in spite of cabals and things, is—in his own peculiar line—the Master's?"

There were so much too many things in this question to be answered at once that they practically checked the discussion, which became particularly difficult in the light of such renewed proof that, though the young man's innocence might, in the course of his studies, as he contended, somewhat have shrunken, the finer essence of it still remained. That was indeed exactly what Peter had assumed and what above all he desired; yet perversely enough it gave him a chill. The boy believed in the cabals and things, believed in the peculiar line, believed, to be brief, in the Master. What happened a month or two later wasn't that he went up again at the expense of his godfather, but that a fortnight after he had got settled in Paris this personage sent him fifty pounds.

He had meanwhile, at home, this personage, made up his mind to the worst; and what that might be had never yet grown quite so vivid to him as when, on his presenting himself one Sunday night, as he never failed to do, for supper, the mistress of Carrara Lodge met him with an appeal as to—of all things in the world—the wealth of the Canadians. She was earnest, she was even excited. "Are many of them *really* rich?"

He had to confess he knew nothing about them, but he often thought afterwards of that evening. The room in which they sat was adorned with sundry specimens of the Master's genius, which had the merit of being, as Mrs. Mallow herself frequently suggested, of an unusually convenient size. They were indeed of dimensions not customary in the products of the chisel, and they had the singularity that, if the objects and features intended to be small looked too large, the objects and features intended to be large looked too small. The Master's idea, either in respect to this matter or to any other, had in almost any case, even after years, remained undiscoverable to Peter Brench. The creations that so failed to reveal it stood about on pedestals and brackets, on tables and shelves, a little staring white population, heroic, idyllic, allegoric, mythic, symbolic, in which "scale" had so strayed and lost itself that the public square and the chimney-piece seemed to have changed places, the monumental being all diminutive and the diminutive all monumental; branches at any rate, markedly, of a family in which stature was rather oddly irrespective of function, age and sex. They formed, like the Mallows themselves, poor Brench's own family—having at least to such a degree the note of familiarity. The occasion was one of those he had long ago learnt to know and to name—short flickers of the faint flame, soft gusts of a kinder air. Twice a year regularly the Master believed in his fortune, in addition to believing all the year round in his genius. This time it was to be made by a bereaved couple from Toronto, who had given him the handsomest order for a tomb to three lost children, each of whom they desired to see, in the composition, emblematically and characteristically represented.

Such was naturally the moral of Mrs. Mallow's question: if their wealth was to be assumed, it was clear, from the nature of their admiration, as well as from mysterious hints thrown out (they were a little odd!) as to other possibilities of the same mortuary sort, that their further patronage might be; and not less evident that should the Master become at all known in those climes nothing would be more inevitable than a run of Canadian custom. Peter had been present before at runs of custom, colonial and domestic—present at each of those of which the aggregation had left so few gaps in the marble company round him; but it was his habit never at these junctures to prick the bubble in advance. The fond illusion, while it lasted, eased the wound of elections never won, the long ache of medals and diplomas carried off, on every chance, by every one but the Master; it moreover lighted the lamp that would glimmer through the next eclipse. They lived, however, after all—as it was always beautiful to see—at a height scarce susceptible of ups and downs. They strained a point at times charmingly, strained it to admit that the public was here and there not too bad to buy; but they would have been nowhere without their attitude that the Master was always too good to sell. They were at all events deliciously formed, Peter often said to himself, for their fate; the Master had a vanity, his wife had a loyalty, of which success, depriving these things of innocence, would have diminished the merit and the grace. Any one could be charming under a charm, and as he looked about him at a world of prosperity more void of proportion even than the Master's museum he wondered if he knew another pair that so completely escaped vulgarity.

"What a pity Lance isn't with us to rejoice!" Mrs. Mallow on this occasion sighed at supper.

"We'll drink to the health of the absent," her husband replied, filling his friend's glass and his own and giving a drop to their companion; "but we must hope he's preparing himself for a happiness much less like this of ours this evening—excusable as I grant it to be!—than like the comfort we have always (whatever has happened or has not happened) been able to trust ourselves to enjoy. The comfort," the Master explained, leaning back in the pleasant lamplight and firelight, holding up his glass and looking round at his marble family, quartered more or less, a monstrous brood, in every room—"the comfort of art in itself!"

Peter looked a little shyly at his wine. "Well—I don't care what you may call it when a fellow doesn't—but Lance must learn to *sell,* you know. I drink to his acquisition of the secret of a base popularity!"

"Oh, yes, *he* must sell," the boy's mother, who was still more, however, this seemed to give out, the Master's wife, rather artlessly allowed.

"Ah," the sculptor after a moment confidently pronounced, "Lance *will.* Don't be afraid. He'll have learnt."

"Which is exactly what Peter," Mrs. Mallow gaily returned—"why in the world were you so perverse, Peter?—wouldn't, when he told him hear of."

Peter, when this lady looked at him with accusatory affection—a grace on her part not infrequent—could never find a word; but the Master, who was always all amenity and tact, helped him out now as he had often helped him before. "That's his old idea, you know—on which we've so often differed: his theory that the artist should be all impulse and instinct. *I* go in of course for a certain amount of school. Not too much—but a due proportion. There's where his protest came in," he continued to explain to his wife, "as against what *might,* don't you see? be in question for Lance."

"Ah, well"—and Mrs. Mallow turned the violet eyes across the table at the subject of this discourse—"he's sure to have meant of course nothing but good. Only that wouldn't have prevented him, if Lance *had* taken his advice, from being in effect horribly cruel."

They had a sociable way of talking of him to his face as if he had been in the clay or—at most—in the plaster, and the Master was unfailingly generous. He might have been waving Egidio to make him revolve. "Ah, but poor Peter wasn't so wrong as to what it may after all come to that he *will* learn."

"Oh, but nothing artistically bad," she urged—still, for poor Peter, arch and dewy.

"Why, just the little French tricks," said the Master: on which their friend had to pretend to admit, when pressed by Mrs. Mallow, that these aesthetic vices had been the objects of his dread.

III

"I know now," Lance said to him the next year, "why you were so much against it." He had come back, supposedly for a mere interval, and was looking about him at Carrara Lodge, where indeed he had already on two or three occasions since his expatriation, briefly reappeared. This had the air of a longer holiday. "Something rather awful has happened to me. It *isn't* so very good to know."

"I'm bound to say high spirits don't show in your face," Peter was rather ruefully forced to confess. "Still, are you very sure you do know?"

"Well, I at least know about as much as I can bear." These remarks were exchanged in Peter's den, and the young man, smoking cigarettes, stood before the fire with his back against the mantel. Something of his bloom seemed really to have left him.

Poor Peter wondered. "You're clear then as to what in particular I wanted you not to go for?"

"In particular?" Lance thought. "It seems to me that in particular there can have been only one thing."

They stood for a little sounding each other. "Are you quite sure?"

"Quite sure I'm a beastly duffer? Quite—by this time."

"Oh!"—and Peter turned away as if almost with relief.

"It's *that* that isn't pleasant to find out."

"Oh, I don't care for 'that,' " said Peter, presently coming round again. "I mean I personally don't."

"Yet I hope you can understand a little that I myself should!"

"Well, what do you mean by it?" Peter sceptically asked.

And on this Lance had to explain—how the upshot of his

studies in Paris had inexorably proved a mere deep doubt of his means. These studies had so waked him up that a new light was in his eyes; but what the new light did was really to show him too much. "Do you know what's the matter with me? I'm too horribly intelligent. Paris was really the last place for me. I've learnt what I can't do."

Poor Peter stared—it was a staggerer; but even after they had had, on the subject, a longish talk in which the boy brought out to the full the hard truth of his lesson, his friend betrayed less pleasure than usually breaks into a face to the happy tune of "I told you so!" Poor Peter himself made now indeed so little a point of having told him so that Lance broke ground in a different place a day or two after. "What was it then that—before I went—you were afraid I should find out?" This, however, Peter refused to tell him—on the ground that if he hadn't yet guessed perhaps he never would, and that in any case nothing at all for either of them was to be gained by giving the thing a name. Lance eyed him on this an instant with the bold curiosity of youth—with the air indeed of having in his mind two or three names, of which one or other would be right. Peter nevertheless, turning his back again, offered no encouragement, and when they parted afresh it was with some show of impatience on the side of the boy. Accordingly on their next encounter Peter saw at a glance that he had now, in the interval, divined and that, to sound his note, he was only waiting till they should find themselves alone. This he had soon arranged and he then broke straight out. "Do you know your conundrum has been keeping me awake? But in the watches of the night the answer came over me—so that, upon my honor, I quite laughed out. Had you been supposing I had to go to Paris to learn *that?*" Even now, to see him still so sublimely on his guard, Peter's young friend had to laugh afresh. "You won't give a sign till you're sure? Beautiful old Peter!" But Lance at last produced it. "Why, hang it, the truth about the Master."

It made between them for some minutes a lively passage, full of wonder for each at the wonder of the other. "Then how long have you understood—"

"The true value of his work? I understood it," Lance recalled, "as soon as I began to understand anything. But I didn't begin fully to do that, I admit, till I got *là-bas.*"

"Dear, dear!"—Peter gasped with retrospective dread.

"But for what have you taken me? I'm a hopeless muff—that I

had to have rubbed in. But I'm not such a muff as the Master!" Lance declared.

"Then why did you never tell me—?"

"That I hadn't, after all"—the boy took him up—"remained such an idiot? Just because I never dreamed *you* knew. But I beg your pardon. I only wanted to spare you. And what I don't now understand is how the deuce then for so long you've managed to keep bottled."

Peter produced his explanation, but only after some delay and with a gravity not void of embarrassment. "It was for your mother."

"Oh!" said Lance.

"And that's the great thing now—since the murder *is* out. I want a promise from you. I mean"—and Peter almost feverishly followed it up—"a vow from you, solemn and such as you owe me here on the spot, that you'll sacrifice anything rather than let her ever guess—"

"That *I've* guessed?"—Lance took it in. "I see." He evidently after a moment had taken in much. "But what is it you've in mind that I may have a chance to sacrifice?"

"Oh one has always something."

Lance looked at him hard. "Do you mean that *you've* had—?" The look he received back, however, so put the question by that he found soon enough another. "Are you really sure my mother doesn't know?"

Peter, after renewed reflection, was really sure. "If she does, she's too wonderful."

"But aren't we all too wonderful?"

"Yes," Peter granted—"but in different ways. The thing's so desperately important because your father's little public consists only, as you know then," Peter developed—"well, of how many?"

"First of all," the Master's son risked, "of himself. And last of all too. I don't quite see of whom else."

Peter had an approach to impatience. "Of your mother, I say—*always*."

Lance cast it all up. "You absolutely feel that?"

"Absolutely."

"Well then, with yourself that makes three."

"Oh *me!*"—and Peter, with a wag of his kind old head, modestly excused himself. "The number's at any rate small enough for any individual dropping out to be too dreadfully missed. Therefore, to put it in a nutshell, take care, my boy—that's all—that *you're* not!"

"I've got to keep on humbugging?" Lance wailed.

"It's just to warn you of the danger of your failing of that that I've seized this opportunity."

"And what do you regard in particular," the young man asked, "as the danger?"

"Why, this certainty: that the moment your mother, who feels so strongly, should suspect your secret—well," said Peter desperately, "the fat would be on the fire."

Lance for a moment seemed to stare at the blaze, "She'd throw me over?"

"She'd throw *him* over."

"And come round to us?"

Peter, before he answered, turned away. "Come around to *you*." But he had said enough to indicate—and, as he evidently trusted, to avert—the horrid contingency.

IV

Within six months again, none the less, his fear was on more occasions than one all before him. Lance had returned to Paris for another trial; then had reappeared at home and had had, with his father, for the first time in his life, one of the scenes that strike sparks. He described it with much expression to Peter, touching whom (since they had never done so before) it was the sign of a new reserve on the part of the pair at Carrara Lodge that they at present failed, on a matter of intimate interest, to open themselves —if not in joy then in sorrow—to their good friend. This produced perhaps practically between the parties a shade of alienation and a slight intermission of commerce—marked mainly indeed by the fact that to talk at his ease with his old playmate Lance had in general to come to see him. The closest if not quite the gayest relation they had yet known together was thus ushered in. The difficulty for poor Lance was a tension at home—begotten by the fact that his father wished him to be at least the sort of success he himself had been. He hadn't "chucked" Paris—though nothing appeared more vivid to him than that Paris had chucked him: he would go back again because of the fascination in trying, in seeing, in sounding the depths—in learning one's lesson, briefly, even if the lesson were simply that of one's impotence in the presence of one's larger vision. But what did the Master, all aloft in his senseless fluency, know of impotence, and what vision—to be called such—had he in all his blind life ever had? Lance, heated and indignant, frankly appealed to his godparent on this score.

His father, it appeared, had come down on him for having, after so long, nothing to show, and hoped that on his next return this deficiency would be repaired. *The* thing, the Master complacently set forth was—for any artist, however inferior to himself—at least to "do" something. "What can you do? That's all I ask!" *He* had certainly done enough, and there was no mistake about what he had to show. Lance had tears in his eyes when it came thus to letting his old friend know how great the strain might be on the "sacrifice" asked of him. It wasn't so easy to continue humbugging—as from son to parent—after feeling one's self despised for not grovelling in mediocrity. Yet a noble duplicity was what, as they intimately faced the situation, Peter went on requiring; and it was still for a time what his young friend, bitter and sore, managed loyally to comfort him with. Fifty pounds more than once again, it was true, rewarded both in London and in Paris the young friend's loyalty; none the less sensibly, doubtless, at the moment, that the money was a direct advance on a decent sum for which Peter had long since privately prearranged an ultimate function. Whether by these arts or others, at all events, Lance's just resentment was kept for a season—but only for a season—at bay. The day arrived when he warned his companion that he could hold out—or hold in—no longer. Carrara Lodge had had to listen to another lecture delivered from a great height—an infliction really heavier at last than, without striking back or in some way letting the Master have the truth, flesh and blood could bear.

"And what I don't see is," Lance observed with a certain irritated eye for what was after all, if it came to that, owing to himself too; "what I don't see is, upon my honor, how *you,* as things are going, can keep the game up."

"Oh, the game for me is only to hold my tongue," said placid Peter. "And I have my reason."

"Still my mother?"

Peter showed a queer face as he had often shown it before—that is by turning it straight away. "What will you have? I haven't ceased to like her."

"She's beautiful—she's a dear of course," Lance allowed; "but what is she to you, after all, and what is it to you that, as to anything whatever, she should or she shouldn't?"

Peter, who had turned red, hung fire a little. "Well—it's all simply what I make of it."

There was now, however, in his young friend a strange, an adopted insistence. "What are you after all to *her?*"

"Oh nothing. But that's another matter."

"She cares only for my father," said Lance the Parisian.

"Naturally—and that's just why."

"Why you've wished to spare her?"

"Because she cares so tremendously much."

Lance took a turn about the room, but with his eyes still on his host. "How awfully—always—you must have liked her!"

"Awfully. Always," said Peter Brench.

The young man continued for a moment to muse—then stopped again in front of him. "Do you know how much she cares?" Their eyes met on it, but Peter, as if his own found something new in Lance's, appeared to hesitate, for the first time in an age, to say he did know. "*I've* only just found out," said Lance. "She came to my room last night, after being present, in silence and only with her eyes on me, at what I had had to take from him; she came—and she was with me an extraordinary hour."

He had paused again and they had again for a while sounded each other. Then something—and it made him suddenly turn pale—came to Peter. "She *does* know?"

"She does know. She let it all out to me—so as to demand of me no more than 'that,' as she said, of which she herself had been capable. She has always, always known," said Lance without pity.

Peter was silent a long time; during which his companion might have heard him gently breathe, and on touching him might have felt within him the vibration of a long low sound suppressed. By the time he spoke at last he had taken everything in. "Then I do see how tremendously much."

"Isn't it wonderful?" Lance asked.

"Wonderful," Peter mused.

"So that if your original effort to keep me from Paris was to keep me from knowledge—!" Lance exclaimed as if with a sufficient indication of this futility.

It might have been at the futility Peter appeared for a little to gaze. "I think it must have been—without my quite at the time knowing it—to keep *me!*" he replied at last as he turned away.

Joseph Conrad

AMY FOSTER

Kennedy is a country doctor, and lives in Colebrook, on the shores of Eastbay. The high ground rising abruptly behind the red roofs of the little town crowds the quaint High Street against the wall which defends it from the sea. Beyond the sea wall there curves for miles in a vast and regular sweep the barren beach of shingle, with the village of Brenzett standing out darkly across the water, a spire in a clump of trees; and still farther out the perpendicular column of a lighthouse, looking in the distance no bigger than a lead pencil, marks the vanishing point of the land. The country at the back of Brenzett is low and flat; but the bay is fairly well sheltered from the seas, and occasionally a big ship, windbound or through stress of weather, makes use of the anchoring ground a mile and a half due north from you as you stand at the back door of the "Ship Inn" in Brenzett. A dilapidated windmill near by, lifting its shattered arms from a mound no loftier than a rubbish heap, and a Martello tower squatting at the water's edge half a mile to the south of the Coastguard cottages, are familiar to the skippers of small craft. These are the official seamarks for the patch of trustworthy bottom represented on the Admiralty charts by an irregular oval of dots enclosing several figure sixes, with a tiny anchor engraved among them, and the legend "mud and shells" over all.

The brow of the upland overtops the square tower of the Colebrook Church. The slope is green and looped by a white road. Ascending along this road, you open a valley broad and shallow, a wide green trough of pastures and hedges merging inland into a vista of purple tints and flowing lines closing the view.

In this valley down to Brenzett and Colebrook and up to Darnford, the market town fourteen miles away, lies the practice of my friend Kennedy. He had begun life as surgeon in the Navy, and afterwards had been the companion of a famous traveller, in the days when there were continents with unexplored interiors. His papers on the fauna and flora made him known to scientific societies. And now he had come to a country practice—from choice. The penetrating power of his mind, acting like a corrosive fluid, had destroyed his ambition, I fancy. His intelligence is of a scientific order, of an investigating habit, and of that unappeasable curiosity which believes that there is a particle of a general truth in every mystery.

A good many years ago now, on my return from abroad, he invited me to stay with him. I came readily enough, and as he could not neglect his patients to keep me company, he took me on his rounds—thirty miles or so of an afternoon, sometimes. I waited for him on the roads; the horse reached after the leafy twigs, and, sitting high in the dogcart, I could hear Kennedy's laugh through the half-open door of some cottage. He had a big, hearty laugh that would have fitted a man twice his size, a brisk manner, a bronzed face, and a pair of gray, profoundly attentive eyes. He had the talent of making people talk to him freely, and an inexhaustible patience in listening to their tales.

One day, as we trotted out of a large village into a shady bit of road, I saw on our left hand a low, black cottage, with diamond panes in the windows, a creeper on the end wall, a roof of shingle, and some roses climbing on the rickety trellis-work of the tiny porch. Kennedy pulled up to a walk. A woman, in full sunlight, was throwing a dripping blanket over a line stretched between two old apple trees. And as the bobtailed, long-necked chestnut, trying to get his head, jerked the left hand, covered by a thick dogskin glove, the doctor raised his voice over the hedge: "How's your child, Amy?"

I had the time to see her dull face, red, not with a mantling blush, but as if her flat cheeks had been vigorously slapped, and to take in the squat figure, the scanty, dusty brown hair drawn into a tight knot at the back of the head. She looked quite young. With a distinct catch in her breath, her voice sounded low and timid.

"He's well, thank you."

We trotted again. "A young patient of yours," I said; and the doctor, flicking the chestnut absently, muttered, "Her husband used to be."

"She seems a dull creature," I remarked, listlessly.

"Precisely," said Kennedy. "She is very passive. It's enough to look at the red hands hanging at the end of those short arms, at those slow, prominent brown eyes, to know the inertness of her mind—an inertness that one would think made it everlastingly safe from all the surprises of imagination. And yet which of us is safe? At any rate, such as you see her, she had enough imagination to fall in love. She's the daughter of one Isaac Foster, who from a small farmer has sunk into a shepherd; the beginning of his misfortunes dating from his runaway marriage with the cook of his widowed father—a well-to-do, apoplectic grazier, who passionately struck his name off his will, and had been heard to utter threats against his life. But this old affair, scandalous enough to serve as a motive for a Greek tragedy, arose from the similarity of their characters. There are other tragedies, less scandalous and of a subtler poignancy, arising from irreconcilable differences and from that fear of the Incomprehensible that hangs over all our heads—over all our heads. . . ."

The tired chestnut dropped into a walk; and the rim of the sun, all red in a speckless sky, touched familiarly the smooth top of a ploughed rise near the road as I had seen it times innumerable touch the distant horizon of the sea. The uniform brownness of the harrowed field glowed with a rose tinge, as though the powdered clods had sweated out in minute pearls of blood the toil of uncounted ploughmen. From the edge of a copse a wagon with two horses was rolling gently along the ridge. Raised above our heads upon the skyline, it loomed up against the red sun, triumphantly big, enormous, like a chariot of giants drawn by two slow-stepping steeds of legendary proportions. And the clumsy figure of the man plodding at the head of the leading horse projected itself on the background of the Infinite with a heroic uncouthness. The end of his carter's whip quivered high up in the blue. Kennedy discoursed.

"She's the eldest of a large family. At the age of fifteen they put her out to service at the New Barns Farm. I attended Mrs. Smith, the tenant's wife, and saw that girl there for the first time. Mrs. Smith, a genteel person with a sharp nose, made her put on a black dress every afternoon. I don't know what induced me to notice her at all. There are faces that call your attention by a curious want of definiteness in their whole aspect, as, walking in a mist, you peer attentively at a vague shape which, after all, may be nothing more curious or strange than a signpost. The only peculiarity I perceived in her was a slight hesitation in her utterance, a sort of preliminary stammer which passes away with the first word. When sharply spoken to, she was apt to lose her head at once; but her heart was of the kindest. She had never been heard to express a dislike for a single human being, and she was tender to every living creature. She was devoted to Mrs. Smith, to Mr. Smith, to their dogs, cats, canaries; and as to Mrs. Smith's gray parrot, its peculiarities exercised upon her a positive fascination. Nevertheless, when that outlandish bird, attacked by the cat, shrieked for help in human accents, she ran out into the yard stopping her ears and did not prevent the crime. For Mrs. Smith this was another evidence of her stupidity; on the other hand, her want of charm, in view of Smith's well-known frivolousness, was a great recommendation. Her short-sighted eyes would swim with pity for a poor mouse in a trap, and she had been seen once by some boys on her knees in the wet grass helping a toad in difficulties. If it's true, as some German fellow has said, that without phosphorus there is no thought, it is still more true that there is no kindness of heart without a certain amount of imagination. She had some. She had even more than is necessary to understand suffering and to be moved by pity. She fell in love under circumstances that leave no room for doubt in the matter; for you need imagination to form a notion of beauty at all, and still more to discover your ideal in an unfamiliar shape.

"How this aptitude came to her, what it did feed upon, is an inscrutable mystery. She was born in the village, and had never been further away from it than Colebrook or perhaps Darnford. She lived for four years with the Smiths. New Barns is an isolated farmhouse a mile away from the road, and she was content to look day after day at the same fields, hollows, rises; at the trees and the hedgerows; at the faces of the four men about the farm, always the same—day after day, month after month, year after year. She never showed a desire for conversation, and, as it seemed to me, she did not know how to smile. Sometimes of a fine Sunday afternoon she would put on her best dress, a pair of stout boots, a large gray hat trimmed with a black feather (I've seen her in that finery), seize an absurdly slender parasol, climb over two stiles, tramp over three fields and along two hundred yards of road—never further. There stood Foster's cottage. She would help her mother to give their tea to the younger children, wash up the crockery, kiss the little ones, and go back to the farm. That was all. All the rest, all the change, all the relaxation. She never seemed to wish for anything more. And then she fell in love. She fell in love silently, obstinately—perhaps helplessly. It came slowly, but when it came it worked like a powerful spell: it was love as the Ancients understood it: an irresistible and fateful impulse—a possession! Yes, it was in her to become haunted and possessed by a face, by a presence, fatally, as though she had been a pagan worshipper of form under a joyous sky—and to be awakened at last from the mysterious forgetfulness of self, from that enchantment, from that transport, by a fear resembling the unaccountable terror of a brute. . . ."

With the sun hanging low on its western limit, the expanse of the grass-lands framed in the counterscarps of the rising ground took on a gorgeous and sombre aspect. A sense of penetrating sadness, like that inspired by a grave strain of music, disengaged itself from the silence of the fields. The men we met walked past, slow, unsmiling, with downcast eyes, as if the melancholy of an overburdened earth had weighted their feet, bowed their shoulders, borne down their glances.

"Yes," said the doctor to my remark, "one would think the earth is under a curse, since of all her children these that cling to her the closest are uncouth in body and as leaden of gait as if their very hearts were loaded with chains. But here on this same road you might have seen amongst these heavy men a being lithe, supple and long-limbed, straight like a pine, with something striving upwards in his appearance as though the heart within him had been buoyant. Perhaps it was only the force of the contrast, but when he was passing one of these villagers here, the soles of his feet did not seem to me to touch the dust of the road. He vaulted over the stiles, paced these slopes with a long elastic stride that made him noticeable at a great distance, and had lustrous black eyes. He was so different from the mankind around that, with his freedom of movement, his soft—a little startled—glance, his olive complexion and graceful bearing, his humanity suggested to me the nature of a woodland creature. He came from there."

The doctor pointed with his whip, and from the summit of the descent seen over the rolling tops of the trees in a park by the side of the road, appeared the level sea far below us, like the floor of an immense edifice inlaid with bands of dark ripple, with still trails of glitter, ending in a belt of glassy water at the foot of the sky. The light blur of smoke, from an invisible steamer, faded on the great clearness of the horizon like the mist of a breath on a mirror; and, inshore, the white sails of a coaster, with the appearance of disentangling themselves slowly from under the branches, floated clear of the foliage of the trees.

"Shipwrecked in the bay?" I said.

"Yes; he was a castaway. A poor emigrant from Central Europe bound to America and washed ashore here in a storm. And for him, who knew nothing of the earth, England was an undiscovered country. It was some time before he learned its name; and for all I know he might have expected to find wild beasts or wild men here, when, crawling in the dark over the sea wall, he rolled down the other side into a dyke, where it was another miracle he didn't get drowned. But he struggled instinctively like an animal under a net, and this blind struggle threw him out into a field. He must have been, indeed, of a tougher fiber than he looked to withstand without expiring such buffetings, the violence of his exertions, and so much fear. Later on, in his broken English that resembled curiously the speech of a young child, he told me himself that he put his trust in God, believing he was no longer in this world. And truly—he would add—how was he to know? He fought his way against the rain and the gale on all fours, and crawled at last among some sheep huddled close under the lee of a hedge. They ran off in all directions, bleating in the darkness, and he welcomed the first familiar sound he heard on these shores. It must have been two in the morning then. And this is all we know of the manner of his landing, though he did not arrive unattended by any means. Only his grisly company did not begin to come ashore till much later in the day."

The doctor gathered the reins, clicked his tongue; we trotted down the hill. Then turning, almost directly, a sharp corner into High Street, we rattled over the stones and were home.

Late in the evening Kennedy, breaking a spell of moodiness that had come over him, returned to the story. Smoking his pipe, he paced the long room from end to end. A reading-lamp concentrated all its light upon the papers on his desk; and, sitting by the open window, I saw, after the windless, scorching day, the frigid splendour of a hazy sea lying motionless under the moon. Not a whisper, not a splash, not a stir of the shingle, not a footstep, not a sigh came up from the earth below—never a sign of life but the scent of climbing jasmine: and Kennedy's voice, speaking behind me, passed through the wide casement, to vanish outside in a chill and sumptuous stillness.

". . . The relations of shipwrecks in the olden time tell us of much suffering. Often the castaways were only saved from drowning to die miserably from starvation on a barren coast; others suffered violent death or else slavery, passing through years of precarious existence with people to whom their strangeness was an object of suspicion, dislike or fear. We read about these things, and they are very pitiful. It is indeed hard upon a man to find himself a lost stranger, helpless, incomprehensible, and of a mysterious origin, in some obscure corner of the earth. Yet amongst all the adventurers shipwrecked in all the wild parts of the world, there is not one, it seems to me, that ever had to suffer a fate so simply tragic as the man I am speaking of, the most innocent of adventurers cast out by the sea in the bight of this bay, almost within sight from this very window.

"He did not know the name of his ship. Indeed, in the course of time we discovered he did not even know that ships had names—'like Christian people'; and when, one day, from the top of Talfourd Hill, he beheld the sea lying open to his view, his eyes roamed afar, lost in an air of wild surprise, as though he had never seen such a sight before. And probably he had not. As far as I could make out, he had been hustled together with many others on board an emigrant ship at the mouth of the Elbe, too bewildered to take note of his surroundings, too weary to see anything, too anxious to care. They were driven below into the 'tween-deck and battened down from the very start. It was a low timber dwelling—he would say—with wooden beams overhead, like the houses in his country, but you went into it down a ladder. It was very large, very cold, damp and sombre, with places in the manner of wooden boxes where people had to sleep one above another, and it kept on rocking all ways at once all the time. He crept into one of these boxes and lay down there in the clothes in which he had left his home many days before, keeping his bundle and his stick by his side. People groaned, children cried, water dripped, the lights went out, the walls of the place creaked, and everything was being shaken so that in one's little box one dared not lift one's head. He had lost touch with his only companion (a young man from the same valley, he said), and all the time a great noise of wind went on outside and heavy blows fell—boom! boom! An awful sickness overcame him, even to the point of making him neglect his prayers. Besides, one could not tell whether it was morning or evening. It seemed always to be night in that place.

"Before that he had been travelling a long, long time on the iron track. He looked out of the window, which had a wonderfully clear glass in it, and the trees, the houses, the fields, and the long roads seemed to fly round and round about him till his head swam. He gave me to understand that he had on his passage beheld uncounted multitudes of people—whole nations—all dressed in such clothes as the rich wear. Once he was made to get out of the carriage, and slept through a night on a bench in a house of bricks with his bundle under his head; and once for many hours he had to sit on a floor of flat stones dozing, with his knees up and with his bundle between his feet. There was a roof over him, which seemed made of glass, and was so high that the tallest mountain pine he had ever seen would have had room to grow under it. Steam machines rolled in at one end and out at the other. People swarmed more than you can see on a feast day round the miraculous Holy Image in the yard of the Carmelite Convent down in the plains where, before he left his home, he drove his mother in a wooden cart—a pious old woman who wanted to offer prayers and make a vow for his safety. He could not give me an idea of how large and lofty and full of noise and smoke and gloom, and clang of iron, the place was, but some one had told him it was called Berlin. Then they rang a bell, and another steam machine came in, and again he was taken on and on through a land that wearied his eyes by its flatness without a single bit of a hill to be seen anywhere. One more night he spent shut up in a building like a good stable with a litter of straw on the floor, guarding his bundle amongst a lot of men, of whom not one could understand a single word he said. In the morning they were all led down to the stony shores of an extremely broad muddy river, flowing not between hills but between houses that seemed immense. There was a steam machine that went on the water, and they all stood upon it packed tight, only now there were with them many women and children who made much noise. A cold rain fell, the wind blew in his face; he was wet through, and his teeth chattered. He and the young man from the same valley took each other by the hand.

"They thought they were being taken to America straight away, but suddenly the steam machine bumped against the side of a thing like a great house on the water. The walls were smooth and black, and there uprose, growing from the roof as it were, bare trees in the shape of crosses, extremely high. That's how it appeared to him then, for he had never seen a ship before. This was the ship that was going to swim all the way to America. Voices shouted, everything swayed; there was a ladder dipping up and down. He went up on his hands and knees in mortal fear of falling into the water below, which made a great splashing. He got separated from his companion, and when he descended into the bottom of that ship his heart seemed to melt suddenly within him.

"It was then also, as he told me, that he lost contact for good and all with one of those three men who the summer before had been going about through all the little towns in the foothills of his country. They would arrive on market-days driving in a peasant's cart, and would set up an office in an inn or some other Jew's house. There were three of them, of whom one with a long beard looked venerable; and they had red cloth collars round their necks and gold lace on their sleeves like Government officials. They sat proudly behind a long table; and in the next room, so that the common people shouldn't hear, they kept a cunning telegraph machine, through which they could talk to the Emperor of America. The fathers hung about the door, but the young men of the mountains would crowd up to the table asking many questions, for there was work to be got all the year round at three dollars a day in America, and no military service to do.

"But the American Kaiser would not take everybody. Oh, no! He himself had a great difficulty in getting accepted, and the venerable man in uniform had to go out of the room several times to work the telegraph on his behalf. The American Kaiser engaged him at last at three dollars, he being young and strong. However, many able young men backed out, afraid of the great distance; besides, only those who had some money could be taken. There were some who sold their huts and their land because it cost a lot of money to get to America; but then, once there, you had three dollars a day, and if you were clever you could find places where true gold could be picked up on the ground. His father's house was getting over full. Two of his brothers were married and had children. He promised to send money home from America by post twice a year. His father sold an old cow, a pair of piebald mountain ponies of his own raising, and a cleared plot of fair pasture land on the sunny slope of a pineclad pass to a Jew innkeeper, in order to pay the people of the ship that took men to America to get rich in a short time.

"He must have been a real adventurer at heart, for how many of the greatest enterprises in the conquest of the earth had for their beginning just such a bargaining away of the paternal cow for the mirage or true gold far away! I have been telling you more or less in my own words what I learned fragmentarily in the course of two or three years, during which I seldom missed an opportunity of a friendly chat with him. He told me this story of his adventure with many flashes of white teeth and lively glances of black eyes, at first in a sort of anxious baby-talk, then, as he acquired the language, with great fluency, but always with that singing, soft, and at the same time vibrating intonation that instilled a strangely penetrating power into the sound of the most familiar English words, as if they had been the words of an unearthly language. And he always would come to an end, with many emphatic shakes of his head, upon that awful sensation of his heart melting within him directly he set foot on board that ship. Afterwards there seemed to come for him a period of blank ignorance, at any rate as to facts. No doubt he must have been abominably seasick and abominably unhappy—this soft and passionate adventurer, taken thus out of his knowledge, and feeling bitterly as he lay in his emigrant bunk his utter loneliness; for his was a highly sensitive nature. The next thing we know of him for certain is that he had been hiding in Hammond's pig-pound by the side of the road to Norton, six miles, as the crow flies, from the sea. Of these experiences he was unwilling to speak: they seemed to have seared into his soul a sombre sort of wonder and indignation. Through the rumors of the countryside, which lasted for a good many days after his arrival, we know that the fishermen of West Colebrook had been disturbed and startled by heavy knocks against the walls of weatherboard cottages, and by a voice crying piercingly strange words in the night. Several of them turned out even, but, no doubt, he had fled in sudden alarm at their rough angry tones hailing each other in the darkness. A sort of frenzy must have helped him up the steep Norton hill. It was he, no doubt, who early the following morning had been seen lying (in a swoon, I should say) on the roadside grass by the Brenzett carrier, who actually got down to have a nearer look, but drew back, intimidated by the perfect immobility, and by something queer in the aspect of that tramp, sleeping so still under the showers. As the day advanced, some children came dashing into school at Norton in such a fright that the schoolmistress went out and spoke indignantly to a 'horrid-looking man' on the road. He edged away, hanging his head, for a few steps, and then suddenly ran off with extraordinary fleetness. The driver of Mr. Bradley's milkcart made no secret of it that he had lashed with his whip at a hairy sort of gipsy fellow who, jumping up at a turn of the road by the Vents, made a snatch at the pony's bridle. And he caught him a good one, too, right over the face, he said, that made him drop down in the mud a jolly sight quicker than he had jumped up; but it was a good half a mile before he could stop the pony. Maybe that in his desperate endeavours to get help, and in his need to get in touch with someone, the poor devil had tried to stop the cart. Also three boys confessed afterwards to throwing stones at a funny tramp, knocking about all wet and muddy, and, it seemed, very drunk, in the narrow deep lane by the limekilns. All this was the talk of three villages for days; but we have Mrs. Finn's (the wife of Smith's waggoner) unimpeachable testimony that she saw him get over the low wall of Hammond's pig-pound and lurch straight at her, babbling aloud in a voice that was enough to make one die of fright. Having the baby with her in a perambulator, Mrs. Finn called out to him to go away, and as he persisted in coming nearer, she hit him courageously with her umbrella over the head, and, without once looking back, ran like the wind with the perambulator as far as the first house in the village. She stopped then, out of breath, and spoke to old Lewis, hammering there at a heap of stones; and the old chap, taking off his immense black wire goggles, got up on his shaky legs to look where she pointed. Together they followed with their eyes the figure of the man running over a field; they saw him fall down, pick himself up, and run on again, staggering and waving his long arms above his head, in the direction of the New Barns Farm. From that moment on he is plainly in the toils of his obscure and touching destiny. There is no doubt after this of what happened to him. All is certain now: Mrs. Smith's intense terror; Amy Foster's stolid conviction held against the other's nervous attack, that the man 'meant no harm': Smith's exasperation (on his return from Darnford Market) at finding the dog barking himself into a fit, the back-door locked, his wife in hysterics; and all for an unfortunate dirty tramp, supposed to be even then lurking in his stackyard. Was he? He would teach him to frighten women.

"Smith is notoriously hot-tempered, but the sight of some nondescript and miry creature sitting cross-legged against a lot of loose straw, and swinging itself to and fro like a bear in a cage, made him pause. Then this tramp stood up silently before him, one mass of mud and filth from head to foot. Smith, alone amongst his stacks with this apparition, in the stormy twilight ringing with the infuriated barking of the dog, felt the dread of an inexplicable strangeness. But when that being, parting with his black hands the long matted locks that hung before his face, as you part the two halfs of a curtain, looked out at him with glistening, wild, black-and-white eyes, the weirdness of this silent encounter fairly staggered him. He has admitted since (for the story has been a legitimate subject of conversation about here for years) that he made more than one step backwards. Then a sudden burst of rapid, senseless speech persuaded him at once that he had to do with an escaped lunatic. In fact, that impression never wore off completely. Smith has not in his heart given up his secret conviction of the man's essential insanity to this very day.

"As the creature approached him, jabbering in a most discomposing manner, Smith (unaware that he was being addressed as 'gracious lord,' and adjured in God's name to afford food and shelter) kept on speaking firmly but gently to it, and retreating all the time into the other yard. At last, watching his chance, by a sudden charge he bundled him headlong into the wood-lodge, and instantly shot the bolt. Thereupon he wiped his brow, though the day was cold. He had done his duty to the community by shutting up a wandering and probably dangerous maniac. Smith isn't a hard man at all, but he had room in his brain only for that one idea of lunacy. He was not imaginative enough to ask himself whether the man might not be perishing with cold and hunger. Meantime, at first, the maniac made a great deal of noise in the lodge. Mrs. Smith was screaming upstairs, where she had locked herself in her bedroom; but Amy Foster sobbed piteously at the kitchen-door, wringing her hands and muttering, 'Don't! don't!' I daresay Smith had a rough time of it that evening with one noise and another, and this insane, disturbing voice crying obstinately through the door only added to his irritation. He couldn't possibly have connected this troublesome lunatic with the sinking of a ship in Eastbay, of which there had been a rumor in the Darnford market place. And I daresay the man inside had been very near to insanity on that night. Before his excitement collapsed and he became unconscious he was throwing himself violently about in the dark, rolling on some dirty sacks, and biting his fists with rage, cold, hunger, amazement, and despair.

"He was a mountaineer of the eastern range of the Carpathians, and the vessel sunk the night before in Eastbay was the Hamburg emigrant-ship *Herzogin Sophia-Dorothea,* of appalling memory.

"A few months later we could read in the papers the accounts of the bogus 'Emigration Agencies' among the Sclavonian peasantry in the more remote provinces of Austria. The object of these scoundrels was to get hold of the poor ignorant people's homesteads, and they were in league with the local usurers. They exported their victims through Hamburg mostly. As to the ship, I had watched her out of this very window, reaching close-hauled under short canvas into the bay on a dark, threatening afternoon. She came to an anchor, correctly by the chart, off the Brenzett Coastguard station. I remember before the night fell looking out again at the outlines of her spars and rigging that stood out dark and pointed on a background of ragged, slaty clouds like another and a slighter spire to the left of the Brenzett church-tower. In the evening the wind rose. At midnight I could hear in my bed the terrific gusts and the sounds of a driving deluge.

"About that time the Coastguardmen thought they saw the lights of a steamer over the anchoring ground. In a moment they vanished; but it is clear that another vessel of some sort had tried for shelter in the bay on that awful, blind night, had rammed the German ship amidships ('a breach'—as one of the divers told me afterwards—'that you could sail a Thames barge through'), and then had gone out either scathless or damaged, who shall say; but had gone out, unknown, unseen, and fatal, to perish mysteriously at sea. Of her nothing ever came to light, and yet the hue and cry that was raised all over the world would have found her out if she had been in existence anywhere on the face of the waters.

"A completeness without a clue, and a stealthy silence as of a neatly executed crime, characterize this murderous disaster, which, as you may remember, had its gruesome celebrity. The wind would have prevented the loudest outcries from reaching the shore; there had been evidently no time for signals of distress. It was death without any sort of fuss. The Hamburg ship, filling all at once, capsized as she sank, and at daylight there was not even the end of a spar to be seen above water. She was missed, of course, and at first the Coastguardmen surmised that she had either dragged her anchor or parted her cable some time during the night, and had been blown out to sea. Then, after the tide turned, the wreck must have shifted a little and released some of the bodies, because a child—a little fair-haired child in a red frock—came ashore abreast of the Martello tower. By the afternoon you could see along three miles of beach dark figures with bare legs dashing in and out of the tumbling foam, and rough-looking men, women with hard faces, children, mostly fair-haired, were being carried, stiff and dripping, on stretchers, on wattles, on ladders, in a long procession past the door of the 'Ship Inn,' to be laid out in a row under the north wall of the Brenzett Church.

"Officially, the body of the little girl in the red frock is the first thing that came ashore from that ship. But I have patients amongst the seafaring population of West Colebrook, and, unofficially, I am informed that very early that morning two brothers, who went down to look after their cobble hauled up on the beach, found a good way from Brenzett, an ordinary ship's hencoop, lying high and dry on the shore, with eleven drowned ducks inside. Their families ate the birds, and the hencoop was split into firewood with a hatchet. It is possible that a man (supposing he happened to be on deck at the time of the accident) might have floated ashore on that hencoop. He might. I admit it is improbable, but there was the man—and for days, nay, for weeks—it didn't enter our heads that we had amongst us the only living soul that had escaped from that disaster. The man himself, even when he learned to speak intelligibly, could tell us very little. He remembered he had felt better (after the ship had anchored, I suppose), and that the darkness, the wind, and the rain took his breath away. This looks as if he had been on deck some time during that night. But we mustn't forget he had been taken out of his knowledge, that he had been sea-sick and battened down below for four days, that he had no general notion of a ship or of the sea, and therefore could have no definite idea of what was happening to him. The rain, the wind, the darkness he knew; he understood the bleating of the sheep, and he remembered the pain of his wretchedness and misery, his heartbroken astonishment that it was neither seen nor understood, his dismay at finding all the men angry and all the women fierce. He had approached them as a beggar, it is true, he said; but in his country, even if they gave nothing, they spoke gently to beggars. The children in his country were not taught to throw stones at those who asked for compassion. Smith's strategy overcame him completely. The wood-lodge presented the horrible aspect of a dungeon. What would be done to him next? . . . No wonder that Amy Foster appeared to his eyes with the aureole of an angel of light. The girl had not been able to sleep for thinking of the poor man, and in the morning, before the Smiths were up, she slipped out across the back yard. Holding the door of the wood-lodge ajar, she looked in and extended to him half a loaf of white bread—'such bread as the rich eat in my country,' he used to say.

"At this he got up slowly from amongst all sorts of rubbish, stiff, hungry, trembling, miserable, and doubtful. 'Can you eat this?' she asked in her soft and timid voice. He must have taken her for a 'gracious lady.' He devoured ferociously, and tears were falling on the crust. Suddenly he dropped the bread, seized her wrist, and imprinted a kiss on her hand. She was not frightened. Through his forlorn condition she had observed that he was good-looking. She shut the door and walked back slowly to the kitchen. Much later on, she told Mrs. Smith, who shuddered at the bare idea of being touched by that creature.

"Through this act of impulsive pity he was brought back again within the pale of human relations with his new surroundings. He never forgot it—never.

"That very same morning old Mr. Swaffer (Smith's nearest neighbor) came over to give his advice, and ended by carrying him off. He stood, unsteady on his legs, meek, and caked over in half-dried mud, while the two men talked around him in an incomprehensible tongue. Mrs. Smith had refused to come downstairs till the madman was off the premises; Amy Foster, far from within the dark kitchen, watched through the open back-door; and he obeyed the signs that were made to him to the best of his ability. But Smith was full of mistrust. 'Mind, sir! It may be all his cunning,' he cried repeatedly in a tone of warning. When Mr. Swaffer started the mare, the deplorable being sitting humbly by his side, through weakness, nearly fell out over the back of the high two-wheeled cart. Swaffer took him straight home. And it is then that I come upon the scene.

"I was called in by the simple process of the old man beckoning to me with his forefinger over the gate of his house as I happened to be driving past. I got down, of course.

" 'I've got something here,' he mumbled, leading the way to an outhouse at a little distance from his other farm buildings.

"It was there that I saw him first, in a long, low room taken upon the space of that sort of coach-house. It was bare and white-washed, with a small square aperture glazed with one cracked, dusty pane at its further end. He was lying on his back upon a straw pallet; they had given him a couple of horse-blankets, and he seemed to have spent the remainder of his strength in the exertion of cleaning himself. He was almost speechless; his quick breathing under the blankets pulled up to his chin, his glittering, restless black eyes reminded me of a wild bird caught in a snare. While I was examining him, old Swaffer stood silently by the door, passing the tips of his fingers along his shaven upper lip. I gave some directions, promised to send a bottle of medicine, and naturally made some inquiries.

" 'Smith caught him in the stackyard at New Barns,' said the old chap in his deliberate, unmoved manner, and as if the other had been indeed a sort of wild animal. 'That's how I came by him. Quite a curiosity, isn't he? Now tell me, doctor—you've been all over the world—don't you think that's a bit of a Hindoo we've got hold of here?'

"I was greatly surprised. His long black hair scattered over the straw bolster contrasted with the olive pallor of his face. It occurred to me he might be a Basque. It didn't necessarily follow that he should understand Spanish; but I tried him with the few words I know, and also with some French. The whispered sounds I caught by bending my ear to his lips puzzled me utterly. That afternoon the young ladies from the rectory (one of them read Goethe with a dictionary, and the other had struggled with Dante for years), coming to see Miss Swaffer, tried their German and Italian on him from the doorway. They retreated, just the least bit scared by the flood of passionate speech which, turning on his pallet, he let out at them. They admitted that the sound was pleasant, soft, musical—but, in conjunction with his looks perhaps, it was startling—so excitable, so utterly unlike anything one had ever heard. The village boys climbed up the bank to have a peep through the little square aperture. Everybody was wondering what Mr. Swaffer would do with him.

"He simply kept him.

"Swaffer would be called eccentric were he not so much respected. They will tell you that Mr. Swaffer sits up as late as ten o'clock at night to read books, and they will tell you also that he can write a cheque for two hundred pounds without thinking twice about it. He himself would tell you that the Swaffers had owned land between this and Darnford for these three hundred years. He must be eighty-five to-day, but he does not look a bit older than when I first came here. He is a great breeder of sheep, and deals extensively in cattle. He attends market days for miles around in every sort of weather, and drives sitting bowed low over the reins, his lank gray hair curling over the collar of his warm coat, and with a green plaid rug round his legs. The calmness of advanced age gives a solemnity to his manner. He is clean-shaved; his lips are thin and sensitive; something rigid and monachal in the set of his features lends a certain elevation to the character of his face. He has been known to drive miles in the rain to see a new kind of rose in somebody's garden, or a monstrous cabbage grown by a cottager. He loves to hear tell of or to be shown something that he calls 'outlandish.' Perhaps it was just that outlandishness of the man which influenced old Swaffer. Perhaps it was only an inexplicable caprice. All I know is that at the end of three weeks I caught sight of Smith's lunatic digging in Swaffer's kitchen garden. They had found out he could use a spade. He dug barefooted.

"His black hair flowed over his shoulders. I suppose it was Swaffer who had given him the striped old cotton shirt; but he wore still the national brown cloth trousers (in which he had been washed ashore) fitting to the leg almost like tights; was belted with a broad leathern belt studded with little brass discs; and had never yet ventured into the village. The land he looked upon seemed to him kept neatly, like the grounds round a landowner's house; the size of the cart-horses struck him with astonishment; the roads resembled garden walks, and the aspect of the people, especially on Sundays, spoke of opulence. He wondered what made them so hardhearted and their children so bold. He got his food at the back door, carried it in both hands, carefully, to his outhouse, and, sitting alone on his pallet, would make the sign of the cross before he began. Beside the same pallet, kneeling in the early darkness of the short days, he recited aloud the Lord's Prayer before he slept. Whenever he saw old Swaffer he would bow with veneration from his waist, and stand erect while the old man, with his fingers over his upper lip, surveyed him silently. He bowed also to Miss Swaffer, who kept house frugally for her father—a broadshouldered, big-boned woman of forty-five, with the pocket of her dress full of keys, and a gray, steady eye. She was Church—as people said (while her father was one of the trustees of the Baptist Chapel)—and wore a little steel cross at her waist. She dressed severely in black, in memory of one of the innumerable Bradleys of the neighbourhood, to whom she had been engaged some twenty-five years ago—a young farmer who broke his neck out hunting on the eve of the wedding-day. She had the unmoved countenance of the deaf, spoke very seldom, and her lips, thin like her father's, astonished one sometimes by a mysteriously ironic curl.

"These were the people to whom he owed allegiance, and an overwhelming loneliness seemed to fall from the leaden sky of that winter without sunshine. All the faces were sad. He could talk to no one, and had no hope of ever understanding anybody. It was as if these had been the faces of people from the other world—dead people—he used to tell me years afterwards. Upon my word, I wonder he did not go mad. He didn't know where he was. Somewhere very far from his mountains—somewhere over the water. Was this America, he wondered?

"If it hadn't been for the steel cross at Miss Swaffer's belt he would not, he confessed, have known whether he was in a Christian country at all. He used to cast stealthy glances at it, and feel comforted. There was nothing here the same as in his country! The earth and the water were different; there were no images of the Redeemer by the roadside. The very grass was different, and the trees. All the trees but the three old Norway pines on the bit of lawn before Swaffer's house, and these reminded him of his country. He had been detected once, after dusk, with his forehead against the trunk of them, sobbing, and talking to himself. They had been like brothers to him at that time, he affirmed. Everything else was strange. Conceive you the kind of an existence overshadowed, oppressed, by the everyday material appearances, as if by the visions of a nightmare. At night, when he could not sleep, he kept on thinking of the girl who gave him the first piece of bread he had eaten in this foreign land. She had been neither fierce nor angry, nor frightened. Her face he remembered as the only comprehensible face amongst all these faces that were as closed, as mysterious, and as mute as the faces of the dead who are possessed of a knowledge beyond the comprehension of the living. I wonder whether the memory of her compassion prevented him from cutting his throat. But there! I suppose I am an old sentimentalist, and forget the instinctive love of life which it takes all the strength of an uncommon despair to overcome.

"He did the work which was given him with an intelligence which surprised old Swaffer. By-and-by it was discovered that he could help at the ploughing, could milk the cows, feed the bullocks in the cattleyard, and was of some use with the sheep. He began to pick up words, too, very fast; and suddenly, one fine morning in spring, he rescued from an untimely death a grandchild of old Swaffer.

"Swaffer's younger daughter is married to Willcox, a solicitor and the Town Clerk of Colebrook. Regularly twice a year they come to stay with the old man for a few days. Their only child, a little girl not three years old at the time, ran out of the house alone in her little white pinafore, and, toddling across the grass of a terraced garden, pitched herself over a low wall head first into the horsepond in the yard below.

"Our man was out with the waggoner and the plough in the field nearest to the house, and as he was leading the team round to begin a fresh furrow, he saw, through the gap of a gate, what for anybody else would have been a mere flutter of something white. But he had straight-glancing, quick, far-reaching eyes, that only seemed to flinch and lose their amazing power before the immensity of the sea. He was barefooted, and looking as outlandish as the heart of Swaffer could desire. Leaving the horses on the turn, to the inexpressible disgust of the waggoner he bounded off, going over the ploughed ground in long leaps, and suddenly appeared before the mother, thrust the child into her arms, and strode away.

"The pond was not very deep; but still, if he had not had such good eyes, the child would have perished—miserably suffocated in the foot or so of sticky mud at the bottom. Old Swaffer walked out slowly into the field, waited till the plough came over to his side, had a good look at him, and without saying a word went back to the house. But from that time they laid out his meals on the kitchen table; and at first, Miss Swaffer, all in black and with an inscrutable face, would come and stand in the doorway of the living-room to see him make a big sign of the cross before he fell to. I believe that from that day, too, Swaffer began to pay him regular wages.

"I can't follow step by step his development. He cut his hair short, was seen in the village and along the road going to and fro to his work like any other man. Children ceased to shout after him. He became aware of social differences, but remained for a long time surprised at the bare poverty of the churches among so much wealth. He couldn't understand either why they were kept shut up on weekdays. There was nothing to steal in them. Was it to keep people from praying too often? The rectory took much notice of him about that time, and I believe the young ladies attempted to prepare the ground for his conversion. They could not, however, break him of his habit of crossing himself, but he went so far as to take off the string with a couple of brass medals the size of a sixpence, a tiny metal cross, and a square sort of scapulary which he wore round his neck. He hung them on the wall by the side of his bed, and he was still to be heard every evening reciting the Lord's Prayer, in incomprehensible words and in a slow, fervent tone, as he had heard his old father do at the head of all the kneeling family, big and little, on every evening of his life. And though he wore corduroys at work, and a shop-made pepper-and-salt suit on Sundays, strangers would turn round to look after him on the road. His foreignness had a peculiar and indelible stamp. At last people became used to seeing him. But they never became used to him. His rapid, skimming walk; his swarthy complexion; his hat cocked on the left ear; his habit, on warm evenings, of wearing his coat over one shoulder, like a hussar's dolman; his manner of leaping over the stiles, not as a feat of agility, but in the ordinary course of progression—and all these peculiarities were, as one may say, so many causes of scorn and offence to the inhabitants of the village. *They* wouldn't in their dinner hour lie flat on their backs on the grass to stare at the sky. Neither did they go about the fields screaming dismal tunes. Many times I have heard his high-pitched voice from behind the ridge of some sloping sheep-walk, a voice light and soaring, like a lark's, but with a melancholy human note, over our fields that hear only the song of birds. And I would be startled myself. Ah! He was different; innocent of heart, and full of good will, which nobody wanted, this castaway, that, like a man transplanted into another planet, was separated by an immense space from his past and by an immense ignorance from his future. His quick, fervent utterance positively shocked everybody. 'An excitable devil,' they called him. One evening, in the tap-room of the Coach and Horses (having drunk some whisky), he upset them all by singing a love-song of his country. They hooted him down, and he was pained; but Preble, the lame wheelwright, and Vincent, the fat blacksmith, and the other notables, too, wanted to drink their evening beer in peace. On another occasion he tried to show them how to dance. The dust rose in clouds from the sanded floor; he leaped straight up amongst the deal tables, struck his heels together, squatted on one heel in front of old Preble, shooting out the other leg, uttered wild and exulting cries, jumped up to whirl on one foot, snapping his fingers above his head—and a strange carter who was having a drink in there began to swear, and cleared out with his half-pint in his hand into the bar. But when suddenly he sprang upon a table and continued to dance among the glasses, the landlord interfered. He didn't want any 'acrobat tricks in the tap-room.' They laid their hands on him. Having had a glass or two, Mr. Swaffer's foreigner tried to expostulate: was ejected forcibly: got a black eye.

"I believe he felt the hostility of his human surroundings. But he was tough—tough in spirit, too, as well as in body. Only the memory of the sea frightened him, with that vague terror that is left by a bad dream. His home was far away; and he did not want now to go to America. I had often explained to him that there is no place on earth where true gold can be found lying ready and to be got for the trouble of the picking up. How, then, he asked, could he ever return home with empty hands when there had been sold a cow, two ponies, and a bit of land to pay for his going? His eyes would fill with tears, and, averting them from the immense shimmer of the sea, he would throw himself face down on the grass. But sometimes, cocking his hat with a little conquering air, he would defy my wisdom. He had found his bit of true gold. That was Amy Foster's heart; which was 'a golden heart, and soft to people's misery,' he would say in the accents of overwhelming conviction.

"He was called Yanko. He had explained that this meant Little John; but as he would also repeat very often that he was a mountaineer (some word sounding in the dialect of his country like Goorall) he got it for his surname. And this is the only trace of him that the succeeding ages may find in the marriage register of the parish. There it stands—Yanko Goorall—in the rector's handwriting. The crooked cross made by the castaway, a cross whose tracing no doubt seemed to him the most solemn part of the whole ceremony, is all that remains now to perpetuate the memory of his name.

"His courtship had lasted some time—ever since he got his precarious footing in the community. It began by his buying for Amy Foster a green satin ribbon in Darnford. This was what you did in his country. You bought a ribbon at a Jew's stall on a fair-day. I don't suppose the girl knew what to do with it, but he seemed to think that his honourable intentions could not be mistaken.

"It was only when he declared his purpose to get married that I fully understood how, for a hundred futile and inappreciable reasons, how—shall I say odious?—he was to all the countryside. Every old woman in the village was up in arms. Smith, coming upon him near the farm, promised to break his head for him if he found him about again. But he twisted his little black moustache with such a bellicose air and rolled such big, black fierce eyes at Smith that this promise came to nothing. Smith, however, told the girl that she must be mad to take up with a man who was surely wrong in his head. All the same, when she heard him in the gloaming whistle from beyond the orchard a couple of bars of a weird and mournful tune, she would drop whatever she had in her hand—she would leave Mrs. Smith in the middle of a sentence—and she would run out to his call. Mrs. Smith called her a shameless hussy. She answered nothing. She said nothing at all to anybody, and went on her way as if she had been deaf. She and I alone in all the land, I fancy, could see his very real beauty. He was very good-looking, and most graceful in his bearing, with that something wild as of a woodland creature in his aspect. Her mother moaned over her dismally whenever the girl came to see her on her day out. The father was surly, but pretended not to know; and Mrs. Finn once told her plainly that 'this man, my dear, will do you some harm some day yet.' And so it went on. They could be seen on the roads, she tramping stolidly in her finery—gray dress, black feather, stout boots, prominent white cotton gloves that caught your eye a hundred yards away; and he, his coat slung picturesquely over one shoulder, pacing by her side, gallant of bearing and casting tender glances upon the girl with the golden heart. I wonder whether he saw how plain she was. Perhaps among types so different from what he had ever seen, he had not the power to judge; or perhaps he was seduced by the divine quality of her pity.

"Yanko was in great trouble meantime. In his country you get an old man for an ambassador in marriage affairs. He did not know how to proceed. However, one day in the midst of sheep in a field (he was now Swaffer's under-shepherd with Foster) he took off his hat to the father and declared himself humbly. 'I dare-say she's fool enough to marry you,' was all Foster said. 'And then,' he used to relate, 'he puts his hat on his head, looks black at me as if he wanted to cut my throat, whistles the dog, and off he goes, leaving me to do the work.' The Fosters, of course, didn't like to lose the wages the girl earned: Amy used to give all her money to her mother. But there was in Foster a very genuine aversion to that match. He contended that the fellow was very good with sheep, but was not fit for any girl to marry. For one thing, he used to go along the hedges muttering to himself like a dam' fool; and then, these foreigners behave very queerly to women sometimes. And perhaps he would want to carry her off somewhere—or run off himself. It was not safe. He preached it to his daughter that the fellow might ill-use her in some way. She made no answer. It was, they said in the village, as if the man had done something to her. People discussed the matter. It was quite an excitement, and the two went on 'walking out' together in the face of opposition. Then something unexpected happened.

"I don't know whether old Swaffer ever understood how much he was regarded in the light of a father by his foreign retainer. Anyway the relation was curiously feudal. So when Yanko asked formally for an interview—'and the Miss, too' (he called the severe, deaf Miss Swaffer simply *Miss*)—it was to obtain their permission to marry. Swaffer heard him unmoved, dismissed him by a nod, and then shouted the intelligence into Miss Swaffer's best ear. She showed no surprise, and only remarked grimly, in a veiled blank voice, 'He certainly won't get any other girl to marry him.'

"It is Miss Swaffer who has all the credit of the munificence: but in a very few days it came out that Mr. Swaffer had presented Yanko with a cottage (the cottage you've seen this morning) and something like an acre of ground—had made it over to him in absolute property. Willcox expedited the deed, and I remember him telling me he had a great pleasure in making it ready. It recited: 'In consideration of saving the life of my beloved grandchild, Bertha Willcox.'

"Of course, after that no power on earth could prevent them from getting married.

"Her infatuation endured. People saw her going out to meet

him in the evening. She stared with unblinking, fascinated eyes up the road where he was expected to appear, walking freely, with a swing from the hip, and humming one of the love-tunes of his country. When the boy was born, he got elevated at the 'Coach and Horses,' essayed again a song and a dance, and was again ejected. People expressed their commiseration for a woman married to that Jack-in-the box. He didn't care. There was a man now (he told me boastfully) to whom he could sing and talk in the language of his country, and show how to dance by-and-by.

"But I don't know. To me he appeared to have grown less springy of step, heavier in body, less keen of eye. Imagination, no doubt; but it seems to me now as if the net of fate had been drawn closer round him already.

"One day I met him on the footpath over the Talfourd Hill. He told me that 'women were funny.' I had heard already of domestic differences. People were saying that Amy Foster was beginning to find out what sort of man she had married. He looked upon the sea with indifferent, unseeing eyes. His wife had snatched the child out of his arms one day as he sat on the doorstep crooning to it a song such as the mothers sing to babies in his mountains. She seemed to think he was doing it some harm. Women are funny. And she had objected to him praying aloud in the evening. Why? He expected the boy to repeat the prayer aloud after him by-and-by, as he used to do after his old father when he was a child—in his own country. And I discovered he longed for their boy to grow up so that he could have a man to talk with in that language that to our ears sounded so disturbing, so passionate, and so bizarre. Why his wife should dislike the idea he couldn't tell. But that would pass, he said. And tilting his head knowingly, he tapped his breastbone to indicate that she had a good heart: not hard, not fierce, open to compassion, charitable to the poor!

"I walked away thoughtfully; I wondered whether his difference, his strangeness, were not penetrating with repulsion that dull nature they had begun by irresistibly attracting. I wondered. . . ."

The Doctor came to the window and looked out of the frigid splendour of the sea, immense in the haze, as if enclosing all the earth with all the hearts lost among the passions of love and fear.

"Physiologically, now," he said, turning away abruptly, "it was possible. It was possible."

He remained silent. Then went on—

"At all events, the next time I saw him he was ill—lung trouble. He was tough, but I daresay he was not acclimatized as well as I had supposed. It was a bad winter; and, of course, these mountaineers do get fits of homesickness; and a state of depression would make him vulnerable. He was lying half dressed on a couch downstairs.

"A table covered with a dark oilcloth took up all the middle of the little room. There was a wicket cradle on the floor, a kettle spouting steam on the hob, and some child's linen lay drying on the fender. The room was warm, but the door opens right into the garden, as you noticed perhaps.

"He was very feverish, and kept on muttering to himself. She sat on a chair and looked at him fixedly across the table with her brown, blurred eyes. 'Why don't you have him upstairs?' I asked. With a start and a confused stammer she said, 'Oh! ah! I couldn't sit with him upstairs, sir.'

"I gave her certain directions; and going outside, I said again that he ought to be in bed upstairs. She wrung her hands. 'I couldn't. I couldn't. He keeps on saying something—I don't know what.' With the memory of all the talk against the man that had been dinned into her ears, I looked at her narrowly. I looked into her short-sighted eyes, at her dumb eyes that once in her life had seen an enticing shape, but seemed, staring at me, to see nothing at all now. But I saw she was uneasy.

" 'What's the matter with him?' she asked in a sort of vacant trepidation. 'He doesn't look very ill. I never did see anybody look like this before. . . .'

" 'Do you think,' I asked indignantly, 'he is shamming?'

" 'I can't help it, sir,' she said, stolidly. And suddenly she clapped her hands and looked right and left. 'And there's the baby. I am so frightened. He wanted me just now to give him the baby. I can't understand what he says to it.'

" 'Can't you ask a neighbour to come in to-night?' I asked.

" 'Please, sir, nobody seems to care to come,' she muttered, dully resigned all at once.

"I impressed upon her the necessity of the greatest care, and then had to go. There was a good deal of sickness that winter. 'Oh, I hope he won't talk!' she exclaimed softly just as I was going away.

"I don't know how it is I did not see—but I didn't. And yet, turning in my trap, I saw her lingering before the door, very still, and as if meditating a flight up the miry road.

"Towards the night his fever increased.

"He tossed, moaned, and now and then muttered a complaint. And she sat with the table between her and the couch, watching every movement and every sound, with the terror, the unreasonable terror, of that man she could not understand creeping over her. She had drawn the wicker cradle close to her feet. There was nothing in her now but the maternal instinct and that unaccountable fear.

"Suddenly coming to himself, parched, he demanded a drink of water. She did not move. She had not understood, though he may have thought he was speaking in English. He waited, looking at her, burning with fever, amazed at her silence and immobility, and then he shouted impatiently, 'Water! Give me water!'

"She jumped to her feet, snatched up the child, and stood still. He spoke to her, and his passionate remonstrances only increased her fear of that strange man. I believe he spoke to her for a long time, entreating, wondering, pleading, ordering, I suppose. She says she bore it as long as she could. And then a gust of rage came over him.

"He sat up and called out terribly one word—some word. Then he got up as though he hadn't been ill at all, she says. And as in fevered dismay, indignation, and wonder he tried to get to her round the table, she simply opened the door and ran out with the child in her arms. She heard him call twice after her down the road in a terrible voice—and fled. . . . Ah! but you should have seen the stirring behind the dull, blurred glance of those eyes the spectre of the fear which had hunted her on that night three miles and a half to the door of Foster's cottage! I did the next day.

"And it was I who found him lying face down and his body in a puddle, just outside the little wicker gate.

"I had been called out that night to an urgent case in the village, and on my way home at daybreak passed by the cottage. The door stood open. My man helped me to carry him in. We laid him on the couch. The lamp smoked, the fire was out, the chill of the stormy night oozed from the cheerless yellow paper on the wall. 'Amy!' I called aloud, and my voice seemed to lose itself in the emptiness of this tiny house as if I had cried in a desert. He opened his eyes. 'Gone!' he said, distinctly. 'I had only asked for water—only for a little water. . . .'

"He was muddy. I covered him up and stood waiting in silence, catching a painfully gasped word now and then. They were no longer in his own language. The fever had left him, taking with it the heat of life. And with his panting breast and lustrous eyes he reminded me again of a wild creature under the net; of a bird caught in a snare. She had left him. She had left him—sick—helpless—thirsty. The spear of the hunter had entered his very soul. 'Why?' he cried, in the penetrating and indignant voice of a man calling to a responsible Maker. A gust of wind and a swish of rain answered.

"And as I turned away to shut the door he pronounced the word 'Merciful!' and expired.

"Eventually I certified heart-failure as the immediate cause of death. His heart must have indeed failed him, or else he might have stood this night of storm and exposure, too. I closed his eyes and drove away. Not very far from the cottage I met Foster walking sturdily between the dripping hedges with his collie at his heels.

" 'Do you know where your daughter is?' I asked.

" 'Don't I!' he cried. 'I am going to talk to him a bit. Frightening a poor woman like this.'

" 'He won't frighten her any more,' I said. 'He is dead.'

"He struck with his stick at the mud.

" 'And there's the child.'

"Then, after thinking deeply for a while—

" 'I don't know that it isn't for the best.'

"That's what he said. And she says nothing at all now. Not a word of him. Never. Is his image as utterly gone from her mind as his lithe and striding figure, his carolling voice are gone from our fields? He is no longer before her eyes to excite her imagination into a passion of love or fear; and his memory seems to have vanished from her dull brain as a shadow passes away upon a white screen. She lives in the cottage and works for Miss Swaffer. She is Amy Foster for everybody, and the child is 'Amy Foster's boy.' She calls him Johnny—which means Little John.

"It is impossible to say whether this name recalls anything to her. Does she ever think of the past? I have seen her hanging over the boy's cot in a very passion of maternal tenderness. The little fellow was lying on his back, a little frightened at me, but very still, with his big black eyes, with his fluttered air of a bird in a snare. And looking at him I seemed to see again the other one—the father, cast out mysteriously by the sea to perish in the supreme disaster of loneliness and despair."

GLOSSARY

abstraction: A generalized idea or quality drawn from a number of particular persons or things that share this characteristic. (See also *allegory* and *symbol.*)

action: One of the raw materials of fiction, the other being persons or *things.* Verbs describe the interaction between things; nouns describe the things.

allegory: A simpler form of the symbolic process, in which concrete persons or things consistently represent *abstractions.* The situation involving these persons or things creates a drama that acts out a moral, a message, or an attitude.

alliteration: The occurrence of closely repeated consonant sounds, usually those at the beginnings of words.

allusion: A reference to a person or event that is likely to be known to the reader. By inviting comparisons it expands and enriches meanings. Allusions commonly draw on history, literature, mythology, or religion.

ambiguity: A word or group of words that contains two or more possible meanings. Writers often use ambiguity deliberately for ironic effect.

artificial aspects: The properties of fiction that reveal the author's hand as he shapes the story and arbitrarily restrict the experience for special effect: an example is the compression of time. (Compare *real aspects.*)

assonance: The occurrence of repeated vowel sounds within a word or in a succession of words.

attitude: The author's disposition toward or opinion of the characters and situations he has created. (See also *theme* and *thesis.*)

cacophony: The tonal discord achieved by the deliberate juxtaposition of harsh-sounding words.

central intelligence: The narrative *point of view,* rendered in the third person, that restricts the story to the *private world* of one character.

cliché: An expression that is so common or overworked that it has lost most of its impact. Authors may have their characters speak in clichés for ironic and usually demeaning effect.

comparisons: The use of *allusions, metaphors,* and *similes* that succinctly draw parallels or contrasts between things or events. These comparisons enrich a story by introducing events or things not literally present in the story's setting.

conflict: The interaction of persons, values, or things in a story, creating tensions that typically lead to a *revelation.* (See also *plot* and *revelation.*)

connotation: A highly suggestive associative meaning that some words carry in addition to their *denotation.*

consonance: The repetition of consonant sounds within a word or in a succession of words. (Compare *alliteration.*)

continuing action: The variation of *point of view* that presents the story as if it were taking place at the present moment. (Compare *recalled action.*)

denotation: The dictionary definition of a word. If a word has more than one basic definition, it's use may give rise to *ambiguity.*

dramatic distance: The variation of *point of view* that produces an ironic tension between what the narrator thinks are the facts and what the reader knows are the facts. This discrepancy invites the reader to judge the narrator and often to consider him somewhat unreliable.

dramatic irony: The *irony* created when a character in a story is ignorant of something that the reader knows. The most complicated plots employ dramatic irony rather than *surprise* or *suspense* for effect. When the narrator himself is the object of dramatic irony, the discrepancy in knowledge is called *dramatic distance.*

euphony: The tonal harmony achieved by the deliberate juxtaposition of pleasant-sounding words.

figurative language: Comparisons drawn, usually through *allusion, simile,* or *metaphor,* whereby the author introduces things that are not literally present in the setting.

first person: The variation of *point of view* that presents the story through a narrator identified as "I." (Compare *third person.*)

imagery: The details that play on the five senses: *sight, sound, touch, smell,* and *taste.* Carefully patterned imagery often signals the author's *attitude.*

impression: The narrative technique by which an author reveals the events to the reader. These events may be staged in the *public world,* witnessed within the confines of a character's *private world,* or filtered through the *narrator's mind.*

irony: The introduction of a variant or surprising word, idea, or event that results in a reversal of expectation. Forms of irony include *irony of situation, irony of style, dramatic irony,* and the *verbal ironies* of *understatement, overstatement,* and *opposite statement.* Deliberate *ambiguity* is sometimes ironic.

irony of situation: A situation in which the reverse of what was expected occurs.

irony of style: A contrast between style and content through which a writer comments on the events. A frivolous, slangy, or artfully simple style may be used to treat serious or lofty subjects for such an effect; conversely, a solemn, pompous, or overblown style may be used for trivial subjects.

literary symbolism: The technique of using a pattern of concrete objects or actions to suggest or convey an additional abstract meaning.

metaphor: The substitution of one image or detail for another essentially unlike it whereby the author introduces something that is not literally present in the setting.

narrator's mind: The *impression* that tells a story directly through the narrator, rather than through the *public world* or the *private world.* (See *impression, private world,* and *public world.*)

omniscience: The variation of point of view in which the all-knowing narrator can skip at will among the various *private worlds* of different characters.

onomatopoeia: The musical effect, common in poetry and often present in prose, that duplicates or imitates the sound of a thing by the sound of the word that names or describes it.

opposite statement: A *verbal irony* that describes a person, thing, or action in terms opposed to its actual attributes.

overstatement: A *verbal irony* that describes a thing in deliberately excessive terms; a hyperbole.

paradox: The successful reconciliation of seemingly irreconcilable ideas.

pace: The speed at which a story is told. The *scenic method* of pace, often employing dialogue, is slow and sharply focused; the *summary method* is faster and covers a great deal in a few words.

personification: The representation of an abstract quality or idea by a human figure or the endowment of an inanimate object with human qualities.

plot: A story with values; that is, the pattern of actions significantly interconnected within a story. This interconnection typically leads to a *conflict* and a *revelation.*

point of view: The mind, or intelligence, selected by the author, through which the action of the story is presented to the reader. This selection involves the choice of both narrator and narrative technique. The author may choose from among *first person, third person, central intelligence, and omniscient* narrators; for a narrative technique he may choose between *recalled action* and *continuing action* and may or may not employ *dramatic distance.*

private world: The *impression* that focuses on the inner world of a character—his thoughts, his reveries, his hidden feelings. (See *impression, public world,* and *narrator's mind.*)

public world: The *impression* that lends itself to easy dramatization by focusing on the external world of its characters. (See *impression, private world,* and *narrator's mind.*)

real aspects: The properties of fiction that remind us of those actual experiences and impressions of life common to us all. (Compare *artificial aspects.*)

recalled action: The variation of *point of view* that presents the story as an action or experience that has already happened and is being remembered. (Compare *continuing action.*)

repetition: The use of recurring sounds or words that set up patterns in prose fiction, contributing to the meaning, unity, and musical effect.

revelation: Structurally, an element of *plot* that grows out of *conflict;* thematically, an insight that discloses the author's comment on some aspect of human behavior. The revelation may come to both a character in a story and the reader or to the reader alone.

scenic method: The slow pacing of events, which gives the reader a strong sense of immediacy. The scenic method typically employs dialogue and a refined focus on specific *imagery.* (Compare *summary method.*)

sight: The form of *imagery* that calls attention to visual aspects for sensory effect. Because it is the most common form of imagery, sight is usually noteworthy as a fictional technique only when it falls into patterns—especially patterns of color, brightness, or shape.

simile: A *comparison* that names both a literal thing and its figurative counterpart. These essentially unlike objects are usually linked by the words *as* or *like.* The figurative counterpart in the simile introduces into the story something that is not literally present in the setting.

smell: The form of *imagery* that calls attention to odors for sensory effect.

sound: The form of *imagery* that calls attention to things heard for sensory effect; second only to *sight* imagery in its frequency.

structure: The arrangement of the larger elements in fiction, such as *plot* or *point of view,* which combine to give a story its shape. (Compare *texture.*)

summary method: The fast pacing of events, typically appearing in long paragraphs devoid of dialogue, that affords a panoramic view and often covers a great deal of time in a short span. (Compare *scenic method.*)

surprise: The least sophisticated structure of a *plot,* which presents the *revelation* unexpectedly instead of developing it gradually and logically from the other elements in the story. (Compare *suspense* and *dramatic irony.*)

suspense: A complication of *plot* that effectively delays the *revelation,* causing the reader's curiosity and anxiety to increase. (Compare *surprise* and *dramatic irony.*)

symbol: A thing or action that strongly suggests, through its repetition and pattern in a story, something abstract in addition to its concrete meaning. Natural symbols, like the rising sun or falling autumn leaves, are common in our world and experience; they are sometimes used deliberately by writers for *literary symbolism.*

syntax: The arrangement of words in a sentence. Variations in syntax can give a varied sense of *pace* in a story.

taste: The form of *imagery* that calls attention to flavors for sensory effect.

texture: The arrangement of the smaller elements of fiction, such as *words, imagery, comparisons,* and *verbal ironies,* that make up the linguistic and stylistic fabric of fiction and contribute to a story's tone. (Compare *structure.*)

theme: The implied *attitude* of the author, which is woven into the story by his choice of technique and suggested to the reader through the *revelation.* (See *attitude, revelation,* and *thesis.*)

thesis: The *attitude* of the author, stated explicitly in the story. A thesis sentence is one that accurately conveys this attitude. Prefaced by "I believe . . .," it may be read as the author's own statement of his story's *theme,* supported by his choice of technique.

things: One of the raw materials of fiction—persons, places, and other components of our everyday environment—represented by nouns. Things interact with one another to create the *action* of fiction.

third person: The variation of *point of view* in which all the characters are referred to by name or by "he" or "she." (Compare *first person.*)

touch: The form of *imagery* that calls attention to the body's tactile reactions for sensory effect.

understatement: A *verbal irony* that describes a thing in terms that are deliberately and markedly low-keyed or unemphatic.

verbal ironies: The use of *overstatement, understatement,* and *opposite statement* for the succinct expression of an attitude somewhat at variance with the truth.

vision: An individual author's unique way of regarding life. His vision represents the composite of all that he has known, thought, felt, and experienced. Each story can reflect only a part of an author's total vision.

words: The basic building blocks of fiction, on which all of its art finally depends. The force of words extends far beyond their basic meanings, or *denotations.* Words may achieve musical effects through *alliteration, assonance, repetition, euphony,* or *cacophony* and enrich meaning through deliberate *ambiguity, connotation, allusions, metaphors,* and *verbal ironies.*

INDEX

A 0
B 1
C 2
D 3
E 4
F 5
G 6
H 7
I 8
J 9